AMULET BOOKS
LONDON

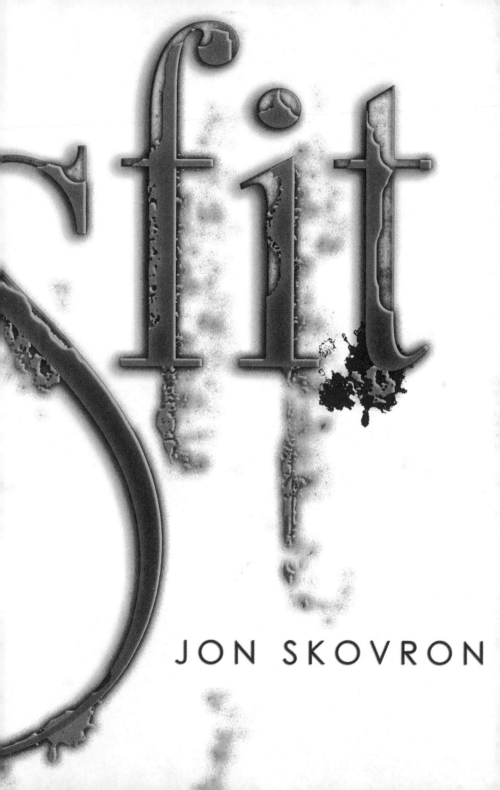

fit

JON SKOVRON

The Library of Congress has catalogued
the hardcover edition of this book as follows:
Skovron, Jon.
Misfit / by Jon Skovron.
p. cm.
Summary: Seattle sixteen-year-old Jael must negotiate normal life in Catholic school while learning to control the abilities she inherited from her mother, a demon, and protect those she loves from Belial, the Duke of Hell.
ISBN 978-1-4197-0021-7 (alk. paper)
[1. Supernatural—Fiction. 2. Demonology—Fiction. 3. Catholic schools—Fiction. 4. High schools—Fiction. 5. Schools—Fiction. 6. Single-parent families—Fiction. 7. Seattle (Wash.)—Fiction.] I. Title.
PZ7.S628393Mis 2011
[Fic]—dc22
2010048691

ISBN for this edition: 978-1-4197-0120-7

Text copyright © 2011 Jon Skovron
Display type design by Sammy Yuen
Book design by Chad W. Beckerman

The text in this book is set in 11.5-point Cochin.

Printed and bound in U.S.A.
10 9 8 7 6 5 4 3 2 1

ABRAMS
THE ART OF BOOKS SINCE 1949
The Market Building
72-82 Rosebery Avenue
London, UK EC1R 4RW
www.abramsbooks.co.uk

For my grandmother and staunchest
supporter, Leokadjia "Lillian" B. Kelley,
whose indomitable strength came
at such a high cost

—J.S.

contents

"The gods of the old religion become the demons of the new religion."

—margaret murray

"Gods can turn into evil demons when new gods oust them."

—Sigmund Freud

misfit

taking the medicine

1

Jael Thompson looks at her reflection in the bathroom mirror and frowns. She pushes back her curly black hair and stares into her green eyes so hard that the rest of her features blur.

"You know what I heard?" she says. "That what you see in the mirror isn't what you really look like. That since mirrors flip everything, you're looking at a flipped version of your face. Like, the exact opposite."

"What?" says her best friend, Brittany Brougher. She walks into the bathroom armed with several bottles of hair product, plastic gloves, and a towel. "Where do you get this stuff, J?"

Jael shrugs, pushing the tip of her nose to one side, then the other.

"Some NPR show," she says.

"Seriously," says Britt. She elbows Jael away from the mirror and lines up the bottles on the sink. "Your dad needs to get you guys a TV."

"Right, like that'll happen," says Jael. "He won't even get me leave-in conditioner."

"And so, my gift to you," says Britt, spreading her hands to present the bottles. "Happy early birthday!"

"Thanks, Britt," says Jael, turning the bottles so that she can examine the labels.

"Well, honestly, I hope this is the right stuff," says Britt. She takes a moment to adjust her own perfectly styled honey-blond hair. "I tried to describe your hair to the lady at the store, and she was all, 'So is she black or mixed?' Which I thought was kind of a lame thing to say. *Mixed*."

"What did you tell her?" asks Jael.

"I said I didn't think you were black, but maybe like Middle Eastern or something, but I didn't really know for sure. And she was all, 'What do you mean, you don't know?' and I said *you* didn't really know either and why's she so hung up on the labels anyway and she just kind of gave up and shoved this stuff at me."

"Yeah, well, it definitely can't make things worse." Jael grabs a fistful of her hair. "I can't even run a comb through this anymore. It's like a giant black cotton ball on my head."

"So did you really ask your dad to get you something and he said no?"

"Yep," says Jael. "He gave me this look, you know, like I was asking for some bizarre extravagance."

"Oh my God, I can totally see it," says Britt. She scrunches her face into a frown and glares at herself in the mirror. "Jael . . . ," she says, in a pretty good imitation of Jael's father's flat, gruff voice. "Jael, money is tight. Do you really *need* these things?"

"No, you're right, Dad," says Jael in a chipper, squeaky voice. "It's actually really convenient that I can store all my pens and pencils in my hair. In fact, you know what? I'll just grow my hair a little longer so you don't even have to get me folders this year!"

Britt breaks into a laugh. "I would pay you so much money to say that to him!"

"Oh yeah, 'cause that would go over really well," Jael says.

"Who cares," says Britt, turning away from the mirror to look at her friend directly. "What's he going to do, take away your allowance?"

"Ha, what allowance?"

"Exactly! So stand up to him for once."

"It's just . . ." Jael stops and looks down at her hands, opening and closing them. "Whatever. It's no big deal. . . ."

Britt raises an eyebrow. "It's just what? You're scared of him."

"No!" says Jael. "I mean, sort of. Look, he's all I've ever had, you know? And when I piss him off, he totally shuts down on me. And it's . . . it's really lonely."

"You *know* I get that, J," says Britt. She sits Jael down on the toilet seat and begins to work the conditioner into her hair. "I feel the same way about my mom. It's always just been me and her against the world. But that was when I was a helpless little kid. Then I started growing up and we went through this bad period where we were always fighting. But we got through it, and now we have respect for each other, you know?"

"My dad actually respecting me?" says Jael. She winces as Britt's fingers catch a snarl. "I'm pretty sure that's never going to happen."

• • •

The next morning is October 16th, Jael Thompson's sixteenth birthday. She climbs out of bed and nearly trips over the pile of clothes on her floor. Not that she has many clothes. Not that she has much floor. In fact, between the twin bed, the dresser, and the desk with her ancient computer, there's just enough room to turn around.

She pulls out her school uniform from the pile of clean clothes: white blouse, a navy-blue plaid skirt, and these god-awful knee-high navy-blue socks. She's supposed to pull the socks all the way up, but that itchy feeling on her shins drives her nuts, so she only does it when she has to. She's gone to Catholic schools all her life and she knows how to play the game.

She heads down the narrow metal spiral staircase to the bathroom on the main floor. The house used to be a one-bedroom ranch with a storage attic, but at some point the landlord converted the attic to a second bedroom. Her room is tiny and drafty, and it sucks to go down the twisting staircase in the middle of the night to pee, but she loves it anyway. Because when they moved to this house two years ago, she and her dad each got their own room for the first time.

Downstairs she checks her hair in the hallway mirror. The conditioning treatment Britt put in seemed to work last night, but her hair rallied overnight and came back crazier than ever this morning. She gives it a few halfhearted scrunches, then sighs and heads for the kitchen.

She pours herself a bowl of generic cereal. Her dad is convinced that it tastes as good as the brand-name stuff. Of course, he doesn't eat it. He's already at school, contemplating how best to bore the students of Our Lady of Mercy High School with obscure points of Church history. Next year, Jael will have to take his class, and she really can't imagine anything worse than that—except sharing a bedroom with him again. But the only reason she can afford to go to Mercy is because the children of faculty members don't pay tuition.

She sits down at the kitchen table and starts to slurp up the cereal, which has already turned to mush. Then she notices a yellow Post-it note stuck to the center of the table. In her dad's blocky, all-caps handwriting it reads COME HOME RIGHT AFTER SCHOOL. WE HAVE TO TALK.

Jael peels the note off the table and stares at it for a moment, fighting the hot, heavy feeling it creates in her stomach. She'll be damned if she's going to let this rattle her, today of all days.

"Oh yeah, and happy friggin' birthday, daughter," she says aloud. Then she crumples up the note, drops it into her soggy cereal, and dumps the whole mess into the sink.

Our Lady of Mercy High School looks like it belongs in some grimy, low-income neighborhood in New York or Boston rather than next to the cute, craftsman-style houses of northeast Seattle. Jael finds that kind of endearing. She doesn't really fit in either.

She crosses the school parking lot and weaves her way through the brand-new SUVs and sports cars owned by unappreciative, overprivileged students who will probably wreck their vehicles before they graduate. She pulls up the hood on her red sweatshirt and jams her hands into her pockets as a prickle of jealousy climbs up her throat. She turns sixteen today, and whatever the "We Have to Talk" note that her dad left is about, she's positive it's not "Let's Talk About Getting You a Car!"

Jael hops up the front steps and through the main doors. Then she hears "Miss Thompson!"

It's Father Aaron, the dean of discipline. He stands just inside the front door, where he stands every morning so he can glare at every student as they arrive at school. He's committed like that. The harsh fluorescent lights glare off his bald head. He takes a slow bite of an apple. As Jael listens to the crunching sounds, she notices little white flecks of apple bits trapped in his walrus mustache.

"Socks, Miss Thompson," he says.

"Yes, Father." She drops her bag on the floor and yanks up her socks to her knees with both hands.

"We want to present a ladylike appearance, don't we, Miss Thompson?" A few flecks of apple land on the floor next to Jael's black leather buckle shoes.

"You bet, Father," she says. "I strive for ladylike at all costs."

Father Aaron munches his apple and frowns at her for a moment, like he's debating whether to nail her for her snarky tone. He is not a fan of sarcasm. But then he just shakes his head and says, "Get to class."

"Yes, Father."

She picks up her bag and walks down the hallway past a long line of dark mahogany doors with frosted windows until she gets to her homeroom. Most of the students are already in their seats, scrambling to finish last night's homework, chatting with neighbors, or texting on their cell phones. Ms. Spielman, the geometry teacher, sits at her desk at the front of the class, shuffling through some quiz papers. Her long brown hair is shot through with streaks of gray, and she wears flowy earth-tone cottons and a bright purple scarf. It's that Earth Mother look that's so popular in Seattle. It can look frumpy, but Ms. Spielman somehow pulls it off.

Jael makes her way to her desk at the back of the classroom. As she sits down, she hears "Hey, Betty."

Rob McKinley has called her "Betty" practically since they met. He claims it's a term of endearment that skaters give girls.

"Hey, Rob," she says.

"Happy b-day," he says, giving her that crooked grin he does so well.

"Thanks." She almost mentions that he's the first person to wish her a happy birthday today, but decides that makes her sound truly pathetic.

"So," he says, "are you doing anything cool for your b-day?"

"Oh yeah," says Jael. "I'm having a pizza party. There will be a sack race, a water-balloon toss, and fabulous door prizes. Wanna come?"

"Uh . . . ," he says, giving her a slightly baffled look. Rob is a total airhead skater boy, complete with blond bangs and an effortless sunny smile. In Jael's experience, those types are usually incapable of talking about anything other than sports or video games. But Rob is also some kind of math and science genius, and she hasn't figured out yet how skater boy and math wiz fit together.

"Joking, Rob," she says. "Just joking."

"I knew that," he says, a little defensively. "So what *are* you doing?"

"Nothing."

The PA system crackles.

"Good morning, students," Principal Dawson's voice announces over the speaker. Everyone calls him Principal Oz because the only time students see him is at graduation. The rest of the year he's just a scratchy, metallic voice over the PA. "Please stand and join me in prayer. *Our Father, who art in Heaven . . .*"

He drones on with the Our Father while everyone gets to their feet. His voice is barely audible over the squeak and groan of chairs, and he goes so fast that he's done by the time most people fold their hands. Everyone then switches to the Pledge of Allegiance.

"One reminder," the PA says after the Pledge is finished. "Don't forget that fifth period will be canceled tomorrow for All-School Mass. That is all. Thank you and have a good day."

Chairs and desks squeak and clank as everyone sits back down.

"Really, Bets," says Rob. "You should do *something* for your b-day."

Jael thinks about the "We Have to Talk" note again.

"Trust me," she says. "Doing nothing on my birthday is way better than some of the alternatives."

"Like?" he challenges.

"Like on my eighth birthday, when my dad put me in the car

and told me we were moving from Tucson, Arizona, to Buffalo, New York. Immediately."

"Buffalo? Is that where you lived before you moved to Seattle?"

"No, I lived in London before I moved here."

"Got it. So were you born in Arizona, then?"

"No, I was born in Siberia."

"Okay, wait," says Rob. "So you were born in *Siberia*? And then you moved to Tucson, and then—"

"No, I lived a few other places before we moved to Tucson."

"A *few*?" Rob squints at her, like he just can't even conceive of it. "How many places have you lived?"

"You know," says Jael, "I've never really counted."

"Why did you move so much? Was your dad military or something?"

"He was a monk," Jael says.

"Um . . ." Rob rubs his temples. "I'm totally lost now."

"That's okay," says Jael. "I've pretty much been lost my whole life."

Rob grins at her. "So, okay, let me see if I've got this right. First, you—"

A voice cuts in. "Miss Thompson and Mr. McWhiley. It's Ms. Spielman. "Whenever you're ready, we can begin geometry class."

"Sorry, Ms. Spielman," says Rob. "I got it. Lock and load."

And just like that, Rob is completely engrossed in the wonders of geometry. Like someone flipped the switch from chatty skater boy to math geek and now nothing exists but angles and algebra. Jael is always amazed at how he can change focus like that. It's irritating, sure, but there's something about it that she also finds impressive.

The buzzing fluorescent lights work their drowsy magic on Jael as Monsignor Francis Locke drones on about the life and times of Jesus. The Mons, as students refer to him, is a sweet old guy, more or less the exact opposite of Father Aaron. Jael isn't sure what someone has to do to go from "Father" to "Monsignor." She just knows it's some kind of honorary thing that the pope gives out. But even though the Mons is so nice and so holy, or maybe *because* he's so nice and holy, Jael also finds him incredibly boring.

"For Jesus had said to him," the Mons reads from the Bible, "'Come out of this man, you impure spirit!' Then Jesus asked him, 'What is your name?'" The Mons looks around the class with a slight smile on his face, as if to say, *Oh boy, here comes my favorite part!* Then he continues.

"'My name is Legion,' he replied, 'for we are many.' And he begged Jesus again and again not to send them out of the area.

"A large herd of pigs was feeding on the nearby hillside. The demons begged Jesus, 'Send us among the pigs; allow us to go into them.' He gave them permission, and the impure spirits came out and went into the pigs. The herd, about two thousand in number, rushed down the steep bank into the lake and were drowned."

Jael keeps her face neutral, but internally she cringes. She'd rather listen to Ms. Spielman ramble on about the Pythagorean theorem or Ms. Randolph drone on about the periodic table than sit through this Bible stuff. Geometry and chemistry are kind of boring, but the religious stuff gets way too personal, especially passages like the one the Mons just read. She's begged her dad a bunch of times to let her go to public school. Seattle Public isn't that bad, and some of the magnet schools are really great. But he says she *needs* to be in an environment like this. Like taking medicine to prevent seizures. He's never said what he's afraid would happen if she didn't go to Catholic school. She's never had the guts to ask.

"Miss Thompson." The Mons's gentle voice breaks into her thoughts. "Why do you suppose that Jesus cast the demon into a herd of swine?"

"Uh . . . because the Jews don't eat pork anyway, so it wasn't really a waste for them?"

"Is that a question or a statement, my child?"

"It's a statement," she says.

"Then believe in what you say," he says. "Make it sound like a statement."

"Okay, Monsignor."

"And, as always, Miss Thompson, your answer is extremely insightful. The Jews do regard pigs as unclean animals. But when we discuss demons, the answers inevitably reach deeper than we first think. Consider this: We know by the name 'Legion' that there are many demons within this man. So the evil in a single human being fills two thousand of the most unclean animal. What might this suggest? Mr. Buchanan?"

"That a man is more evil than a pig?" asks Seamus Buchanan.

Seamus looks like the ultimate redheaded Irish Catholic boy. He claims that he wants to be a priest someday. Jael can't understand why someone would tell people that, even if it's true.

"Indeed," says the Mons. "You are on the right track. Perhaps you are all too young to truly grasp this idea. During my time as a missionary in Peru, I often came face-to-face with the true darkness that lies within humanity. I had a small parish in a tiny neighborhood in Iquitos called Belen. An interesting place. Tropical storms caused the area to flood so frequently that the natives built their tiny houses on stilts. Half the year I had to use a rowboat to get to my home. But they were thankful for the flooding when it prevented the the Shining Path, a murderous band of the communist guerrillas, from reaching their homes during a raid."

He looks at them with his gentle gray eyes and it's the kind of sad wisdom that Jael has only seen before in movies.

"Ladies and gentlemen, the Shining Path did terrible things to the people of Iquitos. Things no human should be capable of."

Jael tries to hold back. Her father has told her over and over again that she can't draw attention to herself like this. But . . .

"Monsignor, I don't get it," she blurts out. "Are you saying that the communist army was possessed by demons?"

"Very astute, Miss Thompson," says the Mons with a gentle smile. But then his face grows serious again. "Yes, I'm afraid it was nothing less than corruption from those most base and vile creatures." He scans the room gravely for a moment, then his smile breaks through again. "But take heart. The miracle of this passage in the Bible, and what I want to impress most upon you, is that with God's will, we can exorcise those horrible demons and send them back to the darkness from which they came."

It's hard to hear the sweet old Mons go on about this kind of stuff. But of course, like most people, he doesn't know the truth.

Jael's mother was a demon.

The Mons turns his kind old eyes back to Jael. "Does that make sense, Miss Thompson? Do you understand?"

"Yes, Monsignor," says Jael, putting on the poker face she's had eight years to perfect. "Demons are bad. Everybody knows that."

half truths

2

On her eighth birthday, Jael Thompson found out she wasn't like other girls.

"I have the name of an angel!" she boasted to her father after school at dinner.

"What?" said Paul Thompson. His hard, square-jawed face usually didn't show much emotion. But at the word "angel," his eyes went wide and he froze, his fork and knife in mid cut through his tamale.

"Mrs. Perez says so," said Jael. She bit down on a green bean and chewed as she said, "You know the Ark of the Covenant?"

"I am . . . familiar," he said. He went back to eating his tamale, but his eyes had a strangely intense look. Jael decided it meant he was fascinated by what she had to say.

"It's a big box that has the broken Ten Commandments of Moses in it," she said.

"Yes . . ."

"Well, Daddy," she said, trying her best to return the intense gaze he was giving her, "the lid of the box has two angels on it. Do you know what their names are?"

He blinked, then stared at her for a moment. "I don't, actually."

She smiled triumphantly. "Their names are Zarall and *Jael*. Can you believe that, Daddy? Can you?"

"Amazing," he said. His voice sounded mild, but a muscle in his jaw twitched.

"I think angels are the coolest, Daddy. Especially Michael and Gabriel." She frowned as she ate another green bean. "But Uriel is pretty cool too. He guards the Garden of Eden with his flaming sword. I think I'd like to have a flaming sword, Daddy. Don't you think that would be cool, Daddy? To have a flaming sword? Daddy?"

"Um." Her father's expression was locked in a grimace, but Jael barely noticed. She was too busy showing off everything she'd learned about angels. It wasn't every day that her father paid this much attention to what she said.

"And there's Azrael, of course," she continued. "But he seems a little scary to me. And what about all those other angels? The ones that stay in Heaven all the time and never leave but just sing and sing and sing?"

"Jael—"

"You know, Daddy, there's seven levels of angels that don't do anything but sing all the time, like infinity and *forever*. Why is that, Daddy? Why do the angels have to sing all the time? Don't they ever get tired?"

"Jael, please stop talking about angels."

"But they're just so cool! And there's all different kinds. Archangels, of course, Daddy. But also? There's cherubim, and seraphim, and ophanim, and you know you can pray to them? Pray to angels just like God, and—"

"*Enough!*" Her father was on his feet, glaring down at her, angrier than she'd ever seen him. His wide shoulders went up and down with each breath. "Never speak of angels in this house again! *Never!* Is that understood?!"

She stared up at him for a moment. Then her eyes welled up with tears.

"Jael," he said. "Don't cry. Don't . . ."

She ran out of the apartment.

Everything in Tucson was beige. The sidewalks, the streets, the houses—everything except the vast blue sky. Jael ran crying out the beige door, down the beige apartment building steps, and through the beige corridor that was her street.

She didn't run for long, though. It was late afternoon and the desert heat lay on her heavily, as if she were moving through a brick oven. She slowed down to a walk for the last block to the neighborhood playground. It was her favorite place, probably because it was the only place that wasn't beige. The massive modern climbing structure was a blast of primary colors, with a red rock wall, a blue tire swing, and three swirling yellow slides. It was sheltered by a massive black mesh canopy that kept off the hard desert sun. Jael spent a lot of time at the playground, alone.

On this day when she came to the playground, it was different. A second structure stood off to the side. It didn't fit in with the rest. The regular play structure was made of plastic and painted metal, but this new contraption was made of a weird mix of wood, stone, and pitted iron. It looked old and not very safe, but Jael couldn't resist something new to explore. She walked toward it.

Suddenly, a sparrow dropped down from the sky and nearly hit her on the head. She gave a little yelp and swatted at it. It gave her a long, warbling chirp in response. Then it landed at the top of one of the yellow spiral slides. It cocked its head at her expectantly.

"What?" she said. Like a lot of lonely kids, she had a habit of talking to animals. Sometimes she even talked to inanimate objects. "I'm just going to check out the new one first."

The sparrow gave her another shrill chirp, then flew off.

"Whatever," she said, trying to make the word sound like it did when the older girls at her school said it. She walked purposefully toward the jumble of wood, stone, and iron.

As she started to climb up, sparkling brown eyes snapped open near her foot. Jael gave a little shriek and stumbled backward. The structure slowly began to shift and rise until it had reassembled into the shape of a giant ox. Jael started to back away carefully toward the playground exit.

But then it spoke.

"Happy birthday," it said in a slow, measured voice.

That made Jael stop.

"Do you know me?" she asked.

It shook its massive stone head. "I knew your mother."

"My mother?" she asked, her eyes going wide. Her father never spoke about her mother, other than to say that she died when Jael was born. Whenever Jael asked about her, he only said they would talk about it when she was older. So Jael didn't know anything about her, whether she was nice or mean, pretty or ugly, smart or dumb. Without any real facts, it was left to her imagination to conjure up her mother. She had imagined a thousand different mothers by this point, each more beautiful and perfect than the one before. A long line of angelic women who would one day swoop down and take her someplace safe, where everyone was kind.

"What do you know about my mother?" she asked the giant ox creature.

"She was once a queen."

"No . . . ," said Jael. A thrill ran through her. Maybe one of her favorite imaginary mothers was the real thing. But she stopped herself. Even if it was magic, this thing was still a stranger. And sometimes strangers lied. He could be making it all up. "Oh yeah?" she said carefully. "Queen of what?"

The creature laughed so low and loud Jael could feel it in her chest. "Such a spitfire," he said. "You are a lot like her."

"I am?" said Jael, unable to keep the dreamy tone out of her voice. She moved a little closer.

"Certainly," he said. "There was a time when we all admired her greatly."

"'We'?" asked Jael. "Are there other things like you?"

He cocked his massive square head to one side. "Oh," he said. "You don't know."

"Know what?" she asked. "Who are you?"

"You can call me Baal. I was a servant of your uncle for a time."

"A servant?" she asked. Then, "I have an uncle?"

He stared at her for a long time, not saying anything.

"Well?" she said.

Still in his measured monotone, he said, "This is disappointing. I had hoped to toy with you a little, halfbreed. But I think it would be lost on you. So I might as well just kill you."

His brown eyes suddenly flared orange. His mouth stretched open, bits of stone and iron grinding within. Then he charged.

Jael stood frozen in terror, unable to move.

Something small and feathered hit her on the head. The sparrow from before. That jolted her into action, and she dove to one side. Baal slammed into the playground structure, primary colors crunching down on him. He rose to his feet, tossing chunks of plastic and metal in all directions with his iron horns.

Jael scrambled to her feet and sprinted for the gate. It seemed impossibly far away and Baal was rapidly closing the gap.

"You can't outrun me!" he said. "You're mine, halfbreed!"

"Not today, hellspawn!"

The hard, clear voice echoed through the playground. Jael's father stood at the entrance, his face calm. He hurled a small glass bottle over Jael's head. It smashed into Baal's face. Liquid sprayed out, and smoke rose up around his head. He gave a pained howl, then stumbled and fell.

Jael's father scooped her up and tossed her over his shoulder like a sack. He sprinted down the street to where the car was double-parked, the engine running. He tossed her into the passenger seat and climbed in on his side. Then he gunned the engine, and the car tore down the street.

They drove for hours on the highway across the desert plains, north toward Phoenix. The sun was setting red across the horizon when Jael finally found her voice.

"Daddy?" she asked. "What . . . was that?"

"A demon," he said tersely. He kept his eyes on the road. "We stayed there too long. I knew it, but I just . . ." He shook his head. "We can't make that mistake again. We got too comfortable."

"He said he knew Mom," she said. "He said she was a queen."

"Demons will say anything to get you off your guard," her father said.

"Was she?" she asked. "A queen?"

He didn't say anything.

"I bet Mom would answer my questions," she said. "I bet she'd be nice to me and she wouldn't keep making me move to new places all the time, and yell at me for talking about angels. I wish she was here to take me away to her palace!"

"Jael, your mother was a demoness."

It hung like that in silence for a long time. Her father still stared ahead at the road.

"My . . . mom?" she asked finally. "Was a demon? Like that . . . *thing* back there?"

"Not exactly like Baal. She looked like a person, most of the time. But yes. She was a demoness."

"But you said she died when I was born."

"Demons can die too," he said quietly. His eyes softened for a moment as he stared at the highway in front of them.

"Was she . . . bad?"

"She tried to do good," he said. Then his face hardened again. "And because of that, she made a lot of other demons very angry. If we stay in one place too long, demons might find us and kill us. That's one reason we have to keep moving."

"What's the other reason?"

"Because if we stay anywhere too long, normal people might figure out what you really are."

"What am I?"

"Your mother was a demon. That makes you half demon."

The desert plains flew by, receding on either side into the encroaching darkness. Jael felt like she was falling, even though she could still feel the car seat beneath her.

"Am *I* bad?" she asked.

"No, of course not!" he said, finally turning to look at her.

"Can I still go to church?" she asked.

"Yes," he said. "Jael, nothing has changed. You're not any different. You just know more about yourself now."

"But won't the priests get mad if they find out I'm a demon who goes to church?"

"First, you're only half demon. Second, they won't find out. Because we will be very careful not to say anything. To anyone." He turned and gave her a hard look. "Won't we?"

"Yes, Daddy." She was silent for a moment. Then, "Daddy?"

"Yes?" His voice was beginning to sound strained.

"Am I . . . going to Hell?"

"No, Jael," he said. "I will do everything in my power to make sure that doesn't happen."

"But—"

"Listen, this is all very complicated stuff that you're not really old enough to understand. I am doing what's best for us. For *you*. All you need to do is trust me. Don't worry about the rest."

"Do I at least have, you know . . . special powers?" she asked.

"No," he snapped. "No powers, no horns, no nothing. You're just like any other girl, but your mother was a demon. That's it. No more questions. Is that clear?"

"Yes, Daddy."

They drove on like that for some time. Finally, her father took a deep breath. "Look, Jael. I'm sorry. I wish things weren't so complicated. That we could just be normal people. But we just . . . can't." He drove on for a while longer. "If you want to talk about angels, that's fine. You can do that. Okay?"

But Jael didn't respond. She didn't know if she wanted to talk about angels anymore.

As the desert night settled in and the gleaming headlights cut through the emptiness all around them, it felt like the darkness would never lift.

And in a way, it never did. Her father never again spoke about her mother after that night. Occasionally, Jael would ask him questions, thinking she had to be old enough to hear the answers by then. But every time, he would tell her there wasn't much point in worrying about it, and to just do her best to be a good person.

Once again, Jael's imagination conjured up a thousand different mothers. But after that night, none of them were kind or angelic. None of them would swoop down and rescue her from this life. She understood that much, at least.

the gift

3

"So guess what I did last night after you left," says Britt as she sits down at the lunch table.

"I give up," says Jael. She holds up her slice of cafeteria pizza and idly watches the grease drip onto the plate. She might be the only teenager who ever lived who doesn't really like pizza. Her dad says it has something to do with her being half demon, although, as usual, he never explains why.

"Well," says Britt. She holds up her hands like she's framing a scene from a movie. "So. James calls me and—"

"Wait," says Jael. "James who?"

"James Gregory? Hello? Noseguard for the varsity football team?"

"Oh," says Jael. "He's a senior?"

"Of course," says Britt.

"Of course," repeats Jael.

"Anyway, he calls me and wants to know, do I want to go for a drive in his new Magnum?"

"Gee," says Jael, dropping her slice of pizza back onto her plate. "I think I can see where this is going."

"Well, obviously." Britt's pink-lipstick smile tightens for a moment and she tugs at her white blouse sleeve. Jael notices that the sleeve is hovering a little too high above the wrist. Britt's mom must be trying to stretch it for one more school year. That might be why it looks like Britt's boobs are about to bust out of her shirt. That's one thing Jael never has to worry about, at least. Her dad will do just about anything to stretch a buck, but he draws the line at letting clothes get tight enough to show his daughter's body shape.

"But J," Britt is saying, "he is so cute, in that big-football-player kind of way." She puts her hands on Jael's and squeezes. "And his Magnum is amazing. *And*, he bought me dinner and everything at some fancy restaurant with cloth napkins and the whole deal." She takes a bite of her cheese-speckled cafeteria pizza and chews for a moment. "I mean, I went down on him too, but whatever."

"Sure," says Jael, trying to sound casual. "Whatever."

"Don't give me that look," says Britt.

"What look?" protests Jael. "There's no look!"

"The prude look."

"I'm not a prude."

"Jael, you've never even kissed a boy."

"That's not true!"

"Oh yeah? When?" says Britt.

"Seventh grade! Albert Crain!" says Jael, like it's a game show.

"Who the hell is Albert Crain?"

"It was back when I lived in England. Back when I still tried to get in with the popular crowd every time I went to a new school. But since I was American, it was like they already hated me to start with, so I was desperate. One of the other girls dared me to kiss Albert Crain, this kid who always had a runny nose."

"And you took the dare?"

"It was just a little peck," says Jael. "But the other girls laughed for hours about it. Well, really, they laughed at me for hours. But they didn't accept me into their group. They just called me Mrs. Crain for a while, then ignored me. Plus, the whole rest of the time I was at that school, I constantly had to dodge Albert, who was convinced that I was secretly in love with him."

They sit in silence for a moment as Jael pokes gloomily at her pizza with her fork.

"That so doesn't count," says Britt.

"No," says Jael. "I guess not."

"This is depressing. Let's talk about something else!" Britt says with a forced brightness. "What are you doing for your birthday?"

"Nothing, really."

"Well, you have to do *something*."

"That's what Rob said."

"Oh really?" asks Britt. She leans back in her seat and gives Jael a smirk. "How interesting . . ."

"Come on," says Jael. "Just because he actually talks to me doesn't mean he wants to go out with me."

"He doesn't know what he wants," says Britt. "He's super cute, but he's a total space cadet. Trust me. You just need to take charge."

"Yeah, right."

"He's into you. How could he not be? You're gorgeous."

"Britt . . ."

"Seriously. I look like every other blond Nordic girl in the Pacific Northwest. But you, with your exotic looks—"

"You mean my big Arab nose."

"Shut up. You're beautiful. And I would *kill* to have your figure."

"What figure is that? Scrawny and boyish?"

"You have *muscles*, J. That is so totally hot. And you know a guy like Rob isn't intimidated by that shit. He is perfect for you! You just have to lead him in the right direction, and I guarantee he will gladly follow."

"I'm not leading him in some direction. I don't even know if I like him like that."

"Oh please," Britt says.

"Even if I did, what would I ask him to do?" says Jael. "I don't have any money, so we couldn't go out. And I couldn't invite him over to watch a movie or TV, obviously. It would be like, 'Hey, Rob. Wanna come over to my place and sit around and do nothing? If we're real quiet, we might even be able to hear my father in his room praying, even though he doesn't believe in God.' Yeah. That would be a fantastic date."

"I'll bet he'd take you out."

"How weird would *that* be? Asking him out, then asking him to pay?"

"Okay, fine," says Britt, slouching back down in her chair in defeat. "But still, you should do *something* on your birthday.

How about you come over to my place again after school. We'll eat junk and watch stupid TV."

"I wish," says Jael. "But my dad said not to make any plans tonight."

"For real?" says Britt, perking up again. "Maybe he's got some amazing present for you or something."

"Like a new suitcase."

"Shut up," says Britt. "Don't even go there."

"What? Why not?" says Jael. "It's been two years. Time to move again."

Britt shakes her head. "He wouldn't do that to you right in the middle of high school. Even *he's* not that mean."

"You have no idea," says Jael.

"Why does he have this freaky obsession with moving?" asks Britt.

"Because he's crazy," says Jael.

"Oh, God, now you've got me paranoid," says Britt. "You better call me afterward. If my phone goes to voice mail, it's because my mom's hogging it, so just e-mail me."

"I'll try," says Jael. "But you know, my old computer—"

Britt waves her hand. "Hey, you know what? Don't even worry about it. Because it's not going to be a suitcase. It's going to be something awesome. You just wait."

"But—"

"J, trust me." Britt squeezes Jael's hand. "You are due for some awesome."

Jael forces a smile. She's always admired the way Britt can stay optimistic, no matter what.

"Sure," she says, trying to match Britt's upbeat tone. "You never know."

Jael gets home just as it starts to rain. The inside of the house is dark except for the light spilling in from the kitchen doorway. Her father never turns on lights unless he has to. He's never said why, but Jael assumes it's to save money on electricity. Or because he's morbid.

The old wooden floorboards in the foyer squeak with each step, announcing her arrival as she makes her way to the kitchen. The kitchen light shines harshly from a single uncovered bulb over the sink. Her father sits at the white kitchen table. He was never a guy to show a lot of emotion, but the past few years, it's gotten even worse. He never lets anything out anymore. Jael can't figure out why he hasn't just exploded by now.

"Jael," he says quietly.

His hands rest on the table, and next to them, Jael sees a small wooden box. A birthday present after all? She feels a sudden surge of hope, but pushes it down. She needs to play it cool. Just because he has a present for her doesn't mean they're not moving. In fact, it could even be a consolation prize for ripping her out of the life she's been trying to make these past two years.

"Hey, Dad," she says, and only gives the box a quick glance on her way to the fridge. She gets out a fig and takes a bite, letting the mellow sweetness of its juice gather on her tongue as she tries to keep herself calm.

He gestures to the chair across the table. "Please sit."

She walks slowly over to the chair and sits down. The window is directly behind her and she can hear raindrops striking the wide, flat leaves of the hostas in the tiny front garden.

She takes another bite of her fig as she examines the box more closely. It's about the right size for jewelry, but it's plain and unfinished wood, with two tarnished silver hinges on one side and a silver clasp on the other side. A small silver padlock lies next to the box, open, with a key still in it.

"Happy sixteenth birthday," he says.

"Thanks," she says.

"So . . . ," he begins, then stops.

Usually, he speaks with absolute precision. The hesitation unnerves her more than anything else has. She gets the feeling this is something even bigger than a moving announcement.

"I have been holding this," he says, and his hands move to rest gently on the box, "for you. I promised I would give it to you on your sixteenth birthday."

He doesn't say anything more. His face is blank, except for a slight tic in one eyelid.

"Who?" she asks. "Who did you promise?"

"Your mother."

Jael suddenly feels like that scared little girl in the car at night in the desert.

"My . . . mom?"

"This was . . ." His voice crackles like an old record and he clears his throat. He brushes some imaginary dust from the small wooden box. Then he says, "It was hers."

He pushes the box closer to Jael. With his eyes still fixed

on hers, he releases the clasp and opens the lid. Inside, the box is lined with a woven silver fabric. And in the middle rests a rough-cut burgundy gem about the size of a baby's fist, attached to a silver necklace chain. The sight of it pulls at something deep inside Jael. Her face is suddenly warm. The need to touch it almost feels like a compulsion.

"Can I . . . ," she says, her hands outstretched.

"Yes," he says.

She reaches into the box and carefully lifts the necklace out by the chain. The gem feels impossibly light for its size. She holds it up and the gem spins slowly. The burgundy color seems to throb from deep within, softening even the harsh white kitchen light with its warm glow.

"It—It's beautiful," she says.

"Yes."

"Oh, Dad . . . this . . . this is the best present I've ever . . ." She looks at him and she must be getting soft because there are suddenly tears in her eyes.

"I'm glad you like it," he says, giving her a tight, forced smile.

"And . . . she . . . wanted me to have this? She said so?"

"She made me swear that I would give it to you when you turned sixteen," he says. "And so I have."

The chain is all one piece, with no clasp. But it's long enough for Jael to slip over her head. Her hands are shaking as she goes to put it on.

"*No!*" Her father lunges across the table and grabs her wrist, hard.

She stares first at his hand clenched around her wrist, then at the violent clash of emotions on his face. She almost doesn't recognize him.

"Dad?" she whispers.

She watches the realization of what he's done wash over him. He releases her wrist, then slowly sits back in his chair. He stares at his hand, like he can't believe it's his.

"I'm sorry," he says, almost to himself. For just a moment, there is something dark and broken in his eyes. Then his face slides back to neutral. "You can't wear the necklace."

"What do you mean I can't wear it? Not at all?"

"No. It's not . . . safe."

"So why did you give it to me?"

"Because I promised I would."

"But how is it dangerous?"

"You are not to wear it. End of discussion."

She cups the gem in her hands and stares into its dark, impenetrable center. "I can't believe this," she says, at first more to herself. Then she looks up at him. "I can't believe . . . *you*." She presses her thumbs onto the gem, rubbing them back and forth like a worry stone. "You finally give me something from my mother. After sixteen years, finally. Something." She looks back down at the necklace. "I would have taken anything, you know," she says softly. "A picture, a piece of clothing, a letter. It didn't have to be a *thing*, even. I would have been happy with a few stories about her. You always refuse to talk about her. I mean, are you so ashamed of my mother? Of what she was?"

"Of course not. You don't understand—"

"How can I, when you won't tell me anything? I don't even

know what she looked like. . . ." She presses the gem to her chest as a white-hot rage crawls up her spine. The anger feels good. It makes her feel strong. Powerful. Justified. She looks at him, staring hard into his eyes. "And now you give me this necklace. The one thing I can have of my mother. But I can't wear it, and you won't even tell me why."

"Jael, it's complicated. I don't think —"

"No." Jael stands up, clutching the necklace in her fist. "Go to hell, Dad."

She runs out of the kitchen. He yells something after her, but she's just trying to hold back the tears until she's up the spiral staircase and safely locked in her room.

Jael lies in bed, dangling her necklace in front of her eyes, staring absently into its dark, cloudy center.

She cried for a little while. Then she tried to call Britt, but the number was busy. Her stupid old computer wouldn't even boot up, so e-mail was out. By the time she'd gone through all that, she was tired. She decided that she wasn't going to do homework. It was her birthday present to herself. She got in her pj's and went to bed ridiculously early. So there.

But now she can't sleep. The window is open next to her bed, and she can hear the cool evening wind rustle through the leaves outside. There's a strange light in the sky, a slight tinge of yellow that makes the familiar view of rooftops out of her window seem almost magical. The air smells electric, and the whole sky gathers its strength, waiting for the signal. A thunderstorm is coming.

Jael loves thunderstorms. She can't say why, exactly. Maybe it's yet another weird demon thing her father never bothered to explain. But there's just something about thunderstorms that she finds soothing. And even though it rains nearly nonstop from October to May in Seattle, thunderstorms happen only once or twice a year. This storm, on this day, almost feels like a birthday present.

The first few drops of rain hit the window screen and stick in the tiny black squares, creating odd pixilated patterns. As the rain picks up speed, the patterns expand until the entire screen is drenched and begins to drip. A little spray makes it through, and drops prickle her face.

Then the lightning and thunder come, emerging from seething purple clouds. They roll and flicker in a soothing rhythm, lighting up the sky in quick bursts. Jael holds her necklace up to see how the lightning reflects off of it.

But it doesn't. Instead, it almost seems to absorb the light. In fact, there's something about the center that plays tricks on her eyes. It almost looks like something is moving in there.

She turns on the lamp next to her bed. Then she squints back down at the center of the gem. No, it's no trick. There really is something moving inside. She squints hard, trying to make it out. Gradually, the tiny swirling shapes within sharpen and come into focus until she's staring at a red-tinted miniature version of her kitchen.

There's a moment of dizzy vertigo and the world seems to lurch forward. Then it's as if she's in the tiny kitchen herself, hovering like a ghost.

Her father sits at the table, just like she left him. But now there are other things in front of him: a small ceramic bowl, a bottle of alcohol, gauze, surgical tape, a knife.

He picks up the knife and looks at it for a moment, turning it slightly so the light flashes along the edge. He positions the bowl of water in front of him and holds his hand over it. Then, whispering something quietly under his breath, he draws the knife slowly across his palm until a thin trickle of blood runs down and dribbles into the bowl of water. He continues to mutter under his breath as he squeezes his hand into a hard fist so that a little more blood drips into the bowl. He carefully cleans his hand with the alcohol and wraps it up in gauze. Then he stares back at the bowl of blood and water, waiting.

The surface of the liquid shivers, and gradually the swirls of blood coalesce into a perfect ring. Something that isn't exactly a voice, but more like an audible ripple in the air, says, "Yeah?" It's a harsh, deep, masculine sound.

"It's done," says Jael's father.

"You gave her the necklace?"

"Yes."

"Strange. I didn't hear anything. Didn't you release it?"

"I gave her the necklace," says her father. "That was all I promised her mother I would do."

There is a pause, while the blood in the bowl writhes for a moment. Then it re-forms.

"You are such a little shit. You might as well have spit on your wife's grave. You know she wanted you to—"

35

"If she wanted me to do anything more, she would have told me," says her father.

"What happened to you? I never liked you, but I at least used to respect you. Now you're nothing but a pathetic, cringing mortal."

"That's enough, Dagon."

"You think this is the end of it?"

"Yes, I do." He turns away, gazing up at the uncovered lightbulb.

"You know you can't avoid this. There are greater things at work here than just you and your cowardice."

"Right, your grand dream of Reclamation," says Jael's father, his voice bitter and mocking. "You hold on to that, Dagon. I know it's all you have left."

"And what do you have left?"

"I have *her*. She's real. And you'll never drag her into your bullshit."

"Bullshit? I believe in the Reclamation and so did your wife. You did too, once. But when it came down to making a real sacrifice, you just couldn't—"

Her father backhands the bowl off the table, spilling the watery blood onto the kitchen floor. He stands and looks down at the puddle, his fists clenched so tightly that the knuckles are white. Then he clasps his hands behind his head, closes his eyes, and takes a slow breath. He gets some cleaning solution and a sponge from underneath the sink. Then he scrubs the bloodstained floor on his hands and knees. He scrubs harder and harder, and his shoulders start shaking like he's crying, but his eyes are dry and filled with rage. . . . Jael can almost taste it, metallic and hot, coiling itself around him, tighter and tighter, until . . .

There's another dizzy lurch, and she's back in her bed, staring at her necklace. But it's empty now.

She hears her father's footsteps on the metal spiral staircase. She quickly switches off her light, lies down, and turns so her back is to the doorway. She hears him open the door and walk slowly, quietly, over to her bed. He stands there for a couple of minutes. Jael concentrates on keeping her breath slow and even, like she's asleep.

Faintly he whispers to her, "I love you."

And then he leaves. She listens to his footsteps going down the metal spiral staircase, then across the hardwood floor downstairs. Finally, she hears his bedroom door slowly close.

She curls up into a little ball, holding the gem of her necklace pressed tightly to her chest. Her father always said they had to hide from demons. So why did he just contact one? Who is this Dagon, and why does he know so much about her and her parents?

It takes her a long time to go to sleep.

confessions

4

The night the demon came to his room, Father Paul was reading Saint Augustine's *Confessions*. It was a book that Paul had always admired. Saint Augustine was one of those guys who saw himself clearly. A man who didn't flinch away from his mistakes. A man of deep contemplation and bold action. Paul could think of a few monks in his monastery who could stand to give it another read. Most of them, actually.

Paul had come to the monastery fresh out of seminary, his heart burning with passion for the wisdom of the great Church Fathers. He had this idea in his head that they would all sit around every night by the fire with a mug of brown ale and talk deep theological concepts. But what he found was a bunch of jaded, lazy old farts who would rather sit in the common room and watch TV every night.

He tried to start discussions. Talking was forbidden during meals, but between services, or in the common areas, he would try to engage some of them in something more than sports stats. They tolerated him politely for a few weeks. Then the abbot pulled him aside and explained to him how things worked around there, and said that if he didn't like it, he was more than welcome to transfer to another monastery.

He should have taken the abbot up on the offer. But Paul wasn't the kind of guy who gave up easily, even when sticking with it was against his best interests. So he stayed on, trying to show by example how a man dedicated to theological pursuit should act. It had been a year since then, and it hadn't been easy. Or effective. Lately, there had been times when he was tempted to loosen up a little. But Paul was good at resisting temptation.

Or so he thought.

It started with a strange dream—dark and warm, like floating in a river of silk. A soft, cool breeze caressed his face, lingering on his lips. Then the air meandered almost teasingly down his chin, onto his naked chest, and farther down his stomach, taut with tension, until finally—

Paul sat up in his small cot, shivering as he clutched the heavy wool blanket that covered him. His breath echoed harshly in the tiny room and his heart pounded so hard, he could almost taste it on the back of his tongue. It took several minutes before his pulse began to slow down. It was the most vivid dream he'd ever had. He shook his head, like it would clear the lingering feeling of sensual longing, and made the Sign of the Cross just out of habit.

He was about to settle back down to sleep when he happened to glance in the direction of his desk and saw a pair of blazing green eyes. They were like a cat's, but larger and brighter. They stared at him unblinkingly out of a dark cloud of shadow, bodiless and luminescent.

Paul knew that he was staring at something supernatural. In his heart of hearts, he felt he had been preparing for this battle his whole life. He held up the small crucifix that hung from his neck and tried to keep his hand from shaking.

"In the name of the Father, the Son, and the Holy Spirit," he said. "Reveal yourself!"

"If you wish," came a clear, light voice.

Slowly the shadows coalesced into the most beautiful woman Paul had ever seen. She had long, wild black hair that seemed to writhe with a life of its own. Her face was finely cut, yet strong, like an Arabian princess from some legend. She sat on the corner of his desk wearing only jeans and a T-shirt in the cold night air. She leaned back on her hands in a way that pulled the T-shirt tight across her breasts. Her legs dangled easily over the edge, spread wide in a casual, suggestive sort of way. She regarded him calmly, one black eyebrow arched and an amused smile on her full, burgundy lips. Her green cat eyes burned into him, making it difficult to think.

Paul had never encountered a demon before, but there was no doubt in his mind that this was what she was. A succubus.

"So you're the one the others talk about. The *good* priest. They all hate you, you know," she said casually. "And who can blame them? Nobody likes to be reminded what a worthless bag of meat they are."

"In the name of Jesus Christ, be gone, demon!" he said, losing some of the firmness in his voice.

"You know, that stuff only works on the lesser demons," she said. "And anyway, I prefer demoness."

"You have no power over me!" he said, the tremor in his voice unmistakable.

"Clearly not," she said. "My seduction failed. Honestly, it's the first time in almost three decades. I'm a bit shocked." Then she winked at him. "And impressed. It takes an incredibly strong will for a mortal to resist me."

"In the name of the Holy Spirit, I command you to tell me your name!" He remembered reading somewhere that knowing a demon's name granted some power over them.

"As I already said, calling on your deity doesn't do much for me," she said. "But I certainly don't mind telling you my name. If "—she held up a finger—"you ask politely."

He stared at her for a moment, not sure if she was mocking him. At last he said, almost tentatively, "Will you please tell me your name?"

Her smile broadened. "Why, for such a gentleman, of course! My name is Astarte."

"You're named after the Phoenician goddess?" he asked.

"Oh, you've heard the name? It seems so few priests these days have," she said with a mischievous glint in her eyes. "But to answer your question, I am not named after the Phoenician goddess. I *am* her. And many others besides."

"Many?" said Paul. "But . . ." He hesitated for a moment, caught between the duty he felt to repel this demon and the scholarly curiosity that had always been his greatest weakness. At last he said, "I don't understand."

"In Greece I was known as Aphrodite, and in Rome I was Venus. In Egypt, they called me Isis. In India, I was sometimes called Durga, at other times Gauri, and occasionally even Kali."

"All of these?" he asked, unable to hide the awe in his voice. "How old are you?"

She frowned. "Now, that's a little rude, don't you think?"

"So is sneaking into my room in the middle of the night and attempting to seduce me," said Paul.

"Many mortals would be grateful for the opportunity," she said.

"I am not many mortals," Paul said.

"So I am beginning to see," she said.

"So these ancient cultures mistook you for a goddess?"

"No, Father Paul. I *was* a goddess."

"But you're just a demon."

"That's what I am *now*," she said. "Because that is what people *want* me to be. That is what they choose to believe."

"That makes no sense. Reality defines belief, not the other way around. How could—"

"Well, Father," she interrupted as she glanced out of the tiny rectangular window in his room, "this has been a delightful chat, but I think I'll take my leave."

"Oh . . . ," said Paul. "Good." But he couldn't quite hide the disappointment in his voice.

"Good-bye, Paul," she whispered. Then she was gone.

It took a long time for him to get back to sleep. Whenever he closed his eyes, the afterimage of those glittering green eyes floated ghostlike behind his lids. He got only an hour of sleep before he had to get up and go to chapel for morning services. Even during prayer he couldn't stop thinking about his encounter with the demoness. More than once he missed joining the others in response.

That afternoon, the lack of sleep caught up with him and he dozed off in the library. The thick collection of papal edicts slipped from his hands and landed on the linoleum with a sharp slap. He woke with a jolt and glanced around to see if the few other priests in the library had noticed. But either they were too engrossed in their studies, or they pretended to be. Did they suspect? It sounded like the demoness visited many of the priests in this monastery. Paul was certain that the others spent the time in wicked sexual acts instead of theological discussion. But if the others did suspect anything, they would most likely assume he was breaking his vows of chastity as well. It surprised him how much that possibility bothered him. Why did he care what those hypocrites thought of him? And yet, he did.

Well, it was over. He had successfully repelled the succubus. Fascinating as the brief discussion had been, he needed to put the whole thing behind him.

Of course, it wasn't that easy. Because that night, she came back.

Paul sat at his little desk in his little room, poring over Augustine's *Confessions* again, trying to keep his mind off the demoness. Augustine had started life as a pagan—rich, selfish, given to indulging in every vice. In the *Confessions*, he describes his reluctant journey from ignorant heathen to one of the greatest theologians the Church has ever had.

Normally, Paul took comfort in the story because it reminded him of his own humble beginnings. Not that he had ever been rich. He had spent most of his childhood in the purgatory of the foster-care system. But he had been selfish and godless. It wasn't until he ended up in juvie for assault that old Father Green took him under his wing and showed him that life was more than just the struggle to survive. Father Green hadn't always been the nicest guardian, but he turned Paul's life around completely. He had taught Paul the sublime joy of intellectual pursuits, and on his deathbed, he had made arrangements for Paul to go to seminary. It was Father Green who first compared Paul to Saint Augustine. And ever since, when Paul's spirits were at low ebb, he found himself sifting through the *Confessions*.

But that night, as he sat at his desk, feeling the walls of his cramped room closing in on him, the words of Augustine seemed hollow, stuffed with self-satisfaction, and—

"Arrogant prick," came the clear, warm female voice behind him.

Paul nearly fell out of his chair as he turned around. Astarte lounged on his cot as if it were some queenly bower that needed only a few beefy, shirtless men fanning her with palm leaves to complete the picture.

"Augustine was," she said. "Not you."

"You!" he said, flushed with horror and a strange thrill. Some futile attempt at a prayer for banishment began to form on his lips, but then her statement filtered through his welter of emotions. "You . . . knew Saint Augustine?"

"Not well," said Astarte. "And certainly not in a friendly sort of way. He was like one of those people who quits smoking and suddenly acts as though he can't stand to be around it at all."

"He was trying to rise above his unfortunate beginning," said Paul, unable to prevent the defensive tone in his voice. "You can't let the past hold you down."

"That's true," she said. "But it's dangerous to reject it completely. For example, take Saint Thomas Aquinas. Now *there* was a priest! But terribly stubborn. When he first started his brewery, I said to him . . ."

They talked for hours about various Church theologians, popes, and saints. He found her wealth of knowledge and unique perspective spellbinding. He was having the type of discussion he had longed for since he entered the monastery. He simply couldn't resist.

It wasn't until the pink predawn light began to leak in through the window that she finally slipped away. Through the next day, Paul barely managed to stay awake. But once the sun went down, Astarte returned again to set his mind on fire.

And she came every night after that. Paul was troubled by it at first. He felt it was risky to spend so much time with an agent of Satan. But it seemed almost a sin to pass up so much firsthand knowledge. He even began to tell himself that he was getting to know the enemy so that he could better fight them. To that end, he began to ask her questions about Hell.

"Is it the orderly pit of eternal suffering that Dante described?" he asked.

She smiled, a little sadly. "No, it's not like what Dante and so many others have depicted. Far more interesting in form, but far less useful in function, I'm afraid."

Paul couldn't quite understand what she was saying, so he tried a different tack. "Are there a lot of demons, then? How many, would you say?"

"What an interesting question," she said, her eyes growing sadder still. "It's never occurred to us to have counted ourselves. I wonder if there are fewer of us now than there used to be, or whether we are just . . . lesser."

"What about Satan?" asked Paul.

"Lucifer Morningstar, you mean? What about him?"

"Does he plan to conquer the world someday?"

"Lucifer? Make plans?" She laughed a little, but it was still tinged with a strange melancholy. "That seems unlikely. Although, I wouldn't know. It has been a very long time since he has spoken to me." She looked away, a muscle twitching in her neck.

"I'm sorry," said Paul. "I didn't realize it would upset you to talk about these things."

She turned to him suddenly, then, her green eyes wide and glistening with tears. A single one escaped and rolled down her smooth brown cheek as she reached out and laid her hand on his.

"Thank you," she said.

"For what?" he asked. "For upsetting you?"

She smiled, and this time the warmth broke through the sadness. "You have a very curious blend of compassion and honesty, yet you are not fragile and weak-willed like so many others."

"Uh," he said. "Thank you, I think."

She laughed and shook her head. "But what about you? We've talked so much about me, but hardly anything about your life."

"I'm afraid my life is nowhere near as interesting as yours," he said.

"If there is one thing that I have learned in my long life," said Astarte, "it's to appreciate nuance." She was quiet for a moment, just looking at him. Then she sat up suddenly. "I wonder if you'll allow me to look."

"At what?" he asked a little nervously.

"Your life."

"You mean my memories? You can do that?"

"Sort of . . . ," she said. "If you let me, I can look at your soul."

"My soul?"

She shrugged. "It's up to you. I certainly wouldn't force something like that."

"And . . . you would see *everything*?"

"More or less," she said. "Not necessarily in a literal way. It's more like I would feel your experiences the way you felt them."

He leaned back against the desk. His first impulse was to refuse. Making himself that vulnerable to a demoness seemed dangerous to the point of stupidity. But then, what did he have to hide? In fact, the more he thought about it, the more appealing the idea seemed. There would be someone in the world who knew and understood him completely. No pretense, no misunderstanding. One person he could be—had to be— completely honest with.

He looked over at her on his cot. She sat up straight, perfectly still, no longer lounging or acting coy. She looked at him with her piercing, unnatural eyes and he somehow knew that she would understand him.

"Okay," he said. "God help me . . . Okay."

She smiled then. And it wasn't the sly smile he always saw before, but one more simple and serious.

"I must warn you," she said. "It can be rather . . . intense for mortals to experience, perhaps even a little alarming at first. The best thing to do is not panic and simply allow it to happen. Go with the flow, as they say."

He nodded, not really trusting himself to speak.

"Come," she said, and patted the spot next to her on the cot. "Sit."

He hesitated.

"You trust me to look into your soul but not sit next to you on a bed?" she asked, that teasing smile coming back a little. "Perhaps you need to rethink your priorities."

He gave her a wry smile and sat down next to her on the bed.

"Good," she said, her voice soothing. "Now, look into my eyes."

He looked.

And the world melted into a churning maelstrom, devoid of order or meaning. There was no up or down, no solid ground to gauge distance or perception. A terrifying vertigo took hold and he struggled to scream, except there was no air, no throat, no mouth, no him—

"Paul!" Astarte's voice pierced through the storm of chaos. "Paul, it's still just me. It's okay, Paul. Don't fight it."

Her voice was like a warm, firm hand that cupped his leaking sanity and gathered it back together. Far away, he heard his own voice say "Okay . . . I'm okay. . . ."

"Good," she whispered. "Now, are you ready to stop hiding behind this storm?"

"You mean . . ."

"Yes, you're the one creating it," she said. "I suspected this was under the surface, but you do hide it well."

"So what do I do?"

"Just let me in, Paul. Just let me in."

"Oh."

"What are you hiding, anyway?"

"Nothing, really."

The storm evaporated in a flash. Behind it, there was pure, joyous light. It filled the hollow chasm of cold loneliness in his heart that he had tried to fill with money, with drugs, with God. But it had never been enough. This was enough. It expanded endlessly within him, encompassing him until he was just a part of it. It sang in a voice unlike anything he had ever heard.

Th.. .. ..

He was back on Earth, in the monastery, in his tiny room, on his old, creaking cot, sitting next to the most beautiful and wondrous creature in the world.

"I . . ." He felt exhausted, as if he had just run a marathon. "I didn't know it would be like that," he said. Then he swayed and started to fall backward.

Astarte caught him and laid him gently down on the cot. There were tears in her eyes.

"Neither did I," she whispered.

Then he lost consciousness.

He woke up hours later, a hard beam of sunlight streaming in through his tiny window. He sat up slowly and looked over at the clock. He had missed morning prayers. In fact, it was nearly lunchtime.

At lunch, the abbot said grace, but Paul barely noticed. He ate as if in a trance, recalling every impossible detail of the previous evening perfectly. It had been like what he always imagined the Apostles had felt when they had been filled with the Holy Spirit. Try as he might, he could not convince himself that the experience had been bad. But what, then, did that mean for him if letting a demon see your soul wasn't bad? In fact, the very idea that Astarte was evil seemed absurd to him now. If demons weren't evil, what about all the other beliefs he had been taught? Was any of it true? He didn't know what to believe anymore. He had so many questions for her. He waited eagerly for the setting sun, so he could drop his burden onto the graceful but inconceivably strong shoulders of Astarte.

Except that night, she didn't come.

He waited for her until dawn finally emerged, its wan rays burning away the last of his hope. His body ached and his eyes burned with weariness. He dragged himself to morning prayers and then down to the dining hall for breakfast and, this time when the abbot said grace, each word was like a hammer. He stared at his food, unable to muster up the effort to eat.

In retrospect, it seemed obvious what a fool he had been. She had failed to seduce his body, so she seduced his mind, his heart, and his faith. She had gotten what she wanted. Why come back? She had done such a thorough job that even now, he couldn't bring himself to hate her.

The clink and clank of silverware on dishes was like needles in his ears. He kept glancing at the other priests around him. Had she visited one of them last night? Mark another fallen soul on the tally sheet and move on to the next conquest? Because make no mistake, he had fallen. He was doomed to love a demoness. He would spend his remaining days here in this living graveyard of dead faith with all these other broken souls. Maybe, every once in a while, she would visit him again. To taunt him, perhaps. Or to offer the sin of flesh that he had refused before. And God help him, this time he would accept. But God would not help him, of course. Because now he was well and truly damned. He would slowly drift through his life like a ghost until death finally carried him down to the deepest pits of Hell.

No. That wasn't him. A coward's defeat might be good enough for these other wretched creatures, but not him. He did not simply sit and wait for things to come to him. He would meet his fate head-on.

He stood up suddenly, leaving a full plate of food behind. Some of the priests glanced up at him, but they remained silent as he left the dining hall. Maybe they knew, maybe they didn't. He no longer cared.

Once he was out of the monastery, he crossed the cobblestone courtyard and passed through the front gate, then turned north into the wide, rolling meadow that led to the side of the mountain.

It took him nearly until sunset to cross the meadow and hike up the narrow switchbacks that zigzagged up the mountain. His mouth was so dry that he could hardly swallow, and his feet were so swollen that they felt like they might burst through his shoes. But finally, he reached a spot that was high enough and accessible enough for him to jump.

His one small hope, which he held in his heart like a clam holds a pearl, was that on his way to Hell, he might see Astarte one last time. If he did, he would look into those sparkling green eyes and show her his soul one more time and maybe she would feel, if only a for a brief instant, the torment she had caused him.

He stepped to the edge, too tired and miserable to feel more than a tiny tremor at the empty space that stretched down and ended far below on a bed of jagged rocks and thorny brush.

He jumped.

Then there was a flash.

Something slammed into his chest and he flew backward onto the ledge. He lay there, gasping for air. A creature of roaring fire loomed over him. It shook its fist at him and shrieked, "You stupid mortal!" It jabbed a burning finger at him, singeing his robe.

He stared up at it uncomprehendingly for a moment and then he looked past the fire and saw the green eyes beneath.

"Astarte?"

"Of course!" she raged at him. "Who else would it be?"

"Did you come to gloat?" he yelled. "To taunt me?"

"Taunt you?" she said, her flames calming slightly. "What are you talking about?"

"Is your demon heart too cruel to even see it?" he said. "I love you!"

"Oh," she said, and the fire went out completely. She stood before him as he had always seen her, in jeans and a T-shirt, except her hair was unkempt and her eyes were red and puffy, as if she had been crying.

"Well, that's it, then," she said quietly. She sat down next to him on the hard mountain rock. "We're in deep shit. Because I love you, too."

pure chemistry
5

Jael stares at the chemistry worksheet in front of her. Symbols and initials that somehow relate to the periodic table squat on the page, silent and unhelpful. All around her, she hears the scratch of pens on paper. Her own pen is poised in the air, ready to begin a flurry of scrawling at any moment. It's been that way for half the class period.

All night she kept having this strange . . . well, "dream" isn't exactly the right word for it. It was more like a memory. But not hers. Her father's? She barely recognized him. And was that her mother that she saw? It seems too much to hope for. One thing she's sure of, the dream has something to do with the necklace. She woke up with the jewel clenched so tight in her fist that her knuckles were white.

"Okay, class," says Ms. Randolph, the chemistry teacher. Ms. Randolph should be in some research lab exploring cutting-edge discoveries instead of teaching basic concepts to unwilling teenage captives. She even looks a little like a mad scientist, with dark, pouchy eyes and wild orange corkscrew hair. "You may use the second half of the class period to finish up the worksheet with a partner."

"Need help, Betty?" asks Rob, sliding into the chair across from her at the black wooden lab table.

"In so many ways," says Jael.

"How was your b-day?"

"It was pretty crappy. But I did get a cool birthday present."

"Yeah? What?"

"Oh . . . ," says Jael. "It's . . . a necklace."

"Awesome," says Rob. His eyes search her neckline. "So . . . where is it?"

"Um." Jael's hand goes unconsciously to her throat. "I'm not really wearing it. Yet. At least . . . uh . . ."

"Sorry," says Rob. "I don't mean to be all up in your business or anything. If you don't want to tell me . . ."

"No, no, it's not a huge deal," says Jael. "I mean, it *is*, but . . . well, my dad gave me this necklace that belonged to my mom. And, uh, I've never had anything of hers before. So it's . . . I don't know. Pretty intense for me. And I guess . . . it reminds him a lot of her. So he doesn't want me to wear it."

"Wow," says Rob. "So he must be still totally in love with her after all these years, huh?"

"Huh," says Jael. "Maybe you're right." The idea takes her by surprise. What if the reason he never talks about her mother isn't because he's ashamed of her or what she was. Maybe he's just brokenhearted. Maybe he loved her mother so much that he'll *never* get over it. And while it sucks that Jael gets the short end of that stick, it also strikes her as kind of romantic, in that sad, emo sort of way.

"Hello?" says Rob. "Bets?"

"Sorry," says Jael. "Just spaced out for a second."

"Did you eat breakfast today? Because, you know, I used to skip breakfast all the time, but then I started getting these dizzy spells and . . ."

His expression is so sincere that she laughs.

"What?" he asks.

"How about you help me with this chem stuff," she says.

"Right, right, right. Lock and load." He leans over and scans her worksheet.

"Why do you always say that?" Jael asks. "'Lock and load.'"

"Huh?" He looks up at her, his blond bangs flopping into his eyes. He brushes them aside. "Oh, just my little thing that helps me get my game face on."

"Your game face? For chem?"

"When I'm in the zone, it all makes sense. But the problem is, I get easily distracted."

"ADD or something?"

He shrugs. "Whatever you want to call it. I don't do diagnosis and meds. It's my thing to deal with and I'll deal with it."

"That makes sense."

Rob gives her a grin. Then he nods to her worksheet. "So, like, Bets. It looks like you don't have any answers written down."

"That's why you're here." She smiles and pats the worksheet.

"Come on. You gotta try, at least."

"Rob, seriously. I just don't get it."

"You have to get excited about it, that's all."

"Excited? About chemistry? I mean, I appreciate it in

theory; it makes medicine and things like that. But calculations with the periodic table, not so much."

"That's not really what I mean," says Rob. "That stuff is cool and all, but what I'm talking about is . . . well, it's kinda like magic."

"Magic?" Her heart skips a beat. "Uh, what do you mean?"

"Okay"—Rob holds up his hand—"I can see you're totally sketched out. I know it sounds hokey or whatever . . ."

"No, I'm interested," says Jael. "Trust me."

"All right," says Rob. "Well, you know, back in the day, there were these people. Sorcerers, witches, shamans, and what-not, who thought they were making magic potions. But what they were really doing was chemistry. They just didn't fully understand it." As he continues to talk, his eyes get bright and his usual grin widens into something open and boyishly excited. "They'd mix this frog skin with that leaf, and poof, it cured some disease. They thought it was the prayers they were saying or the spirit of the lizard or whatever that did it. But it was actually the chemical reaction between the skin and the leaf."

"I can kind of see that . . . ," says Jael. "So magic is really just science we don't understand yet?

"Exactly!" says Rob, excited in a way that Jael's never seen before. "And, and, and—there's still so much that we don't understand. Fifty years ago, we hadn't even mapped the genome. I mean, what's it going to be like fifty years from *now*? Theories as big as a multiverse or as small as subatomic particles? We just have no idea! We can't even imagine!"

"So . . . do you think this is just about potions, or could it be other kinds of stuff? Like . . ." She can't bring herself to look at him as she asks the next part, so she picks at the hem of her skirt. "You know, like, uh . . . I don't know . . . magic talismans. Or, I don't know . . . magic people?"

"You know what I think?" asks Rob, and his voice is so quiet yet so raw that her eyes are drawn back to him. "I think that all these barriers we put up between us and what we believe is impossible. It's all bullshit. Like putting on blinders. Because we're scared."

"Of what?"

"Of what we're capable of. You know?"

"I . . ." She doesn't want to be scared. She wants to feel the open excitement she sees in Rob's eyes instead. A slow blush creeps up onto her face, but she forces herself to keep looking at him. "I don't know if I get what you're saying. But I really want to."

His smile is like the sun after a storm.

"Cool," he says. "Now, seriously. Let's lock and load."

"And that was it?" demands Britt. "Then he just started doing the chem worksheet?" There's a mound of little white packets of Parmesan cheese next to her plate, and she begins slowly, methodically tearing them open and dumping them on her spaghetti noodles until the powdery white cheese sits like a tiny Mount Rainier.

"Yep," says Jael. She stirs the dry, orange spaghetti noodles on her plate without much interest. "Not another word about anything other than the periodic table."

"Boys," Britt says. She twirls a big mound of spaghetti on her fork and takes a bite. Then she says, "I never pegged Rob for one of those New Age freaks, though."

"What do you mean?"

"Oh, you know. Those hippie types that believe in magic crystals and shit." She wiggles her fingers at Jael, like she's casting a spell.

"Yeah . . ." Jael gives a forced little laugh. "Pretty weird."

"And totally a sin."

"Right," Jael says.

Religion is the one topic that Jael and Britt don't really talk about. Despite the fact that Britt hooks up with boys on a regular basis, she is hard-core Catholic. Obviously, that would kind of conflict with Jael's parentage.

"But he's totally cute. And super sweet," Britt adds quickly. She stirs the mound of Parmesan into her noodles for a moment and a frown starts to wrinkle her pale forehead.

"How's, uh . . . what's his name? Varsity noseguard guy," Jael asks.

"James Gregory?"

"Yeah, him."

"Douche."

"Whoa, what? I thought you liked him."

"I did until yesterday after school when he told me he couldn't take me out anymore because he was getting too much shit from the rest of his team. But get this: He said we could still fool around if I want."

"He actually said that?"

"Yeah."

"Britt . . . I'm sorry. That's really shitty. He sounds like an idiot. You deserve way better."

"Yeah," says Britt without much enthusiasm. But then she takes a deep breath and works her face back into something that looks kind of like a smile. "So what about you? How was your night? My mom was hogging the phone, talking to some guy from Chicago. So what was that 'We Have to Talk' note all about?"

Jael gives a bitter little laugh. "That's funny. I kind of forgot about the note. But what's even funnier is that we hardly talked at all."

"Well what *did* happen?! You're killing me here!"

"Um . . . he just gave me this necklace from my mom."

"Oh my God, that's amazing!" Britt says. "I bet it's gorgeous! So where is it? Why aren't you wearing it?"

"He said I can't wear it."

"What? He is such an asshole!" She looks pissed, like *she's* the one being banned from wearing it. "Did he say why?"

"Not really," says Jael. "I guess I didn't really give him the chance."

"What do you mean?"

"Well, when he said that, I kind of flipped out and told him to go to hell."

"Damn right!" Britt says. "You go."

"Yeah," Jael says. "I went."

"J, I am so proud of you for sticking up for yourself, finally. How does it feel? I bet it feels amazing."

"I definitely feel . . . I don't know . . . different," says Jael.

"Talking to boys, standing up to your dad." Britt reaches across the table and squeezes her arm. "You keep up this momentum. I can just feel it, J. This is going to be your year."

The next class period is canceled for the All-School Mass in honor of Saint Francis of Assisi. Jael isn't an expert on saints, but this particular one was permanently burned into her brain when she was little. Her father bought her a picture book called *The Life of Saint Francis*. Saint Francis was this rich guy who gave up everything, including his clothes, then ran around naked in the forest with the animals. She still remembers page seventeen, which showed Saint Francis's naked ass as he preached in front of a small cluster of animals. The picture embarrassed her so much that she shoved the book up on the highest level of her bookshelf. But that night, she couldn't stop thinking about it. She wanted to make sure that she really did see it. So once her father was asleep, she took it to bed with her, pulled the covers over her head, turned on her flashlight, and stared at the drawing of a naked saint in the woods exposing himself to a bunch of animals in a book that her father had bought in a religious bookstore. To this day, whenever anyone mentions Saint Francis, she thinks of that picture.

The chapel takes up an entire wing of the school and looks even more gloomy and gothic than the rest of the building. The tall stained-glass windows don't let in much light and the slick slate floor seems to hold a lingering chill. At the far end is a massive crucifix with a statue of a bleeding, nearly naked Jesus, suspended by thick chains over a simple stone altar.

misfit

Despite being half demon, Jael doesn't mind Mass. For one thing, she hopes that it chills out any weird demon stuff that might creep up in her. But probably even more important, it's just always been one of the few constants in her life. For about an hour, she knows exactly what's going to happen and how she's supposed to respond. When the priest gets to the middle of Mass, she's down on the hard kneelers, staring at nothing, muttering the Nicene Creed along with every other student in the school. She's reached that mental place of absolute zone-out, totally on autopilot as she mutters, "We believe in one God, the Almighty Father, maker of Heaven and Earth, of all that is seen and unseen. . . ."

Then she smells something burning.

She looks around, but none of the altar servers are burning incense. And anyway, it's not that spicy sweet smell. This is more like a fireplace mixed with melting plastic. Other people start shifting around in their seats, and someone behind her coughs.

"Your bag," hisses Britt next to her. "It's something in your bag."

Jael looks down and sees a tendril of smoke curling out from under the flap of her messenger bag. She doesn't know what's going on in there, but she's sure that she doesn't want to deal with it in the middle of All-School Mass. She grabs her bag, climbs over Britt and out into the aisle, then heads toward the exit at the back of the chapel.

"Miss Thompson," says Father Aaron as he holds up a hand to stop her, a frown beneath his walrus mustache.

"Sorry, Father," she mutters. "Female trouble."

He flinches and immediately steps aside. It's a cheap shot, but as long as she uses it sparingly, it's always effective.

Once she's out of the chapel, she sprints down the main hallway of the school and into the bathroom. She checks the stalls to make sure no one is hiding out, then she dumps everything from her bag onto the floor. She swats away a puff of smoke and scans the contents.

She sees her necklace first and grabs it. She should have left it at home. What was the point of carrying it around with her if she couldn't wear it? But moments before she left that morning, she changed her mind and shoved it in her bag anyway.

She examines it carefully now, but it seems fine. Then she looks down at the rest of the stuff and sees a roughly circular shape burned into her history textbook. It's still smoking a little, and the edges of the hole glow orange. She kneels down and flips through the book. It's one of those thick, five-hundred-page monsters, and the hole goes down to about page three hundred, with brown scorch marks another twenty pages deep.

She hurriedly spreads out the rest of the things in her bag. A few of the pens are halfway melted, a notebook is a little crispy at one edge, and her lip gloss is destroyed, but the history book seems to have absorbed most of the damage.

But damage from what?

She stands up and nervously rubs her thumb across her necklace. She notices tiny black bits stuck to some of the chain links and she absently begins to pick them off. Then she realizes that they look like burned paper. She looks back at the history book. She kneels down again and holds the gem over the hole. It fits perfectly.

She slowly stands up and stares at the gem. Deep in the center, she can just make out an angry red pulse.

"What are you?" she says. "Where did you come from?"

The pulse grows larger until the entire gem flashes red in slow, regular beats. She sees a slight movement in the center, and a sickening fear shoots up through her stomach. Not now. Not here in the school restroom, in the middle of the day. . . .

That weightless vertigo feeling hits again and she finds herself somewhere else. But it's not like anyplace she's ever seen. It appears to be a cavern about the size of a football field. The ceiling is ridged with off-white, curved beams—like being inside a giant rib cage. Six-foot-high gray stalagmites protrude from the ground in regular intervals. She can't tell if they're made of stone, wood, or bone. Balanced on top of each one is a crab shell the size of a car. Some of the shells are mottled with red and orange, others with green and blue. All of them leak thick black smoke and sprout tongues of flame. Something like grease drips from them and runs down the sides of the pillars.

Then she hears heavy footsteps accompanied by a dry, scraping sound. A figure roughly the shape of a person, but more than eight feet tall and massively built, walks down the line of shells, its face hidden in shadow. For a moment Jael panics, thinking it will see her. But then she remembers that it's just like last night. Even though it all *seems* so real, she's not really there.

The creature shuffles down the line of columns, stopping at each one to examine the giant crab shell on top. It pokes a stick of some kind into one of the shells, and she hears screams and whimpers in response. As the creature gets closer, she sees that what she thought was clothing or armor is actually fish scales covering its entire body. The scales are yellow and have a sickly, dried-out look. The creature's thick arms stretch out to either side, ending in thin, curved claws.

The fish creature uses the stick to lift up the top half of one of the shells. A puff of black smoke escapes, followed by something fast and wriggling. The creature slams the shell back down, trapping whatever it is back inside. Then it stands there for a moment, staring at the closed, smoking shell. It scratches its hairless, earless head with one claw.

Then it turns suddenly and looks directly at Jael with black, impenetrable sharklike eyes.

A pathetic little squeak of fright escapes from Jael's throat.

"Well, well, well," the creature growls in a voice like sandpaper. "It looks like you're more clever than your father thinks."

It smiles. Cracked fish lips stretch wide, showing rows of needle teeth as long as her fingers.

"He won't give you the answers you need. When you're ready for the truth, use the necklace to call me. Just call for Dagon. . . ."

The hard heat of the cavern drops away and she is left huddled on the bathroom floor, shaky and cold. But the visions of that place and that creature still fill her mind. It's all she can do to keep from hyperventilating.

The door opens.

65

"Jael?"

Ms. Spielman. Jael hears the soft clack of her sandals coming closer. Ms. Spielman kneels down next to her.

"Jael, what's wrong?"

Jael looks back at her with wild, frightened eyes. "I don't know," she manages to say in a halting whisper. Then a strange laugh bubbles out for a moment before she's able to stop it. "I don't know."

"Okay, Jael, you're okay," says Ms. Spielman in a voice as soft and soothing as honey. It helps a little. "I'm here. What can I do to help?"

"Don't . . . t-t-tell my dad about this," Jael says.

"About? . . ." says Ms. Spielman. Then she notices the burned history book. "What happened?" she asks, unable to keep the shock out of her voice.

Jael says nothing.

"Okay, well, forget it for now," says Ms. Spielman, her voice back to soothing sweetness. Almost singsong. She places her cool, soft hand on Jael's cheek and smiles at her. "Why don't we get ourselves together a little, huh? Put your necklace back on and we'll clean up the rest of your stuff."

"It wasn't . . . ," Jael begins. But if she puts the necklace back in her bag, it could start burning things again. She's already come this far; she might as well go all the way. So she holds the chain up in both hands and slowly puts it over her head. The gem rests against her chest and feels so nice on her skin that she lets out a quiet sigh.

"Feel better?" asks Ms. Spielman.

Jael nods.

Then the two of them gather up Jael's stuff in silence and put it back into her bag.

"Jael, I have to get to my next class," says Ms. Spielman. "But I think Father Ralph has this period free. Would you like to talk to him for a bit?"

"Okay," she says. She feels like she has to talk to somebody. And Father Ralph might actually be the perfect person.

Jael slouches in a neon-green IKEA chair in Father Ralph Frizetti's office. Father Ralph is the youngest of the three priests and he does his best to make both education and Catholicism as accessible and hip as possible. But he tries a little too hard to "keep it real," as he says. He always wears the regular priestly black with the white collar, but he also wears a funky cartoon character belt buckle, as if to let students know that he can be fun, too. And the single hoop earring and scruffy hipster beard just don't look right on him. But at least Jael can relate to him. Unlike the drill sergeant Father Aaron or the saintly Mons, Father Ralph just seems like a regular person who happens to be a priest.

Father Ralph leans back on the edge of his desk, scratching his beard thoughtfully. They've been sitting like this for more than five minutes in complete silence. But if Father Ralph is getting impatient, he doesn't show it.

At last, feeling like an idiot but not knowing any other way to start, Jael says, "Father, do you believe in . . . uh, supernatural stuff?"

He looks surprised by the question. "Well, Jael, yes, as a matter of fact, I do."

"Really?"

"I believe that God counts as supernatural."

"Oh," says Jael. "What about . . . magic?"

"I prefer the word 'miracle.'"

"Right," says Jael, her faint hope of real communication with Father Ralph already starting to fade. She gives it one last try. "What about stuff like evil spirits and, uh . . . demons?"

He looks at her for a long time, like he's trying to figure out if she's messing with him. Eventually he says, "Well, in a way, I do."

"In a way?"

"Hell isn't a place, you know."

"It isn't?"

"No, it's a state of mind. A state of being. Hell is the absence of God."

"Okay . . ."

"So, technically, you don't even have to be dead to be in Hell."

"You don't?"

"Nope. You just have to have alienated yourself from God to the point where you no longer see Him or feel Him in your heart."

"Uh-huh," says Jael. She doesn't like how he's trying to maneuver the conversation. "And do you feel Him in your heart, Father?" she asks with maybe a little snottiness.

He pauses for a second, adjusting his SpongeBob Square-Pants belt buckle, then smiles and says, "Of course. Now, the question is, Jael, do you?"

"Look, Father. It's all kind of complicated for me. You know, there's a lot of . . . family history."

"Your father has made his doubts about the Church known to the rest of the faculty. Doubt is healthy, and it's only natural for you to begin to explore similar questions."

"Okay, but what if some things in the Bible were . . . wrong. You know? Like what if demons weren't really . . . evil? At least, not all of them."

"Well, Jael, I don't really believe in demons."

"Okay, so you think they're just a state of mind, too?"

"Well," says Father Ralph, rolling his eyes. "Some of the older members of our faculty would disagree with me, but the way that I interpret scripture is that Satan is not an actual person who walks and talks and creeps into your room at night to tempt you into doing evil things. Satan, demons, and all of those scary things are merely symbols of the weakness within us. Our human weakness that comes from Original Sin. We separate it from ourselves and give it the label of Satan, or monster, or any number of things. But Satan is no more real than, say, Superman. They're both icons that we, as members of this society, all identify with because they reflect something about ourselves. We are all a little bit like Superman. And we are all a little bit like Satan, too." He smiles a little smugly, probably thinking he's picked a good comparison. Then he glances at the burgundy gem around Jael's neck.

"Wow," he says. "That's a very pretty necklace."

"Thanks," says Jael. "I think it might be from Hell."

69

the avenging love
6

Paul liked to watch his wife sleep. Astarte was such a complicated being that sometimes it was difficult to see her clearly. But when she slept, all of those layers dropped away. Her perfect tan face smoothed out and almost seemed to radiate peace.

He brushed back a ringlet of her black hair and wondered if demons dreamed and, if so, what they dreamed of. He'd have to ask her later when she woke up. Let her sleep for now. They had been traveling hard for weeks.

He gently kissed her cheek, then slipped on pants, a sweater, and his overcoat. It probably wasn't wise for him to go out alone. But he was tired of being cooped up in the hotel. Back at the monastery, all those years ago, he had been able to stay in confined spaces for days on end. Now even the respectably sized hotel room pressed in on him. He couldn't decide if that was a sign of growth or something else.

"Paul?" Astarte whispered sleepily from the bed.

He paused at the door. "Yeah, hon?"

"Pick me up some breakfast while you're out."

"Sure," he said, and quietly slipped out.

Their hotel was just off Union Square. He wandered the park and square aimlessly for a little while, then down Broadway, no real purpose or destination in mind. The morning air had a nice brisk bite to it that kept him moving. There was something so comforting about the anonymity of New York City. He could be anyone from anywhere. It didn't really matter.

"Father Paul?"

He stopped, the hand in his overcoat pocket going to the little vial of holy water he always kept with him. Then he slowly turned, ready for fight or flight, whichever seemed more practical. But it was Father Poujean, an old friend from seminary. The dark-skinned Haitian priest sat at a small table outside a café, the only occupant on this chilly early morning. He flashed a bright smile, then took a demure sip of his espresso.

Paul walked over to him and they clasped hands. "It's just Paul now. Remember?"

"Yes, yes," Poujean said. "Still playing the same old game, eh?" He gestured to the other seat at the table. "Please."

"You think we should settle down?" asked Paul as he sat at the table. "Get real jobs and buy a house in the suburbs?"

Poujean stirred his espresso in silence for a moment. "You know, it doesn't matter how many rogue demons you destroy. It won't earn you a get-into-Heaven card. So why do you do it? Why do you risk your life like that?"

Paul shrugged. "We do it because somebody has to keep them in line, and we are uniquely qualified for the job."

"It can't pay well," he said.

"No," agreed Paul. "It doesn't. But we get by."

Poujean gave him a searching look. "How do you earn anything at all?"

"She handles the financial aspects of the business," said Paul with a wry smile. "I don't pester her for details."

Poujean sipped his espresso. Then he said, "Do you really think you're making a difference?"

Paul leaned back in his chair and rubbed his temples. "I don't know. Sometimes I do. But . . ."

"There's more of them coming over," said Poujean.

"They're getting bolder," said Paul. "More confident."

"People aren't expecting demons at the supermarket, Paul. So they don't see them."

"Sometimes I think people would believe in aliens before they'd believe in demons."

"That's how it is now," said Poujean. "But what are they doing, these rogue demons? What are they playing at?"

"I don't know," admitted Paul. "They're changing tactics. It's not just possessing some poor mortal and terrorizing the locals for a bit of fun, like it used to be. All of a sudden they're turning up in financial institutions, in real estate, in politics. I think they've been working their way into the infrastructure for some time, but lately they've been getting bolder. They're changing the world from the inside, and it seems like they're being organized by someone in Hell with real authority."

"To what end?"

"Astarte has theories. She believes it's all coming to a head sometime soon. That everyone is digging in. Bracing for something big."

"What do you think?"

"I think it's been over a century since she's been in any sort of influential position in Hell. The few demons she still kept in touch with cut her off when she made our relationship known. Most demons think that falling in love with a mortal is blasphemy. The only one who still talks to her is her brother, Dagon. He's nice enough, but not real bright. So she doesn't really have any hard evidence on any of it. She's just taking shots in the dark."

They sat in silence for a little while. The waiter came over and asked if Paul wanted to order.

"Better not," said Paul. "I have to get going. I promised I'd bring back some breakfast before we head out."

Once the waiter had left, Poujean asked, "On a case, I assume?"

"We got the lead back in Tel Aviv and followed it to Moscow. Had a little tussle with some low-level imps there. Nothing too serious. Astarte was able to get some more out of them, though. Seems like whatever their game is, it's something with real estate and urban planning here in the city."

"I know a man who might be able to help with that particular area. Real estate and such," said Poujean.

"To be . . . understanding?" asked Paul.

"Of ex-monk mages with demonic spouses?" asked Poujean. "I think he's flexible enough to handle it."

"Interesting," said Paul. "Mind introducing us?"

"Well, I did have plans today. . . ."

"But there is that little matter of me saving your ass from that spider cult back in Paris a few years ago," said Paul.

Poujean nodded. "There is that. Although if memory serves, I believe it was actually your lovely wife who saved my ass."

"Yeah, yeah," said Paul. "We're a package deal. Not intended for individual sale."

"She does excel at saving people's asses, though," said Poujean.

"You're telling me," said Paul.

Astarte was waiting in the lobby when Paul and Poujean entered the hotel. Instead of her usual jeans and T-shirt, she wore a long, heavy skirt and a simple white blouse. Her usually wild black hair was pulled up into a tight ponytail. She smiled warmly at Poujean, her green cat eyes twinkling.

"Ah, Father Poujean," she said, extending her hand. "So good to see you again."

Poujean kissed the back of her hand and said, "The pleasure is all mine, as usual, Erzulie Freda."

Paul handed her a bunch of bananas and gave her a quick kiss. "Why are you dressed like that?" he asked.

"Don't you like it?" she asked with an impish grin.

He regarded her for a moment. The austere clothes made the fine angles of her face even more pronounced, and since her green eyes were the only splash of color, they seemed to sparkle even brighter than usual. He shrugged. "You're still beautiful."

She smiled and laid her hand gently on his cheek. "My husband, master of the artless compliment."

"Ah," said Poujean. "But you know he always tells the truth."

"Of course," she said. "One of the many reasons why I

keep him around." She slipped her arm through Paul's in the strangely formal way that she always did when there were other mortals around. "The reason, my dearest, that I am wearing this drab attire is because we're going to Crown Heights and I thought it best to blend in somewhat."

"Crown Heights?" asked Paul. "Why would—"

"How did you know?!" asked Poujean, his eyes wide.

She grinned. "Magic," she said, and winked.

Poujean looked imploringly at Paul.

"That's the best explanation you're going to get out of her," Paul said. "So I take it this guy you're taking us to see is in Crown Heights?"

Poujean nodded, looking a little disappointed that Astarte had stolen his thunder. As they walked to the subway station, Poujean filled them in on the climate of the neighborhood. There were two main ethnic groups in Crown Heights—the Hasidic Jews and the West Indians. And they didn't get along.

The Hasidim were one of the most conservative sects of Judaism. In their community, a great deal of importance was placed on attire and social interaction between the genders. The women wore long dresses and covered their heads. The men wore black suits and hats and grew full beards. On the other hand, the West Indians were considerably more liberal. There had been long-standing tensions between the two groups. Then, in 1991, there was a car accident in which a Hasidic man killed a West Indian child. A three-day riot followed.

"It's been a few years since the riots," said Poujean as

they descended the station steps to the underground subway platform. "But tensions remain."

Soon the number 4 train pulled in, and they boarded an empty car. The subway train rocketed through the tunnel that connected Manhattan and Brooklyn beneath the East River. The lights flickered out for a moment. When they came back on, Paul noticed there were two people in the car who hadn't been there before. They stood at the far end of the car, casually reading the advertisements above their heads. One was a tall, thin man with a long nose, a pronounced overbite, and glittering amber eyes. The other one was short and round, not so much fat as simply thick, with droopy, florid jowls and lavender eyes. Both of them were clearly demons.

Paul squeezed Astarte's hand and she immediately squeezed back. She knew. When they got out at the Franklin Avenue station, the demons followed but maintained a good distance.

"We're being tailed," Paul muttered to Poujean.

Poujean nodded. "I saw them. They must be fairly powerful to manifest without a human host."

"I know those two," said Astarte. "The tall one is Amon, the fat one is Philotanus. They *are* powerful, but clearly time has not made them more intelligent if they thought we wouldn't notice them slipping in like that."

"Will holy objects affect them?" asked Poujean.

"I should think most would," she said.

"Good. Then they won't be able to follow us for long."

Poujean led them out of the station and onto the promenade,

a strip of sidewalk along the main thoroughfare of Eastern Parkway. The street was lined with old apartment buildings and the occasional grocery store, all with bars on the windows. A few Hasidic families walked along the promenade, glancing at the mixed crew as they passed.

The two demons followed at a distance until Poujean turned and led his friends up the front steps of an old brownstone. As Paul and Astarte walked through the front door, Poujean pointed to the small box nailed above the doorway.

"There's a little piece of blessed Torah above every door in every Hasidic home," he said.

"Spiritual security system," said Paul.

"Precisely," said Poujean. "And much less gruesome than painting the door with lamb's blood." He glanced at Astarte. "It still baffles me as to why none of these objects affect you."

She shrugged. "I'm just not that kind of demon."

Paul knew the real reason. It was because she predated all Judeo-Christian religions, and was therefore immune. Of course, saying "Because I'm too old" was not something Astarte would ever say.

They entered the building and ascended an old, creaky staircase to the third and topmost floor.

"We're meeting with Rabbi Kazen, a very progressive voice in his community," said Poujean. "He's rather eccentric, and a little too in love with his books. But he's a good, kind man. He and I have been working together to try to ease some of the tensions between our two communities. If this case of yours is somehow connected to real estate in Brooklyn, there's a good chance the Hasidic community is involved, or at least aware of it. And if they are aware, so is he."

Poujean knocked quietly at a door covered with peeling yellow paint.

There was a sound like a pile of books falling over, then slow, heavy footsteps. A moment of silence as the person presumably peered through the peephole, then . . . "Ah!" Paul counted the sounds of three dead bolts and a chain sliding open, then at last the door flew wide. A large man with a flat, bearded face stood in the doorway in shirtsleeves and suspenders, his arms outstretched.

"Father Poujean!" he bellowed in a deep baritone, and embraced Poujean in a rough bear hug, slapping him several times on the back.

"Good to see you, Rabbi," said Poujean, wincing slightly.

"And who did you bring me?" asked Kazen. He glanced briefly at Paul, but then he saw Astarte and his eyes went wide. "An interesting pair, to say the least!" His eyes flickered anxiously to Poujean, who nodded.

"Come, then, come!" He gestured inside. They followed him into a living room with no furniture, only stacks of books. "Who needs shelves, yes?" Rabbi Kazen said, and chuckled. "This way, I don't even need furniture." He sat down on a stack of books and gestured for them to do the same.

"Rabbi," said Poujean. "This is an old friend of mine from seminary, Paul Thompson. And this is his wife, the lovely—"

"I am not blind," said Kazen, still jovial, but with a strange edge to his voice. "And I certainly need no introduction to Lilith, the First Woman."

Astarte nodded. "Rabbi."

"Ah, my dear," he said, rubbing his hands together briskly. "The knowledge that must be contained behind that radiant face. I could ask you a thousand questions and still not be satisfied."

"Quite so," said Astarte. "But what about an exchange of one for one?"

"Only one?" he said with good-humored anguish. "Well, I will have to make it a good one, then."

"Rabbi," said Paul, "we're tracking a large and well-connected group of demons. They seem to be getting heavily involved in a lot of financial activities—real estate, stocks, that sort of thing."

"That seems a bit complex for them," said Kazen.

"Right," said Paul. "This actually seems to be a coordinated effort. We're trying to determine who is in charge of it. Our concern is that this is being organized at a higher level. Perhaps even by one of the Grand Dukes."

"Hmm," said Kazen. He leaned back on his stack of books and stroked his beard. "There is one group that has been trying to push into Hasidic turf, actually. Of course, there's more than money at stake for us. We need this neighborhood in order to maintain our way of life. So they haven't been very successful yet. But they've got someone in the Haitian community who's been stirring up old resentments the past few weeks and I fear that things could get unpleasant."

"One of mine?" asked Poujean in surprise. "Do you know who?"

"A fellow named Emile Rameau, I believe," said Kazen.

Poujean frowned. "That's strange . . ." He looked at Paul and Astarte. "I know this man. He's not the sort to get mixed up with demons in any sort of serious way. If he's working for them, they're pressuring him somehow."

"Or possessing him," said Paul.

Poujean's eyes widened. "We should see him immediately."

Paul nodded and stood up, extending his hand to Kazen. "Thank you very much for the information."

"Just a moment!" said Kazen with a sly grin. He turned to Astarte. "What about my question? One for one?"

Astarte leaned back and crossed her arms. "Ask away," she said, and smiled in that cold way of hers that told Paul quite clearly that this poor, knowledge-thirsty rabbi was about to be taught a lesson.

"Well!" said Kazen eagerly. "One question only . . . hmmm . . . which to pick . . ." He tugged on his beard for a moment, his thick brows furrowed. "Ah! I've got it!" He sat up and smoothed his shirt and pants, as if preparing himself for a historic event. "Oh, Lilith, First Woman and Queen of the Lilitu, where is the Garden of Eden?"

"The Garden?" asked Astarte, her smile still present, but taking on an even harder edge than before.

"Hon . . . ," said Paul, placing a hand on her arm.

"But my love," said Astarte. "I did promise I would answer."

"Yes, yes!" said Kazen, his eyes gleaming eagerly. "Can you tell me where it is or what it looks like?"

"Better than that," she said. "I can show you."

"Oh yes!" he said exultantly.

"Look into my eyes," she said in a voice that almost purred.

He did, and the lines of tension in his face lessened until it was almost slack and his eyes grew distant.

"The Garden," said Astarte. "Omphalos, the center, the origin of all . . . it lies at the point where Heaven, Hell, and Gaia—the mortal realm—intersect."

Kazen's eyes widened, seeing something in his mind's eye.

"It is a place," continued Astarte, "that follows all rules and none. The crossroads of order and chaos, light and dark, good and bad. It is, as Lao-tzu once said, the source from which both mystery and reality emerge. A darkness born from darkness. The beginning of all understanding."

Kazen's eyes changed slowly from dreamy amazement to unease.

"In that darkness," said Astarte, "lives Abbadon the Destroyer. He stands upon countless worlds of mortal souls. His eyes are the torment of a million dead gods and goddesses, and his mouth is a gaping wound in a reality that consumes time itself."

Kazen's face twisted up with fear. He covered his eyes with his suddenly trembling hands, but it did not block the images that were in his head. "Please . . . ," he whispered.

"And past him," said Astarte relentlessly, "the Void, the unmaking of everything. To look upon it is to know one long, endless moment of death as the universe itself dies."

"Please," moaned Kazen, tears coursing down his bearded cheeks. "Please, no more."

"Yes," said Astarte abruptly. "A wise choice." She waved a hand in front of his face. He shuddered, then began sobbing.

"Astarte," said Paul, giving her a reproachful look.

"What?" she said, blinking innocently. "He asked."

"He also just helped us with the case," Paul said.

She rolled her eyes. "Okay, perhaps I was a little harsh."

"Yes," Paul agreed. "You had your fun, but . . ."

"Fine," she said crossly. She leaned over the still-sobbing Kazen. "Rabbi," she said gently, "look at me."

"No, no," he said weakly. But he looked.

"It's okay," she said, and stroked his bearded cheek. "It is best for mortals not to know some things. You will remember this lesson, but not the images I showed you. It will be like a dream, in which the feeling is recalled vaguely and without detail. Now sleep on your nice, safe, scholarly books and take comfort in their simple embrace."

Kazen's face slowly softened and his eyes closed. She gently laid him down amidst his piles of books.

"Thank you," said Paul.

She shrugged, then kissed him. "One of the many reasons I keep you around."

"God . . . ," said Poujean. He looked at her with a new appreciation and a bit of unease.

"Let's go see this Emile of yours, Father," said Astarte, and she walked out of the apartment.

"Y-y-yes, of course," said Poujean. As he and Paul followed her down the steps, he whispered, "Does she do this a lot?"

"Only when they ask for it. She still feels a responsibility to enlighten mortals. I've tried to suggest that it doesn't have to be so . . ."

"Cruel?" asked Poujean.

"Yeah," said Paul. "She's having a little trouble with the concept."

When they got back out onto Eastern Parkway, the two demons who had followed them from the subway were gone.

"They're somewhere around," said Astarte.

They walked down the parkway promenade, out of the Hasidic section and into the Haitian section. The same old buildings lined the streets, although they seemed a little more run-down. Out of many windows came the thumping music of raga—similar to Jamaican reggae, but harder and more aggressive. Poujean led them to the largest apartment building on the block, five stories high.

"I'm not sure how Emile is mixed up in all this," said Poujean. "He's a very fine, stable member of my church. Sells a few traditional remedies on the side, but nothing serious. Certainly nothing that would make me think he was dealing with darker aspects of Vodoun. He is no *bokur*." He turned to Astarte. "Please, Erzulie Freda. Be kind to him. For my sake."

"Why, Father Poujean," she said, and smiled sweetly. "I'm *always* kind. Except when they ask me not to be. And I don't think we'll have to worry about that in this case."

"Why do you say—" began Poujean. Then they heard a scream coming from within the building.

They pushed through the heavy front doors and charged

down the hallway. Poujean led them up to the second floor and through another hallway to a scuffed white wooden door. The screams were coming from behind it. Poujean pounded on the door.

"Emile! Marie! It's Father Poujean! Open the door!"

They heard the sounds of frantic fumbling with the locks, then the door swung open. A middle-aged Haitian woman stood in the doorway, panting, the sleeve of her shirt torn.

"Father! Thank God!" she said between breaths. "It's Emile!"

"What happened?" asked Poujean as they piled into the narrow foyer of the apartment.

"He's been mounted by the *loa* before," said Marie, "but they've never taken control of him this violently! I had to lock him in the bedroom!"

Almost in response, a sharp crash of breaking glass came from down the hall.

"Did this come on suddenly?" asked Paul. "Or did it happen gradually?"

"Who . . ." She glanced worriedly at Poujean.

"It's okay," he said. "This is Father Paul, an old friend from seminary. Please answer the question."

"W-w-well," she said, "he had been acting a little moody the past few weeks, and that's not like him. But it was nothing like this."

"And when did he lose control?"

"Only just a little bit ago."

"They knew we were coming," Paul said to Astarte and

Poujean. "They've been prepping him for something and we forced their hand. Poujean, come with me. We'll see if we can't kick whoever's in there out. Astarte . . ." They exchanged a quick look and she nodded.

Astarte turned to Marie. "Come, dear," she said in a soothing tone. "Let's go to the kitchen. I don't suppose you have any fresh fruit? I'm famished."

Marie looked helplessly at Poujean.

"It's okay, Marie. You and your husband are in good hands."

Astarte led Marie into her own kitchen, murmuring quietly to her. Paul and Poujean followed the screams and pounding to the bedroom. As they walked, Paul pulled two long, fat rosaries from his overcoat pockets and handed them to Poujean.

"I'll stun him and you tie him down to something heavy," he said tersely.

Poujean took the rosaries, looking nervous.

Paul didn't break his stride as he knocked aside the chair that held the door closed, opened the door, and stepped into the dark room. It stank of piss and vomit. A naked man crouched on top of the bed. His head snapped in Paul's direction like an animal's would. His eyes were bloodshot and a thick, clear liquid leaked from them. He was chewing on something and had blood smeared on his face and a headless pigeon in his hand. A snarl curled his lips.

"In the name of the Father, the Son, and the Holy Spirit, be gone!" shouted Paul, splashing holy water on the man. "In the name of Muhammad, Siddhartha, Lao-tzu, and Confucius, of Zeus and Jupiter, of Shiva, and Osiris, in the name of the faith of all those named and unnamed, I cast you out, you parasite, you scavenger, you bottom-feeding scum of mortality!"

The possessed man reeled. His eyes rolled back into his head until only the whites showed, and he fell on the bed in convulsions.

"Poujean! Now!" barked Paul.

Poujean hurriedly tied the possessed's wrists to the metal headboard, then stepped back to the other side of the room.

Another moment and the convulsions subsided. The possessed took stock of the rosaries that secured him to the bed, and a strange bleating sound, like a goat's cry, escaped his lips. Then he turned his eyes to Paul.

"I've heard of you," he said. "Astarte's pet exorcist. Very cute. But I think you'll find that I—"

"In the name of Yahweh, El, and Brahman!" roared Paul, throwing more holy water. "Be gone!"

The possessed howled in pain. "When I break free from here, I will dine upon your entrails, you mortal incubus!"

"Are we going to go on like this for a while?" asked Paul in a milder tone. "Or are you going to save us all the trouble and get out now? I don't have all day."

"You will find me much more difficult to dislodge than the lesser imps you are accustomed to, mortal," he hissed.

"Sure, sure," said Paul, sounding bored. "Nice bluff, but I can smell you from here, Bifrane."

The possessed's eyes widened in outrage. *"Bifrane?!* You think I am some decrepit peddler of corpses?! You will pay for that insult, you gobbet of flesh! Tremble in fear, mortal, for I am Asmodeus, master of gamblers and whores, corrupter and despoiler of life!"

Paul sighed and shook his head. "It's almost disappointing how often that trick works."

"What?"

Paul walked over and placed his hand on top of the thrashing head of the possessed. "With thy name, Asmodeus, I bind thee to this mortal shell."

"No!" screamed the possessed. "You filth, you whoreson, you—"

"And be quiet," said Paul.

The possessed's mouth moved, but no sound escaped.

Paul walked over to the corner of the room where Poujean stood awestruck. He sat down heavily in a small, wooden chair and said, "That's a lot more tiring than it looks."

"I . . . I don't understand," said Poujean. "You just trapped him inside Emile's body?"

"Yes."

"And now?"

"We wait for the other two to come running."

Poujean rubbed his temples and leaned against the door frame. "I think I'm a bit out of my league."

"The fact that this doesn't happen to you on a regular basis is a good thing," said Paul. Then he leaned back in the chair and closed his eyes.

There were a few moments of quiet, during which the possessed gave up thrashing and simply glared at Paul and Poujean with a sulky expression. Then the front door of the apartment blew inward with such force that splinters skittered all the way down the hallway to the bedroom. Paul launched himself out of his chair and stepped into the hallway.

"Hellspawn!" he yelled, brandishing his vial of holy water.

Two figures—the tall, gaunt Amon and the short, thick Philotanus—stepped over the wreckage of the door and into the apartment. Philotanus hung back a bit while Amon strode down the hallway toward Paul and Poujean, smiling wolfishly.

"Where is she, mortal? Where is that traitorous bitch?"

As he walked past the kitchen, a thick jet of flame blasted from the doorway and slammed him into the far wall.

"Right here, Amon," said Astarte from the doorway.

Smoke trailed from Amon's clothes, hair, and skin. He snarled, showing long canines. Then he leaped at her, his fanged mouth stretching wide into a wolf's muzzle. She stood perfectly still until he was only inches from her, then she thrust her fist down his throat. His jaws clamped down on her shoulder, fangs sinking through her shirt and into her flesh. Bright red bloomed on her white blouse. But then she shifted her weight slightly, her shoulder tensed, and Amon's eyes went wide.

"Ah," she said cheerfully. "Do you know what I have a hold of in there?"

He whimpered but continued to bite down on her shoulder.

"Neither do I," she said. "But let's see what happens when I twist."

He barked in pain, his jaw opening with a jerk.

"This isn't Hell," she said quietly, "and your master isn't here to protect you."

Then Paul felt a hard grip around his neck. A thick, oily voice behind him said, "And you have gotten soft here on Gaia."

Paul couldn't turn his head, but he didn't need to. The other end of the hallway was empty now, and the rancid stench told him that Philotanus had just appeared directly behind him, and probably held Poujean as well.

"Release the mortals, Philotanus," said Astarte, "or be destroyed."

"Your weakness for these cattle sickens me," said Philotanus. "When Belial hears of it, he will punish you severely."

"Belial and the other Grand Dukes are nothing but usurpers. They have no right to claim mastery over me or any other demon."

"The Grand Dukes were invested with their power by the authority of Lucifer Himself!" said Philotanus.

Astarte gazed at him for a moment. "You really do believe Belial's lies, then, don't you, Philotanus? You have forgotten that we weren't always like this. Once we were glorious."

"We were fools," said Philotanus, and spat.

"The Grand Dukes have you, then," she said, her eyes sorrowful. "Completely."

"They have us *all*," he said. "Even if you are too stubborn to accept it yet."

She sighed, her eyes trailing off to stare at nothing for a moment. Then she flexed her shoulder. Amon began to howl, but it was cut short into a gurgle as she hauled a yard of intestines out. He shuddered convulsively and fell to the floor.

"That was foolish," said Philotanus. "Now these mortals will die."

"No," said Astarte quietly, "you will."

Her eyes met Paul's and she nodded.

That was the signal he had been waiting for. He pulled a long silver-bladed crucifix from a sheath strapped to his thigh and plunged it into the round belly behind him. He heard a retching sound, and putrid black bile splashed his back. He ignored that and sawed slowly upward while whispering, *"Memento, homo, quia pulvis es et in pulverem reverteris!"* Remember, man, you are dust and to dust you shall return.

Philotanus released his grip, trying to escape, but Paul spun around, the prayer growing to a roar on his lips as he struck the demon with all his might. Paul could smell the corruption on this one. He was a schemer, a torturer, and a molester of children. Paul worked without pause, hacking away with his bladed crucifix, letting his loathing and hatred fuel each blow until finally there was nothing left but quivering chunks of demon flesh.

"Paul." Astarte's voice penetrated through his rage. "Enough. He won't be coming back."

Paul stopped, his breath whistling harshly through clenched teeth. As his peripheral vision returned, he could see Poujean looking at him in horror. He ignored it and instead looked to Astarte. "Amon escaped," he said in a flat voice, and pointed with his dripping, bladed crucifix at the spot where only a small pile of intestines remained.

"It will take him a long time to heal from that," said Astarte in a soothing voice. "And in the meantime, he will suffer quite a lot."

Paul grunted. Then he pointed his crucifix at the possessed, who was still chained to the bed, eyes wide. "What about him?"

Astarte looked over at the possessed, her face neutral. "What *about* him?" she asked.

"The penalty for forcibly possessing a mortal," he said, "is destruction."

Astarte continued to look at Asmodeus. He looked back at her through the mortal frame that held him prisoner. His eyes were now dark and deep and empty, like the night sky.

"Will you let him speak for a moment?" she asked Paul.

Paul's eyes narrowed, but he nodded curtly, then made the sign of the cross and said, "Speak, Asmodeus."

Astarte walked over to the bed. "Well, Asmodeus?" she asked. "Will you follow Philotanus into oblivion?"

"Does it matter?" asked Asmodeus. "I see now what this was. They knew you were onto their operation here. I was bait to draw you out. I was expendable, expected to fail. But why? I have faithfully served His Grace. I have done everything in my power to earn his favor."

"You know why," she said, almost gently. "Belial will never truly accept you."

"Because of what I once was," Asmodeus said hollowly. "A halfbreed."

"Yes."

"But I sacrificed my mortal side," he said, his eyes screwing up with anguish. "I destroyed half of myself. Can there be any worse torment?"

"Belial's hatred for halfbreeds is endless. No amount of suffering on your part will ever satisfy him."

He nodded. "And yet, what else could I do? If I had not tried to appease him, he would have killed me outright." He closed his eyes. "No matter what I do, I can never escape what I am. I have tried, and I have failed. Worse, I have defiled myself beyond repair. My existence is bereft of meaning. Let your avenger destroy me. It makes no difference to the universe."

Astarte looked at him for a moment. "Perhaps you are mistaken," she said at last. "Perhaps you still have tasks to complete." She turned to Paul. "Spare him. For me."

Paul's eyes widened. His mouth set hard, as if he was in pain. The hand that held the crucifix tensed up and the blade quivered. Then he took a deep breath and nodded.

"For you," he said quietly. "Anything."

He wiped his blade on the bedsheet, slid it back into its sheath, then walked to the other side of the bed.

Asmodeus looked to Paul on his left and Astarte on his right, his expression baffled.

"I give you your life, Asmodeus," said Astarte. "A day will come when you will be able to repay this debt. Until then, bide your time and serve your cruel master as best you can."

"I do not understand," said Asmodeus.

"Oh?" said Astarte, one eyebrow arched. "Perhaps you understand better than anyone." She held his gaze for a moment and something passed between them.

"No!" he said. "You—"

"Yes," said Astarte calmly.

He stared up at her, his face merely a frame for those bottomless eyes. "I feel your sorrow," he said at last.

"I feel no sorrow," she said firmly. Defiantly. "I feel joy."

An expression of awe slowly grew on the possessed's face. "Can such a thing be? Can your heart be so bold?"

"Of course."

He looked up at the ceiling, and a strange little smile formed on the possessed's lips. "Astarte, you have given me something rarer than my life this day. You have given me hope."

"There will be many dark times ahead," she said. "Remember that hope. Keep it close."

"Always," he said.

Paul looked back and forth between them, his eyes narrowed.

"Please release him now, my love," Astarte said.

Paul nodded curtly, leaned over, and laid his hand on the possessed's forehead.

"Swear that you will never possess another mortal man or woman," he said.

"I swear," said Asmodeus.

"I release you," Paul said.

The possessed convulsed, then fell unconscious. A fine mist coalesced above Emile's head. For a moment, Asmodeus appeared in his true form—a creature with three heads: man, ram, and bull. He bowed in thanks first to Paul, then to Astarte. Then his form dissipated.

"What was all that about?" asked Paul.

Astarte looked at him then in that way she had, her fierce green demon eyes piercing down to his soul. It stripped away all the safeguards he held up during the fight. She disarmed his heart until he stood before her, the same man who had thrown himself off a cliff because he loved her too much. Still holding his gaze, she walked slowly around the bed until she stood in front of him. She held out her hands and he took them immediately in his.

"I'm pregnant," she said.

It hung there in a silence that stretched on for a long time. Then Poujean, off in the corner, cleared his throat. "Would it be appropriate to offer my congratulations?"

"Of course it would," said Astarte. Her eyes were still locked on Paul's, and there was a vulnerability in them that he had never seen before.

"Part demon, part mortal," he said.

"Yes," she said. "A halfbreed."

"Forbidden by Hell," he said. "And Heaven."

"Yes," she said.

"They will hunt us," he said.

"Yes, they will," she said.

"They will kill us," he said.

"They will *try*," she said.

He slowly knelt down and pressed his forehead to her stomach.

"You will see," she said, stroking his hair. "This is our destiny. This child will set right that which has been wrong for so many centuries now."

"I love you," he whispered. "Nothing else matters."

a date and destiny
7

"Ms. Thompson! Study hall is for work, not sleep!"

Jael jerks awake, Father Aaron's voice ringing in her ears. She mutters an apology as she massages the indentation on her cheek from her geometry book. Another one of those visions. Or memories. Whatever they are. She wasn't even aware of falling asleep this time. One minute she was studying isosceles triangles, the next she was watching her dad chop a demon to pieces.

Her hand touches the gem that hangs around her neck and again she wonders what it is and where it came from. Hell, like she told Father Ralph? She said it more to freak him out than because she believed it. But is it really such a stretch? And why is it the one thing her mother made her father promise to give her? Maybe these visions she's been having are supposed to happen. Maybe it's what her mother wanted.

For the rest of the afternoon, she can't shake the gruesome visuals the necklace showed her. First that fish monster in that place with the giant crab shells. Then her parents, clearly in love, and killing demons together. In a weird kind of way, it's like a dream come true. She's always wanted to know more about her mother. And seeing her father as a badass exorcist mage (or whatever that Haitian guy called him) definitely explains a lot about the way he is. She wishes she could have known him back then. Of course, she wishes she could have known her mother at all.

"Hey, Betty! Wait up!"

She's just leaving school after the last bell when she hears Rob's voice. She turns and sees Rob standing at the top of the steps with some of his skater buddies. He waves to her, then pulls his board from the strap on his backpack, jumps, lands the board on the stair handrailing, and slides down.

"Mr. McKinley!" yells Father Aaron from his post by the door. "Not on school property!"

"Sorry, Father," calls Rob over his shoulder as he lands at the bottom of the steps next to Jael.

"Wow," says Jael. "Um, hey."

Rob kicks the board up and catches it with one hand, then brushes his hair out of his eyes. "Hey," he says, "you doing anything?"

Jael stares at him for a moment. "What, like right now?"

"Sure, right now."

"Uh, no," she says. "Not really."

"Oh yeah? Well, you wanna . . . uh, hang out?"

"Hang out?" repeats Jael. "Like, you and me?"

"Yeah, you know," says Rob. "A buddy of mine just started working the dinner shift at Denny's. He can score us some free grub, as long as we don't care what it is. Just, whatever's easy for him to make extra of without people noticing."

"Free dinner at Denny's?" Why is she unable to say something even remotely intelligent right now?

"Well, it's not fancy or anything, but I thought, you know . . ." He tries to smile again but this time there's a hint of nervousness to it. "I mean, if you don't like Denny's, we could do something else."

"No," says Jael. "Denny's sounds just about perfect."

She smiles, and that wipes the nervousness away from his smile.

"Excellent," he says.

The Denny's is just like any other: thin green carpet, brown Formica tables, and bright fluorescent lighting that still makes the place seem dim somehow. Jael and Rob sit in a corner booth and sip burnt coffee. Even though they've talked a thousand times at school, it feels completely different to be off school grounds, sitting across from him in the cramped booth. A tingle of nervousness runs through her, and she's glad she has the comforting weight of the necklace against her skin.

A guy with a buzz cut and dressed in a Denny's apron comes over. Jael's seen him climbing out of one of the many expensive SUVs in the school parking lot.

"Yo, Robbie!" says the guy as he leans across the table and clasps Rob's hand.

"Chas!" says Rob. "I'm feelin' that apron, bro!"

"I know, right?" says Chas. "It's totally hot."

"I'm gonna have to borrow it sometime," says Rob.

"No way, man. This shit is Denny's employees only. We have to take a blood oath. Like the Masons."

"Sounds serious," says Rob.

"Totally. So, you finally decided to take me up on my offer, huh?"

"Finally? It's only been two weeks."

"For free grub? I would have jumped on that in, like, two days."

"Yeah, well . . . ," says Rob. "Hey, do you know Jael?"

"I have not had the pleasure," says Chas. He turns to her and grins in a weird way, like he knows something. "I'm Chas."

"Thanks for the food hookup," says Jael.

"All right, folks," says Chas. "You just chill and act like whatever I bring you is something you ordered. Let the feasting begin!"

Once Chas leaves, Rob turns to Jael.

"So, was that you splitting early from church?"

"Uh, yeah," says Jael. "You saw that?"

"Everything okay?"

"Sure, I just . . . wasn't feeling well. Didn't want to throw up in chapel, you know?" The lie tastes bitter in her mouth. Rob is such an honest, open guy, it seems wrong somehow. But what else can she say? *Sorry, the demonic necklace I inherited from my mom was about to burn the chapel down?* Even though Rob said a lot of open-minded things about magic this morning, the truth would be pushing it. But maybe someday she'll be able to talk about this stuff with him.

That thought sends a thrill through her. To talk to someone.

To tell her secret. To have just one friend she can be one hundred percent real with. Before this moment, she hadn't even considered that possibility.

"Hey," Rob says, "at least you missed the Mons going on forever with the Petitions."

"Oh, yeah," says Jael, relieved to be back on familiar topics like complaining about teachers. "Sometimes I wonder if he actually knows anyone who *isn't* sick or dying."

"He's led a pretty crazy life, I guess. Some of his stories about being a missionary in Peru? That is just some messed-up shit."

"He hasn't really said a lot about it to us," says Jael. "Just kind of hints at it."

"Yeah, he and I talked a few times. He was trying to get me to come back to the Church and believe again. I guess he thought telling me a few intense stories about being a missionary might spark my interest."

"It didn't?" asks Jael.

"Nah. I mean, those Shining Path guys were pretty messed-up. They would kill and torture all these people. Not soldiers or anything, just normal people. Hack them up with machetes. But I don't think it had much to do with them being atheist. I think it was because they were poor, oppressed, and pissed off to the point of insanity."

"The Mons is definitely old-school religion."

"But even still, he's got this weird Zen thing going," says Rob. "I feel like he's been through some serious shit and come out on the other side totally at peace."

"I wish he could give some of that peace to Father Aaron," says Jael.

"The Mons might be extra holy," says Rob, "but he can't do miracles."

They continue to stay on safe topics throughout dinner, almost like it's just an extended version of the kind of conversations they have in homeroom. Dinner is heavy on the fried appetizers, and Jael isn't used to that, so by the time they finish, she feels a little ill. Rob admits that he isn't feeling great either, so they take their time walking home.

The rainy season has begun, so the sun sets earlier every day. Even though it's only six o'clock, the sky is dark as they walk through the neighborhood. The cool evening air and a full stomach have finally loosened Jael's nerves a bit, so she says, "Hey, I just uh . . . wanted to say how cool I thought it was what you said this morning about chemistry. And, uh, magic."

Rob shrugs. "It's my thing, I guess. Other than skating, of course."

"So . . ." Jael struggles to think of how to put it in a way that won't make her sound completely crazy. "So if you believe all that stuff, do you believe in God?"

"Seriously?" asks Rob. He squints at her in the dim street light.

"Yeah," says Jael. "I mean, I'm not Catholic or anything, so don't worry about offending me."

"Yeah, I figured that," he says with a little smile. "The way I look at it, it doesn't really matter if God exists or not. I'm still going to do what I think is right."

"I guess that makes sense," says Jael. "Sort of."

"How about you?"

"When I was a little kid, I used to believe it all," she says. "God, the pope and Jesus stuff . . . All of it."

"Sure, me too," says Rob. "That's normal."

"No, I mean I was *into it*. Like on Good Friday, when the priest would go around to the Stations of the Cross, talking about Jesus getting whipped, the crown of thorns, all that stuff? By the time he got to nailing Jesus's hands to the wood, I'd be crying. Like every time."

"Whoa," says Rob, but Jael can't tell if he's surprised or impressed. "So what happened?" he asks. "When did you stop believing?"

"I don't know," she says. "It's . . . complicated for me. I don't know what I believe anymore."

"I don't think it matters that much. The stuff you do is way more important than the stuff you believe."

"But don't you do things based on your beliefs?"

"I'd say it's the other way around. You believe things to justify what you do."

"Huh," says Jael. They walk on in silence as she tries to unravel that statement in her head.

They get to her house and Jael feels like she's supposed to invite him inside. But she knows her dad wouldn't like it. He's already going to be pissed at her for going out without letting him know. And with a boy, even. Best not to push it any further.

"Well," she says finally, "I should probably get some homework done or something."

"Okay, okay, yeah, sure," says Rob.

"Thanks for, uh . . ." She isn't sure how to phrase it. After all, the word "date" was never officially used, so it's possible he doesn't think of it as one. "I had fun," she says.

"Me too," says Rob. "So, like . . . does this mean we can hang out again?"

"Yeah," Jael says. "That'd be cool." Then she turns to go.

"Hey, wait," he says.

Jael turns back and the look on his face makes her think that maybe he's going to ask her if he can kiss her and if he does, she has no idea what she's going to say.

"Is that . . . Is that your mom's necklace?"

"Oh," says Jael. Her hand goes to her throat. "Yeah."

"Can I see it?" asks Rob.

"Um . . ." She feels a slow flush creep onto her face. This could be even more uncomfortable than if he'd asked for a kiss and she's tempted to dodge. But that clear, honest look in his eyes pierces her careful cool, leaves her feeling off balance and open in a way she's not used to. She nods and holds the chain up so that the gem dangles, turning gently in the moonlight.

He tilts his head to one side and leans in close. So close that she can smell his spicy deodorant.

"Do you know what kind of stone it is?" he asks.

"Uh, no," she says. She feels so vulnerable with him this close. She can't decide if she should look at him or look away. "I guess ruby?"

He shakes his head, he eyes still locked on the necklace. "No, I don't think so. It's hard to tell in this light, but I think the coloring is a little dark for a ruby. I don't think I've ever seen anything like it."

"You know a lot about jewelry?" she asks, half teasing.

"Gemstones? Yeah. I know some," he says casually. Like all boys are interested in jewels. "So," he says, and returns her teasing smile with one of his own. "You decided to wear it anyway, huh?"

"Oh," says Jael, leaning away. "I didn't really . . . well . . ."

"No, no, I totally get it," he says. "There's just something about it that's . . . I don't know. It's just cool."

"Yeah," says Jael.

"How could you resist, right?" The playful smile again.

"No, really, it wasn't like that. It was just a situation where it would have been really weird not to put it on."

"Maybe so," says Rob. "But you still haven't taken it off."

"No," says Jael. "I haven't."

He nods, suddenly serious. "Thanks for showing it to me."

"Sure," says Jael.

"Your mom gave it to you?"

"Yeah."

"Do you remember her?"

Jael shakes her head. "She died when I was a baby."

"Sorry," says Rob.

"I used to think it was good that I don't remember her," says Jael. "Because I thought then I'd never miss her. But I was wrong."

"How so?"

"I do miss her."

"Missing someone you never knew . . . ," says Rob. "What does that feel like?"

"It's hard to describe," says Jael. "Sometimes, it feels like I'm missing a part of myself."

He nods, and they just stand there looking at each other. The yellow streetlight reflects off his blond hair, and his jawline and cheekbones stand out sharply from the shadows.

"What was her name?" Rob asks.

It's been a long time since anyone has asked her that. It's been a long time since she's said it aloud.

"Astarte," she says, and just like always, she gets a little tingle down her spine.

"Wow," says Rob. He shivers just a little, like he got the same tingle. "Cool name."

"Yeah," says Jael. "It's a little weird, but I like it."

"I bet she chose your name."

"Why's that?"

"Because you have a weird cool name too."

She can't quite look at him as she says, "Thanks."

He shrugs, and that wide-open grin comes again. "Okay," he says, and takes a few steps backward. "See you tomorrow." Then he pulls his skateboard from his backpack and coasts down the sidewalk and into the night.

Jael turns smoothly, like there are wheels under her own feet, and glides into the house. As she makes her way slowly through the darkened living room, she decides she has to call Britt. She can almost hear her smug "I totally called that!" now.

But as Jael places her first foot on the spiral staircase, it's her father's voice she hears.

"Jael."

She stops and turns around. He stands in the kitchen doorway. He's backlit by the harsh bare lightbulb, so she can't quite make out his expression, but his arms are folded across his chest and she knows that's never a good sign.

"It's late," he says. "Where were you?"

"Dinner with a friend," she says, attempting a casual tone.

Her father's head tilts back slightly, so that the light shows his face and she can see just how pissed he is. "I don't think so," he says. "I called Britt's house. She was there. You weren't."

"I do have other friends, Dad."

He raises an eyebrow, and there's just a hint of amusement on his face, like he doesn't believe her. "Oh really?" he asks. "Who?"

"You probably don't know them," she says, shifting her weight back and forth.

"It's a small school. I'm sure I do."

"It's a boy, okay?" She says it quickly, forcing herself to keep both feet firmly on the ground.

"A boy?" The furrows in his brow dig in deep, and he leans his hand on the door frame, like he has to steady himself. That's when Jael sees that his hand is bandaged. From when he cut himself to contact that demon. For some reason, it's this tiny little concrete detail that reminds her that she isn't the only one who needs to be interrogated.

"Jael, we've talked about this," he's saying. "You are not to date until—"

"What happened to your hand?" she asks, her tone calm.

"Don't change the subject on me," says her father, shifting his weight so his hand drops down and out of view. "You deliberately broke one of the few rules—"

"What happened to your hand, Dad?" This time, her tone is sharp, each consonant spit out with precision as cold certainty settles in the pit of her stomach.

"I was fixing something and the screwdriver slipped," he says. "Now listen—"

"You're lying!" she says.

"Excuse me?" he says, his eyes wide in disbelief.

"That's not how it happened, Dad. And I'm starting to think you lie to me a whole lot. You told me we're hiding from demons. So why were you talking to one last night?"

"How did you? . . ." He looks horrified. And for some reason that makes her feel really good.

She pulls the necklace out from under her shirt. "This necklace showed me. The one you said wasn't safe. I guess you meant it wasn't safe for *you*."

"You put it on?" says her dad. "Jael, I told you never to—"

"Stop it! It's over, Dad. I'm done playing your little game. You always tell me I'm too young to understand. You've been saying that since I was eight. When are you going to get it through your head that I'm not a kid anymore? Whatever it is, I can handle it."

"It's not as easy as that, Jael," he says. "And if you had obeyed me in the first place, you—"

"What, Dad? I'd still be in blissful ignorance? Well, let me tell you, it's not that blissful. I'm sick of it. Stop bullshitting me and tell me what is really going on!"

She juts her chin out and braces herself. She's never sworn at him like that before and she expects him to get pissed. But instead, his face softens. His eyes fill with an anguish that's so painful to see, she wants to take it all back.

"Oh," he says in little more than a whisper. Then he looks away, his hand groping for the door frame again.

"Dad?"

"You just . . ." His voice is hoarse. "I just saw it for the first time. How much you look like her."

"Dad . . ." This isn't what she wanted at all. To hurt him like this.

"Your mother . . ." His eyes stare off at nothing and his voice is hollow. "You want to know something true? About your mother?"

"Look, Dad," she says uneasily.

"I told you she died in childbirth. That was a lie," he says. "The truth is that she died when you were three months old. She was murdered."

A silence settles in as that last word penetrates.

"Someone . . . killed my mother?" she asks finally.

"Yes. There. Some truth." He looks at her at last, his face bitter. "Are you happy now?"

"No!"

"Truth does not bring happiness, Jael." He turns away again. "Now, go to bed and let's forget all of this." He waves her off. "No punishments. No blame. We'll act like tonight didn't happen."

For just a second, she feels a strange sort of relief. Like, *Oh, good, we can go back to the way things were.* But then she thinks he must be insane.

"There's more, isn't there, Dad? What's so bad about being a . . . halfbreed?"

Her father flinches at the word but says nothing.

"Is that what they call me?" she asks. "The demons?"

"Yes," he says.

"So what's all that about halfbreeds being forbidden by Heaven and Hell? Should I be worried about something?"

"Jael, please, can we at least just talk about this tomorrow?" He reaches out to her. It's a gesture he rarely does and it's so hard for her to resist. But she steps away.

"I have a right to know," she says.

"It's just . . ." He's losing and he knows it. "Jael, I can't just . . ." His face is pleading with her, but this time the weakness only pisses her off more.

"If you can't tell me, maybe someone else will. Like that fish monster in my necklace. What was his name?"

"Jael, don't do that—" This time he's the one who backs up.

"Dagon, or something, wasn't it?" she asks, like she's taunting him.

"Jael, stop this right now!"

She stares hard at the necklace. "Dagon, are you in there? I'm ready to hear the truth!"

"You . . . have no idea what you've just done," her father says quietly.

Something shifts behind the easy chair. At first it just looks like a shadow. But the darkness slowly gathers and grows larger and more dense. That's when Jael starts to wonder if she really did just do something very stupid.

The darkness solidifies into the massive, hulking fish creature she saw earlier in the necklace. But there is a big difference between seeing it inside a gem and seeing it towering above you with gleaming black shark eyes and rows of glinting, needlepoint teeth that splay out in all directions. Her mind goes completely blank as she wails and stumbles toward the door.

"Jael, wait!" calls her father.

Something strong closes around her waist and stops her. She struggles to break free and screams so loud and long that it feels like she's going to pop a blood vessel.

"*Help!*" she wails. "*Oh God oh Jesus HELP ME!*"

Her father's voice: "Be careful with her!"

"I am! I am!" snarls the creature. "She's wriggling!"

"Jael, listen to me!" her father shouts over her screams. "Please, just calm down! Just listen!"

She can't, though. All she can think about is the demon that has her by the waist, its rotten stench gagging her as it lifts her off the ground. She screams and sobs. She thrashes her body, swings her fists, kicks her feet. This lasts for several minutes until she finally runs out of steam. Her voice trails off into a faint moaning whimper and she droops over like a wilted flower.

"There now," says the creature. "That's better."

She's slowly turned around until she stares into the face of the demon. Its black lidless eyes reflect her own terrified, tear-stained face.

"It's okay," says the demon around its mouthful of savage teeth. "I'm not going to hurt you." Then it carefully, almost gently, places her back on the ground.

Her legs are wobbly, and she has to brace herself against the wall with her hand to keep from falling over. Her father stands next to the monster with a look of weary resignation.

"Who . . . ," she says, her voice hoarse from screaming. "What is that?!"

"That is your uncle Dagon," says her father. "On your mother's side."

biRth

8

Paul Thompson had seen a lot in his thirty-five years of life. He had been to nearly every country in the mortal world, and quite a few in Hell as well. He had seen wonders most people thought impossible, and he had seen horrors born from the collective nightmares of humanity. He had felt searing hatred, crushing despair, and all-consuming love. But none of it prepared him for the first time he held his daughter.

They had been holed up in a cave in Siberia while Astarte gave birth. The labor took two days. A blizzard howled outside, but it was a whisper compared to her screams. They were so loud and had been going on for so long that Paul was forced to stuff his ears with cotton to keep from going deaf. But finally, the first tiny cries of a baby rang out in the dark cave. Hell's physician, Uphir, wordlessly held out Paul's daughter to him. She looked so small and pink in the demon's long gray hands. Paul's hands shook a little as he took her and cradled her awkwardly in his arms. Her bright green eyes, just like her mother's, gazed up at him in wonder as her hands opened and closed. He stroked the sparse, plastered-down black curls on her head.

"Paul," said Astarte, her voice heavy with exhaustion. "Is it? . . ."

"She," said Paul, "is perfect." Then he laid the baby gently on her chest. The baby immediately began to nurse, and a look of contentment spread across Astarte's face.

Uphir stood up, his large yellow eyes gazing at them coldly under his wrinkled forehead.

"As your physician, I recommend that you remain here for at least eight hours," he said in a dry voice. "But if you don't leave within the next hour, Belial will find you and kill you."

"Thank you, Uphir," Astarte said. "I know you have put yourself in danger by helping us."

"I have repaid my debt to you," he said. "Now I wash my hands of the entire tragedy." He turned and walked out of the cave into the howling wind, then dissipated like the blinding snow that swirled through the night air.

"Ah, screw that guy," said Dagon from his spot in the corner. "Don't let him get you down, sis."

"Of course not," she said, gazing with absolute peace at her baby.

"Kinda fragile-looking," remarked Dagon as he heaved his large scaly frame up and walked over to where she lay.

"Do you have to get so close?" snapped Paul.

"Hey, just trying to get a look at my niece," said Dagon.

"I don't think —"

"Paul," said Astarte. "You promised."

Paul looked at his wife for a moment, his face tense. Then

he sighed. "Yes. I did." He gently kissed his little family, then stood up so that Dagon could sit down next to them.

"Wow!" said Dagon as he sat down. "No teeth!"

"They grow those later," said Astarte.

"Or claws," he said.

"Now you're just being silly. What halfbreed ever has claws?"

"I don't know," he said with a shrug. "Haven't met very many. Not exactly like there's a lot of them."

She looked down at her baby. "No," she said. "There's not. Belial has made certain of that."

There was silence except for the wind, which still howled outside the cave, hissing and spitting ice.

"Do you think you can move soon?" Paul asked.

"I don't have a choice," Astarte said. "Let's wait until she finishes eating, though."

Paul nodded tersely and began to pack their few belongings.

"So, what's the kid's name?" asked Dagon.

".Jael," said Astarte. "Jael Thompson."

Dagon's mouth opened wide in a glittering fanged grin. "Seriously?"

"Do you like it?" she asked.

"I love it," he said. And then he laughed, a rumble that reverberated so loudly in the small, icy cave that Paul winced, even with the cotton in his ears.

But Baby Jael stared up at her uncle in wonder. Then she smiled and let out her own little hiccup of laughter.

• • •

Paul sat with his baby in the suffocating heat of the tent because at least it was out of the stinging sands that blew in all directions. The baby cried, her shrill wail like needles in his ears. He whispered soothingly to her, rocked her, put her down, picked her up again, but she continued to scream. He fed her, changed her diaper, burped her. It didn't help. So eventually he just gave up. He sat on one of the rugs and leaned against the tent pole, placed her on his lap, and let her screams drown out all thought.

Dagon slipped into the tent and winced at the sound. "I could hear her miles away."

"Sound carries in the desert," Paul said numbly.

"What's wrong with her?"

"You mean other than the fact that it's a hundred and twenty degrees out?"

"That makes no difference to her," said Dagon.

Paul sighed. "Astarte can get her to stop, but I can't. Not when she gets like this."

"Where is she anyway?"

"Somewhere out in the dunes," said Paul. "She said she needed some solitude to think about what we do next."

"Yeah, I agree that we need a better plan than 'keep running.' But Belial is almost here. We have to move soon."

Paul nodded and stroked Jael's curly black hair. They sat there without speaking for a while. The tent walls flapped rapidly in the high desert winds. After a while, Baby Jael fell into a fitful sleep. Paul gazed down at his angelic half-demon daughter. She was so vulnerable, so helpless. When he allowed himself to think about exactly what was after her, he felt a deep ache in his chest. The threat came not from some petulant imp or even a low-ranking earl like Philotanus. No, it was one of Lucifer's favorites. Belial, Grand Duke of the Northern Reaches of Hell. A demon so powerful, he was almost an elemental force—like cold, hard winter itself. A creature so obsessed with purity and perfection that he would stop at nothing to destroy Jael simply because she was a halfbreed. So they ran, and he followed. How much longer could they last?

Evening had started to settle into the desert when Astarte appeared at the tent entrance.

Dagon stood up immediately. "We have to go," he said.

"I know," she said, looking strangely at peace. "But it's going to have to wait a little bit longer."

"Cutting it really close," Dagon muttered, but sat back down.

She kissed Paul gently, then took the baby into her arms, whispering in a voice so soft that Paul's mortal ears couldn't pick it up. But Jael squirmed slightly, opened her jade green eyes, and smiled and cooed. Astarte smiled back, and a single tear dropped onto Jael's forehead.

"You okay?" asked Paul.

"I think I have a plan that will keep her safe," she said. "At least for a while."

"Oh?" said Dagon, a strangely suspicious tone in his voice.

"If I draw the demon aspect out of her, Belial won't be able to locate her directly," she said.

"But . . . ," began Dagon, but he stopped while some nonverbal exchange took place between the siblings.

"But what?" demanded Paul.

"But . . . she'll be just like a mortal."

"Will it work?" asked Paul.

Dagon simply shrugged.

"Will Belial still be able to track us?" asked Paul.

Another strange look between Astarte and Dagon. Then she said, "For now, it will just make it harder."

"But you think it's worth it?" asked Paul. He felt helpless, not even sure if he knew what they were talking about.

"I do think it's worth it," she said quietly. She looked down at Jael and smiled as tears suddenly sprang back up into her eyes. "My sweetest joy." She carefully laid her down on one of the rugs. From her deep desert robe pockets, she pulled a small wooden jewelry box lined with silver, and a silver chain with an empty pendant setting.

"Did Vulcan make that for you just now?" asked Dagon.

She nodded.

"He must have owed you pretty big."

She smiled bitterly. "Everyone in Hell either owes me or hates me."

"Or both," agreed Dagon.

She laid the jewelry box and silver chain on the rug next to Jael. Then she opened the snaps of Jael's onesie so that her tiny chest was exposed. Astarte gazed at her for a long time and tears started to fall again.

"Sis," said Dagon quietly, "if you're going to do it, you gotta do it now."

She nodded and, tears still sliding down her face, plunged

her hand into the baby's chest. It passed through as if it were water, but Jael let out a scream so piercing that Paul had to cover his ears. Then Astarte slowly pulled out a brilliant, burgundy thread of light. There was a little resistance at the end and Jael cried even louder. But a quick tug and the thread of light was free. Jael's cry slowly trailed away to a shivering whine.

"Paul," said Astarte as she wrestled with the thread of light. "Please . . . I can't stop what I'm doing. Comfort her."

Paul jolted as if coming out of a trance, then swooped up his baby. Jael nuzzled her face into his arm and whimpered quietly.

Astarte gathered the thread into the palm of one hand, then pressed her hands together. Her face tensed up with effort and her green eyes blazed. Harsh grunts escaped from her lips and her arms shook. At last she let out a sigh and held out a fist-size, rough-cut burgundy gem to Dagon. As soon as he took it, she sank back into Paul. He shuffled his loads so that he had Jael in the crook of one arm and Astarte nestled into the other. Dagon picked up the silver chain and fixed the gem inside the pendant setting. Then he placed the necklace into the jewelry box and closed the lid. He looked at Paul, his black shark eyes unreadable.

"We have to go," he said. "Now."

Extracting Jael's demon aspect did seem to slow Belial down somewhat. But it also slowed the family down. Jael didn't have the same resistance to weather that she'd had before. She required more food, more sleep. In fact, she regressed completely to mortal baby development. She no longer babbled or laughed, and she couldn't hold up her head. Paul had to assure Astarte several times that this was normal for a two-month-old mortal baby. So while the chase slowed, they gained no lead.

But Astarte seemed less and less concerned about it. In fact, she seemed calm almost to the point of disconnected. It was so unlike her that Paul began to get suspicious. Finally, one night while they were camped in the Highlands of Scotland, nestled up in the mountains, miles from the nearest town, he decided to force the issue. Dagon was out scouting, so it was just the two of them and Baby Jael, sitting by a campfire that burned the rich peat that was so plentiful in that area.

"Okay, what's going on?" Paul said.

"What do you mean?" Astarte asked as she gently rocked Jael in her arms.

"You're keeping something from me."

"Oh?"

"Yes. And Dagon's in on it. That's why he hasn't been around as much. We all know he's a terrible liar."

"He is a terrible liar," she agreed.

"But you're not," he said.

She said nothing, but continued to rock Jael.

"Why won't you tell me?" he asked. "You think I won't be able to handle it?"

"Yes," she said. "That's exactly what I think."

"How can you possibly say that after everything we've been through together?"

"Because this is something very different."

"I don't understand," he said, fighting to keep the quaver

out of his voice. "We have never kept things from each other before."

"I will tell you. Very soon, I think," she said. "But I fear it will take a lot longer for you to accept."

Later that evening, after the fire had burned down and they were settling into sleeping bags, Dagon appeared in the tent opening, his bulky silhouette shimmering in the moonlight.

"He's here," he said with quiet tension.

"What?" Paul jumped to his feet, startling Jael awake. "How did he gain that much?"

"It doesn't matter," said Astarte calmly. She handed Jael over to Dagon, who cupped the baby awkwardly in his massive, clawed hands. Then she turned to Paul and held his face in her hands.

"My love," she said. "You must promise me something."

"What are you talking about?" he demanded.

"Promise me that you will give her the necklace on her sixteenth birthday."

"Why are you talking like this?" he said, panic edging into his voice.

"When she is old enough, you must allow Dagon to help her understand her demon aspect.

"Astarte! Stop this! Stop—"

"Please," she said. Tears streamed down her cheeks. "Please don't make this any harder."

"But *why?*" he asked, his voice strangled.

"This is larger than you, or me, or even our baby," she said. "She has a destiny to fulfill. Now promise me. Please, Paul. Let me face him knowing that my sacrifice is worthwhile. Promise."

"I promise," he said, his voice ragged with misery.

"Thank you," she said. "My dear own love. You are like no other in this world." Then she kissed him long and hard. He tried to hold on to her, but of course she was stronger than him and she pushed him away at last.

"Dagon," she said hoarsely. "Take them now. Please."

Dagon cradled Jael carefully against his chest, then grabbed Paul with his free hand. Paul struggled, but the scaled arm clamped down on him like steel.

Paul had one last glimpse at the love of his life as she stood at the entrance to their tent. There was a look of hard resignation on her tear-streaked face.

Then everything was a howling, wind-lashing blur.

Asmodeus, the broken halfbreed whom Astarte had spared the year before in Brooklyn, was the only witness to what happened next. His natural form was a three-headed creature—ram, bull, and man. But since he sacrificed his mortal half, he was far too weak to appear in that form on Gaia. What's more, he had sworn to the priest that he would never possess another human again. So he stood on a nearby hilltop in the body of a ram as he watched Dagon streak off with the priest in one arm and the baby halfbreed in the other. He watched Astarte walk out into the clearing near the smoldering campfire. She simply stood, waiting. She didn't have to wait long.

Belial landed in a bolt of white lightning. He was twice her height, glinting in the moonlight like a creature made of ice and razor blades. The moment he touched down, Astarte sent him reeling with a blast of fire. He recovered quickly, then hurled a blast of sleet that tore into her flesh and left her bloody and fighting to stay on her feet. They fought for some time, fire against ice. The skies flickered and rumbled as they grappled. But the last few centuries had given Belial a strength and stamina few could match. Finally, he broke through a wall of fire and grabbed her by the neck. Then he began to slowly tear her apart and consume her, limb by limb. The last piece was her left arm. He started from the shoulder, cramming it down his throat. But when he had almost reached the elbow, she still somehow had enough presence to bend her arm, reach around his head, and tear off his ear just as he swallowed the last of her, and the ear with her.

He bellowed in pain and rage, clutching at the wound on the side of his head. Then he tore apart the tent, looking for the halfbreed. When he didn't find her, his roar shook the mountains like an earthquake.

Asmodeus watched it all. He marveled at what Astarte had done that night. It was not just a battle that had taken place, but a complex and powerful ritual, with herself as the sacrifice. This is what she had meant when she had spoken to him, agreeing to spare him. That a time would come when he would be able to repay his debt and find renewed purpose.

First, he would spread the word of what he had seen this night, quietly, carefully, to sympathetic persons. The Grand Duke of the Northern Reaches had been outwitted. And what was more, his precious own perfection had been marred.

Change, real and inescapable, had been wrought this night.

Asmodeus had experienced much in his long existence. He knew the beginning of an epoch when he saw it. The fall of the Grand Dukes of Hell was at hand, and the infant halfbreed would be the catalyst. It seemed impossible that such a creature could survive long enough to reach maturity. But on that night, Asmodeus swore that he would do whatever he could to make sure that she lived long enough to come into her own power and fight for herself.

Rebirth

9

Jael lets the necklace drop back down to hang from her neck. She looks first at her father, then at Dagon.

"Why did she do it?" she asks. "Why did she stay behind to die?"

Her father stares at the necklace, his expression unreadable. "I don't know," he says.

"She had to," says Dagon. "Belial couldn't trace you anymore, but he could still trace her."

"There had to be another way," says her father.

"There was also something about what she did, ripping off his ear, and the way she did it," says Dagon. "I don't really understand it myself, but I know it was something that had to happen."

"But why did that demon want to kill me so badly?" says Jael. "I was just a baby."

"Because you're half mortal, half demon," says Dagon. "You knew that, right?"

"Why is it so bad to be a halfbreed?"

"It's not bad!" says Dagon. "But it's unusual. The only time one is created is when a mortal and demon truly love each other. You can guess how often that happens. In the past, some of those halfbreeds became really powerful and caused a lot of trouble for the established order. Basically, you're a wild card. Belial and the other Grand Dukes have plans in motion, and you're just the kind of person who could screw them up."

"Don't fill the girl's head with your Reclamation destiny garbage," says her father. He turns to Jael. "Look, Belial is the ultimate perfectionist. He has a homicidal obsession with purity. Belial has made it a personal mission that demon blood will never get corrupted by mortals again."

"And you're saying this Belial is still out there somewhere looking for me?"

"Yes," says her father. "Which is why we've been hiding all these years. Why we have to move so much. Because he will never give up. Not just because are you a halfbreed. But also because your mother mutilated him. He wants revenge."

"So what do we do?" she asks.

"Give her the letter," says Dagon.

Her father looks like he wants to object. But instead he presses his lips into a tight, thin line and nods. Then he turns and picks up the Bible that always sits on the coffee table. He flips through the onion-skin pages until he finds a specific page and pulls out an old, yellowed paper.

"This is from your mother," he says, extending the folded paper.

Jael's hands tremble as she takes it from her father. On it is written:

To Jael Thompson, on her sixteenth birthday.

The handwriting is small, jagged, and strangely ornamental, almost like that old manuscript style, except messy. Jael takes a deep breath to steady her hands. Then she carefully unfolds the paper, which crackles and feels both rough and delicate from age. The pages are laced with scribbles, scratched-out words, and smears of ink.

> *Dearest Jael,*
>
> *You are sixteen now. I must confess that it is strange to imagine you as a teenager while I look at you now, as a baby, lolling around on a blanket, drooling and puking on yourself! But that is one of the many precious marvels of humanity that I have come to appreciate.*
>
> *My daughter, it is time for you to reclaim that which you have been denied all these years. It is time for you to embrace your demon aspect. I'm sure it was difficult for you all these years, knowing what you are capable of, but not being able to accomplish it. Remember that it has been difficult for your father as well. I am certain he has done the best he can, but my death will be hard on him. It may indeed be a wound that never heals. He has carried a burden no mortal should ever be asked to carry. But believe me when I tell you, I could see no alternate course of action. It was my death that guaranteed your life.*
>
> *So I must leave you in the care of your father and your uncle Dagon. If you have not met your uncle, you soon will. You must try not to judge him immediately. He is ugly, he can be difficult sometimes, and can be rude most*

times. But listen to him. He is incapable of lying and has seen more civilizations rise and fall than he would care to count. There is no one in all of Hell who cares for you more. He will be your guide as you learn what it means to be a demon. And that is what you must do now. It will be dangerous, of course. But it is time for you to accept what you are. To go forth and be the wondrous creature you were meant to be.

There is so much more I want to tell you. But I must trust that your father and your uncle will, between the two of them, lead you on the right path.

Hell is a dangerous place and many in it will hate you simply because of what you are. They will call you "halfbreed," which is a very inaccurate name. Do not ever think of yourself as half of anything. You are all human, and all demon. You have every right to both heritages. Remember, my dearest, that you were created from a love that is seldom found on this earth or anywhere else. With time, patience, and courage, there is no telling what you are capable of.

Love,

Your mother,

Astarte Thompson

Of all the things contained in the letter, the phrase that Jael reads over and over again, and finally speaks, just to hear it, is "Your mother."

It sounds almost like a prayer.

"Jael," says her father. "I know this must be a lot to take in. Perhaps we should stop for the night—"

"Are you kidding?" says Dagon. "Now we free her demon half!"

"Wait a minute, Dagon," says her father. "Let's not—"

"What happens when we do that?" asks Jael.

Dagon shrugs. "I'm not sure. Maybe nothing. Maybe a lot of stuff."

"Will I . . . " She's not sure how to say it without making it totally offensive. "Will I look like you?"

"Ah . . . ," says Dagon, and his smile fades. He shakes his head. "No, I look like this for a different reason. It's not hereditary. You'll probably look more like your mother."

"And will I have, like . . . powers?"

His fanged grin returns. "Never know until we try."

"Jael," says her father, "I really think—"

"How do we do it?" asks Jael.

"Let's see that necklace again," Dagon says.

She pulls the gem up from under her blouse. It feels warm to the touch. "You're going to put this back into me?"

"Yep."

"But then . . ." She frowns. "Won't that other demon, Belial, be able to find me?"

"Yes, exactly!" says her father. "Belial is waiting for this to happen!"

"It's not as simple as that," Dagon says to her father. "Sure, he'll hear it, all right. But he won't know what it is exactly or where it's coming from. There will be way too much noise for him to get any useful information out of the event. But all that's beside

127

the point." Then he turns to her. "Jael," he says. It's the first time he's said her name. Most people pronounce it "Jail," but Dagon pronounces it "yah-EL," from the old Hebrew. Jael's always been slightly uncomfortable with her name, like it doesn't fit. But when her uncle says it, it sounds right. It sounds beautiful. "Jael," he says again. "It's time to become your whole self. Haven't you always felt it? An emptiness? Like you've lost something?"

She nods.

"You can't go on living half a life. Being a demon is part of who you were meant to be. And if you don't do it now, you lose the chance to be a whole being forever."

"What do you mean I lose it forever?" asks Jael.

"Your demon half will start to fade soon," says Dagon.

"We don't know that for sure!" says her father.

Dagon looks at him, his face full of disgust. "It's been away from her long enough. Maybe even too long already. Did you really think this was a permanent solution? Why do you think Astarte insisted on this age? She was pushing it as far as she could without risking irreparable damage." He turns back to Jael. "This is what your mother wanted. I trust her completely. Your father did too, once upon a time."

"I did until she betrayed me," says her father.

"Still, after all these years, you can't bring yourself to see it," says Dagon sadly. "To believe that it's possible."

"Here we go again," says her father, rolling his eyes. "You and your grand fantasies. There is no destiny, no prophecy, no Reclamation. You're deceiving yourself if you think we're anything more than accidental misfits!"

Dagon says nothing. Just looks at him with his shiny, black eyes, his face alien and unreadable. Then he turns to Jael.

"Well?" he asks her. "What do you want to do?"

"I want to be what my mother said," she says quietly. "The . . . how did she say it? . . . 'wondrous creature' she thinks I'm meant to be. That's what I want."

"Jael," says her father. There's a pleading tone in his voice. "You don't have to decide right now. A few more days won't hurt. Take some time to get your bearings, think it through. Because you won't be able to change your mind later."

"I'm tired of waiting," she says. "And I'm tired of doing it *your* way all the time." She takes off her necklace and holds it out to Dagon.

He smiles appreciatively as he takes it from her. "This is nice work. She was so good at this kind of stuff." With his thumb, he bends back the silver clasps that anchor the gem to the chain. He holds the gem out to her father.

"Here," he says. "You have to do it."

Her father reluctantly takes the gem from Dagon's hand. He walks over to her, looking tired and a little sick.

"Are you sure this is what you want?" he asks her. "It's going to change everything."

"Good," she says. She pulls the collar of her shirt wide.

"It's also probably going to hurt," he says. "A lot."

"Do it," she says.

He places the gem on her bare skin just below her throat.

"I release you."

The world crashes down around her.

She can't breathe.

She can't see.

She can't move.

Her skin is slowly peeled from her body. She knows something low and guttural must be coming out of her mouth. She can feel it ripping its way out of her lungs and past her throat. But she can't hear it because there is a roar in her veins like a hurricane. Then she hears a crack, like the first strike of thunder. A bright, pure light pierces her, fixes her on a single point of space and time, and she is screaming still, though not from pain, but from fear and wonder. Like she's just been born.

The storm within her recedes until she is left with only the sound of her own breath. She opens her eyes.

Everything is the same, but it looks different now—clearer, sharper, more alive. It's like the world had always been covered in a thick layer of dust before, and now it's all been wiped clean. She sees the tiny cracks in the paint on the ceiling and hears the water flowing through the pipes in the wall. Dagon smiles at her, his sharp toothy grin consuming most of his face. She smiles back. Then she looks at her father and she is amazed at how old and weak he looks. Sadness hangs around him like a haze.

"Dad . . . ," she says.

"You look . . . ," he says, "just like her." Then a tear rolls down his weathered cheek and it's the most beautiful thing that she has ever seen. It glitters like a precious crystal and drops from his chin with a grace that makes her catch her breath. She watches it hit the floor, spreading out until it is absorbed by the wood.

"I want to see the moon," she says suddenly, and turns and walks out the front door. She hears Dagon call out to her, but his voice isn't nearly as interesting as the squeak of the front steps beneath her feet or the damp smell of the night with the faintest trace of salt from Puget Sound.

She stands on the sidewalk in front of the house and looks up. Clouds trail across the sky like the memories of dreams. The moon shines as bright as the sun, but with a grace and gentleness that the sun could never show. She sees in its pockets and craters old battle wounds from meteors that hit long ago, before the age of humanity. Before life on this planet. She looks deep into the night sky and she can feel the vast, limitless space like it's something that continues beneath her skin. In that moment, she understands what infinity means. She understands how small a part she is within it, hurtling through its depths. All control on this planet is an illusion. As that understanding grows, so does a sense of helpless vertigo. Like her vision is pulling her forward, off balance, as though she feels the roundness of the Earth, and every step must be taken carefully or she'll fall right off. . . .

She shakes her head, closes her eyes, tries to rid herself of the sensation. But she can still see the night sky beneath her eyelids, drawing her out into the cold, uncaring stars. She can't even remember what reality is supposed to look like. Even as she stands on the sidewalk with her eyes squeezed tight, a part of her is being pulled farther and farther through the cosmos until she feels so stretched out that she could snap.

She screams, and screams, and screams.

Dimly she's aware of thick, scaled arms wrapping around her and dragging her back into the house and to the kitchen table.

"Look," she hears Dagon's voice say, piercing through the panic.

There's a small bowl of water in front of her. It pulls her attention immediately and focuses her down until she's only aware of the countless minute movements of the water. The surface ripples gently, and it feels like a waterfall is pouring over her, cleansing her, breaking her free of everything else. She shudders and sighs.

"Okay now?" Dagon is directly behind, still holding her.

She nods, her eyes on the water.

His arms slowly release her.

"What's that burning smell?" she asks.

"Me," says Dagon.

Jael looks up. There are scorch marks on his arms and chest. Small swaths of scales are peeling off to reveal blistered flesh beneath.

"What happened?"

"You," he says. Then he grins. "Cool, huh? Your whole body went hot when I grabbed you. Great reflexes you've got, kid. A natural." He slaps her on the back, a look of pride on his face.

A strange flush of satisfaction runs through her and she realizes it's nice to have someone look at her like that, even a fish monster.

"What happened to me?" she asks. "Out there?"

"Mortals have a lot of safety mechanisms, like perception filters. If they were to ever understand the whole universe at once, they'd probably go crazy and die. It's a lot to take in, and most of them just aren't built for it. A demon doesn't have all those filters, though. We don't have limitations on what we can see or understand. My guess is that since most demons are thousands of years old, we've had time to adjust. You, on the other hand, are just jumping into the deep end on your first time out. Every halfbreed is different. There's going to be a lot of unexpected surprises."

"Right . . . ," says Jael. She looks back at the bowl of water. She sticks a finger in, breaking the surface.

"Well, let's start packing," says her father, walking over to her. He's shaken off his earlier sadness and now he's all business. "We can be gone by sunrise."

"What?" says Jael. "What do you mean 'pack'?"

"We have to move, of course."

For a moment, it's hard for her to catch her breath. It brings her back to the reality of her life like a sharp pain. Two really good friends—one of them possibly even a boyfriend in the making. And she's about to lose them. "But Dad . . . ," she says, trying to find her voice.

"I think we should try somewhere less populated," her father is saying. "Maybe rural Australia or Alaska, We homeschool from now on, that's certain. And then—"

"And *then* what, Dad?" says Jael. "What about college?"

"You can get degrees online these days, can't you?"

"How am I going to get a job?" She's just throwing things out there, trying to trip him up long enough for her to figure out what she needs to say to stop this from happening.

"It'd have to be something that you can do from home, obviously," he says. "Perhaps Web design, or copywriting, or telemarketing, or something like that."

"That's it?" says Jael, not even trying to hide the misery in her voice. "That's my whole life you've got figured out?"

"I know it's disappointing," he says, laying his hand on her shoulder. "We all have dreams that just can't come true. But trust me, I've had sixteen years to think about this, and it really is the best option."

"Sure," says Dagon with exaggerated casualness. "If you want to live like a shadow."

"Dagon, don't butt in," says her father. "You aren't—"

"I'm not *what*, Father Paul?" Dagon asks. He places a massive, clawed hand on the table and leans across to stick his fanged muzzle right up close to her father. "I'm not allowed? Entitled? Wanted? I'm her uncle, and your time being the one and only voice in her life is over. That was the agreement. That was the promise we made to Astarte."

Dagon and her father glare at each other for a moment, Jael and the table in between them. Then Dagon turns back to Jael.

"Listen, kid," he says. "You don't want that kind of life. Always hiding and sneaking and running away. It's not even fit for a mortal, and you're much more than that. Your daddy's kept you safe, and that's great, but now it's time to fly the nest."

"You want her to go to Hell?" says her father. "You're insane!"

"Of course not Hell proper," says Dagon to her father. Then back to Jael. "But kid, I know this little group that's kind of . . .

neutral to the whole thing. Heaven, Hell, halfbreeds . . . they don't judge. You stay with them while you're getting yourself together. I'll visit when I can. We'll work on getting your abilities focused and in control. And then . . ."

"And what?" says her father. "Go out and pick fights with other demons? Or maybe get them to accept her, like that poor bastard Asmodeus did?"

"No!" says Dagon. "Not like Asmodeus! That's not an option."

"Isn't that the guy who—"

"So what then, Dagon?" her father interrupts, his voice rising as he scowls up at the monster twice his size. "If it were up to you, you'd just throw her on some backwater burnt-out husk of Hell and let her go native until someone catches on and rips her to pieces! And you even want to bring the Deadlies into it? You can't be serious."

"They're fine now!" says Dagon defensively.

"Who are the Deadl—"

"Dagon," her father interrupts again, "she isn't welcome in Hell and you can't guarantee her protection."

"You can't protect her either," says Dagon. One clawed hand digs into the wood of the table, the other clenches into a fist. "If you actually think that hiding in Alaska is going to save you from Belial, then you're even dumber than I thought!"

"Really," says Jael. "I don't think Alaska—"

"At least *I* have a plan," her father says. "You haven't even thought this through. You want to make it up as you go along, just like you always do. And look where it's gotten you."

"I've made my choices and I stick by them!" growls Dagon.

"You don't know anything about mortals!" shouts her father. "You don't know anything about taking care of a child—"

"Hey," says Jael, "I'm not a—"

"Oh, yeah, Father Paul," says Dagon, putting his hands on his hips and leering at him. "Because you've been a model parent. So supportive and loving."

"Damn you!" says her father. "I've done everything—"

"Everything but accept her for who she really is. Everything but believe in what Astarte was trying to do," says Dagon. "What I am *still* trying to do."

"Get it through those thick scales of yours!" says her father. "There isn't going to be a Reclamation! You will never be gods again! I won't stand by and watch you throw her life away on your delusions!"

"STOP IT!" shouts Jael.

Her father and her uncle look down at her in surprise, almost as if they had forgotten she was there.

"You're not even trying to figure this out anymore. You're just fighting," she says as she stands up and walks away from them. Then she turns back, her arms folded on her chest. She gives them both a level stare. "Well, since neither of you seems to have a good plan, what about *my* idea?"

They look at each other, then back at her.

"And?" says her father. "What is your idea?"

"I'm just going to stay right here."

"Jael," says her father. He takes a step toward her. "You

don't really have the full picture yet of the kind of danger you're in—"

"No, I think I get it, Dad. Scary monsters are after me, my life span is probably going to be short, and there's nothing either of you can do to stop that. So if I've only probably got a few years at best, I want to at least try to enjoy it."

"That's fine, kid," says Dagon, "I get that. But don't you want to do something more interesting? Go places?"

"I have *been* places. I have *done* interesting things. And I am so *lonely*," she says, and she has to fight to keep the tears away. "My mom said I have a right to my mortal life and my demon life. I want both. I want to learn about being a demon. I want to know everything I can about my mother and my family. But I also want friends my own age! Real friends, for once. We've been here two years and I'm so close, Dad. If I leave now, you take it all away again."

"You're saying you want to keep going to Our Lady of Mercy?" asks her father, not bothering to hide his shock.

"Hey, come on," says Dagon, nudging him. "A demon in Catholic school? Could be good for some laughs."

Her father glares at him.

"Okay, okay," says Dagon. "In all seriousness, I think this could work. Maybe not for a long time, but for a little while. It might even be the best option. Think about it. We know who everyone is. We know who might become a problem."

"But how is she going to fit in?"

"She's half mortal. Holy objects don't affect her."

"We don't know that for sure," says her father. "In fact, as far as her traits and abilities, we don't know *anything* for sure. We're flying completely blind here. Unleashing her on an unsuspecting population of mortal high school students could be catastrophic."

"Unleash me?" says Jael. "Jesus, Dad, you make it sound like I'm some kind of menace."

"Of course you aren't," he says, maybe a little too quickly. "But . . ."

"But what, Dad?"

"Yeah, Father Paul," says Dagon, a touch of hardness in his voice. "But what?"

Her father looks at them with a helpless expression.

"Please, Dad," says Jael. "Give me a chance to show you this can work."

He is silent for a little while and just stares off into a corner of the room, his face tense. Then at last he takes a breath and says, "If we do this, you will have to promise me something."

"What?"

"You cannot talk to anyone about this. Believe me, people will not understand. There will be times when you'll be tempted, for whatever reason. But no matter how nice they seem, once you turn their world upside down like that, they will not thank you for that. The truth will terrify them, and they will project that fear on you. Is that clear?"

"Yeah, I get it. Dad, I've had to keep this to myself since I was eight. I'm pretty good at it by now."

"It's different now," says her father. "We don't know what you might be capable of. People could get hurt."

"There you go talking about me like some kind of walking disaster again!"

"Just . . . promise me," says her father. "The moment someone even gets suspicious, or if you accidentally do something that makes you stand out in any way, you will tell me."

"Us," says Dagon.

"Us," says her father reluctantly.

"I promise," says Jael.

He stares at her for a moment longer, then nods. "Fine. We'll try it. For now."

Jael lets out a slow breath and her stomach knots start to unkink.

"Thanks, Dad," she says.

Her father says nothing. Instead he goes back to staring into the corner. Jael follows his line of sight and realizes he's staring at the broken silver pendant clasp from the necklace. Jael wonders what it means to him to see it there, empty and useless.

"I think," he says at last, "that if Jael is going to insist on going to school tomorrow, we should get to bed."

life as a succubus
10

The next morning, it takes Jael a while to get out of bed. Not because she's tired. In fact, she feels more awake, more energized, than she ever thought possible. No, what keeps her from getting out of bed is the fact that everything looks, sounds, and smells amazing. Last night she had been too distracted by the argument to really take it all in. But now, the way the sunlight glances through the window, the way dust motes drift through the air, and even the weaving cracks of the hardwood floor seem so fascinating that she can hardly tear herself away from them. It's as if these inanimate objects call to her in some strange way.

Eventually she makes it through her morning routine and down to the kitchen. She finds her father sitting at the table, flipping through student assignments.

"Jael," he says quietly.

"Morning, Dad. Running late?"

"No," he says.

If he never needed to leave so early, Jael wonders, why did he? She almost wants to ask, but doesn't. She's in too good a mood to spoil it.

140

She reaches into the cupboard for a cereal bowl, but the thought of eating cereal suddenly nauseates her. Instead she scans the fridge, looking for something more appealing. The figs are all gone, but there's a bunch of asparagus, and for some bizarre reason they look really tasty. She grabs the whole bunch, sits down at the table, and begins to chew them raw.

"Your mother was the same way," her father says quietly. "She only ate live food."

Jael freezes, a stalk of asparagus halfway to her mouth. "Live?"

"No meat," her father says quickly. "She never ate meat. And nothing cooked or cured or frozen. Just fresh fruit and raw vegetables."

Jael continues eating. She's never really cared for asparagus much, but now it tastes incredible. Rich and sharp, with plenty of satisfying crunch.

"Does this mean I'm an herbivore?" she asks.

"I believe so," he says.

"Are all . . . um . . . demons herbivores?"

"Ah, no," says her father. "Definitely not."

The way he says it, Jael is afraid to ask for more details. Instead, she just eats her vegetables in silence. After a little while, she says, "Where's, uh . . . Uncle Dagon?" She's still getting used to having an uncle, human or demon.

"Hell," he says. "He had to work."

She eats another stalk of asparagus. Then she says, "Is he coming back?"

"When he can."

"Okay." She's not sure why the idea of having a giant, hulking fish monster shambling around the house makes her feel better, but it does. She finishes the last of her asparagus, then stands up and grabs her bag.

"Bring extra snacks," says her father. "You'll probably get hungry more often now."

"Sure. Fine." She carries her bag over to the fridge and dumps a bunch of grapes into it.

"Just . . . be careful today," her father says. "Don't draw too much attention to yourself."

"Dad, if there's one thing I've learned from you dragging me from school to school my whole life, it's how to blend in."

"Right, like the way you blended in yesterday at Mass."

"Yeah, yeah," she says, and heads out the door, relieved to get away from him and all his negativity. She feels amazing. Better than she ever has in her entire life. She can handle anything. School is going to be a breeze.

But a problem surfaces as she walks to school. She thought the objects in her room were interesting. Outside, it's much more intense. The green of the trees; the yellows, reds, and blues of the small houses; and the rainbow cascades of flowers all sparkle in the faint sunlight. Every smell hits her nose like a surprise. Pine, *bam!* Rose, *bam!* Grass, *bam!* The sounds of insects and cars, birds and planes, all work together harmonically and rhythmically, as if improvised by jazz musicians. It's all so fascinating that she has to force herself to keep walking; she knows that once she stops, she'll never make it to school.

She's so impressed with the simple gardens in her neighborhood that she expects to be blown away by her new view of the sleek sports cars and SUVs that pack the school parking lot. But as she weaves through the clusters of vehicles—some empty, some containing students applying last-minute makeup or sucking down one last cigarette—the hulking clumps of metal all seem somehow frail. Like they could collapse on their occupants at any moment.

Jael watches Rob's friend Chas climb out of his shiny black SUV. The massive vehicle seems like it's barely holding together. And come to think of it, Chas himself, who seemed so cool yesterday, looks like he's barely holding together as well. There's something precarious and desperate about both him and the vehicle. A panic just below the skin. It's such a distinct feeling, almost like she can smell it on him.

It occurs to her that she is now just standing on the walkway in front of the school and openly staring at Chas and that Chas is staring back at her. She quickly turns and hurries up the front steps. She has to prove to her father that she can blend in, remember?

As she passes through the front door, she realizes that her socks aren't pulled up. She braces herself for the inevitable reprimand from Father Aaron. But it doesn't come, so Jael just keeps going. She resists the urge to look back and see if Father Aaron is paying attention.

On her walk to homeroom, Jael notices that Chas isn't the only one. Other people she passes in the hallway are staring at her. Full on, blatantly staring. Is she unconsciously doing

143

some weird demon thing? Are horns at this very moment sprouting from her head? She detours into the bathroom.

She looks in the mirror. Nothing has changed since the morning except her hair, which seems even more unruly than ever. But there are no glowing demon eyes, no horns or scales or bat wings sprouting from her head. She wets her hands and takes a few pathetic swipes at her hair. It's hopeless, though, and anyway, she has about three minutes to get to homeroom. She's just going to have to deal with the occasional stares from her classmates.

But "occasional" isn't the word for it. As she continues down the hall, everyone she passes gives her a look almost like amazement. No, more like hunger. Like she's a candy bar. Or a supermodel. Is she doing this to them? Her mother was a succubus. So has Jael inherited some kind of succubus vibe? Well, if that's the worst part of being a demon, she's in pretty good shape. So she's magically gotten hotter overnight. How bad can that be, really? People will probably get over it pretty quickly.

Once in the classroom, she heads for her chair, trying to pretend like most of the room isn't staring at her.

Then she hears Rob's voice. "Hey, Betty. How's—"

The moment she looks at him, he freezes. His mouth is open and his eyes are so wide she can see the whites all the way around.

"What?" she says.

He blinks a few times and closes his mouth.

"Wow," he says. "Uh . . ." Then he freezes again.

"Hello?" she says.

"Uh-h-h-huh . . ." He sputters like a broken-down car and then just looks away.

Throughout class, other students keep turning and glancing at her, trying to look like they aren't staring and failing miserably. Rob, on the other hand, stares fixedly at his desk.

"Rob," says Ms. Spielman. "Can you tell me what that angle is?"

"Uh . . . Sorry, Ms. Spielman. Could you repeat the question?"

"What is going on with everyone today?" says Ms. Spielman. "Are you all asleep?"

No, thinks Jael. *They're trying not to stare at the demon freak.*

When the bell rings, Jael lets everyone else leave first. Even then, people look over their shoulder at her so much that they bump into one another. When the rest of the students have all filed out, she gets up to go.

Ms. Spielman says, "Jael, can you stay for a minute?"

"Sure," she says.

Ms. Spielman squints at her for a moment, but thankfully she doesn't have the same hungry look on her face that everyone else does.

"How did your talk with Father Ralph go?"

"Oh," says Jael. "Okay, I guess."

"Jael," says Ms. Spielman, and then she hesitates, like she's trying to decide if she's going to say something or not. "I like your father enormously. He's a wonderful teacher and a very bright man. But I could see how it would be . . . difficult to live with him. I imagine there's a lot of pressure on you right now. So you need to have someone—and I'm not saying it's me or one of the priests—but you need to have someone to talk to. To be completely open and honest with."

"Yeah," says Jael. "I think things are going to be better now. My uncle came into town and he's straightened up some stuff for me."

"Well, that's great," says Ms. Spielman. "You know, your father never mentioned that he had a brother."

"Oh, he doesn't. It's my mom's brother."

"Your . . . ," she starts to say, then stops. Then she just smiles and nods. "Wonderful." Jael has noticed that most people react that way when she brings up her mother. Like they have to be extra gentle with her. Then Ms. Spielman's smile drops away. "But you still need to talk to Father Ralph again."

"Why?"

"Because you demolished his textbook."

"Oh," says Jael. "Right."

As she makes her way to her social ethics class, weaving in and out of boys who are so spellbound by her that they seem unable to even move out of the way, she decides that she's already over this hotness vibe or whatever it is. Maybe for other girls this is a dream come true. But for Jael it's just creepy.

She bursts into the classroom like it's some kind of refuge. But as she makes her way to her seat, she hears chairs shift and conversations trail off. She pulls out her Bible, flips it open, and pretends that she's totally engrossed in it.

The Mons comes drifting into the classroom, looking as

peaceful and serene as usual. He turns to face the class, a gentle smile on his lips.

"Good morning, ladies and gentlemen," he says. "Today, we will be talking about—"

Then he sees Jael. He doesn't do the hotness stare. Instead, his kind old face twists into a look of utter horror. Jael buries her face back in her Bible. The room is completely silent for what seems like an eternity. Then at last she hears the Mons clear his throat.

"Yes, as I was saying," he says. His peaceful smile returns, but there's something forced and unconvincing about it. "Today we are discussing the parable of the Good Samaritan." He keeps the smile up, but throughout class, while he talks on and on as usual about the kindness of Jesus Christ, his eyes keep darting back to Jael. And there is no kindness in his gaze.

When the bell rings at the end of class, Jael thinks he's going to ask her to stay behind. She can't imagine what he knows or thinks he knows, and she braces herself for something crazy. But instead of approaching her, he's the first one out the door. In a way, that worries her more. Could someone like the Mons really spot the demon in her that easily? She promised her father that she would tell him the moment someone seemed suspicious. It hasn't even been a whole day yet, and already things feel like they're getting out of control. Maybe her plan really is stupid. Maybe she really should just give up and resign herself to life as a telemarketer in Alaska.

No. She's not going to give up that easily. And maybe this can all be fixed. If she's doing some invisible demon thing unconsciously, her uncle can probably tell her how to stop doing it. *Just get through the end of the day,* she thinks. After all, it's just people looking at her funny. No one's actually doing anything.

"Hi, Jael."

"Hey, Jael."

"Yo, Jael."

The boys are over the shy stage. They wave to her or call out to her in the hallway as she walks to lunch. How do they even know her name? It isn't like she's ever talked to any of them before. She's never even had a class with most of them.

But by this point, there's something even more pressing than her sudden popularity. She's already eaten the extra bunch of grapes she brought, and now she's starving. It's not like any hunger she's ever felt before. Her entire body is cold and aching, crying out for fuel. She stalks through the cafeteria line, but even a quick glance at the lasagna turns her stomach. She moves right along to the dessert station, where she has her choice between a piece of chocolate cake, an apple, or a banana. Of course, each student is only supposed to take one.

"Hey, Chuck," she says to the lunch cook. "I know this is against the rules, but can I just have an apple and a banana and forget everything else?"

"Uh . . ." Chuck's mouth hangs open. He looks like he's just gone brain-dead. "S-s-sure, Jael. Have as much as you want!"

"Seriously?" asks Jael. She feels strangely like she's taking advantage of him, but the hunger is painful.

"You bet. As much as you can carry."

"Thanks, Chuck," she says. Feeling elated and sketched-out at the same time, she snatches up a pile of fruit and quickly walks over to the table that Britt has staked out.

"Wow," says Britt. "I can't even explain how good you look today."

"Um," says Jael, attacking an apple.

"For real," says Britt. "What are you doing? Is it makeup? Some new skin cream?"

"We both know my dad wouldn't buy that stuff," says Jael around a mouthful of apple.

"So, what is it?" asks Britt. "Come on, you're supposed to tell your best friend these kinds of secrets."

Secrets. Jael is used to keeping secrets, but she feels like she's nearing some kind of breaking point. Maybe if she just tells Britt . . . but she promised her father she wouldn't. That was the deal with staying here. A vague look from the Mons is one thing, but just flat-out telling someone? And what if her father's right? What if Britt totally flips out and turns on her? She is hard-core Catholic, after all.

"I just blossomed, I guess," she says at last. She takes another big bite of her apple and swallows. She can actually feel her blood sugar rise and her muscles loosen. "Grew into myself or something."

"I'll say," says Britt. Then she gives Jael a wicked smile. "Say . . . didn't I see you leaving school with Rob McKinley yesterday?"

"Uh, yeah," says Jael.

"So?!" says Britt. "How'd it go?"

"Oh, fine," says Jael. It seems like her date was weeks ago, rather than just last night. "It was cool."

"What'd you do?"

"We just went to Denny's."

"That's it?"

"Yeah. It really was . . . nice." But what now? This morning he couldn't even look at her.

"Come on, do I have to beg? Details?"

"Really, we just walked to Denny's, had something to eat, then he walked me home. He's a really nice guy. And actually pretty deep, in his own way."

"Do you think you guys will go out again?"

"I hope so."

"Listen. He's a total flake. Don't take it personally if he . . . you know . . . well, I've just heard that he gets distracted and loses interest in a girl quickly. You should ask him out next time. Keep things going."

"Sure," says Jael. "Maybe I will."

"Really?" asks Britt. She doesn't look convinced.

"Yeah," nods Jael. "Really."

Britt squints at her again. "There really is something different about you today. . . ."

"Hey, Jael."

Jael looks up. A big jock stands at their table.

"Yeah?" she says, biting into her second apple.

"Uh . . ." He looks like he's trying very hard to be cool. "You, uh, doing anything tonight?"

She stares at him for a moment, totally incredulous. Then she says, "Get lost," and goes back to her apple.

"Uh . . . ," he says, like he doesn't quite believe what he's just heard.

"No, really," says Jael. "Bye."

He wanders off, looking bewildered.

"Are you crazy?" asks Britt. "That's Andy Link!"

"If you say so," says Jael.

"The best soccer player Mercy has had in, like, forever."

"Right," says Jael, rolling her eyes. "Because that's totally my type."

"Who cares," says Britt. "He's hot, he's rich, he's popular! What more do you need?"

"Actually, I'm pretty sure those are the three things I don't need." She tosses aside her apple core and decides to switch it up with a banana. She never used to like bananas, but now it's hard to stop herself from shoving the whole thing in her mouth at once. Just as she's taking a big bite, she hears "Hey, Jael."

"What?!" she says around a mouthful of banana and looks up. It's Seamus Buchanan.

"Sorry, Seamus," she says. "Didn't mean to snap, I just . . ."

But he's giving her the look.

"I . . . uh . . . That is . . . I was wondering if —"

"No," she says. "Whatever it is, no."

Seamus nods, almost gratefully, and stumbles away.

"You know," says Britt. "He's never dated anyone. Never even asked anyone out."

"Well, good," says Jael. "Glad I didn't give him the chance to break his record."

But Britt doesn't laugh. In fact, she doesn't even smile. It takes Jael a moment to place the expression on her face, because she's never seen it before. Britt is jealous. How can Jael explain to her that it isn't her fault? That it's all weird demon magic . . .

Yeah, sure, thinks Jael. *Because then Britt would be completely relieved.*

Jael finds that if she keeps her head down and walks fast enough, it prevents guys from stopping her in the hall to ask her out. Even still, they continue to call out to her as she passes, some of them pleading, others almost angry. She can't live like this. If her uncle can't fix this, she'll have to start walking around with a paper bag over her head. That would probably attract less attention.

"Jael?"

She keeps walking. She just doesn't have it in her to tell one more guy to go away.

"Jael."

This one is persistent. She quickens her pace.

"Miss Thompson!"

Jael stops. That's a teacher's voice. She slowly turns back. Father Ralph is at the other end of the hallway. When she looks at him, he flinches. She can see the crazy stare in his eyes, but he fights it back.

"Miss Thompson," he says, his voice a little unsteady. "Please come here."

He gets more uncomfortable the closer she gets to him. By the time she's directly in front of him, a deep red flush covers his face. He doesn't look her in the eyes, but instead stares down at the book in his hands. The history text with the big hole burned into it.

"Didn't you hear me calling?" he mumbles.

"Sorry, Father. I thought you were a student."

"Oh . . . well . . ." He stares at the book like he's trying to remember why he's holding it. Jael notices he's wearing a Superman belt buckle today. For some reason, that strikes her as kind of pathetic. He was so confident yesterday. So sure of his little speech about magic and miracles, Satan and Superman. And now he is face-to-face with something that he doesn't believe exists. Somewhere deep inside, he is aware of that, and she can smell his confusion. His fear.

He clears his throat and asks, "What class are you going to right now?"

"English."

"I need to speak with you for a moment. I'll write you an excuse."

Jael follows him into his office and sits in the green chair across from his desk. He doesn't lean on the edge of his desk this time, though. Instead, he immediately sits down behind it. Like he wants to keep something between them.

"We still need to talk about this." He places the book on his desk. There is a strained sound to his voice. "You obviously can't work with this one, so it needs to be replaced."

"Okay," says Jael.

"Now, I realize . . ." It's like he has to force himself to continue talking. "I realize that you and your father don't have a lot of money, and the school fees to replace a lost book are a little overpriced, honestly. But there is a used bookstore in the U District where you can probably find one much cheaper. So I suggest you bring this one along." He pushes it across the desk to her, still not looking up. "To make sure you have the correct edition."

"Thanks, Father," says Jael. She shoves the book in her bag. "That's really cool of you to think of that. I'll do it this weekend."

"Wonderful," he says. A muscle in his jaw twitches spastically.

"Is that all you wanted, Father?" she asks.

"Um . . ." The bell rings out in the hallway and he flinches. "Yes."

He looks like he could freak out at any moment, but she wants to make sure of one thing before she leaves.

"So, Father?"

"Yes?" He's sweating now.

"Sorry about that . . . uh, joke I made yesterday. You know, about my necklace being from Hell and all. You know I didn't mean that literally, right? It's like you said: Lucifer and Hell and all that stuff. It's just a state of mind."

"Right," he says through clenched teeth. "No, of course. I didn't think for a moment you actually believed . . ."

"Oh, good," says Jael. "I'll get the new book this weekend. I promise, Father."

"Great," says Father Ralph. He's clutching his desk like it's the only thing keeping him from falling out of his chair. His eyes keep flickering over at her, then away, like he's afraid to look at her but he can't help himself. It's strange. Jael can almost see the things going on in his head. In fact, she catches his gaze for just a second and . . .

She gets a confused welter of images of her . . . naked. . . .

She's out the door in a second, feeling sick. The class period has started, so the hallway is empty. She leans her hand against the wall, closes her eyes, and takes a deep shaky breath. She knows that priests are just people and everyone has weird thoughts, and whatever freaky succubus thing she's doing is making it worse. But there is a part of her, the stupid little girl who cried on Good Friday, that still holds on to some sad hope that priests are somehow better than the rest of the screwed-up human race. And even though she's past this and she knows better, it just pisses her off. She wants to go back in there and somehow *show* that liar his own thoughts. Ram them down his goddamn hypocritical throat. . . .

A burning smell hits her nose and she jerks her hand away from the wall. Underneath is a black scorch mark on the paint.

"Oh, God . . . ," she whispers. She stares at her hand. Waves of heat pour off it like an asphalt road in summer.

"Miss Thompson!"

Jael jerks her head up, holding her hand behind her back.

Father Aaron stands at the other end of the hallway, his arms crossed, glaring at her.

"Go to class, Miss Thompson," he shouts down the hallway.

"Y-y-yes, Father."

He turns sharply and walks down another corridor, out of sight.

Jael looks back at the scorch mark on the wall. She rubs at it to see if it will come off. But it's burned in so deep, it looks permanent. This is all permanent. This is her life now, and things will never go back to the way they were. Her father warned her. She has nobody to blame but herself.

She carries that realization with her the rest of the school day. It settles on her like a weight. It sinks into the muscles in her back until it feels like someone's knotted them in a tight French braid. She avoids any contact with anyone for fear of seeing some weird sex thing in their eyes. She avoids touching anyone so she doesn't accidentally burn them. She feels so isolated. So trapped within her secret. All she wants to do is escape. Get home where at least she doesn't have to pretend like everything's okay.

But then, as she's leaving, she sees Rob with his skater buddies. She feels this intense craving for him. It twists up in her stomach and all she wants to do is take him back to that cozy booth in Denny's and talk about stupid school stuff and weird chemistry ideas all night. She's walking briskly toward him before she's even made a conscious decision to do so.

"Hey, Rob," she says.

All the boys go silent and stare at her, except Rob, who looks everywhere else but at her. There is panic in his hazel eyes.

"Rob, can I talk to you a minute?" she asks.

"Uh . . ." It's almost like her presence causes him physical pain. "I . . . uh . . . have to, uh, do something . . . uh, right now. Sorry." And he hops on his board and takes off.

"Shit," she says.

As she watches him escape, she gradually becomes aware of the fact that his friends are still staring at her.

"So, Jael," says Chas. "You, uh, doing anything tonight?"

• • •

Jael hoped that the walk home by herself would give her some peace. But cars slow down as they pass, like they're looking at a traffic accident, and one even runs a stop sign. When another car almost drives up onto someone's lawn, she decides that's all she can take. She hitches her bag up on her shoulder and runs home. She makes it to her front door in minutes, not even winded, but she doesn't take the time to appreciate that because she is suddenly so hungry she feels like she's about to pass out. She bursts into the house, stumbles to the kitchen, and throws open the refrigerator. She finds a bunch of broccoli and just stands there devouring it, stalk and all, with the fridge door still open.

"How was school?" she hears her father behind her.

"Terrible," she says between mouthfuls.

"I knew it!" he says. He paces around the tiny kitchen, cracking his knuckles. "I could see it coming a mile away. I can't believe I even let you—"

"Nothing happened, Dad. It was just . . . awkward."

He stops and gives her a suspicious look. "What do you mean by that?"

"I have to talk to Uncle Dagon," she says.

"That would be all be okay in the next few days."

"No, right now. I can't do this for another couple of days."

"Do what? Jael, you promised that if there's a chance someone suspects—"

"It's not like that," says Jael. "Nobody suspects."

"Well, then? What is the problem?"

"It's just . . ." Her father is the last person on earth she wants to talk to about this. She can't even look at him. "Please, I just need him."

"I have no way to contact him right now," he says, almost like he enjoys saying it.

"What about that thing you did with blood in the bowl?"

"If you do it more than once in a lunar cycle, there can be problems."

"Problems?"

"Accidentally contacting the wrong demon."

"Well, then I'll do it."

"Absolutely not," says her father. "I will not have you cutting yourself for any reason. It's the weekend. Whatever this problem is, clearly it's not so dire that you feel the need to share it with me. You can just stay home until your uncle shows up on his own to fix it."

"Fine, I'll just do it without your help," says Jael.

"You haven't the slightest idea what you're doing," says her father. "You don't even know the incantation."

"Maybe I don't even need that stuff. Maybe only normal people need that stuff," says Jael. "Mortals." She spits out the word with a contempt that makes her father's eyes go wide. It surprises her, too, but to cover that up, she gets to work like she has some idea what she's doing. She fills a bowl with water and grabs a paring knife from the drawer. She sits down at the table and holds her hand out over the bowl.

"Jael . . . ," says her father.

Before she can change her mind, she takes a deep breath, closes her eyes, and drags the knife across her palm.

There's no pain, just a strange screeching noise.

She opens her eyes hesitantly, expecting to see gushing blood and other nastiness. Her hand is unharmed, but the knife is now a flat, warped piece of metal.

"Damn," she says. "Shit, damn, damn, damn—"

"See?" says her father. "I told you to stay home. I told you that you had no idea what you were getting into. You're in way over your head, Jael, and I have no idea how we're going to—"

Jael flings the ruined knife across the kitchen, sending it skittering across the floor and into the hallway. She presses her palms against the table and blinks rapidly to clear the emerging tears. "Thanks for the support, Dad," she says between clenched teeth. "You know, it's almost like you don't want me to get this. Maybe you don't want me to get any of it. My family. My mother. Half of myself."

She stares at him for a long time, waiting for him to defend himself. But he doesn't. He just stands there with that stupid tough-guy look of his. That hurts a lot more than she thought it would.

"Dad?" she says, her voice starting to crumble.

It hangs in the air like that for a moment, then he looks away and quietly says, "Silver. It has to be a silver knife to cut through your skin."

There's a brief flutter of hope in Jael's chest, but it sinks immediately. "We don't have any silver, do we?"

Without a word, her father leaves the kitchen. She hears his slow, deliberate footsteps as he walks into his bedroom and pulls open a dresser drawer. A few minutes later he comes back holding a narrow ivory case. He takes the lid off and holds it out to her. Inside, on a red satin cushion, is a small silver knife with a bone handle.

"This . . ." She takes it from him. "This was . . ."

"Your mother's," says her father. "She used it only for her own bloodletting, when spells called for it."

Jael places the case on the table and takes out the knife. It seems impossibly thin and delicate, but when she presses her finger against the tip, it draws blood immediately.

"Ah!" she says, and holds her hand over the bowl. "Will this be enough?"

"Not if I were doing it," says her father. "But maybe for you."

"So now I'm supposed to say something?"

"Yes. *'Prodeo, Dagon piscis rex.'*"

"What?"

"It's Latin."

"What does it mean?"

"Literally, it means 'Come to me, Dagon, Fish King.' "

"Well, can't I just say that?"

"Formal prayer in Latin always worked best for me," he says.

"Well, I'm going to try it in English," she says. "Because if I have to do everything in Latin, that's gonna suck."

She squeezes her finger and the blood wells up. A single drop falls into the bowl of water and she says, feeling a little silly:

"Uncle Dagon, Fish King. Come here, I need to talk to you." Then, "Please."

The water immediately bubbles and froths like it's boiling. Jael lets out a little yelp and leaps back. Two clawed hands emerge from the bowl, stretch up into the air, and reach out to grab the edge of the table. Then a head that's much too big for the bowl emerges, elongating as it passes the rim. It's followed by one shoulder, then another, and so on, until at last Dagon stands in front of them, his ragged fish scales dripping blood. He shakes himself violently, spattering blood on the Formica.

Then he turns his black shark eyes on her and says, "Christ on a cross, could you have found something smaller to squeeze me out of?"

"Sorry," says Jael. She feels a strange thrill at seeing her uncle. She wonders if maybe it's the relief of having someone around who is more monsterish than her. "I didn't realize you'd actually show up. I thought it would be like when Dad does it."

"Demon blood is a much better conductor than mortal blood," says Dagon.

"Right . . . ," says Jael.

"So what's the emergency?" he asks.

"Well . . ." She glances at her father. "Maybe we could go talk about this somewhere else," she says.

"No, Jael," says her father. "If you truly want me to help you, if you want my support, then I need to know what's going on."

She tries to meet his gaze and fails. "You're not going to like it," she mutters.

"Add it to the list of recent events," he says.

She keeps her eyes firmly fixed on Dagon. "The guys at school were really into me today."

"Of course." Dagon grins, teeth glinting in the harsh kitchen light. "You're pretty."

"No," says Jael. "I mean, like, they wouldn't leave me alone. Like they *couldn't* leave me alone."

"I'll bet," says Dagon. Then he laughs in a sea-lion bark. "I mean, you are a succubus after all."

"Oh God," says her father.

"Those poor teenage boys!" says Dagon, still laughing. "They must have been in agony!"

"It's not funny," says her father.

"Oh, Father Paul, don't be such a little priss," Dagon says. Then he turns to Jael. "Did you have your hair down like you do now?"

"Yeah," says Jael. "What's that got to do with it?"

"That's where it's coming from," says Dagon.

"My hair?"

"The longer and looser it is, the more potent that kind of magic gets."

"So . . . if it were really short, the boys would leave me alone?"

"Well, you'll never be a wallflower again no matter what, kiddo. Sorry. But yeah, your affect on mortals would be less intense."

"Good enough," says Jael. She turns and walks out of the kitchen.

"What are you doing?" her father calls out.

But she doesn't answer. Instead, she goes into the bathroom and pulls out the clippers her father uses to cut his hair. A moment later, a shower of black, frizzy locks start to fall to the tile floor. She takes it slowly, one strip at a time, front to back. At first, her heart is racing because she can hardly believe what she's doing to herself. So many bad-hair-day mornings she thought of it. But every time, she chickened out. She continues to cut her hair, and after a while her heart slows. She's able to appreciate the odd sensations of the clippers sliding across her scalp and the sudden cool freshness that follows in its wake. Once she's finished, she rubs the shock of short spiky hair, letting it prickle her palm. She looks at herself in the mirror and sighs deeply, feeling like she's shed several pounds.

She notices her uncle Dagon watching her, his massive shape taking up most of the doorway. In moments like this, when he's completely still and silent, she remembers all over again how alien he is to her, and how little she understands him. What was it her mother's letter had said? That he has seen more civilizations rise and fall than he cares to count. She can't even conceive of what that might be like.

"It doesn't look too bad," she says.

"I'm no expert on mortal aesthetics," says Dagon. "But I think you'd have to do a lot worse than a haircut to make yourself ugly."

"Yeah, but it's just the demon magic stuff that makes people think I look prettier, right?" says Jael. "It's not like I can claim any credit for it. It's not me."

"This 'demon magic stuff' you're talking about is not

something separate. It's as much a part of you as your lungs or your teeth. So keep that in mind. And sure, your beauty is in the eye of the beholder. All beauty, and all ugliness, is subjective. There is no other kind."

"Well, anyway, it didn't do much good for me today," she says.

"I thought the boys were falling all over each other."

"Except the one guy that I actually like," says Jael.

"Oh?" says Dagon, cocking his head to one side. "There's a guy?"

"Yeah, well, I know you can't lie, but don't mention to my dad that I actually like a boy. He'd totally flip."

"I'll try to avoid the topic," says Dagon. "You might have noticed, he and I don't talk too much anyway. So what happened with this boyfriend?"

"He's not a boyfriend," Jael says quickly. "I mean, I thought maybe there was a chance. . . . But he couldn't even stand to be near me for more than a few seconds."

"That so?" asks Dagon, and he smirks, his lower teeth poking out on one side.

"What?"

He shrugs. "If he already liked you before . . . well, maybe he was a little overwhelmed."

"Huh," she says, looking back at herself in the mirror. "Could it be that intense?"

"Kid, you got no idea. And when you actually start using it on purpose—look out, world."

"Yeah, well, I don't think I'll ever use it on purpose. That would be totally creepy."

"Listen, kid," says Dagon. "I'm supposed to be at work right now, so I have to split. But we can start your training tomorrow. Get a little better control of all this."

"Work, huh?" asks Jael. "What do you do, anyway? Like, torture dead people or something?"

"Torture dead people?" asks Dagon, his eyes going wide.

"Isn't that what demons do?"

"The crazy stuff these mortals think up!" he says. His face curves into a wicked frown and he glances down the hallway toward the kitchen, where her father still is. "Kid, you have to stop listening to these mortals. They have no idea what they're talking about. Especially the priests."

"But . . . isn't that what Hell is? The place of eternal torment?"

"Hell's no picnic, but it's not *that* bad."

"So . . . bad people don't go there when they die?"

"Of course not," he says. "Trust me, we have enough problems on our own without taking on garbage from Gaia."

"Gaia?"

"The mortal realm."

"Okay, so when people here on . . . uh . . ."

"Gaia."

"Right. Gaia. When we die, where do we go, then?"

"Dead people? How would I know?"

"What about Heaven?"

"What about it?"

"Well, do people go there?"

"No idea. Never been there."

"Um . . ." Jael rubs her temples. "I'm totally confused now. If Hell doesn't exist to punish the wicked, what's it there for?"

"You know," says Dagon, giving her a teasing smile. "I've often wondered the same thing about Gaia. What's it there for?"

She just stares at him.

"What?" He shrugs. "If you can answer my question, I'll try to figure out yours."

"Fine," she says. "So what do you do in Hell, then?"

"I'm Hell's baker."

"You're kidding."

"I'm not."

"So when I saw you in that place with the giant shells and all, that was your kitchen?"

"I share it with Hell's cook, Nysrock, but otherwise, yep. That's my domain."

"Wow," says Jael. "How bizarre. I mean, you don't really think about Hell having an actual kitchen."

"I wasn't always a baker," he says. "Before Belial and the other Grand Dukes consolidated their power, things were different. Once, I was . . ." Creases appear in the dried scales of his face for a moment, causing some of them to crack and flake off. Then he shrugs. "Well, I wasn't a fish, that's for sure. But that's a long story and I've got to get back to work because I've got about two thousand loaves in the oven. So let's figure out where we're going to meet tomorrow. We're gonna need a big, natural space without people. Any ideas?"

"In a city?" asks Jael. "There isn't much. Do I have to get there by myself?"

"Afraid so," says Dagon. "The only way I know to transport someone is through Hell, and I don't want to risk anyone catching sight of you."

"Yeah, I don't know how I feel about going to Hell anyway, even if there aren't any tortured dead people," Jael says. "I don't want to count on my dad, so it's got to be somewhere I can get by bus. Maybe Discovery Park?"

"How big is that?"

"I don't know . . . like, five hundred acres?"

"That's it?"

"That's a lot for a city."

Dagon sighs. "If that's the best we can do."

"So where should we meet?" asks Jael.

"You just find a spot without mortals around," says her uncle. Then he winks. "And get ready to make some magic."

Then he's gone, leaving behind only a faint fishy odor.

"Yeah," she whispers to herself as she looks in the mirror. She runs her hand through her new spiky hairdo, feeling it slide freely through her fingers for the first time since she can remember.

"Magic."

She has no idea what that even means. But she thinks she just might be ready for it.

a bad hair day

11

"Well, brother," said Astarte. The desert wind whipped at her thick, curly black hair as she gazed at the vast stone temple before them. "It seems you are doing well these days."

Dagon grinned broadly, a twinkle in his amber eyes. "It doesn't equal the majesty of Babylon, but it's pleasant enough. The Philistines are a fascinating and cultured people."

"Yes," said Astarte. "It helps that they adore you so much that they built this gorgeous temple for you."

"Yes," said Dagon. "They have good taste. And they're quite the artisans, as well. Come inside and I'll show you row upon row of finely crafted pottery, all with my dashing good looks painted on them."

"Oh," said Astarte, arching her eyebrow. "Do you think I should? I'd hate to go blind from all that beauty."

"Hmm," said Dagon, and tugged at his short trimmed black beard, his chiseled brown face serious. "Perhaps we should only look at the first floor."

She punched him in the shoulder. "You are impossible," she told him. "Lead the way to this rogues' gallery."

The pair started down the wide, dusty road, their white

robes gleaming in the harsh sun. As they walked by, mortals stopped their activities and bowed low. When they passed between the massive wooden pillars at the front of the temple, a chorus of joyful voices greeted them. The chorus continued to sing as Dagon led Astarte through the temple, pointing out the rows of hundreds of delicate handcrafted pots, bowls, cups, and pitchers that lined the walls. It wasn't until they reached the high stone altar and Dagon nodded in their direction that the chorus stopped and filed silently into an antechamber to rest.

"It's convenient that they keep all these bowls and cups here," said Dagon. "My people make an excellent alcoholic beverage."

"And you encourage drinking in the temple?" asked Astarte. She shook her head. "Next you'll institute holy prostitution."

"It worked for you," said Dagon.

"That was Greece," said Astarte, as if that explained it perfectly. "I'm done with all that now."

"Oh yes," said Dagon. "Your precious Phoenicians. How are they?"

"Busy as always," said Astarte. "I'm a spirit of love, not maternity. I don't coddle, and I prefer my mortals to have a little more autonomy."

"Suit yourself," said Dagon. "I have too much fun hanging out with mine to leave them for too long."

"Dagon," said a low, rumbling voice from the front of the temple. A creature stood at the entrance, like an ox standing upright on its hind legs, but several times larger and made of iron, wood, and stone.

"Ah, Baal!" said Dagon as he walked down the center aisle. Astarte trailed slightly behind. "I'm glad you're here. My sister just stopped by for a visit."

"My lady," said Baal in a slow, measured voice. He bowed his head, and the sound of creaking wood and grinding stone echoed through the temple. "It has been too long since I last beheld your beauty."

Astarte smiled slightly. "Pretty words, sir. Has my brother been coaching you?"

"Yes," said Baal with no trace of embarrassment. "He has taken me under his wing, so to speak. And I am very grateful."

"Baal," said Dagon, "I was thinking a feast would be in order to celebrate my sister's visit. Could you oversee that for me?"

"It would be my pleasure," said Baal without changing his low, flat inflection. "I will begin arrangements straightaway. But first, news from Ashdod."

"Oh?" asked Dagon.

"It's that Samson again," said Baal. "Recently he slew ten thousand of your people with a jawbone."

"What?" said Dagon, his face clouding. "And with only a jawbone?"

"Of an ass, I believe," said Baal.

"The sheer insolence!"

"Who is this Samson?" Astarte asked.

"Hebrew," said Dagon tersely.

"Weren't those the people with the box of sand?" she asked. "The one that injured you back in—"

"Yes, yes, their Ark of the Covenant," said Dagon, and he began to pace back and forth, rotating his hands on his wrists as if recalling the pain. "This one is rather impressive. I question whether he's even mortal."

"I assure you he is mortal," said Baal. "Although it is rumored that he is favored by Heaven."

Dagon snorted. "All Hebrews think they are a favorite of Heaven." He paused in his pacing and frowned. "Still, this one seems able to show some proof of it."

"Are the Hebrews a real threat to your people?" asked Astarte.

"Not really," said Dagon. "They haven't figured out how to make iron, so we have a huge tactical advantage over them, and they aren't nearly as organized as we are. But their whole exclusive one-god-only policy is a serious pain in my ass. They're impossible to work with when they keep telling me I don't exist."

"And of course they wounded your pride with that box of sand."

"That too," said Dagon.

"Perhaps he has a weakness," said Baal. "Like Achilles."

"Maybe," said Dagon. Then he turned and gave Astarte a coy look. "Sister dear, don't you owe me a favor for something or other?"

"No," said Astarte. "Why do you ask?"

"Well, I'll owe you one, then."

Her eyes narrowed. "For what?"

"This Samson can't seem to say no to a pretty face. If he has a weakness, I'll bet you could find out what it is easily."

"Brother, really. We both have better things to do than waste all this time and effort on one mortal."

"But," said Baal, "this mortal is the champion of the Hebrews. . . . "

"Exactly!" said Dagon. "The Hebrews unite under him. If we put him back in his place, no one else will get delusions of grandeur and it will be clear to everybody that their distant god in Heaven isn't going to protect them from a god right here."

"These Hebrews really got under your skin, didn't they?" asked Astarte.

"Please, sister. It will be such an easy task for you."

"Perhaps . . . ," she said.

"You'll do it?" said Dagon, already wrapping her in a rough embrace.

"On one condition," she said, pushing him away slightly.

"What?" he asked, his eyes narrowing.

"If I do this thing, you must promise to stop obsessing over these Hebrews. Let past insults go and move forward. It's not like you to hold a grudge."

"Of course, sister dear. You're absolutely right. Once this is finished, I will turn to more important matters."

"Do you require anything else?" asked Baal. "Or should I begin the arrangements for tonight's feast?"

"Yes, please, by all means," said Dagon, dismissing him with a wave of his hand.

Baal made his slow, creaking way out of the temple.

Once he was gone, Astarte said, "Do you trust this one?"

"Baal?" asked Dagon. "Of course, of course. Believe me, there isn't much activity going on in that stone skull of his."

"I see," said Astarte. Then she smiled. "Well, brother dear. As slow as he moves, the feast probably won't be ready for hours. Would you mind pointing me toward a fruit tree so I can tide myself over until then?"

"Would a fig tree do?" he asked, returning her smile with a grin.

"You know that's my favorite," she said.

"Yes," he said as he put his arm around her shoulder and led her out of the temple to the orchard. "I remember that well."

"It was a rather pivotal moment in humanity, wasn't it?"

"Adam certainly thought so," said Dagon.

Astarte found Samson in an inn on the outskirts of Ashkelon. He sat by himself in a corner, away from the others. His long hair flowed like a waterfall over his thickly muscled shoulders and down his broad back. She could see at once that there was something different about this mortal. Someone had touched him for a very specific task, and that task was near completion. She sensed that she would be the catalyst to bring it to a close. She hated the feeling that she was just a pawn, with little choice of her own. But she had seen heroes before, and fate always seemed to snap at their heels like a rabid wolf until the day the hero grew weary or clumsy and fell into its slavering jaws.

She walked slowly over to his table. It wasn't until she stood directly in front of him that he looked up from his plate of bread and meat.

"Samson," she said, looking directly into his rich brown eyes. "May I sit?"

He looked her over slowly, making no effort to hide his interest. His hunger.

"Yes," he said, and gestured for her to sit. Then he began to eat again.

He reminded her of a lion—large, powerful, and regal, in a coarse sort of way. What puzzled her was that he did not seem like a troublemaker. Rather, he seemed to be the sort who had to be provoked. Perhaps even led. She wondered by whom.

"Are you a whore?" he asked her. There was no judgment in his tone. Simply a desire for clarification.

"I do not require money, if that is your question," she said.

He nodded and stuffed a chunk of meat in his mouth. As he chewed, he said, "What do you require, then?"

"Ultimately, I require . . . attention," she said. "As long as it is sincere, how you choose to administer that attention is entirely up to you."

He nodded again and took a large gulp of wine from his cup.

"How do you know my name?" he asked.

"How does anyone *not* know it?" she asked.

"Is that so?" he asked with only faint interest. "Am I famous?"

"Or infamous," she said.

He smiled at her for the first time. "I like you," he said. "What is your name?"

"Delilah," she said.

It didn't take long for him to ask her up to his room. Once

there, he wasted no time in satisfying his hunger. In fact, it was over rather quickly. And she told him so.

"Rest a short while," she advised as they lay together in the dark.

"You did not feel attended?" he asked.

"Not hardly," she said.

"I am sorry," he said, staring up at the ceiling.

She sat up and placed his head in her lap. "You carry a heavy burden," she said as she stroked his long hair.

"What do you know of it?" he asked.

"Nothing," she said. "But it is clearly written in everything you do."

He was silent for a while as she continued to stroke his hair. At last he said, "Yes."

"But surely you have nothing to fear," she said in a slightly teasing tone. "Everyone knows you have no weakness."

"Oh," he said with a quiet laugh. "I have a weakness."

"For beautiful women," she suggested.

He laughed again. "Besides that."

"And what, pray tell, would that be?"

"Ah, you are a tricky one," he said, but he still smiled.

"I'm glad you noticed a quality other than my breasts," she said.

"If someone were to bind me with fresh bow strings, I would lose my strength."

She laughed. "You, however, are not tricky in the slightest. You don't actually expect me to believe something like that, do you?"

He laughed delightedly. "I truly do like you," he said. "It is a shame you are a woman. You have the spirit of a warrior."

She looked down at him, one eyebrow arched. "Is it really a shame that I am a woman?"

"Of course not," he said, reaching up to touch her cheek for a moment. "Now, truthfully, if you were to bind me with new rope, I would lose my strength."

"That one is even more ridiculous than the first. I sincerely hope you are never called upon to lie in order to save a life, because that person would surely die."

"It is true that I have not been gifted with cleverness," he said. "What you see before you is all there is."

"I find that refreshing," she said.

"I have been dedicated to my God since the day of my birth. A Nazirite always strives for truth and simplicity in all things. And that is where my weakness truly lies. My God gives me my strength and if I ever did something that broke one of my Nazirite vows, such as cutting my hair, He would most certainly take away my strength as punishment."

"So it will grow until the day you die?" she asked.

"God willing," he said.

She remained silent after that, and continued to stroke his hair until the tension in his face eased and he drifted off to sleep. Even after that, she continued to look down at him.

"You have been here the entire time," she said quietly.

Baal stepped out of the shadows, his brown liquid eyes glittering in the darkness.

"Yes," he said. "Your reputation is well deserved."

"And yours, apparently, is nothing but a facade," she said.

"Yes," he said.

The feast to celebrate the capture of Samson was held at the Temple of Dagon in Gaza. Revelers traveled from Ashkelon and Ashdod, as well as Ekron, and even far-off Gath.

Despite the fact that it was the single largest gathering of Philistines in more than a century, Baal managed the festivities with his unflappable authority. Dagon sat in his chair by the altar, surrounded by thousands of cheering, singing Philistines. The upper levels were crowded to overflowing with those who had come to celebrate the downfall of their common enemy. They drank from large casks of wine, cheered on the dancers and musicians, and laughed delightedly at the acrobats.

"Isn't it wonderful, sister?" Dagon shouted to her over the din.

She looked back at him, her eyes sad. "Is it?"

"Come now, you've got to give the mortals a feast now and then to keep them happy."

"What of the mortal in your dungeon? What about his happiness?"

"Bah! He is only one mortal. You and I... yourself." Dagon took a long drink from his cup. "And besides, he killed many of my people."

"I wonder if perhaps he was manipulated into it," she said. "He did not seem to me the type to go looking for carnage."

"Did he get to you, my sister?" asked Dagon with a teasing grin. "Have you fallen for some mortal?"

"Perhaps a little," she said. "Even so, you cannot deny what a sad thing it is to see a hero brought so low."

"Oh come now, my dungeons aren't that bad," Dagon said.

She looked at him for a moment, her brows knitting together. "You haven't seen him, have you?"

"What? Why, no, I haven't. You were the one who insisted I not concern myself with him once he was captured."

"Perhaps you should have one final look. For closure."

"If you like," he said. Then he turned toward the front of the temple. "Baal! Why don't you fetch our guest of honor and bring him up here for a moment?"

Baal looked at Dagon for a long moment, as if he didn't understand. Then he said, "Of course. An excellent suggestion." He turned to a few mortals at his side and spoke quietly with them. As they scurried off, Astarte caught Baal's gaze, and it was cold.

A while later, when most of the celebrants were considerably drunk, the servants brought out Samson.

"What is this?" gasped Dagon.

The Samson who stood before him was barely recognizable. His hair was a ragged patchwork of short clumps. His muscles had wasted away from malnutrition. He was covered with whip marks and bruises. Worst of all, his eyes had been burned out of their sockets. Only an infected mass of scar tissue remained.

"Behold!" boomed Baal's slow, measured voice. "The once mighty Samson brought low before you!"

Throngs of drunken people cheered at his back.

"What cruelty have you wrought upon this poor wretched creature?" said Dagon.

"Only what was just," said Baal. Then he turned to the crowd. "Was it not the Hebrew god who said an eye for an eye? Well, this Samson has dimmed the eyes of thousands of our people, and if he had as many eyes we would burn them all out!"

The crowd roared like rabid animals. They jeered and spit on Samson. He stood straight and tall, but his weak, starved body shook with the effort.

"I don't understand what's going on," Dagon said to Astarte. "My people are artisans and architects, not bloodthirsty barbarians."

"Things change," said Astarte. "And mortals can be fickle."

"Here he is!" Baal said to the crowds, his deep, resonant voice carrying effortlessly through the temple. "The man who slaughtered our people and destroyed our homes! And still he stands, too puffed up with arrogance even now to humble himself before those he has wronged!"

That was when a beautiful handcrafted pot crashed onto Samson's head. A trickle of blood leaked from the gash on his forehead and he swayed. Then another bowl struck him, and another. The pottery crashed into him, shattering against his emaciated frame again and again. The Philistines pulled their priceless artwork from the shelves and from the altars and hurled what they could grab with howls of rage. Samson stumbled and almost fell. He reached out his hands until he caught hold of the massive wooden pillars at the center of the temple. He clung to them as cups, bowls, pots, and vases rained down on him.

"Stop this!" yelled Dagon. "What has come over you all? These are not my Philistines!"

"No," said Baal, his emotionless brown eyes locked on Dagon's amber eyes. "They are mine now."

"You . . . ," said Dagon, but his body was so clenched with rage that he could barely move.

"I used Samson to show your people the foolishness of attachment to aesthetics and beauty. I have shown them what a truly powerful god requires of them. A god worth worshiping."

"How could you do this? I took you in when you had nothing. You were my apprentice!"

"Times are changing," said Baal. "You must change with them. Or die."

Then he turned his back on Dagon and gazed at Samson and the crowds that closed in tighter and tighter around him. They had broken all the pottery in the temple and now beat and kicked Samson while he clung stubbornly to the pillars.

"Yes!" boomed Baal. "Rip him apart with your bare hands! Tear his bleeding flesh from his bones while he still screams! I, your god, command it!"

The crowd surged forward, fighting each other to get to the man.

"Oh, God!" cried Samson. "Remember me, I beg you, and strengthen me only this one last time that I may be avenged!"

"I don't know what your god thinks of all this," said Dagon with a quiet growl. "But I will grant you this request gladly."

Suddenly, Samson stood up straight. His muscles seemed to expand as his hands pressed against the support pillars. The pillars groaned and shuddered, then cracked. But the crowds were too bent on fighting one another to notice. Then the pillars gave way, the ceiling shattered, and the temple collapsed with a sound like thunder.

Dagon and Astarte stood outside the temple as it fell. They caught a glimpse of Baal for a moment, his eyes locked on them as everything crumbled around him. Then he was buried with his shrieking Philistines under a mass of wood and stone.

They stood there for a few minutes, the silence sudden and oppressive.

Then Astarte said, "Come, brother. Baal will dig himself out soon enough. It will be better if we aren't here. You can come to Phoenicia until you decide what to do next."

"I still don't understand," he said quietly, "how it came to this."

"Baal was right. Change is coming."

"What will we do?" he asked.

"I don't know," she said.

a lesson in the elements

12

The next morning, it starts to rain. Not the flirtatious occasional drizzle of the past few days, but the steady, sodden mist of Seattle's version of winter. It isn't a harsh cold like many of the places that Jael has lived. In fact, it rarely dips below freezing. Instead, it's just dark, quiet, and wet from October to May.

The bus crosses the George Washington Memorial Bridge, then winds through downtown and past the Space Needle and Monorail. As Jael stares out the window, her demon vision cuts through the mist easily and the city opens up for her. The streets slope dramatically down to canals and waterways that churn endlessly out into Puget Sound. She notices that parts of the coastline are not solid rock, but are instead filled in with dirt and sawdust by arrogant men trying to steal just a little more land from the sea. Their gall amazes her, especially since it's so clear to her how fragile that false land is. It survives on the whim of nature, and it wouldn't take much to wash it all away.

The bus skirts the hilly bungalows of Magnolia and finally plunges into the forest. After a few minutes, it emerges into a big open field in the center of the park. In the summer, the field is covered with sunbathers and people playing Frisbee or football. Now that the rains have come, it's empty and a little sad. Jael is the only person left on the bus, and as she gets off, the bus driver says, "Have fun out there."

"Yeah, thanks," she says. "I'll try."

The bus slowly pulls away, taking its dry warmth and light with it. She's left standing in the damp grass on a dark, gray day, slowly getting wetter and wetter as she stares at the empty forest that borders the field.

Usually, she'd feel tense in an empty park. She'd imagine muggers or rapists lying in wait for her. But now as she looks around, she feels comfortable, despite the weather. In fact, she doesn't even feel alone. At first she can't quite figure out why. Then she realizes: It's the trees.

She knows that trees are alive, of course, but she's never thought about it much before. As she looks at them now, she can see distinct personalities. The way one leans forward makes it seem sad, and the way one shelters another is kind of sweet, like two old people on a bench. By contrast, the manicured lawn feels boring and faceless. She walks toward the trees.

It's a lot drier among the trees. The branches form a thick canopy over her head that blocks out most of the rain.

"Pretty nice for tame trees," says Dagon. He's right next to her, but his sudden appearance doesn't startle her. She expected him to be there. His scales look different now—moist and healthy—and there's a rainbow sheen to them. Maybe it's the rain, or being in a more natural setting, but there seems to be a brightness about him, an energy that makes him appear less like a giant fish man and more like something that belongs on Earth. Or as he called it, Gaia.

"Tame trees?" she asks.

"This isn't real wilderness," says Dagon. "Someone takes care of them. Most of those types force the trees into shapes or arrangements instead of letting them find their own way. This mortal, whoever he or she is, actually gave the trees a lot of leeway. Makes them friendlier."

"Friendly trees," says Jael.

"Sure," says Dagon. "Can't you feel it?"

Jael places her hand on the trunk of the big oak next to her.

"I didn't mean literally," says Dagon.

"No, no," says Jael. "I think I can, though. It's kind of weird. . . ." She frowns. "I don't know how to describe it. It's not really a good or bad feeling. I just feel . . . noticed. Which is weird, because I didn't realize I was being ignored before."

"Nature doesn't care about mortals," says Dagon. "At least not as individuals. They die so quickly compared to a tree. And they don't really do anything."

"What about what scientists say?" asks Jael. "About us killing the Earth?"

Dagon makes a honking sound, like a laugh and a sneeze. "First, when you say 'us,' you're not talking about yourself."

"But I'm still half—"

"And second, the idea that they could kill the planet Earth is the height of mortal arrogance."

"But what about global warming and all that stuff? Isn't that real?"

"Sure it is, but global warming isn't the death of the Earth. It's the death of humanity. It's more like the Earth's way of evicting mortals because they've been lousy tenants. Just because the Earth isn't habitable doesn't mean it's dead. Just not in the mood for guests and freeloaders."

"So if the Earth doesn't care about mortals, why does it care about demons?" asks Jael.

"I wouldn't go so far as to say it cares about us," says Dagon. "It's more like mild curiosity. We live long enough to show up on its radar, so we can affect things in very small ways."

"What do you mean, we can affect things?"

"That's what magic is," says Dagon. "Coaxing the elements into doing something a little different from what they usually do." He moves over to a small stream, his thick, scaly legs surprisingly agile. Then he beckons to her. Jael picks her way through the clumps of moss and thick roots that stick out of the ground with a lot less grace.

"We'll start with the ones that are closest to you." Dagon bends over and scoops up a handful of water. "Look at this." He holds out his clawed, webbed hands with a perfect pool of water collected in the center. "Now, it's natural for water to freeze. Just not something it's used to doing at this temperature. So convince it to do it anyway."

"Convince the water . . . ," says Jael. "What, like, talk to it?"

"If it helps you," says Dagon. "But that's more to keep you focused. Water doesn't understand language, just intent."

"But how does it get my intent?"

"Well, that's the trick, isn't it?" says Dagon.

Jael glares at him.

"What?" Dagon grins. "Nobody said it would be easy."

"Can't you at least give me a hint?"

"It's different for everyone," says Dagon, still smiling. "I wouldn't want to impose my own techniques on you."

"Thanks," says Jael. She stares at the water in Dagon's hand.

"It does help if you're touching it," he says. "At least, at first." He holds out his hands and pours the water into her hands. Since her hands are much smaller and don't have webbing, a lot of it trickles to the ground.

"I can't hold as much as you," she says.

"It would be easier if it were more solid," he agrees. Then he winks at her.

"Right," she says. She looks at the tiny puddle in her hands. Feeling pretty dumb, she says, "It would be easier to hold you if you were solid."

And she's looking at a small disk of ice in her hands.

"I did it!"

"Careful," says Dagon. "Don't start thinking like that. You and the water did it together."

"Right." Then she says to the water, "Sorry. We did it."

"Better," says Dagon. "Now get it to turn to steam."

"Hmm," she says. She stares at the clump of ice for a minute. "Turn to steam," she says.

Nothing happens.

"You can't command it. You have to convince it," says Dagon. "Give it a reason to change."

"So, why would water want to become steam?"

"Freedom, perhaps?"

"I don't get that."

"When water is heated, the molecules speed up and separate from each other. That's steam. So imagine how great it would feel if you could spread out like that, then see if the water's interested in it."

Jael has a hard time imagining being able to let loose that much. To literally explode. It doesn't really seem that fun. In fact, the idea makes her a little uncomfortable.

Then she gets this strange feeling that the ice in her hands disagrees with her. She can't say how, exactly, but a whisper at the base of her skull tells her exactly how much fun it can be to throw yourself to the wind, literally.

"Oh yeah?" says Jael to the ice. "Show me."

The ice dissolves into a single puff of steam. And as it disperses, Jael catches just a hint of the joy it feels.

"Okay, that's pretty cool," she says.

"It's just the beginning," says Dagon. "Water's the most accommodating of the elements. Some of the others are a little more tough to convince."

"Like earth?"

"Right," says Dagon. "Earth doesn't like to change what it's doing. If you want to start an earthquake where one never happened before, you'd have to be pretty damn persuasive."

"But if one was already happening, I could just egg it on?"

"You got it."

"What about growing plants and stuff super fast?"

"That's a little more complicated," says Dagon. "Because you have to coordinate earth, water, and air."

"What about air?" she asks. "It's gotta be pretty flexible, right?"

"It is," says Dagon. "The trick is keeping it on track."

"But it's air. It's everywhere, so what does it matter?"

"I'll show you," says Dagon. "Getting the ice into steam was about getting the water molecules to go faster and farther apart, right?"

"Oh, God, this is turning into a science class."

"Science, magic. Just labels for the same thing."

"Huh," says Jael, thinking of Rob.

"So," Dagon continues, "hot-air balloons work the same way. The air is heated, which makes the air molecules fly around faster and farther apart."

"So, wait," says Jael. "Are you telling me I can do that to make myself fly?"

He spreads his webbed hands wide. "I don't know. Can you?"

She closes her eyes. It's kind of hard to actually feel air unless there's a breeze. So she waits until a strong wind comes up. Then, when she can feel it all around her, she tries to recall that fleeting feeling of joy that she got from the steam.

"You want that, don't you?" she says to the air around her.

Then she's jerked off her feet and up into the sky.

"*Ohhhhhh shiiiit!*" she yells.

She pitches forward, then spins around so fast that the ground beneath her becomes a blur. She pauses about fifty feet up and just hangs there.

Then she drops.

The earth rushes toward her and she screams, "Please, God, no! *Help!*"

There's a flash of orange.

Then she strikes. But instead of hard earth, it feels like warm pudding. She opens her eyes and finds that she's submerged in a glowing orange sludge. She kicks hard through the thick liquid until she breaks the surface. All around her, the forest is the same as it was, except for this small pond of steaming orange.

"That was incredible!" says her uncle, his fanged mouth open in a wide grin. "You're picking this up even quicker than I expected!"

She swims to the edge of the orange pool. "What happened?"

"You got the earth beneath you to liquefy so it would break your fall."

"Liquefy . . ." She looks at the pool around her. "So this is . . . lava?" She scrambles out of the lava and back onto solid earth. "Why didn't it kill me?"

"Are you kidding? Uphir recommends that demons bathe in lava at least once a month."

"Who's Uphir?"

"Hell's physician."

"Huh," says Jaël. Then she realizes something. "I'm naked!"

She drops to a crouch and covers herself as best she can.

"Of course you're naked," says Dagon. "Lava might be fine for you, but your clothes didn't stand a chance."

"What do I do?"

"What do you mean?" he asks, looking a little confused.

"I can't walk around like this!"

"Oh," he says, and scratches his scaly face thoughtfully. "Hmm. Well, you can change your skin to look like clothes."

"I can?"

"Sure. Just get a picture in your head of what it looks like, and then . . . well, it's hard to describe. Just imagine the feeling of your skin changing into it."

Jael pictures her jeans, T-shirt, and raincoat. But nothing happens.

"Try adding more details," says Dagon. "The important thing is to get as specific as possible."

It's hard for Jael to concentrate when she's squatting naked in a forest, but she tries to recall little things about her clothes. She remembers the fraying on one pant leg cuff, the slight stretch in the shirt neck, and the buttons on the jacket. She holds the entire image in her head, then pictures her skin matching it. When she looks down, there it is.

"Wow," she says. She slowly stands up and checks herself over. "And I could make any clothes I want?"

"You could even grow fur and a tail," he says. "You just can't change your size."

She moves around a little, testing the feel of her new clothes. "It's weird. I still feel kind of . . . naked."

"That's because you are," says Dagon. "You just *look* like you have clothes on."

"Well, that's no good."

"Why not?"

"It feels weird. I need to have something on."

A flicker of irritation moves across Dagon's face. "You know, these mortal hang-ups of yours don't really mean anything. You need to let them go."

"They aren't hang-ups," says Jael. "It might be hard for you to understand, but being naked in public is a big deal for a mortal."

"But that doesn't concern you anymore," says Dagon.

"Look, I guess you don't like to think about it, but I *am* half mortal. I'm getting enough crap from my dad about being half demon. I don't need you coming in from the other side hating on mortals."

He looks at her, his black shark eyes unreadable. Then he nods once, slowly, like he's bowing to her. "Fair enough."

He scans the trees around them. "So, real clothes . . ." He stands there for a few more moments, idly scratching at the small gill slits on his neck, then his face brightens. "Here's something we can do. Hold your hands out together."

She cups her hands in front of her, almost like she's receiving communion at church. Then he stretches out his arm, digs his claws into his shoulder, and slowly rakes them down, peeling scales off as he goes. The scales flutter into Jael's outstretched hands. He begins to work faster, switching back and forth between arms, until he's shuckling a pile of scales into her hands. Clots of blood bloom on his arms but are quickly covered as new scales grow in.

"Doesn't that hurt?" she asks.

"Sure," he says, still scraping away. When he's done, she has a heaping pile of scales cupped in her hands.

"There," he says, and smiles in satisfaction. "That should be enough."

"For what?"

He reaches out and picks up a single scale. When he lifts it up, the rest are drawn with it, like a big piece of fabric. He holds it up for her.

"It's not much," he says.

The scales gleam with glittery rainbow swirls.

"It's beautiful," she says.

He drapes it around her. "Just needs something to hold it in place," he mutters. Then, still holding the cloak in one hand, he reaches into his mouth and grasps one of his big shark teeth.

"Wait!" she says, then winces as she hears the crack.

He holds up a large, triangle-shaped tooth. He smiles in satisfaction, a trickle of blood coming from his lips.

"I could have found something else," she says. "You didn't have to rip your own tooth out."

"It'll grow back," he says. "Besides, since it's still a part of me, it'll stick to the scales." He places it at the point under her chin where he's holding two corners of the scale cloth, then lets go. It hangs around her like a cloak.

Jael gathers it around her body. The inside feels surprisingly soft. The outside feels smooth when she slides her hand down and rough, like sandpaper, when she slides it back up.

"It's awesome," she says. "Thank you."

"Well, you can only wear it in the rain. If it gets dried out, it'll look ratty and it'll probably smell. Like me."

"I don't think that'll be a big problem in Seattle," she says. "I don't get why you did this, though. I mean, that had to really hurt."

"Jael." It still gives her a strange shiver when he says her name. Like she can almost get a sense of the person he believes she's capable of becoming. A person who deserves an exotic name spoken with reverence. But now he looks a little sad. "If all you ever do is try to avoid pain, you'll never create something truly worthwhile."

"I don't try to avoid pain," she says quickly. Then she thinks about it for a second. "Do I?"

"You're a brave one, that's for sure," says Dagon. He gently lays his webbed hand on her head, covering most of her scalp. "But you've still got a ways to go. It's one of those things that comes in time." Then he looks around. "And while we're waiting . . ." He turns her head in the direction of the seething orange lava pool that hisses at the occasional drops of rain that slip through the canopy of trees. "I think you better put out that pit before it eats up the forest."

Eventually Jael is able to coax the earth back into a solid state. She can feel its resistance and confusion. After all, she was the one who asked it to liquefy, and that had been a much more urgent request. But finally, almost resentfully, it thickens and cools until it looks like a big patch of slick, black lumps.

"Okay," says Jael. "So why didn't the flying thing work? That's what started all of this."

"It's pretty easy to get air to do something," says Dagon.

"The trick is to keep it doing that thing for more than a few seconds. You got it to lift you up all right, but as soon as it did that, it got bored and wandered off."

"So is real flying even possible?" she asks.

"I've seen a few successes," says her uncle. "And a lot of failures. But who knows, maybe you'll get it someday."

"So there's only one more element, right?" says Jael. "We've done water, air, and earth. The only thing left is fire."

"There's actually two left," says Dagon. "And they're somewhat interrelated. Fire and spirit."

"Spirit? Like a soul?"

"Sure," says Dagon. "If that's what you want to call it. The part that makes us who we are. The spark of life."

"So that's why it relates to fire? The spark thing?" asks Jael.

"Not really," says her uncle. "Here, let's start with this."

He reaches down and picks up a large branch that's fallen to the ground. He brings it up to his lips and opens his mouth wide so that the rows of teeth protrude. He strikes a claw across one tooth, and a few sparks fly. He does it again, and more sparks leap out. A few of them hit a couple of the leaves on the branch. He blows on the leaves gently until the sparks nestle into the green and start smoking. He blows harder and the leaves begin to burn. Soon, flames lick around the edges. Then, at last, the branch catches on fire.

It's the first time Jael has seen fire with her demon eyes, and she's not prepared for its beauty. The swirling, lashing orange and red intertwine in a dance. Bits of blue flicker at the base, and the yellow edges reach endlessly toward the sky. Of all the things she's seen in the past few days, this simple burning stick is the most marvelous.

"What is fire?" asks Dagon. "It isn't an object with mass or weight. It is the visible transformation from matter into energy. So fire isn't a 'what,' really. It's a 'how.' And yet you can see it. You can hear it. And if you're strong enough, you can feel it."

He holds the stick out to her.

"Go ahead," he says. "Invite it over."

A part of her—the mortal part—is screaming at her to step away. But the demon part is too entranced with the fire's beauty. Hesitantly, she reaches out her hand. She's not exactly sure what she says to the fire. Something awestruck and barely coherent, like a giggling fangirl. But whatever it is, it does the trick, and the fire leaps gracefully off the branch and onto her hand.

When it touches her palm, the heat shoots up her arm, straight to her heart. She suddenly feels so light, so free. *So this is what the steam was talking about*, she thinks. She never realized how weighted down she was, how tied up with dumb, pointless details like clothes, money, and status. This means something real. Something perfect.

But then the fire shrinks down until it's just a flicker, and the feeling of euphoria dwindles with it.

"Oh," she sighs. "What happened?"

"You want to keep it going?" Dagon asks quietly.

She nods.

"It's going out because it doesn't have any fuel."

"Should I put it back on the branch?"

"You could do that," says Dagon. "Or you could feed it something else."

"I don't understand."

"Give it back what it gave you," he says. "Give it some encouragement. Give it some joy."

She closes her eyes. Then she takes the little bit of lightness that remains within her and gives it up to the tiny fire in her hand. That offering acts like breath on the flame, bringing it slowly, gently back to life. Her eyes are still closed, but she can feel it grow in her hand, and the thrill within her heart grows with it. But this time, rather than hog it all, she gives that to the flame as well. And the more she gives the fire, the more she has to give. She and the fire grow lighter and stronger, and everything else drops away from her mind until there is nothing but this moment of freedom. She doesn't know why, but she starts to laugh, and then she starts to cry. She must look completely insane, giggling with tears streaming down her cheeks, but she's beyond caring.

"Jael," she hears her uncle say.

She slowly opens her eyes. Her entire body is wreathed in flames that reach up to the darkening sky. She is the fire. She is pure action, roaring and laughing and crying. She stretches out her hands and sings the song of fire, and it is glorious.

After some time, her uncle says, "Okay, time to come back."

Regretfully, she withdraws from the fire, pulls herself back into her body and lets the flames slowly fade away. When at last she stands still and quiet, she is just a girl again.

"That," says Dagon, "is just a dim shadow of what it's like

to feel the last element — spirit. But we'll save that for another time."

Jael looks up at him, pleased with herself but still missing the fire. She tries to smile, but it only comes out halfway.

He grins at her, his jagged shark teeth gleaming in the twilight, with one gap. Then he scoops her up in a massive hug.

"You did good, kid. Now you should probably head out. I think your little explosion was visible for a ten-mile radius."

It takes a while for her to get home. The buses don't run very often on Saturday nights, and none of them are express. But Jael hardly notices. Everything around her looks different. It feels as if the change that began Thursday night is complete. Life is crowded with potential, with magic. There are so many forces just waiting to be tapped, to be put to some constructive use, and she never realized it before. The world is like a giant toolshed filled with babies who don't know how to use the tools, and don't even realize that the tools are anything other than something to stick in their mouths.

As the bus cruises up Eighth Avenue through North Seattle, she watches the rain run down the outside of the window. She draws squiggles and shapes in the condensation with her finger. The bus is empty. But of course, she's not alone. If nothing else, there's the earth beneath her and the air all around her. And in Seattle, more often than not, the rain that falls from the sky. She asks the condensation on the windows if it would like to draw its own pictures. She finds out that it does. So she leans back in her seat and watches images of clouds and mountains and forests slowly appear up and down the bus windows until she's surrounded by a silvery panorama dimly recalled by raindrops.

When the bus lets her off at her stop, she walks slowly down the sidewalk toward her house, taking in all the life she's never appreciated before. The cowering grass and potted plants. The skittish wind that slides around houses and cars. She wonders why the wind doesn't just knock it all down. She knows it could, if it wanted to. If it had a reason.

Then she looks up into the night sky, something she hasn't done since Thursday. She sees it unfold in all directions, expanding endlessly, and for a little while she can follow it. But then it dips down like a roller coaster and she gets a nasty jolt of vertigo. So she hastily returns her attention to ground level. One thing at a time.

When she gets home, her father is still up, sitting in the living room and reading the Psalms from the Bible by candlelight. She closes the front door softly behind her and he looks up. He seems pale and gray and very ordinary.

"Well?" he says. "How did it go?"

"I think," says Jael, "that it was the best day of my life." Then she smiles slightly. "So far."

He stares at her for a moment. She can't tell whether he's happy she did this or not. But she realizes she kind of doesn't care.

"Britt called," he says. "It sounds earth-shattering, whatever it is. I could barely get in two words."

"Everything is earth-shattering for Britt. Especially when it involves boys."

"Well, thankfully we don't have *that* problem at least," he says. "Boyfriends."

"Yeah," says Jael. "Whew." Then she climbs up the spiral staircase to her bedroom.

When she calls Britt, it only rings once before she picks up.

"Oh my God, J, where have you been?"

"Uh . . . out?" says Jael.

"With Rob?"

"Um, no." Jael wants to tell her that maybe things with her and Rob aren't really going to work out. But she can't quite figure out how to phrase it in a way that isn't "because he's freaked out by my amazing succubus powers." And Britt is so wound up, she doesn't give her much time to respond anyway.

"Well," Britt says, "don't quote me on this, but I'm pretty sure I met the One yesterday."

"A new boy? Do I know him?"

"No, he doesn't even go to Mercy."

"So where'd you meet him?"

"Some Church thing. It's not important. What's important is that he is the real deal. Like so gentlemanly and mature, but not all uptight about it. And he has these blue eyes you could just dive into and get lost forever."

"Cool," says Jael. She hasn't heard Britt like this in a long time. Completely nuts over a guy. It's a little annoying, but Jael is also relieved that the weird jealousy vibe she was getting from Britt yesterday is gone. "So, are you guys going out or something?"

"He's picking me up in, like, twenty minutes! He has one

of those Prius hybrid cars. You know, because he's really into environmental stuff. He's so deep, J. And sooo sweet. I *never* thought a guy like that would ever be interested in me, you know?"

"Why not?"

"I don't know . . . I guess because they never have been before."

"Well, you tend to pitch yourself more to the meathead jock types anyway."

"Yeah, I know," says Britt. "They're just so easy, I guess. But I can totally see now that I was wasting my time. Things with this guy are completely different. When I'm with him, I feel like the best version of me. Does that make sense?"

"Sure."

"I can't wait to see him again!"

"That's awesome, Britt. I hope you have fun. Let me know how it goes."

"So . . . if you weren't with Rob today, who were you with?"

The sudden change of topic almost gives Jael mental whiplash. "Uh . . . my uncle."

"You have an uncle? Since when?"

"Since Thursday. He lives out of town. He and my dad don't really get along, but he decided I was old enough that I didn't have to listen to my dad anymore."

"J, that is major. An uncle. Family other than your lame-ass dad. Is he cool? He must be if he hates your dad. Would he adopt you?"

"He's very cool," says Jael. "But I don't think he could adopt me. He works weird hours and lives way out in the middle of nowhere."

"But he's going to be coming to visit a lot?"

"He said as much as he can."

"That's awesome."

"It is," says Jael.

Finally, a moment of silence.

Then Britt says, "Sorry I was such a butt yesterday. I don't know what my deal was. Just grumpy, I guess."

"It's okay," says Jael. "I was kind of out of it too. I didn't get much sleep the night before."

"We're both going through some stuff right now," says Britt.

"Yeah," says Jael.

"It's good, J. Change is good. For both of us."

"Totally," says Jael.

the fifth element

13

After learning how to harness the power of the elements, Jael thought finding a history textbook wouldn't be that big of a deal. But she stands in the doorway of the used bookstore on U-Dub campus, and she has no idea how she's going to find this book. There are no neatly organized aisles, no alphabetical order by author. Instead, bookcases are unlabeled and rest at odd angles, some of them close to tipping over, and all of them are crammed full.

She sees a guy stocking shelves, just tossing stuff randomly into the bookcases. It doesn't seem like he's being lazy, though. It's like he's purposefully being random. He looks like a college student—that scruffy scholar type—a little unshaven, with shoulder-length black hair.

"Excuse me," she says.

The stack of books in his arms tumbles to the floor.

"Oh, sorry!" she says.

"Um," he says as he juggles the few books he's managed to hold on to. "Don't worry . . . it's . . . let me just . . ."

She reaches out and takes the books. He smiles at her.

"Thanks," he says.

"It was my bad anyway," she says.

He bends down and scoops up the fallen books. "No, no, I'm trying to learn how to be more flexible."

"Oh yeah?" she says. "I could use a lesson in that."

"I think a lot of people could," he says as he takes the last of the books from her and slides them onto a shelf. "So . . ." Now he seems to look at her for the first time. His eyes are a piercing pale blue, like a desert sky. "Do you need help with something?"

"Uh, yeah," Jael says. "I can't seem to figure out how to find anything in this place. I was hoping you might be able to point me in the right direction."

"Sure, what are you looking for?"

"Uh . . ." She suddenly feels like the dorky high school kid she is. "My, uh . . . history textbook."

He doesn't seem fazed. Maybe he assumed she's in high school. That's almost worse.

"Do you have the title and the edition?" he asks.

"The book's in my bag . . . ," she says. Then she realizes that she'll have to pull it out and show him. She wishes she'd just tried to look for the book herself, but it's too late now. She pulls the book out and hands it to him.

"Ah," he says as he stares at the large burn hole.

She's not sure why she cares what this random guy in a bookstore thinks, but suddenly she's blushing.

"It was an accident," she says.

"I kind of assumed that," he says. Then he grins, like he understands completely. "Come on. Let's go hunting for books."

He leads her through the maze of shelves and she's glad

she asked for help after all. It would have taken her hours to find anything. But he takes her directly to the textbook section, cleverly hidden behind the romance section. In just a few minutes, he's located the correct edition. He pulls it from the shelf, looks at the glossy picture of the bald eagle on the front, and smirks.

"These books are pretty ridiculous."

"Yeah?" she says. "Why's that?"

"Well, it's such a slanted view of history. And I'm not just talking about the chapters on Vietnam or that 'Manifest Destiny' crap, which was just an excuse for the government to take land from the American Indians. I'm talking the whole thing. Columbus? He didn't do anything except set a precedent for subjugation. Washington? He didn't believe that the common people could actually elect decent leaders. That's why they set up the electoral vote. FDR? The guy pretty much cornered Japan into bombing Pearl Harbor so that he could get America into the war and out of the Depression."

"Wow," says Jael. "I guess you're a history major."

He rolls his eyes. "What can I say? I'm a sucker for old stuff. Anything else you need?"

"Um . . . Do you have a section about, uh, demons?"

She expects him to give her a weird look. But instead, he just says, "Fiction or nonfiction?"

"There are nonfiction books about demons?"

"Sure. Angels, demons, ghosts. All that."

"Huh," she says. "Yeah, sure. Where's that?"

She follows him all the way to the back of the store in a

corner that seems even quieter and more cluttered than the rest.

"This is all the religion and occult stuff," he says. "Were you looking for something specific?"

"Not really," says Jael. "I, uh . . ." She doesn't want him to think she's blowing him off, but she also doesn't want him looking over her shoulder. "I just wanted to browse for a bit."

"Excellent," he says. "That's what this store is for, really. The accidental discovery. So, I'll leave you to it." He turns to go, then stops. "If you need anything else, or, you know, if you get trapped under a bunch of angel books or something, just give me a shout. I'm Jack.'"

"Sure, Jack. Thanks."

He smiles again. "Nice talking to you." Then he wanders off.

If all the guys in college are like Jack, she can't wait to get there. Assuming that she can convince her father that she doesn't need to be locked away in an Arctic fortress.

She squares her shoulders, takes a deep breath, and plunges into the stacks of demon books.

Jael probably should have expected that every book she picked up would describe demons as evil, nasty, and ugly. But somehow it hurts anyway. And it's unfair. She's not like that. Her uncle isn't like that. Well, ugly, sure, and maybe he smells a little nasty. But he's definitely not evil. And while she never met her mother, she knows she wasn't evil.

She looks down at the book in her hand. *A Catalogue of Demons and Fiery Fiends from the Netherworld!* She doesn't actually know any other demons. And she's already gathered that she and her family don't fit in with the crowd. So it could be that her little family are the only nice demons. But if the books got Hell wrong, if it isn't a place where bad people go to be punished when they die, maybe they got demons all wrong too.

She's just about to put the book back on the shelf and give up looking for something helpful. But then she catches sight of a familiar blond skater at the other end of the aisle.

"Rob?"

He glances up at her from a stack of books, and for a brief moment the same frightened expression she saw on Friday clouds his face. But then his smile breaks through.

"Bets!" he says. "You cut your hair!"

"Uh, yeah," she says. She touches it self-consciously.

"Looks awesome," he says.

"For real?"

"You bet."

"Yeah, well," she says. "Guess I needed a change."

"Now you look like a real Betty. Skater chicks usually have short hair."

"Rob, does anybody else use that name? Betty?"

Rob shrugs. "Some people. It's a little old-school."

"And anyway, I've never even been on a skateboard."

"But if you ever were, you'd slay it."

"How do you know that?"

"It's my skater Zen."

She rolls her eyes. "You're such a geek. So, what are you doing here anyway?"

"Speaking of geek," he says.

"No, I didn't mean it like that."

"Hey, it's cool. You're in the same place. So we can be geeks together. Of course, I come here all the time. So that makes me a bigger geek."

"I didn't realize it was a competition, but I'm pretty sure I have you beat. What are *you* looking for?"

"Oh." He suddenly looks uncomfortable. "Old, out-of-print stuff you can't find anywhere else."

"Like what? Old chemistry books?"

"Yeah, sort of. Stuff that bridges that connection between what they knew back in ancient times about magic and what we know about science."

"Sounds cool."

"No, it's totally weird. You don't have to humor me."

"It isn't weird," says Jael. "Not to me, anyway."

"So, what are you doing here?"

"I accidentally trashed my history book, so I have to replace it. How's that for geeky?"

"And so . . . you were looking for it in the occult section?"

"Oh," says Jael, glancing down at the *Catalogue of Demons and Fiery Fiends from the Netherworld!* book she's still holding. "Just, uh, browsing."

"I thought you might be doing some extra credit for the Mons," says Rob.

"Oh yeah, because it's religious stuff?"

"Well, that and the demon thing?"

Jael stares at him for a moment. "Demon thing?"

"You know what the Mons did before he taught at Our Lady of Mercy, right? He was an exorcist."

"Shut up. That's got to be just some dumb school rumor."

"No, it's true," says Rob. "He told me himself."

"The Mons," says Jael. It's a struggle to keep her voice level. She remembers the look he gave her on Friday. "The Mons was an exorcist?"

"Yep, just like those old movies. I guess it started when he was in Peru. The people in his congregation there thought he was some kind of saint, I guess, because he was just performing exorcisms left and right. He was like some granddaddy master exorcist. Isn't that crazy?"

"Uh," says Jael. Her heart is suddenly pounding in her ears so loudly, she hardly hears herself say, "Yeah."

"Sorry," Rob says. "I didn't mean to freak you out."

"I'm not freaking out," she says, a little too quickly.

"You totally are. I thought you didn't believe in that stuff."

"I don't. It's nothing," she says. But it's everything. All at once, that feeling of isolation comes back, like she's hemmed in by all the lies, just like she's surrounded by all these books that hate her and her family. She wants to knock down the lies and tell the truth to the few people who actually matter to her. But they wouldn't understand. They'd all turn on her. Her father said so.

She looks down at *A Catalogue of Demons and Fiery Fiends from the Netherworld!* She can picture all the authors of all these books: a bunch of old white guys with beards and tweed jackets looking down on her in disgust from their dusty little offices. The whole world hates her and they don't even know her. All because of shit like this. Even her father buys it in his own weird way. But it's nothing but hateful anti-demon prejudice. The anger boils up in her so fast and furiously that it takes her by surprise. It wipes away the doubt, the isolation. It makes her feel powerful and free, just like yesterday when she held—

"Shit, Bets, that book is on fire!"

The fear in Rob's voice brings her back. She holds up the book, which crackles with bright blue-white flame. And she realizes that she's not free like a fire. She's just a lonely girl with a lot of problems. She closes her eyes as the tears begin to flow. She slowly pulls back from the fire on the book, starving it. It flickers one last time and dies. She opens her eyes again, and through the tears that won't stop coming she sees the charred book and, beyond that, Rob's face, frozen wide in shock. Maybe the books are right after all. Fiery fiend. Menace. She just destroys things.

"Jael?" Rob's voice is quiet.

She shakes her head, wiping tears away with her sleeves. "I gotta go," she says, and tries to brush past him.

"Hey," he says, and he pulls her to him.

For a moment she resists.

"It's going to be okay," he says, and wraps his warm arms around her.

He has no idea what he's talking about, of course. But somehow she believes him. She sinks into his arms and they stand there like that for a while, her wet face pressed into his flannel, the burnt book dangling from one hand. Finally, he carefully eases her back. He takes the book from her hand and places it up on the top shelf.

"Good thing this section is all the way in the back," he says, a little grin sneaking in. Then he grows serious again. "Now, you want to tell me what just happened there?"

There's a little café a few doors down. It's quiet and empty, which is exactly what Jael needs. The few tables are a worn, scratched wood. The place seems purposefully run-down, with old photographs of Seattle hanging lopsided on the walls, and a chipped and faded totem pole by the entrance. The only person in the café is the woman at the register. She's so engrossed in her paperback romance novel that she doesn't look up until they get to the counter. Rob orders a cup of coffee and Jael orders freshly squeezed orange juice. While the woman is pressing the oranges, Rob says, "Hey, is Max working today?"

The woman squints at him for a second. "You're a friend of his, right? I've seen you here before."

"I'm Rob," he says.

"Right," she says. "He's off on Sundays, but I'll tell him you stopped by."

"Thanks," says Rob.

Jael notices that when the cashier rings them up, she only enters the juice. They grab their drinks and head over to a table in the corner.

"Is it always like that for you?" asks Jael. "Free stuff?"

"What, the amazing McKinley hookup? Yeah, pretty much. It's one of the few advantages of living in the same place your whole life. You know lots of people."

"But don't you feel like you owe them, or something?"

"More like they owe me," says Rob. "I've been doing people's math and science homework since first grade."

"Huh," says Jael.

They sit in silence for a little while. Jael stares into her orange juice, stirring it listlessly with her straw.

Finally, Rob says, "So are you going to tell me what just happened?"

"You're not going to let it go, are you?" she says.

"What, that a book spontaneously combusted in your hand? And you didn't even flinch at it? Uh, what kind of scientist would I be if I let that slide?"

Jael sips her juice through the straw, mainly to give herself a moment to gather her courage. Then she says, "Do you really believe all that stuff about how magic is just unexplained science and we don't really know what's possible?"

"Sure," says Rob. "I mean, it's just a theory. I've never actually seen it in action. Well, maybe until today."

"Yeah."

"So you're saying that what just happened there was magic? Like actual *magic*?"

"Okay, so what if there were certain . . . people who bridged that connection between science and magic?"

"Like a witch?" asks Rob. "Are you going Wicca on me?"

"Not exactly," says Jael. "So, for a long time, people thought witches were evil. Just 'cause they did magic or something that most people couldn't understand."

"A lot of people still think witches are evil. They just don't kill them anymore. At least not in America."

"Right. There's a lot of . . . prejudice to that name. People make assumptions about them."

"Sure, like riding brooms, ugly with warts . . ."

"And evil," says Jael. "Most people assume they're evil."

"Bets, are you sure you're not going Wicca?"

"I'm sure."

"Then just spit it out."

"Rob, I'm a demon."

"Uh . . ."

"Well, half demon. On my mother's side."

"A demon," he says, his eyes getting wide. "As in . . . a creature from Hell . . ."

"Here," she says. "Maybe I should just show you."

Jael looks down at the orange juice in front of her. The juice isn't quite as responsive as water, but it seems interested in her idea. The air in the straw is downright excited about it. So she asks the air to leave the straw, which creates a vacuum that sucks the juice up. It jets a small fountain a couple of inches into the air, then freezes. For a brief, lovely moment, it almost looks like an orange crystal flower sprouting from the glass. Then the weight of it tips the glass over. The flower hits the tabletop and shatters into tiny flecks of frozen juice.

Rob stares at it for a second, his eyes and mouth wide. "Oh shit . . . ," he whispers. He leans in close and touches the shards with his finger. "It's still just juice. . . . You froze it?"

"Yep."

"You can control things on a molecular level?"

"Not control. Influence."

"Bets," says Rob, his eyes bright in that weird way they get during math or chemistry class. "That is so badass." He looks back at the scattered juice crystals. "Will it thaw at some point, or do you have to push it back in the right direction?"

"I think it'll eventually get bored of being like that," says Jael. "But it might take a little while."

"And you can do this with anything?"

"As long as it has some natural element in it. And big stuff like gravity would probably ignore me."

"And this is what demons do?"

"I guess. I mean, I don't actually know very many demons."

"What about possessing people and all that?"

"I don't know. Some demons maybe do it. Like the weaker ones, I think, that can't be here on their own."

"What about the horns and tail?"

"I could make them, if I wanted, but I'm not sure why I would. . . ."

"What you're telling me is that everything I've been told about demons is wrong?"

"Pretty much." She waits. If he's going to turn on her, this is the moment.

But instead of getting angry, he looks kind of hurt.

"What?" she says.

"So . . . all this time, you've just been pretending to be normal?"

"No!" says Jael. "Well, sort of. See, I've known for a long time that my mom was a demon. I just didn't know what that meant for me."

213

She does her best to condense the past five days into something that makes sense. It feels really good to get it all off her chest, but telling it to a "normal" person for the first time, she feels just how bizarre her life really is.

"So what are you going to do about this Belial guy?" asks Rob.

"What am I going to do?" repeats Jael. "You mean, other than spend my life hiding from him?"

"Hide? Are you kidding? He deserves to get his ass kicked!"

"If my mother and my uncle couldn't beat him, how would I do it? I'm not even a real demon, just a halfbreed."

"But you can't let him get away with it. He killed your mom."

When he says it, it hits her in a way it never has before. Hearing it from her father and her uncle was one thing. But when Rob says it, it slips through her defenses somehow, and her eyes suddenly well up with tears.

"Can we . . . ," she says, blinking hard. "Can we just talk about something else?"

"Yeah, sure," he nods. "Totally. So . . ." He thinks for a moment, then says, "Oh! I got it. How does this element thing relate to whatever was going on last Friday? You know, when I couldn't talk to you."

"I don't know," Jael says. "Maybe it doesn't relate."

"Of course it does. Everything relates. That's the whole point."

Jael thinks about it for a moment. "Maybe it has something to do with spirit."

"Spirit?"

"The fifth element."

"Quintessence?" asks Rob.

"What?"

"It's an alchemy thing. Plato called it 'aether.' He thought that the heavens, where the sun and moon and stars were, was filled with aether, and it was also within us. Kind of like the life spark, or the soul."

"I guess that sounds about right," says Jael. "If it really is like another element, then I can influence it. And on Friday, I was accidentally influencing people's spirits."

"Can you see them? People's spirits?"

"I don't think so . . . ," she says, but then remembers that glimpse into Father Ralph's mind. Not something she really wants to repeat.

"Maybe you just have to . . . I don't know." He wiggles his fingers. "Do some magic."

"Maybe," says Jael. "But I'm not sure I should be messing around with stuff too much."

"Are you kidding?" says Rob. "That's the best way to learn! Come on, Bets." He's giving her that look again. The earnest, heart-melting one.

"You do that on purpose," she says.

"What, me?" he says. Then, "Seriously, come on, try."

"Well . . ." Her mother did this once with her father. When they first met. She leans in. "Okay, I think if I can just look into your eyes, maybe I can see something."

Rob props his head up on his hands and stares at her. He flashes a goofy smile and she laughs.

"Stop making that face," she says.

"What face?"

"I don't know, like you're all excited about this."

"I am excited. How could I *not* be?"

"Fine, fine," she says. She doesn't want to admit that she's actually really nervous.

She looks into his eyes. At first she only notices details, like the black specks in his hazel irises and the streaks of green around his pupil. But the longer she looks, the more she relaxes into it. . . .

She feels a dizzy rush, like when she looked into the necklace. It's as if she's falling through the black pupil of his eye into a long tunnel.

And then she sees it.

It moves like flame.

It shimmers like water.

It's as light and free as air.

It's as rooted and strong as earth.

It's the most beautiful thing she has ever seen. It sings to her — not with a voice, but with something simpler and more pure than any sound she knows. The song throbs in her head and she starts to hum along. The spirit grows brighter and louder in response to her accompaniment. As if from far away, she hears Rob's breath, loud and heavy.

"Should I stop?" she hears herself ask.

"No," he says hoarsely. "Don't stop."

So she sings along with his soul and it grows even brighter and more beautiful with each moment, so raw and full that she wants to touch it and she can't help herself. She reaches her hand toward his chest and it passes through without resistance. Her fingertips brush against his flickering spirit; it shivers and so does she.

When she felt fire, it was ultimate freedom. When she touches spirit, it is ultimate communion. Every moment of Rob's life is laid out before her in heartbreaking simplicity. In this moment, she knows him and understands him completely. His inner radiance is the most wondrous thing she has ever seen and she can't help herself. She grabs it with both hands.

Then Rob cries out.

Jael lets go and pulls back into herself. Her pulse pounds in her temples and her face is flushed.

"Rob?" she whispers.

Rob sighs. Then his eyes roll back into his head and his face hits the tabletop with a wet smack.

"Rob, are you okay?" She reaches out and shakes his shoulder. Nothing.

Carefully, she turns his head to the side. His eyes are closed, but he's breathing.

"Rob, please, wake up."

His eyes flutter, then open. They're a little unfocused, like he's had a concussion.

"Jael," he says, only a little louder than a breath.

"Yeah?" She leans in to hear him better.

"Will you marry me?"

She stares at him for a moment, trying to figure out if he's joking. He doesn't look like he is.

"It couldn't have been that cool," she says.

"It was even cooler, but I don't have anything better to offer."

"Excuse me," calls the cashier. "Everything okay over there?"

"Listen, we gotta get out of here," says Jael. "The cashier is totally watching us."

"Yep," says Rob. But he doesn't move.

"I'm serious," says Jael.

"I'm going as fast as I can."

"Are you sure you're okay?" she asks. "Should I call 911 or something?"

"I'm totally fine," says Rob. "It's just going to take a little while to recover, I think. It was like . . . an orgasm . . . times a hundred." He sighs again, and continues to lie on the table.

"Really?" says Jael. "Like a . . ." She isn't sure how she feels about that at all.

"Miss?" says the cashier.

"We're going now," Jael says to the cashier. Then she grabs Rob by the armpits and hauls him out of the café, wondering if she's just royally screwed up everything.

"Wow," Rob mumbles. "Super demon strength."

The cool early evening air brings Rob back somewhat, and he's able to walk, with her help, to the bus stop. By the time they board the bus, he seems to have recovered.

During the ride, they're both quiet. Rob stares out the window at the darkening sky, a look of sleepy contentment on his face, eyes half-veiled by blond bangs.

Jael tries not to stare at him. She can't stop thinking about his soul. Its strange, beautiful song lingers in her fingertips. She presses them to her cheek and closes her eyes, remembering the feeling. It was amazing.

Yet, it also makes her feel . . . dirty. Is it just some weird Catholic guilt thing because he compared it to an orgasm? Or is the mortal part of her trying to tell her that what she did was bad? Because the thing is, she wants to see his soul again. She wants to touch it again. She wants to . . . she doesn't know what, exactly, but it worries her. Some kind of demon hunger has woken up within her. Something ancient and primal that doesn't give a shit about right or wrong. Something that really scares her.

The wind starts to pick up as Rob walks Jael to her house. She finds herself wishing it was only as simple as a walk to her house. That they were just normal, boring teenagers with normal, boring problems. They could be talking about TV right now or wondering if they would pass their math test. It could've been that easy. But it's not.

The breeze pushes gently through her short hair, as if trying to soothe her. It helps a little. She takes a breath of sharp night air and lets it out slowly.

The sound makes Rob look at her.

"Have you told Britt?" he asks.

"No."

"Isn't she supposed to be your best friend or something?"

"I guess. I mean, I promised Dad I wouldn't tell anybody, so he's already going to be pissed I told you. I kind of knew you'd be okay with it for some reason. But honestly, I don't know how she'd handle it. What if she freaks out and tells the whole school?"

"Would she really do that?" He looks doubtful.

"Well, she goes to Mass and all that."

"Are you kidding? She believes all the pope and Jesus stuff?"

"It seems like it," says Jael. "I mean, once, she told me some rumor that one of the varsity soccer players was gay. I didn't really understand why she cared, so I just said 'So?' And she totally flipped out on me. Started yelling all kinds of crazy stuff about homosexuals being an abomination and a blight on the world. I tried to argue with her about it, but she wouldn't listen, so I just gave up. She doesn't really talk about it that much, but underneath it all, she's hard-core conservative."

"But isn't she, like . . ." Rob clears his throat. "I mean, I've just heard that she gets around."

"I guess that's what confession is for."

"Yikes," says Rob. "I almost feel like, what's the point?"

"I don't know," says Jael. "The whole Catholic thing is so weird. Sometimes I think it's more like a culture than a religion. Like, even though I don't believe the prayers or the pope and Jesus stuff, I still kind of feel Catholic. You know? I can't just cut it off. And since I know demons are real, what if the Church got some other parts right too?"

"What, like the Mons being a real exorcist?" asks Rob. "Are you worried he's going to do something? Is that why you flipped out in the store and started burning stuff?"

"Yeah, I guess," says Jael.

"But he just seems so peaceful and old," says Rob. "I bet he doesn't even kill bugs."

"I don't know," says Jael. "The look he gave me on Friday . . . he was like some other person. It was freaky."

"So what are you going to do?"

"I promised my dad that I would tell him if someone started getting suspicious. But if I do . . ."

"You'll have to move again," says Rob.

"Yeah."

They walk in silence for a moment. Then, slowly, Rob reaches over and takes her hand. She tenses up at first. But slowly, she forces her hand and arm to relax. As they go, it gets easier, until it starts to become nice. Even comforting.

"Hey," he says after a little while. "Maybe you just get on the Mons's good side. Bring in your uncle for show-and-tell to talk about what it was really like during biblical times."

"You know what?" says Jael, a smile starting to lift up the corners of her lips. "That would almost be worth it."

The whole rest of the walk home, Jael can't quite get the smirk off her face as she imagines her uncle teaching religion class.

They stop in front of her house. She stares up at her dark, silent windows.

"You wanna come in?" she asks.

Rob looks startled, then says, "Sure. If you think it would be cool with your dad."

"Honestly?" says Jael. "I don't really care if he's cool with it or not."

• • •

A single large candle on the livingroom coffee table is the only light in the house. Jael's father sits on the couch next to it, poring over his lesson plans. When Jael walks in, he says, "Jael, I—"

Then he sees Rob.

"Who is this?"

"Dad, this is my friend Rob."

Her father's eyes widen. "Friend." He says it like he doesn't know what the word means.

"Hi, Mr. Thompson," says Rob uneasily. "I've seen you around at school, but I don't think we've actually met." He holds out his hand and gives his best Rob smile. But her father stays seated, still holding his lesson-plan book. Rob's outstretched hand slowly slips into his pocket.

"So," says her father. "You are Jael's . . . friend?"

"Uh, yes, sir."

"And I get the feeling you know *everything*. Is that right?"

"I, uh, guess so. Or a lot of it anyway."

Jael's father doesn't say anything for a long time. He lays down his book and stands up. His hands are loose at his sides as he takes a few steps around Rob, circling him like he's examining him. Jael assumed this would be tense. But she starts to wonder if he's coming around. Rob's just one of those guys everyone likes. Maybe not even her father is exempt from his charm.

"Well, Rob," her father says quietly, "may God have

mercy on your soul. Because she won't. Now, get out of my house."

"Dad!" says Jael.

"A demoness will cause you more agony by accident than an army of malicious, heartbreaking teenage girls."

"What are you saying, Dad?! Stop it!"

"Who knows," he continues. "You might already be damned to the darkest pits of Hell for even associating with her. The ways of a demoness are devious."

"Rob," says Jael through clenched teeth. "Please. Just go."

"Are you sure?" he says, looking bewildered.

"Please," says Jael.

He nods slowly, then leaves. Jael watches the front door close quietly behind him. She doesn't trust herself to look at her father, so she continues to stare at the closed door.

"I can't believe you just did that," she says.

"Well, perhaps that will teach you to play by the rules."

"I don't even know what you're talking about. 'Damned to the darkest pits of Hell'? People don't even go to Hell!"

"I know that," he says. "I was putting some fear into him. The last thing we need is some lovesick schoolboy following after us."

"Following us?" says Jael. "Following us where?"

"I'll probably need a day or two to lock something down," he says. "But you blew our cover. We have to leave."

"Dad, no! Rob won't say anything!"

"Jael," he says, adopting a firm but reasonable tone, like

they're discussing her grades. "I know exactly what that boy wanted, what he thought would happen."

"I think I can handle myself—"

"Exactly. And when he tries to take what he wants and you knock him on his ass, what happens then? Well, I'm guessing he gets his revenge by revealing you to the world."

"But he's not like that. Why do you always expect the worst to happen?!"

He looks at her sadly and shakes his head. "You just don't get it. You're not old enough to understand what's truly at stake here. How bad it can really get."

"You always say that," she says. "I think you just can't stand not being in control of me."

"You want to know why?" he asks, his tone mild.

"Sure, Dad," she says, rolling her eyes. "Tell me."

"No," he says. "I'll show you."

"What do you mean?" she asks, her boldness faltering.

"Dagon's not the only one who knows some magic. Look into my eyes," he says. "Look into my soul."

"Dad . . ."

"Just do it. I'm sure you've figured out how by now."

So Jael looks into his eyes, down into his soul. It's nothing like Rob's. Instead of bright and glorious, it's heavy and crumbling—full of dark, broken, jagged edges. The song is slow and heartbreakingly sad.

"Good," she hears him say. "Now, I want you to go deeper. Concentrate on one of the biggest, sharpest-looking pieces."

At first, she doesn't quite know what he means. But as she

continues to focus, she realizes that the flickers of light on the edges are actually images. Gradually, the images grow more pronounced, and she can begin to hear sounds with them.

"Now," says her father, "very carefully, reach out and touch one."

She does. And the world melts.

voodoo child

14

Paul sat at the scuffed wooden table and stared at his one-year-old daughter. Jael sat on the dirt floor, playing with her only toy, a threadbare rabbit that had once been pink. The night song of insects came in through the open windows of the shack and, with it, the heat of the Haitian summer evening.

Jael carefully maneuvered her chubby bare legs under her diaper, grabbed the table leg next to her with one round arm, and slowly pulled herself up to a teetering standing position. She looked up at Paul with her solemn green eyes and presented her rabbit.

"Bun," she said.

"Yes," he said. "Bunny."

"Bun," she said. "Nee."

"Very good," he said.

She nodded, satisfied, and dropped back down onto her butt, cooing softly to her rabbit.

The sound of an old car engine approaching covered the insects' song. Paul launched himself from his chair and ran to the window. He watched the car pull up the dirt road, then stepped away from the window. The engine cut out and a car door slammed. Paul slid the dead bolt back and opened the door. Father Poujean came in holding a grocery bag in one arm.

Paul and Poujean clasped hands. Then Poujean handed Paul the bag and crouched down next to Baby Jael. She looked up at him and presented her rabbit.

"Bun," she said. "Nee."

Poujean gently cupped her cheek in his hand, his eyes glistening. He looked up at Paul.

"She is beautiful," he said.

"Yes," said Paul.

"So much like . . . ," Poujean started to say, but when he saw the pain flash across Paul's face, he stopped himself. He looked back down at Baby Jael and ruffled her curly black hair.

"You are a marvel," he told her. "A miracle."

She smiled back, showing her two tiny bottom teeth.

"I'm sorry," said Paul.

"Don't be," said Poujean.

"The last thing I wanted to do was drag you into all of this," said Paul, "but I've run out of places. He can't track us directly anymore, but he's got a legion of demons scouring the world for us. If we stay here too long, they'll come, and I don't want to endanger you, so we'll leave in a day or two. I just . . ." His throat closed up like a fist and his eyes stung.

"It's okay," said Poujean, placing a hand on Paul's shoulder. "Truly."

"I just needed to talk to someone who understood the whole picture. To brainstorm with. I'm not sure what to do now. Parenting . . . it doesn't come naturally to me." A tear finally escaped and he sat back heavily in his chair, pressing his hands to either side of his head.

"Where is her uncle?" asked Poujean.

"Betrayer," spat Paul. "He let it happen. He helped it along."

"But Paul," said Poujean, "perhaps he was only—"

"No," said Paul. "I will not allow him near her."

Poujean said nothing for a long time. Instead, he watched Baby Jael crawl across the dirt floor, dragging her rabbit around with her.

"You can stay here for as long as you want," said Poujean. "No one comes out to this old shack. They all think it's cursed."

"Is it?" said Paul.

Poujean shrugged. "It used to be the home of a powerful *bokur*."

Paul grunted. "Just guilt by association, then," he said. "That's rarely a problem. But we won't stay long. We have to keep on the move, at least until Belial stops pushing the hunt so hard."

"Do you think he'll give up?"

"No, but he can't have every demon in the Northern Duchy crawling through Gaia for too long without upsetting the delicate balance of power in Hell."

"Do you think it's wise to keep on the move like this?" asked Poujean. "I fear it isn't good for the baby."

"What other choice do I have?"

"You could seek protection."

Paul laughed a short, humorless burst. "From who?"

"The Church."

"You can't be serious."

"You'd be surprised. If you get in touch with the right people and present yourself in the right way, they can be quite flexible and accommodating. I have some friends at the Vatican who—"

"No," said Paul, his voice flat. "I know the types you're talking about, and they always have agendas, and their help as often as not ends up being a tie that binds you to them. I won't owe them anything."

Poujean was silent again. He walked over to Jael, who had pulled herself up at the other side of the table. He picked her up and held her. She returned his grave expression for a moment, then reached out and stuck her finger in his nose. He laughed and kissed her on the forehead, then put her back on the ground.

"There is something else we could try," he said.

"Oh?" said Paul.

Poujean picked up the bag from the table. He pulled out some baby food, formula, bottled water, and diapers and placed them to one side. Then he pulled out a bottle of rum, a package of cigars, a top hat, and a pair of round mirrored sunglasses.

Paul picked up the top hat and looked at Poujean questioningly. "This seems a little heavy for you."

Poujean smiled slightly as he took the top hat from Paul and examined it, picking off bits of dirt. "Our encounter with those demons in Crown Heights had a profound impact on me," he said.

"I'm sorry," said Paul. "It wasn't fair to put you through that. Destroying a demon is ugly business."

"That wasn't the part that affected me the most," said

Poujean. "It was your wife's conversation with Asmodeus. For the first time, I was able to see things from their point of view." He walked over to a small altar in the corner of the shack and placed the top hat on top of it. Then he walked back to the table and picked up the sunglasses. "That perspective has opened up a new pathway for me." He popped one of the mirror lenses out of the sunglasses. "A crossroads, if you will." Then he walked over and placed the sunglasses next to the top hat.

Paul picked up the bottle of rum and gazed at the tan liquid. "If you think there's a chance the Baron will listen, let's ask."

"It will take a little while before everything is ready. He can be rather picky at times."

"They all are, each in their own way," said Paul. "I'll take Jael out while you work."

"There's a well down the hill a ways," said Poujean. He pointed to a metal bucket next to the door. "You could go get some water. I'll need it after this, and you'll want to conserve the bottled water as much as possible."

"Good idea," said Paul. He picked up Jael, slid her into the baby carrier, and pulled it onto his back with practiced ease. Poujean brought the rum and cigars to the altar. He lit one of the cigars, took a few puffs, then placed the still-burning cigar on the altar. He lit a cluster of candles beneath the altar. Then he opened the bottle of rum and took a long swallow. He took another swig and spat it on the altar. He picked up a stick with a dried gourd tied to the end of it and began to shake it like a rattle. Then he started to sing quietly.

Paul picked up the bucket, and with Jael strapped to his back, walked out into the dark, hot night.

Paul took his time hiking down through the dark trees to the well. The rhythm of his walk lulled Jael to sleep, as it usually did, and he didn't want to wake her up. Also, he knew Poujean would need some time alone. Contacting Vodoun spirits, or *loa*, as they preferred to be called, was a tricky business. Especially when it was a *loa* as capricious as Baron Samedi, spirit of the crossroads and death. One slip could put the requester in a state far worse than death.

But after an hour or so, the bugs were eating Paul alive and Jael smelled like she needed a diaper change. So he began to make his way back to the shack.

As he carried the water-filled metal bucket back up the hill, he thought he saw some movement over by a group of trees. He stopped, his heart suddenly racing. He waited, but saw nothing more in the darkness. This was a forest, he told himself. There were animals around. After another minute of stillness, he moved on. The dim light from the shack came into view and he picked up his pace. Then he thought he heard something like a twig breaking. He froze again, but heard nothing more, so he continued toward the shack. In his mind, he debated whether his nerves were shot or if he was walking into something really nasty. As soon as he stepped through the door, he knew which it was.

Two young Haitian men held Poujean pinned flat against the table, and one of them was choking him. Poujean's limbs shook and his eyes showed only the whites.

Paul dropped the bucket of water with a clang and the two men turned their heads. Their faces were expressionless, their eyes bloodshot and leaking. They were possessed.

The sound of the bucket falling woke Jael and she began to wail. Paul tried to tune out the screaming baby on his back as he pulled a vial of holy water from his pocket. "In the name of God, Jesus, Muhammad, Moses, and the Buddha," he shouted, flicking holy water on the men, "I cast you out!"

The men hissed like snakes and lurched away, releasing Poujean so that he slid to the floor. Paul pressed his advantage, shouting the prayers of exorcism while Jael continued to yell in his ear. He had them backed into a corner, and in a few more minutes he would have exorcised them. But then he heard a clang from the bucket he had dropped by the door, as if someone had kicked it. He glanced back and saw three more possessed men piling in through the door. He angled his body sideways so that Jael wasn't directly exposed to either group. It was starting to look like a well-laid ambush.

He held his vial of holy water in one hand and drew his bladed crucifix with the other. He didn't want to use the sword on these possessed innocent mortals, but if it came down to their lives or his daughter's, he knew which one he would pick.

"In the name of Isis and Osiris, of Zeus and Hera, I cast you out, spirits!" he shouted first at one group, then the other. They cringed and kept their distance, but he couldn't press one group without exposing Jael to the other group.

He quickly bent down to check Poujean's vitals. He

was breathing, but with a shallow quickness that seemed unnatural, as if he was fighting off possession.

Then the possessed in the doorway were shoved roughly aside and a tall, lean figure with a wolfish grin and amber eyes strode through.

"Amon," said Paul. "I should have killed you when I had the chance."

"Yessss," said Amon. "You should have." His eyes gleamed with glee and the muscles under his face writhed, as if he could barely hold on to his human shape. "But you are mortal and therefore faulty. This was inevitable. I am only glad it is me who will deliver the halfbreed to His Grace. He has offered the feast of your soul as the prize."

"You won't get either," said Paul, brandishing his bladed crucifix.

"You plan to fight me with a baby on your back?" asked Amon. He laughed, a harsh bark. Paul responded with a quick thrust. But his balance was off, his turn slow, and Amon easily avoided him.

"It is rare that I waste much thought on a mortal," said Amon. "But you, I have thought of often."

Paul knew it was hopeless, but hadn't it always been? So he attacked with the fearless desperation of a man cornered. Amon and his possessed slowly closed in around him.

"Philotanus was my brother," said Amon. "You cannot even begin to conceive of the vast knowledge and towering intellect you snuffed out with your clumsy artifacts and prayers. Like all mortals, you only know how to waste things."

Amon lunged and grabbed Paul's wrists. His grip was so strong that Paul's hands went into spasms and he dropped both vial and crucifix. Amon's grin widened, becoming more and more canine, the teeth sharp and protruding from his lips as he drew closer.

Then Paul felt the awkward weight of Jael suddenly lifted from his back.

"No!" he shouted.

One of the possessed scurried out of reach with Jael in his arms. Paul thrashed against Amon's iron grasp and wailed like an animal.

"Oh, this is too delicious!" snarled Amon. "And too loud." He opened his mouth wide and the skin peeled back, exposing the wolf head beneath. Then he sank his teeth into Paul's neck. Paul's screams turned into a gurgle as blood splashed onto the table, the dirt floor, and the still-unconscious Poujean.

Amon dropped the struggling, gasping Paul to the ground, drew his head back, and howled. Then he shed his legs like clothes, revealing a snake tail as thick as a tree trunk beneath.

"I think . . . ," he said, his amber eyes cloudy with bloodlust. "I think I will have this halfbreed for myself." He snatched Jael from the arms of the possessed and opened his jaws wide.

"Hey now!" came a low, rough voice from the other side of the room.

Amon froze, his eyes suddenly clear and frightened. He turned his head and looked in the direction of this new voice.

It was Poujean. But it was not Poujean anymore. He stood tall, his arms folded over his chest, his head cocked to one side in a playfully scolding manner. He wore the black top hat and the mirrored sunglasses with one missing lens, and he held a burning cigar loosely in his teeth.

"What do ya tink you're doing?" he asked in an amused, almost mocking tone. "Tresspassin' on my turf?"

Amon's lip curled up. "This has nothing to do with you, Baron. Leave it alone."

"Oh-ho!" laughed Baron Samedi around his cigar. "Dat so? You goin' ta tell me what ta do?" He took a step closer. "Here? In my land?"

"You're nothing but a recycled New World nightmare," said Amon. "You have no authority over me."

"Well now," said the Baron, "actually, accordin' to da truce between Lucifer and Papa Guede, no demon of Hell can shed blood on da soil of Haiti. And"—he gestured to the gasping, gurgling Paul on the dirt ground—"dat definitely counts."

Amon glared at him for a moment, then pulled himself back into his human shape. "Fine," he said. "We were just leaving anyway." He turned toward the door, casually tucking Jael in the crook of his arm.

"Ah no, not so easy as dat," said the Baron. "Why don't you give me dis precious baby as payment for breaking the truce."

"No thanks," snarled Amon. He shoved the possessed out of his way and ran out of the shack.

"Ah so," said the Baron with an amused twinkle in his eyes. He took a few deep puffs on his cigar. Then he looked at the possessed men. They stared back at him with their blank, bloodshot eyes.

"I'm disappointed in you, children," he said. "Letting foreign devils mount you like dis. It shows a weak will." He picked up the bottle of rum from the altar, took a long swig, then splashed some on each of the possessed. They convulsed for a moment and the air above them rippled thickly with imps escaping back to Hell. Then the mortals dropped to the ground, unconscious.

The Baron turned to the gasping, bloodied Paul. "Hey, I know you," he said, shaking his cigar at him scoldingly. "Erzulie Freda's husband, yes?"

Paul could do nothing but wheeze one last time. Then his eyes started to dim.

"What is wrong with you people?" said the Baron, shaking his head. "I said dis is my turf. I decide who lives and dies. And you, I'll keep around for a while." He pressed the burning cigar into the wound in Paul's neck. The stench of burning flesh filled the shack and Paul convulsed wildly. But when the Baron pulled the cigar away, Paul took a long, shuddering breath and touched his healed neck.

"Dat's better," said the Baron, and he nodded, placing his cigar back in his mouth.

Paul staggered to his feet, rubbing his neck carefully, his face a mixture of shock and relief. But that quickly changed to panic.

"My daughter!" he shouted, and charged for the door.

"Wait now," said the Baron, easily restraining Paul with one hand on his shoulder. "No need to worry. You'll get her back any moment now."

"How?" demanded Paul.

"You wait and see," said the Baron, and he winked.

Off in the distance, Paul heard a sudden wolfish howl of panic that changed abruptly to pain. Paul listened to the short barks and whimpers, while the Baron grinned and chewed his cigar. Then a shape appeared in the doorway. It looked like a mortal woman, but she walked with a strange, shuffling gait. As she stepped into the light of the shack, Paul saw that it was a zombie. Her hair was patchy, her skin peeling away from the bone in strips on her face. In her rotting arms she held Baby Jael. She stroked Jael's hair with bone fingers and smiled down at her with a vague yet unmistakable maternal affection.

"Jesus," said Paul, stunned speechless for the first time in a very long time.

"Ah, thank you, my dear," said the Baron, gently removing Jael from the zombie's arms. "You may go back to your feast. I am quite pleased with you. I suspect your service may be ending soon."

She nodded and slowly turned, then shuffled back through the door and into the night, heading in the direction of the canine howls of misery.

"This is yours, I think," said the Baron as he handed Jael to Paul.

Paul held Jael in his arms, feeling her warm breath against his chest as if for the first time.

"Thank you," he said simply.

The Baron shrugged. "It's good to remind these demons sometimes that I'm still around."

There was another shrieking bark in the distance.

"I didn't know zombies could eat demons," admitted Paul.

"Oh, dey can't, really," said the Baron. "But you know, dey just keep trying anyway."

When Poujean woke a few hours after dawn, he found Paul sitting at the table, holding the sleeping Jael in his arms and staring out the window. Poujean struggled to his feet, rubbing his head.

"Is everything okay?" he asked.

"Yes," said Paul quietly. "Thank you."

"For what?"

"You did it. You brought the Baron here and he helped me. Not exactly in the way we hoped, but that's pretty typical of the Baron."

"Is that why I feel like a cow has stepped repeatedly on my head?" asked Poujean.

"Probably," said Paul.

Poujean tore open a bottle of water and chugged it down without taking a breath.

"You going to be okay?" asked Paul.

"Every muscle in my body aches," said Poujean as he wiped his mouth with the back of his hand. "But in a good way. Like when I was a boy playing soccer. The kind of ache that reminds you that you're still alive. With things to do." He picked up the black top hat that lay on the altar.

"The Church won't like you doing this kind of stuff," said Paul. "It's too dark for them. Too blatantly pagan."

"Yes," said Poujean. "But I hear a call now that is stronger even than when I was called to the priesthood. I cannot ignore it. Perhaps my path leads away from the Church for a while."

"That's funny," said Paul. "Because I think mine is leading me back to them."

"Oh?" said Poujean. He turned from the hat to Paul.

"That's how the Baron helped. In addition to saving my life and my daughter, he convinced me to follow your advice," said Paul.

"Which advice was that?"

"To ask the Church to protect us."

"How did he convince you to do that?" asked Poujean.

Paul looked down at the sweet baby girl in his arms. "He didn't need to say a word. If it weren't for him, I would have lost her last night. I have to humble myself and accept that I can't do this alone. I can't let my feelings toward the Church or my pride get in the way like that again. From now on, I think only of the greater good."

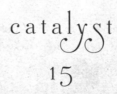

catalyst

15

They stand in the living room, father and daughter, both reeling from the shared experience.

"Dad, I . . ."

"Do you see now?" he asks. "Do you want to bring something like that down on this sleepy little neighborhood? If there is any risk that this Rob could reveal us, it will be more than just embarrassing. It will be deadly."

"But Dad, we can't just keep moving. *I* can't do it. I'll go crazy."

He looks at her, and Jael sees the pain in his eyes. She remembers the heavy song of his soul.

"Please, Dad," she says, in little more than a whisper. "I know you don't want to do this."

But he takes a deep breath and shakes his head. "I'm sorry. I need to you be strong," he says. "I need *you* to think about the greater good now. I will give you tomorrow to say good-bye to your friends. We leave in the evening. Go up to your room and start packing."

Then he sits back down in his chair, picks up his Bible, and begins to read.

She walks slowly up the spiral staircase to her bedroom. Once there, she stares at the clothes on the floor for a long time. She feels her body slowly heat up and she lets it. What does it matter if she scorches a few walls now? She's leaving anyway. Going off to live in some remote land—no friends, no contact with anyone except a bitter ex-priest and a fish monster. Perfect.

Why can't her father just trust her for once? Why can't he believe that someone other than him is capable of doing something right? She can make this work. She knows it. It will never get to the point where crazy demons and zombies are climbing in through the windows. Or if it does, it won't be because of Rob. There has to be a way to convince him of that.

Britt will know what to do. Jael hasn't been sure about telling her all of this, but what's the risk now? If she *doesn't* get Britt's help, she'll be leaving in twenty-four hours anyway.

With a sudden burst of energy, she grabs the phone on her dresser and punches in Britt's number. But she's let herself get too hot. Just as the voice mail kicks in and Britt's mom's cheerful, dippy voice comes on, Jael's phone melts into a shapeless blob.

"Shit," she hisses, and flings it across the room, where it smashes through the monitor of her computer.

Well, there goes that option too.

The anger and frustration boil up inside her and her body gets even hotter. Smoke begins to rise off her clothes. She can't seem to calm down. She's losing control like she did at the bookstore.

"No!" she says. "Please, just . . . cool off." She just throws it out there, not even really expecting anything. But the air responds. *Yes*, it almost seems to say *If it upsets you to be so hot, we can make you cooler.* A moment later, her skin temperature drops so low that there's a light dusting of frost on her jeans.

She sighs deeply. "Thanks," she says, although she's not sure if air really cares about stuff like that.

The heat problem is solved, but she still needs to talk to Britt and she doesn't have either a phone or a computer. She knows her father won't let her out this late. And she's so pissed at him she doesn't even want to see his face right now anyway. So for the first time in her life, she contemplates sneaking out. She peers out her bedroom window. There isn't any ledge and the lone tree in their little yard is not within jumping distance. Not that she's crazy enough to jump at this height, considering her last attempt at flight.

But she did get into the air, didn't she? It was only for a few seconds, but that might be all she needs.

She leans out the window. The wind is up, so it's hard for her to get the air's attention. Eventually, she connects with a swirly little piece and asks it to stop her from falling. Then she quickly steps off the window ledge before the wind gets tired of waiting. She sways somewhat precariously in midair for a moment. Then the air loses interest and lets her fall. But she's already been talking with the air beneath it, so she only drops by a foot. She continues like this, moment-by-moment, step-by-step, until she lands on the ground.

She thanks the earth under her feet for being its dependable self. The earth turns its groggy attention to her for a moment, then goes back to whatever it is earth thinks about.

Jael turns west, toward Britt's house.

• • •

All the windows in Britt's house are lit up like they're having a party. But that's how Britt and her mom keep it all the time, even when it's just the two of them. It looks a lot more cheerful than Jael's own dark, gloomy home. Her eyes have adjusted so well to the night that as she approaches the front door, she has to squint at the light that spills out.

Jael walks up the front steps and across the porch. She has to step around old toys, broken exercise machines, and camping gear, some of which has probably been there for years. Britt and her mom always enter through the back door, where the garage is, so the front porch has become a dumping ground. That's one of the dangers of always living in the same house, she supposes. You never need to purge your possessions, so stuff just keeps piling up.

Jael rings the doorbell, and after a few moments Britt's mother answers the door. Her thick honey-blond hair seems wreathed in light from the room behind her. She smiles with glossy red lips.

"Hi, Jael. What's up?"

Ms. Brougher really is a beautiful woman, in that classic pinup kind of way. All soft curves and bright smiles. She's always made Jael feel especially coarse and unfeminine.

"Hey, Ms. Brougher," says Jael.

"Jael, you're not my student anymore. You can just call me Heather now."

"Sorry," says Jael. "It's habit."

"So, what's up, girl?" says Ms. Brougher. "You're out late on a school night."

"Yeah," says Jael. "Can I talk with Britt?"

Ms. Brougher raises a penciled eyebrow at her. "Hmmm . . . can I take a guess and say that you're having boy trouble?"

"Uh, sure," says Jael. Close enough.

"Well, come on in."

Jael follows her into the living room, which is crowded with overstuffed furniture that makes the small room seem even smaller.

"Britt's on the computer in her room. I'm sure she can pull herself away. Just go on in." She makes a dainty flipping motion with her hand, then leans over and picks up a cordless phone from one of the easy chairs.

"Hey, I'm back," she says into the phone. "Yeah, just one of Britt's little friends, here for some romance advice." She pauses as she listens to the response. "Ha-ha, Jack. Real funny. She is only sixteen, you know." Then she wanders out into the kitchen.

A little tingle runs through Jael at the name Jack. Can it possibly be the same guy from the bookstore? How weird would *that* be? . . . She hopes it isn't, because that would be a little disappointing. A guy like that could do better than Ms. Brougher. Somebody younger. And cooler.

Jael looks around at the living room: at the huge TV that had been a gift from one of Ms. Brougher's previous boyfriends, at the stacks of teen fashion magazines on the coffee table, and at the line of crucifixes and framed pictures of saints hung along the walls. Jael can't decide whether coming here was the best idea she's ever had, or the worst.

When Jael peeks through the doorway into Britt's room, she sees her in the corner, hunched over a keyboard and staring at her computer monitor. It looks like she has about five different instant message windows open at once, as well as e-mail and an article from *Teen Vogue*.

"One sec," says Britt without turning around. Then she clacks furiously on her keyboard.

Jael looks around Britt's room, which is, as always, perfectly organized. Every inch of wall is covered in posters of models or actors, except the space directly over her bed. That place of honor is held by a massive metal crucifix.

"Hookay!" says Britt. "Good night, Internet!" Then she spins around in her chair to look at Jael. "I just told them all I have to sign off to help a girlfriend in crisis."

"Why do you think I'm in crisis?" asks Jael.

"Uh, because you never just show up at my house late at night like this. Now, sit down, you're making me nervous."

Jael sits on the edge of the bed.

"So, what's up?" asks Britt. "Is this about Rob?"

"Yeah, kinda," says Jael, trying to decide where to begin. Blurting it out like she did with Rob probably isn't going to work, and lighting something on fire just to show her would definitely freak Britt out. She should have planned ahead of time how she was going to do this.

"Come on," says Britt encouragingly, "Whatever you guys did, trust me, I've done it."

"Uh . . ."

"I'm your best friend. If you can't tell me, who can you tell?"

"That's just it," says Jael. "I don't know if I should really tell *anyone*."

"Oh my God, are you pregnant?"

"What? No!"

"Okay," says Britt, visibly relieved. "Well, it can't really be any worse than that. So what is it?"

"You know how a lot of people think that witches and stuff like that are evil?"

"Of course," says Britt. "Why wouldn't they?"

"Well, what if they weren't? Not all of them, anyway. What if it was all just some kind of . . . misunderstanding?"

Britt frowns. "How could it possibly be a misunderstanding? The Bible is full of examples of witches and sorceresses. And they're all evil."

"So what if there were others, though, who were good and just didn't get mentioned?"

"Oh, yeah, right. Like, 'Hey, God. I know you're all-knowing and everything, but you missed a few.'" She gives Jael a weird look. "What's this all about? You never talk about this kind of stuff. Is Rob into some weird Satanic cult or something?"

"No!" says Jael. "Maybe witches was . . . a bad example. I was just . . . uh, talking metaphorically."

"J, just talk straight with me. Are you and Rob hooking up or what?"

"No," says Jael. "I mean, not yet. I don't know. I'm just . . . look, honestly, I'm not even sure where to begin. . . ."

"Oh," says Britt, rolling her eyes and nodding her head. "Okay, I get it."

"You do?" asks Jael, pretty sure she doesn't.

"Sure. Sorry, I've been a little slow on the uptake today."

She leans in a little, like they're suddenly speaking more confidentially. "Listen, it's totally normal to be nervous about the first time. But I am here to tell you that there's nothing to be scared of."

"No?" Jael feels like she's lost control of the conversation.

"I mean, it's a little weird," Britt says. "And kind of uncomfortable at first." She makes a sour face. "Okay, being totally honest here, it's a lot uncomfortable. But once you relax into it, you know, it's really . . ." She shakes her head and sighs. "I don't even know how to describe it."

"What are you talking about?" asks Jael.

"Last night!" says Britt.

"Oh, right," says Jael. "Deep Prius guy."

Britt goes into her latest romantic adventure. Hearing Britt talk about sweaty contact in the back of a car is almost more than Jael can stand, so after a while, she stops listening. Without really deciding to do it, she looks through Britt's eyes to see what's behind their cheerful sparkle.

Britt's soul is different from either Rob's or her father's. It flails and quivers like an injured bird, desperate and maimed. As Jael looks deeper, like her father showed her, she starts to see the images encased in the depths of the spirit, stacked up like layers of silver flame. They spill over each other in a confusing welter. She goes for the biggest one and for just a moment she sees the ceiling in a car, a fogged window, and the muffled sound of a girl crying softly into fabric. The sadness cuts into Jael's heart like a knife. And that's when she understands that she's not going to find what she's looking for here with Britt. No solution, no comfort. Even if she could get Britt past the Bible stuff, there's no more room for drama in the Brougher house. It's all booked up.

"That's it," says Britt, all bright eyes and smiles. "No more virginity for me! Boy, what a relief!"

Jael pulls away from her friend's soul and looks into her cheerful face. "You really did it?" she asks. "You had sex with this guy?"

"J, I know what you're thinking, but I'm here to tell you that there's nothing to be scared of. In fact, I can't wait until we do it again, you know?"

"Really?"

"J, he's really so amazing and smart and super nice. His parents are totally evil, though. I don't know how he avoided being all screwed up like them. I think it's because he does so much in the Church. Anyway, seriously, I think I'm in love with him."

"Wow," says Jael. "Love?"

"Just wait until you meet him!" she says. "You'll totally understand. We're perfect. Like you and Rob."

"Yeah . . . ," says Jael.

Is it so hard to believe that Britt has really found someone? Maybe Jael is just jealous, because if she moves, she loses Rob along with everything else.

"He sounds . . . great," Jael says at last. She's about to say she can't wait to meet him, but realizes that she isn't going to, because she'll be gone in less than twenty-four hours. A lump rises in her throat. It's best for her to just fade quietly away and let Britt have her normal life with her normal church boyfriend. To bring her into Jael's world would just be selfish.

So Jael pushes a smile onto her lips. "I should probably get going. School night and all."

"Are you okay, then?" asks Britt. "For real?"

"Yeah," says Jael. "Thanks."

"Hey, what are best friends for?"

"Sure," says Jael. "See you tomorrow."

Jael is about halfway home when she sees the ram. The streetlight shines off its glossy white coat and thick, curled horns. It just stands there, casually, like it's normal for rams to hang out on a street corner in Seattle. It's looking directly at her.

She stops and waits to see what it will do. She isn't scared, exactly. But she also isn't about to take any chances, even on what appears to be a misplaced farm animal. After a few moments, it begins to walk toward her, its hooves clicking loudly.

"Stop!" she says.

It does.

She isn't sure what's weirder, that she talked to the ram or that it understood. But she decides that it's a good sign that it obeyed.

"Who are you? What do you want?"

My name is Asmodeus and I am here to help you.

"How are you talking in my head?"

I am sorry to be so invasive, but your father made me swear never to possess another man or woman, and this animal is unable to articulate sounds clearly enough for you to understand.

"Asmodeus, huh?" she says, taking a few steps closer. That was the demon her mom asked her dad not to kill. "So you were, like, sort of a friend of my mom's?"

Her love for you was something I had never encountered before. I hadn't realized such fierce kindness was even possible. . . . It changed everything for me. So I vowed to watch over you and aid you in whatever small way I can, warning your father when other demons get too close. I even tried to warn you directly once, when Baal found you. But that was not particularly effective.

"When Baal . . . wait, the bird, right? You were that sparrow that kept chirping at me!"

Yes, in urban areas I often choose birds or squirrels to escape notice.

"So why a ram this time?"

In my true form, which I can only take in Hell, I have three heads. One man, one bull, and one ram. By using a ram for this, our first true meeting, I wanted to be something like myself.

"Well, uh, nice to meet you, Asmodeus."

I wish this were no more than a pleasant meeting, little one. But I come to you tonight with a grave warning.

"What's that?"

Belial is coming.

"What?" she says, something cold and hard settling in her gut. "How did he find me?"

Your uncle disappeared from his post in the middle of a shift. That made Belial take notice.

That must have been Friday night, when Jael called him out of the bowl. All for her stupid hair emergency.

Then you made quite a bit of noise while practicing your magic yesterday. It was like a beacon in the skies of Hell.

"So what do I do?"

Run or fight.

"How can I possibly fight this Belial guy? He's like some super demon and I'm just half demon."

Not "just." A halfbreed is not simply half demon and half human. A halfbreed is something else entirely. A rare and potentially dangerous creature. Merlin, Perseus, and many others in your legends were halfbreeds. That is why you are feared and hated so much. The power of the elements is joined with your will. The power of Earth itself.

"Don't get me wrong," says Jael. "Freezing things is cool and all, but I don't think it's going to do much for me in a fight. Especially if this guy is king of the ice or whatever."

It is true that the elements of Gaia have been passive for a long time. But they don't have to be. Perhaps they need only the right catalyst.

Jael thinks about that for a moment. She remembers Thursday night and connecting to the elements, and how she wondered why something as powerful as the wind was so timid.

"You're saying I could get them into action?"

I am saying that if you fight, they will fight with you

The ram turns and begins to walk away.

"Wait!" says Jael. "How do you know so much about halfbreeds?"

The ram stops and lowers its head.

I used to be one.

"Yeah, you said something like that to my mom, but I

couldn't figure out what you meant. You were a halfbreed, but now you aren't?"

I was so desperate to be accepted by Belial and the other Grand Dukes, so afraid of the consequences of what I was, that I destroyed my mortal half.

"How did you do that?"

Just as your mother extracted the demon half from you for a short time, I extracted the mortal half from myself. But instead of protecting it as your father did, I cast mine into the Void.

"Oh," says Jael. She doesn't really know what else to say. "Did it hurt?"

It is still an agony to this day. It is a wound that will never heal.

"But they still didn't accept you, even after that?"

Of course not. And even if they did, my power is now so diminished, I am not of much use.

"I'm sorry," says Jael.

Don't be, little one. Every success of yours buoys my spirit a little more. You make me proud to be a halfbreed, a feeling I never thought possible. Now I must return to Hell, and you must decide what you will do when the Grand Duke comes for you.

The ram shudders and a fine mist coalesces above its head then dissipates.

"Asmodeus?" says Jael.

"Baaa!" says the ram, then runs off into the night, its cloven hooves echoing in the still night air.

As she continues her walk home, Jael wonders if there's any chance that Asmodeus is right. Could she really turn this all around? To not live in fear or on the run? For the first time in her life, to just be still? The idea buzzes warmly in her chest. She would risk just about anything for that.

Jael decides to let herself in through the front door. It's pretty late. Her father has probably gone to bed already. But when she gets inside, she finds that he has fallen asleep on the couch, his worn old Bible open on his chest. The candle on the coffee table is still lit.

"Great, Dad," she whispers. "Real safe."

She walks over to blow it out, but stops and looks at her father. His head is tipped back and to the side, leaving his mouth wide open. He looks different when he's asleep. The tension is gone from his face and he looks years younger. Like the man in the necklace who loved her mother.

Who is this guy? she thinks. She's lived with him her entire life, and yet she feels like she barely knows him at all. She looks down at the flickering candle that watches over him every night. Does the flame know him? No, not really. The fire is new every night and doesn't know or remember anything. The candle doesn't seem to care.

She decides not to blow it out. Instead, she takes it up to her room and puts it on the dresser at the foot of her bed. She could use some distraction, so she asks the fire if it would like to dance for her. It says that as a matter of fact it would. So Jael lies back in bed and watches the flame stretch and shimmy and flicker in a silent dance. It isn't long before all of the day's thoughts and worries slip away and she drifts off to sleep.

The flame, of course, wants to be free of its candlewick

tether. Now that it's been encouraged to move in ways that it doesn't ordinarily, it's worked itself up into a frenzy of hunger.

It begins to stretch higher. It reaches for something it can hold on to. Something it can eat besides the sluggish wax beneath it. It wants to eat the room, and the house, and everything else it can.

But the air in the room has been hanging around far longer than air usually does, partially because of poor ventilation, but partially because it likes Jael. She's such a funny little thing. So serious. So stuck. But artlessly charming, like the rustle of tall, wild grass. The air decides that it doesn't want the fire to eat her, or the room, or the house. It doesn't have anything against fire in general. In fact, they usually get along rather well. But this time is different.

So the air withdraws itself from the fire.

And the fire slowly suffocates and dies.

Britt sits back down at her desk and stares at the image of the pouty male model on her computer desktop. Something is up with Jael. She knows it. Something that Jael didn't say. Britt wonders if she talked too much. If she didn't give Jael a chance to get it out.

She sighs and rubs her eyes. Maybe she should go to bed early tonight. Last night was pretty intense. But instead of shutting down her computer, she opens chat.

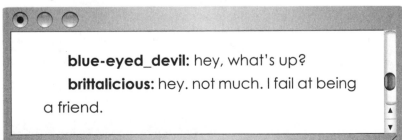

blue-eyed_devil: hey, what's up?
brittalicious: hey. not much. I fail at being a friend.

blue-eyed_devil: why do you say that?

brittalicious: o, my buddy J was trying to talk to me but I just can't shut up and listen sometimes. Why do I always have to make everything about me?

blue-eyed_devil: don't b 2 hard on yourself. if it was really that bad, she would have said something anyway.

brittalicious: I guess so . . .

blue-eyed_devil: I KNOW so. you want to grab a bite somewhere?

brittalicious: well, it is a school night . . .

blue-eyed_devil: come on! I need to get out of the house. my parents totally suck. And that chocolate shop on Greenwood is open until midnight! my treat . . .

brittalicious: bribing me with chocolate . . . you really are a devil, Jack.

blue-eyed_devil: >:D I'll pick u up in 10 minutes.

Britt shuts down her computer. She can't quite stop the stupid little smile that creeps onto her face. This one really is different. She just knows it.

exorcising independence
16

The rain pours down much harder than usual for October. Since Jael lost her raincoat to lava, and she doesn't quite feel comfortable wearing her demon-scale cloak to school, all she has left to wear is her red hoodie. By the time she gets to school, she's completely soaked. She walks through the front door of the school quickly, grateful for the shelter. She peels back her wet hood and runs her fingers through her spiky hair, flicking water droplets everywhere.

"Miss Thompson, front and center," she hears Father Aaron say.

Jael stops and looks down at her socks. She actually remembered to pull them up this morning, but they're so heavy with rainwater that they came down on their own. She slowly turns to face Father Aaron, her leather shoes squishing.

But beneath his usual sour frown, there's something unfamiliar in Father Aaron's expression.

"Keep your head about you today, Miss Thompson," he says. "Be smart."

She stares at him for a moment.

"What? . . . "

256

"The bell's about to ring," he says. "Better hurry, or you'll be late for class."

"But—"

"Miss Thompson, that is all."

"Y-y-yes, Father," she says. She turns to go, then says, "Thanks, Father."

"There's nothing to be thankful for," he says quietly, and his tone sends a chill down her spine. "Now, go to class."

She nods and hurries down the hall to her classroom.

As soon as she sits down at her desk, Rob says, "You okay?" He looks worried.

"No," says Jael.

"Did you get in trouble for telling me everything?"

"Uh, yeah."

"So are you grounded or something?"

"No," she says. "He says we're moving."

Rob just stares at her, like she's slapped him across the face.

"Sorry, I probably should've tried to break that a little more gently," she says. "I just . . . there's no one else to talk to."

"He's moving you guys just because you told one person," says Rob. "Doesn't he know he can trust me?"

"He doesn't trust anyone anymore," says Jael. "I think . . . not since my mom tricked him into letting her die to save us." She puts her head down on her desk. "Maybe it's for the best. This demon my mom knew showed up last night. Asmodeus. He said that Belial knows I'm here. That he's coming for me."

"Isn't that the guy who killed your mom?" asks Rob.

"Yep."

"Oh shit."

"Exactly."

"So, I guess that's freaking you out a little?"

"A little?" says Jael, lifting her head up. "I mean, first of all, here's this giant demon that is so fierce he makes other demons pee their pants, and he is coming to eat me. But what's even worse is I keep thinking of all the other people I'm putting in danger just by hanging around. So maybe it's better that we're moving. What if he showed up when I was hanging out with you?"

"Are you kidding me?" says Rob. "I *want* to be there. I'm gonna cheer you on while you kick his ass!"

"But that's just it. How can I possibly win? My mom and my uncle couldn't take him and they're *real* demons. I'm just a halfbreed."

"But maybe that's better," says Rob.

"That's what Asmodeus said, but I can't see how."

"Okay, check it. Last night after I left your house, I went home and did some serious Google-Fu on halfbreeds."

"You did what?"

"Online research. On halfbreeds. And the only one I could find any record of in the last two thousand years was Merlin."

"As in the guy from the King Arthur stories? I think Asmodeus mentioned something about him."

"Merlin was one of the most famous wizards who ever lived. So maybe you *could* take on this Belial guy. I mean, think about it. Why is it the bigwigs don't want halfbreeds around? Why do they always make a point of killing them when they're just babies? Maybe it's because when they grow up, they're all as powerful as Merlin."

"Maybe," says Jael. "My uncle said each one is different. Just because Merlin was awesome doesn't mean I am."

"Mr. McKinley and Miss Thompson," says Ms. Spielman from the front of the class. "If it's okay with you, I'd like to begin teaching a little math."

"Sorry, Ms. Spielman," says Jael as they both look down at their textbooks.

After a few moments, Rob whispers, "I think you're awesome. And I believe you can do it."

Her first impulse is to chuck something at him. *What does he know, anyway?* But then she thinks, *What do I know?* Maybe Rob could be right. Is that such a crazy idea? That someone else might be right?

After class, they're walking out of the room when Ms. Spielman stops them.

"Jael, would you stay behind a moment?" she asks.

"Uh, sure . . . ," says Jael, looking at Rob.

"Hey, I'll catch you after school?" he says.

"Yeah, okay. Good," she says.

After Rob is gone, Ms. Spielman gives Jael a little smile.

"He's a nice boy," she says.

"Yeah," says Jael, blushing.

"Everything okay?" she asks. "I didn't see your father in the lounge this morning."

"Oh, sure, yeah," says Jael. "I think he took the day off for some reason." To pack.

"Jael," says Ms. Spielman, then she stops for a second and just looks at her. "If you ever want to talk to someone, I'm here. Sometimes it helps to have a . . . female perspective."

"Oh, uh, thanks, Ms. Spielman. I definitely will. Uh, if I need to talk about anything."

Ms. Spielman doesn't quite seem satisfied with this brush-off. She frowns a little, then reaches out her hand as if to touch Jael's cheek. But she stops short.

"You have so much potential, Jael. Once you believe that, you'll take off like a rocket. I promise."

Jael forces a smile at her. "Okay, Ms. Spielman." If she only knew what Jael is up against, she probably wouldn't be that confident.

"Maybe," says Ms. Spielman, "you feel as though no one really understands what you're going through. What obstacles you have in front of you."

"What?" says Jael. It's like Ms. Spielman picked the thought from her head.

"Jael, everyone feels that way sometimes," says Ms. Spielman. "It's all right. If people only had the courage to admit it to each other, none of us would feel quite so alone."

"Sure," says Jael. She suddenly doesn't feel comfortable in the room. "Thanks, Ms. Spielman. Have a good day."

"You too, Jael," she hears Ms. Spielman say as she walks out.

"Halloween," says Father Ralph to his history class, "or All Hallows' Eve." He shifts his belt buckle, which is a cutesy cartoon version of a skull. "It exists in some form or another in just about every culture."

Jael isn't really paying much attention. Britt didn't show up at lunch today. It wouldn't be the first time she's skipped school, but Jael wishes it hadn't happened today. What if Jael doesn't even get a chance to tell Britt that she's leaving? Maybe she should have said something last night after all. . . .

"But," continues Father Ralph, "Halloween wasn't originally about monsters and demons."

That word gets Jael's attention.

"All Hallows' Eve, Dia de los Muertos, or similar holidays," says Father Ralph, "are about those who have died. They are reminders to us all that the dead are always with us."

There are some laughs scattered from the back, where Andy Link and his fellow soccer jocks sit.

"I don't mean ghosts or zombies," says Father Ralph. "The real haunting is the memory of a loved one. And driving away demons is symbolic of us attempting to drive away our own inner demons."

Why does he keep using that word? Jael wonders.

"Why do ghosts frighten so many people?" says Father Ralph. "Is the concept of a spirit coming back from the dead inherently evil? Remember that for much of the Church's history, the Trinity was known as the Father, the Son, and the Holy Ghost. But now, it's the Holy Spirit. So what happened? When did the word 'ghost' become associated with evil?" He looks around the room. "Yes, Jack?"

There's no one named Jack in Jael's class.

She slowly turns around in her seat. In the last row of desks, she sees him. The guy from the bookstore with the long, wild black hair. But he looks as young as a high school kid now and he's wearing a school uniform.

"Well, Father," says Jack. He speaks in a casual, breezy tone, as if he's lecturing the entire class, but the whole time, he stares at Jael with his piercing, pale blue eyes. "The word 'ghost' became more and more associated with evil when society drifted away from a concrete concept of spirituality. As religion became more secularly regimented, the spiritual aspect of Christianity became threatening and alien. Indeed, many who consider themselves to be devoutly religious believe that the spirit realm doesn't exist at all."

"An excellent answer, Jack," says Father Ralph. He and everyone else in the room are acting like Jack has always been in the class.

Jack continues to look at Jael, an ironic smile on his face. Then he slowly winks at her.

"Jael, please face front and pay attention," says Father Ralph.

"Sorry, Father." She turns back around.

For the rest of the class period, the hair on the back of her neck prickles, like she can feel Jack's blue-eyed gaze on her. She has to force herself not to squirm in her seat. Who is this guy? Clearly he's not just some bookstore guy, and there's some kind of magic going on. Is he a demon, or something else? He was really friendly at the bookstore, but now it feels like he's messing with her. Maybe he figured out what she is. She did accidentally light a book on fire in the store, after all. He probably saw that.

But what does he want? She decides to corner him and get some answers at the end of class.

Finally, the bell rings and Jael turns back around.

But Jack is gone.

As the rest of the class files out, Jael stays behind, watching Father Ralph sort through some notes on his desk. After a moment, he looks up at her.

"Oh, hi, Jael," he says casually, like he doesn't remember how he couldn't even look at her on Friday. "Thank you for replacing your book so quickly." Then he goes back to his notes.

"No problem, Father," says Jael. "Um . . . hey, Father?"

"Yes?" he says, still sorting through his papers.

"When did Jack start at Our Lady of Mercy?"

"Jack?" says Father Ralph. He looks up at her for a moment, frowns, and scratches his beard. "Sorry, Jael. I don't think I know a Jack. Is he a freshman?"

Jael stares at him for a second, then says, "Uh, right. Because there's no one in this class named Jack."

He gives her a strange look, like he has absolutely no idea what she's talking about. "Of course not."

"Thanks anyway, Father." Then she turns to go.

"Oh, Jael, wait a moment. I'm glad you stayed behind. I almost forgot."

Jael turns back.

Father Ralph suddenly looks embarrassed. "This is a some-what strange request, I know, but . . . Monsignor asked me to bring you by his office after class. He said there's something very important he needs to talk to you about."

"Oh," says Jael. Mons. The exorcist. A sudden sick fear shoots through her.

It must show on her face, because Father Ralph quickly says, "You're not in trouble. Or at least, I don't think so. Frankly, I'm not sure I understand what it's all about."

"Okay," she says.

"Don't worry." Father Ralph smiles. "I'll be there to protect you from the mean old Mons."

"Great," says Jael, and she forces herself to smile back.

Jael follows Father Ralph to the wing of the school where students are hardly ever permitted: the Residences. All three priests live there in studio apartments. A few old oil paintings of saints on the hallway walls, and a noticeable lack of classrooms, are the only indicators that this isn't a regular part of the school. But to Jael, entering the hallway feels like walking on forbidden ground.

"Monsignor or I will write you an excuse for your next class," says Father Ralph as he leads her down the dim hallway.

Jael nods, but doesn't trust herself to speak.

"Not that this will take long, I'm sure," he says cheerfully.

Maybe he's right. What if Jael is making too much of this? So what if the Mons used to be some exorcist. Would an exorcism even affect her? And anyway, it was a long time ago that he did that kind of stuff. Maybe he sensed something was off on Friday. That's understandable. But she's got that a lot more under control now. He'll probably just ask her some questions. All Jael has to do is be cool and play dumb, and he'll probably let her go.

They're at the entrance to the Mon's quarters now. The door is made of a rich, dark mahogany with no window. Father Ralph knocks, and after a moment she hears the Mons say in his peaceful voice, " Please come in."

See? The Mons sounds downright cheerful.

Father Ralph opens the door, then gestures for Jael to go in first. Despite her inner pep talk, adrenaline crackles in her veins and she walks into the room with a stiff, self-conscious gait. It's dim and stuffy inside. The only furniture is a desk, a small couch, and a bookshelf. One small window lets in the feeble light from outside through old plastic blinds.

Standing next to the window is Britt. She looks at Jael, her mouth set in a hard line.

"What are—" Jael starts to say. Then the door slams shut behind her and she hears a dead bolt click. She turns back and sees Father Ralph by the door, looking very confused and flustered. Next to him is the Mons, dressed in his full priest getup: the robe, the scarf, the whole deal, like he's ready to say Mass. Except the look in his eyes is not the one she sees when he prays for the sick and dying.

"Jael Thompson," he says in a booming voice, his face grim and determined. "Father Ralph, your dear friend Brittany, and I are here, with the grace of God, to help you."

Jael glances at Britt, searching her face for some sign that she might be humoring the Mons. Maybe even that she thinks it's a joke. But the look Britt returns is absolutely serious.

She turns back to the Mons. "Monsignor?" she says lightly. "I don't understand. I don't need any help."

"That is because you cannot see what we see. You cannot see the forces of darkness that have enthralled you."

"Wait," says Jael, "is this an intervention?"

"No," says the Mons. "It is an exorcism."

"What?" says Father Ralph, and turns to the Mons. "Francis, what are you talking about?"

"Look at her, Ralph," says the Mons. "The poor girl is possessed by a demon."

"Francis," says Father Ralph. His eyes are wide with alarm, but his voice is set in a forced reasonable tone. Like he can talk them all down to earth. "An exorcism? This is crazy, not to mention probably illegal. And I'm pretty sure the bishop would not—"

"The bishop," says the Mons, "is a weak, officious worm who has less faith than an atheist."

"Francis, what's gotten into you?" asks Father Ralph, his voice laced with panic now. "Listen to yourself. You sound like some kind of raving zealot."

"No, Ralph," says the Mons. "I sound like a true man of the Church. And if you can't see the cancerous evil pouring out of this girl, then you are no priest at all."

Father Ralph just stares at him, utterly lost. Jael can see it in his eyes. He didn't join the priesthood for titanic battles of good versus evil. He just wanted to help people. He's way out of his depth and he knows it.

The Mons turns back to Jael, and she can see in *his* eyes that it was precisely titanic battles of good and evil that brought him to the priesthood. And he is ready to throw down.

"My child," he says in a stern voice, "we are here to save your soul from the wicked monster that has invaded you."

"Monsignor, I still don't know what you're talking about," says Jael. "I'm not possessed by any monster."

"Jael," says Britt. "We've all seen the way you've changed over the past week. I didn't understand what was going on until Monsignor talked to me about it this morning. That was why you kept talking about witches last night. You were calling out to me for help and I just didn't understand. So let Monsignor help you. He's your only hope for salvation."

Jael wants to tell her that she's a traitorous bitch, then maybe throw her through the window. But this isn't the time for that. She takes a deep breath and turns back to the Mons.

"I don't believe in any of this stuff," she says, unable to keep the tension from her voice.

"If you believe none of this is true . . ." The Mons looks at Father Ralph and Britt while he talks, as if they are his audience. "If you don't believe in demons and the vile powers of darkness, then you have nothing to fear." He turns back to Jael, his old eyes as hard and cold as steel. "If you have nothing to hide, why not go through with it?"

"Fine, whatever," Jael says, striving for indifference, but sounding a bit too shrill.

"Jael," says Father Ralph. "You don't have to do anything you don't want to do." He looks at her pleadingly, like he wants her to back down.

Instead, she looks at the Mons. "Say your stuff."

He nods, and turns his gaze to Father Ralph. "You can leave if you like," he says in an almost mocking tone.

"No, Francis," says Father Ralph. "I'll stay. I won't leave you alone with these girls. And I warn you, if I see anything inappropriate or dangerous happen, I'll be calling the police."

"The police will not be of much help, I'm afraid. But stay if you like. Perhaps you will yet have the opportunity, by the grace of God, to see the truth." He turns back to Jael. "I'm glad you have consented. Now, please sit on the couch. Someone who is in the throes of exorcism often flails around, and I want to minimize the injuries you might inflict on yourself."

"Sure," says Jael. She sits down on the small couch, trying without much success to look relaxed. It's just like Mass, she tells herself. Except she doesn't have to kneel the whole time.

The Mons takes two leather straps and fastens one on each arm of the couch.

"Hold out your hands," he says.

"Francis, you've got to be kidding!" says Father Ralph.

"The couch is for her protection," says the Mons. "These straps are for ours."

"You really do believe this nonsense," says Father Ralph, shaking his head, his expression somewhere between amazement and disgust.

"I believe because I have seen pure evil incarnate," says the Mons. "I have been face-to-face with the darkness, and I know what it is capable of. When the demon takes hold, I don't want Brittany in any danger."

"God will protect me," says Britt.

The Mons turns to her, a bitterly amused smile on his face. "God's will is unknowable."

Britt flinches and lowers her head.

The Mons turns back to Jael. "Your hands, please."

Jael can feel her body instinctually heat up. That's the last thing she needs right now, so she asks the air around her to cool her off. But she's too agitated and the air goes overboard. The temperature of the room drops so rapidly that frost rimes the window and everyone's breath turns to fog as it leaves their mouths.

The Mons looks around, but doesn't seem surprised. He just holds out the straps and says, "Your hands. Quickly."

Jael holds out her hands and she can't stop them from trembling. The Mons sees it immediately. He looks her in the eye and says, "I cannot tell you that there's nothing to fear. Because that would be a lie."

"Jael," says Father Ralph. "Are you sure you want to go through with this?"

Her mouth is so dry, it takes a few swallows before she can say, "Yeah. Do it."

The Mons nods and fastens the straps around her wrists and pulls them tight so that she can't lift her arms. Then he steps a few feet back. He looks at Britt and Father Ralph. "From this point, you must obey my every command if we have any chance to save this girl. Now"—he pulls out a small black prayer book from under his robes—"let us begin."

He holds the book in front of him and reads in a loud, deep voice, "Holy Mother of God!"

Britt and Father Ralph respond with, "Pray for us."

"Holy Virgin of virgins."

"Pray for us."

"Saint Michael."

"Pray for us."

"Saint Gabriel."

"Pray for us."

The funny thing is, it really does seem like Mass. It goes on and on, just like the Petitions, and it slowly builds up a lulling rhythm. Little by little, Jael begins to relax. This isn't so bad, she thinks. And what if the Mons really can get the demon out of her? Almost all of her problems gone in a poof. Is that really such a bad thing? Sure, she'd miss the little bit of magic she's learned. And her uncle would be crushed. But maybe her dad would loosen up. Maybe they wouldn't have to move. And there would be no Jack stalking her, and no worrying about Belial showing up out of nowhere.

Of course, she'd never be able to avenge her mother. In fact, if her mother was still alive, it would probably break her heart. After all, it would be like Jael was rejecting her. . . .

Then an image forms in her mind of her mother. Not the dreamlike visions from the necklace, but something somehow dredged up from her own memory. She can see her so clearly: a woman with black, curly, tangled hair that frames a regal, brown face. Her sharp green eyes have a sadness to them, but there is a smile on her lips like she's just about to laugh. She's strong and fierce and beautiful. And she gave up her life so that Jael could live.

What happens to demons when they die? Maybe they go wherever mortals go. Maybe they return to the elements. Or maybe they burn into nothingness.

For years, Jael has told anyone who will listen that she doesn't believe in an afterlife. That the whole concept is just stupid. But now, the idea that her mother simply does not exist grips her as if she were again staring into the infinite night sky. It's too big for her to grasp and she starts to panic. She clings to the image of her mother like a life preserver. If nowhere else, there is one place that her mother exists. In her.

But then the guilt crashes down on her. Because only a few moments before, Jael wanted to get rid of her mother and everything that went along with her as if her demon half was some kind of sickness. How can she reject the mother she has always longed for?

"I cast you out, unclean spirit!" the Mons yells.

He flicks holy water on Jael's face and it breaks her concentration. The image of her mother begins to slip away.

"Along with every satanic power of the enemy," says the Mons. "Every specter from Hell, and all your fell companions, in the name of the Lord Jesus Christ!"

Jael tries to bring the memory back, but the harder she fights to hold on, the faster it fades away, until finally, she only has a dim recollection of it.

"Hearken, therefore, and tremble in fear, Satan!" yells the Mons. "You enemy of faith, you foe of the human race, you begetter of death, you robber of life, you corrupter of justice, you root of all evil and vice!"

It dawns on Jael that the Mons is talking about her mother.

"Seducer of men! Betrayer of nations! Instigator of envy!"

"Stop," Jael says quietly. A wind begins to pick up. Loose papers flutter around the room like startled birds.

"Font of avarice! Fomenter of discord! Author of pain and sorrow!"

"Stop it now," she says a little louder. The room temperature drops below freezing. A sheen of frost coats everything.

"Depart, seducer!" shouts the Mons, gazing at her with grim determination. "Full of lies and cunning, foe of virtue, persecutor of the innocent!"

"I said stop it!" Jael rips her arms free from the leather straps and stands up.

"Give place, abominable creature!" yells the Mons as he backs away. There is fear in his eyes, but it is dim compared to his hatred. "Give way, you monster!"

"SHUT UP!" Jael screams so loud that the windowpane cracks. She lunges forward and grabs the Mons by his robes with one hand and hauls him in until their faces are only inches apart.

"Depart, impious one, accursed one!" yells the Mons, his spit hitting her face. "Depart with all your deceits! The Lord God commands you!"

"Nobody commands me," says Jael in a voice she barely recognizes as her own. She holds him with one hand. Her other hand rises in a fist. "Not the devil, and not God." Her fist bursts into flames and she thinks it would be so easy just to shove this jet of fire right down his throat.

"Be gone, seducer!" he shrieks.

It would be so easy . . .

Jets of water spray down from the ceiling. The fireball in her hand must have set them off. But the temperature in the room is so low that the spray turns to hissing sleet. She takes a deep breath as the ice crystals pound on her head and back. Then she lets her fire go, lets her anger go.

"Do you actually believe you're doing God's work?" she asks.

"I am a servant of God," he whimpers.

"The only one you serve is your own ego," she says. "I see it in your soul. But you don't have to take my word for it."

She looks deeply into his eyes. He wails and tries to pull away with a desperate energy. She grabs his face with her free hand and forces him to look into her eyes, where he sees the reflection of his own eyes. Together, they look down into the murky depths of his soul.

She riffles through his memories like a bloodhound. She can almost smell the stink of corruption on his soul. But where does it live? What is its root? Then she sees an image of a dead little boy, and she steps into a memory of Peru.

She can feel the heat from the sun, hear the screams of the dying, and smell the patches of blood that streak the stone-paved streets of Iquitos. She looks through the eyes of young Father Francis Locke as he kneels down in the street and tries to bind the stump of a little boy's arm. It was hacked off by one of the Shining Path guerrillas with a machete. The guerrillas have vanished into the forests, as they usually do, leaving many dead, and many more soon to die. This boy probably won't live. Father Locke knows it. The boy knows it. Yet Father Locke continues to bind the bleeding stump because there's nothing else he can do. He has only been a missionary here for one year, but he can hardly remember any other life. There is only this. Gathering the flock again after the communist rebels have wreaked their havoc.

"Father, Father!" A young woman appears next to him. He thinks of her as a woman, anyway, but to Jael she looks like a girl. "We found one! We have him!"

He nods, then finishes the tourniquet for the boy. He lays his hand on the boy's forehead and quickly gives him last rites. Then he stands up and motions for the woman/girl to lead him.

They walk through narrow, winding streets to a small open market area. A large crowd shouts and curses at someone crumpled on the ground. It's a member of the Shining Path, covered in dirt and blood, but still alive.

The crowd wants to know what they should do. Everyone else is dead, they say. The police captain. The governor. Father Locke is in charge now. They want to kill the rebel. And they want absolution.

The rebel, who looks about thirteen to Jael, struggles weakly on the ground. One leg bleeds profusely from a machete gash, and one arm lays useless, ripped up by a gunshot wound.

"Please, Father, I beg you," says the rebel boy. "Give me protection in the name of the most merciful Jesus Christ."

Father Locke stares at the man/boy for a long time. He seems deaf to the shouts and protests of the people who surround him.

His thoughts make no sense to Jael. Something about a temple made of gold with rivers of blood flowing down its sides. Finally, Father Locke lifts up his hand for silence.

"Tie a tourniquet around his leg and arm so he doesn't bleed to death."

"Oh, thank you, thank you, Father!"

"You ask for the mercy of Jesus Christ. And yet, as a communist, you don't believe in God."

"I do, Father! I'm baptized! Before the liberation army took me, I went to Mass every Sunday!"

"Even worse, you received God's grace, and you threw it away for a fickle promise of power."

"No, Father, I swear! I didn't have a choice!"

"I know that," says Father Locke. He turns to the crowd. "My children, how could God allow such a horror as the Shining Path to come upon us? He is testing us. The pagan sorcery of the Incas has not been eradicated completely. We know this. In the mountains, they still practice it. Even some of you still practice it in your own small ways. The Devil is subtle and often appears in guises we don't expect. The darkness of Inca sorcery, fed secretly all these years, has taken shape as an army of cruel militant atheists. The government is fighting a losing battle because they are only using guns and weapons of this mortal plane. But this is a spiritual war, and God expects us to fight. The stakes are not just our lives, but our eternal souls as well."

"Amen!" shouts the crowd.

Father Locke looks down at the bleeding rebel. "But as I said, I realize that you were forced into this."

"Yes!" says the rebel.

"You are controlled by a diabolical power, a demon born from the pagan sorcery of the Incas. But I will free you," says Father Locke. "I will exorcise the demon!"

"Amen!" shouts the crowd.

Father Locke leads a procession down the street. They fan out behind him, singing hymns as they carry the possessed rebel out of Iquitos to the area of Belen, where Father Locke lives. It's during the flood season and Belen is under five feet of water. All the tiny huts that people live in are on rafts or stilts.

The procession carefully loads the rebel into a small wooden boat. Then Father Locke, alone, rows him out in the water to his raised hut.

"Please, Father, I'm not possessed!"

"Of course you are. How else could you have committed such atrocities?"

"No, Father! You don't understand. . . ."

The rebel says more, but Father Locke remembers that an exorcist should never listen to the lies, threats, or bribes that the demon heaps on him.

When they get to Father Locke's hut, the rebel is too weak to move, so Father Locke lifts him from the boat and carries him into a corner of his hut. Then, he begins the exorcism. He's never done one before, but he has the rituals and he's talked to other priests who have done them. He finds the prayers and activities soothing. He hopes that the rebel also finds some small comfort in them as he battles the demon inside himself.

After a while, the rebel is raving like a madman. Thick yellow pus seeps from his tourniquets and Jael begins to understand what's really happening here. But this is only a memory and she can only watch.

After another day, the rebel's arm and leg are purple and decayed in the tropical heat. He has stopped screaming.

Three days later, the rebel dies, and Father Locke takes comfort that at least he saved the boy's immortal soul.

Word spreads of the miracle. Other rebels are brought to him. Some found, some captured, some claiming not to be rebels at all. They are all bruised, battered, and near death. Father Locke saves them all.

It isn't until the flood season is over and the waters recede that a passing police officer sees the pile of bodies that has collected under the stilts of Father Locke's house. . . .

The memories drain away: the heat, the jungle, and the smell of death. Jael, the Mons, Father Ralph, and Britt still stand in the Mons's office with freezing rain spitting down from the sprinklers and a lashing wind that comes from nowhere.

"You . . . ," Jael says. "And you call *me* a monster."

"Oh, God," whispers the Mons. "These are tricks! Demon tricks!"

Jael continues to look into his eyes, pulling out the memories that have been buried so deep for so long so that he can't hide from them any longer. He struggles and pushes against her as she tunnels down into the soft, raw nerves of his identity, taking that image of the pile of rotted, bloated corpses and shoving it as far down as it will go.

"You are a psycho and a mass murderer," she says.

A shriek boils up from deep in his gut, "GOD, NO!"

Then his whole body convulses violently with a strength Jael wasn't prepared for, and he slips from her grasp.

She lunges forward to stop him from falling backward, but her fingertips only graze the wet cloth of his robe.

His head smacks hard onto the wet marble floor and he lies still.

The sprinklers shudder off, the fluttering objects drift back to the ground, and the temperature in the room returns to normal. Jael stands over the Mons, her hand still outstretched as she looks down at him. She smells blood. A line of red seeps from the point where his head hit the floor. The blood thins and spreads as it mixes with the melting ice crystals. She sees her reflection in a puddle tinged with red, and she doesn't look like some righteous creature of magic. She just looks like a scared little girl.

There is a loud pounding at the door, then the hinges break free from the frame and the door falls forward with a smack. Father Aaron stands on the other side, breathing hard from exertion. He holds an enormous iron cross in his hands, splinters from the door stuck on the corners. He surveys the room for a moment, then he tosses the cross on the couch and runs to the Mons. He kneels down and checks his breath and pulse.

"Is he . . . ," whispers Jael. "Is he . . ."

"He's alive," says Father Aaron. Then he turns to look at Britt and Father Ralph. They stare back at him like they don't know him.

"This little adventure of yours is over," says Father Aaron. "Don't speak of this to anyone. Now, go."

They just stare at him.

"GO!" he barks.

They flinch and run out the door.

"Father," says Jael. Her voice trembles. "I didn't mean—"

"You've had a hard day," he says quietly. Almost gently. "Go home to your father."

"Y-y-yes, Father," she says. She turns to go.

"Miss Thompson," says Father Aaron.

Jael stops.

"See you in school tomorrow," he says. "Right?"

"If you think that would be—"

"I do. I'll handle this. That's why I'm here."

It is a long, slow, dark walk home in the rain. School must have let out hours ago, but she can't bring herself to rush. The sound of the Mons's screams still echo in her ears and she can still smell the blood. She feels raw all over, and she has no idea if she just won or lost or if winning or losing even means anything anymore.

When she nears the house, she sees someone huddled under the awning on the front step.

"Dad?"

His head jerks up. Then he runs out into the rain and sweeps her up in a fierce hug.

"Aaron called and told me that you missed your afternoon classes," he mumbles into the top of her head. "Then you didn't come home. I thought . . ." He lifts his head and looks at her, squinting as the rain pounds on his face. Jael has never seen him this frantic before. This openly concerned.

"I'm okay, Dad," she says, although she's not really sure if she is.

He pulls her into the house, pats her down with a towel, and takes off her shoes. She can't help but wonder, who has replaced her father with this kind, nurturing human being?

"Let's get you dry and fed. Are you hungry? Thirsty? Tired? What happened?"

"I'm not really sure what happened," she says. "The Mons locked me in his office and he tried to do an exorcism. And I . . . I think I might have screwed him up. Permanently."

"What did you do?"

"I showed him what his soul looks like."

"Oh," says her father. He's quiet for a moment as he looks at the damp towel in his hands. Then he tosses the towel on a doorknob and says, "So, are you hungry?"

"That's all you have to say about it?"

He looks at her with a strange calmness. "What is there to say? Are you asking me if you did the right thing? Well, if he was so self-deluded that the truth drove him mad, then perhaps it was exactly what he deserved. On the other hand, who can truly say that they know their own soul? I can't. I don't think you can. Perhaps we all delude ourselves. Perhaps we all deserve that fate. Or perhaps no one does." He looks at her. "Is that what you wanted to hear?"

"Yeah," says Jael. "Sort of."

Yep, it's definitely still her father.

"Great. So, food?"

"Yes, please," she says.

Apparently squash is on sale, because the fridge is packed with it. Jael sits down and has a feast with pumpkin squash, acorn squash, butternut squash, and spaghetti squash. The next hour is devoted to peeling skins and eating pulp, seeds, and all. In between bites, she tells her father the details and he listens intently without comment. After she's finished with the story, she quietly eats her squash for a little while. Then she says, "Dad, I don't understand how all that stuff with the Mons happened."

"I've never done missionary work like that," says her father, "but I've heard that it can be very hard to stay out of local politics." He looks at her for a second. "But that's not what you mean."

"No," she says. "I want to know how a crazy mass murderer can become my high school religion teacher."

"Perhaps the locals really did see him as a holy man," says her father. "Perhaps the police were too frightened of the Church in Peru to bring charges against him. Perhaps the Church simply wouldn't listen. You have to remember, every time a priest is convicted of a crime, especially one that seems rooted in the traditions of the Church, the power of the Vatican slips slightly."

"So they could have just covered it up?"

"Possibly," says her father.

"The Church hid a murderer?"

"More likely, those who made the decision simply chose not to learn the details."

"Details? I wouldn't call those details."

"I agree that sometimes it's a terrible practice."

"Sometimes? Please, when is it not terrible?"

"When it saves your life," he says.

"What?"

"After that incident with Amon and the Baron, I followed Poujean's advice and asked the Church to shelter us. How else do you think I could have gotten jobs all over the world on almost a yearly basis? I contact the local bishop, tell him we need to move. He contacts the cardinal, and it goes up the chain until someone in the Vatican finds me a new teaching post."

"But they don't know what I am, right? Not for sure."

"Father Aaron does."

"What? For how long?"

"As long as we've lived here. He receives my confession once a month."

"Jesus, Dad, that's probably something you should have told me."

"Probably," he says.

Jael is about to say something more, but she stops herself. She just criticized her father, swore at him even, and he agreed. No excuses, no denials. He just agreed. So she decides to let it go at that.

"Okay, but it's not like he's telling the pope or anything." Her eyes narrow. "Right?"

"Jael, do you really think, as cautious as the Church is, that they would offer sanctuary to a creature as potentially powerful as you without keeping a close watch? Father Aaron isn't just some parish priest. He's a high-ranking member of the Vatican with an extensive background in military intelligence."

"Father Aaron is an *undercover spy*?"

"Not exactly. It is true that no one else at Mercy is aware of what he really is. But a spy wouldn't let the people he's spying on know who he truly is, and he's never made it a secret to me. He's actually been quite helpful in keeping me informed of Church politics that might affect us. You could even say he's our advocate at the Vatican. In fact, he's one of the main reasons we've stayed here this long. No other Church contact has been this supportive, and that counts for quite a lot."

"So . . . okay, what does the Church want from us? From me?"

His eyes grow distant and he shakes his head.

"That, I don't know," he says.

Then the doorbell rings.

They freeze for a moment.

Jael says, "Who—"

"I'll go see," says her father.

Jael listens to him walk out to the hallway and open the front door. There's a long silence. Just when she's getting really worried, she hears Rob's voice.

"Hi, Mr. Thompson. You don't have to let me in or anything, but can you just tell me if Jael is okay?"

There's another long silence. Then she hears her father say, "Come inside out of the rain, Rob."

"Thanks, Mr. Thompson."

Jael throws down her half-eaten squash and runs out to the

hallway. Rob is there, rain dripping from his jacket onto the front mat.

"Jael," he says. "Are you—"

That's as much as he gets out, because she grabs him and hugs him fiercely. After a few moments, he whispers, "Ribs, Bets. Super demon strength making it hard to breathe."

"Oh, sorry." She lets him go.

Rob takes a deep sigh of relief, then says, "So, you're okay, obviously."

"Yeah," she says. "I am now."

"It was the weirdest thing," he says. "I get this call from Father Aaron. He wouldn't tell me anything other than that I should check in on you. Totally had me freaked out. So what happened?"

"Are you hungry, Rob?" asks her father.

"I'm always hungry, Mr. Thompson."

Her father smiles slightly at that. "Well, come on. I'll make you something. We have all this lunch meat that Jael won't eat now and it'll go bad before I get to it all."

Jael follows them silently into the kitchen. She doesn't want to say anything that might screw up this sudden change in her father's attitude toward Rob. She and Rob sit down at the table while her father makes him a sandwich. During this surreally normal activity, Jael describes the exorcism again. After she's done, Rob says, "I can't believe it. Britt was your best friend."

"I guess she thought she was helping me," says Jael. "I almost told her the last night. But I just felt like . . . I don't know. Like she couldn't handle it. She's already got so much of her own drama to deal with. I felt like adding my own to it just wasn't right." She picks a little bit of pulp off the husk on her plate. "This is so much worse, though. Maybe if I had told her before . . ." She stares at the shell of squash. "Well, it's too late now."

"I think your instincts were right," says her father. "There might be a few exceptional cases." He hands Rob a plate with a neatly made sandwich. But I think that most people will react the way I warned you about. It's simply too much for them."

"Like Father Ralph, huh?" says Rob. "I always kind of thought he was a punk."

"Yes," says Jael's father. "He will be the one to watch. He's never really bought into the more traditional aspects of the Church. This will certainly change his views, but for better or for worse, we'll just have to see."

"Dad," says Jael. "Does that mean . . ."

"I think there will be difficulties and risks wherever we go," he says. "You've shown me that you have the courage to face them. And I'm getting a little tired of running."

"Oh, Dad!" She can't help herself. For the first time since she was a little girl, she reaches out and hugs him.

"So what's going to happen to the Mons?" asks Rob.

"Oh," says a growling voice from Rob's water glass. "I'm hoping for an eternity of suffering."

Rob stumbles back, tripping over his chair as two clawed hands emerge from the drinking glass. Dagon slowly pulls himself through the narrow opening limb by limb, squeezing out like scaly yellow toothpaste until he's leaning casually against the table. He picks up Rob's half-eaten sandwich and shoves it into his mouth. His shark teeth shred it to ribbons.

"Uncle D," says Jael, "that was a totally unnecessary entrance."

He grins, leans over, and wraps her in his ragged, flaking arms. "You did good today, kid. I'm just on a coffee break, so I can't stay. But I wanted to tell you that."

"Ohshitohshitohshit," whispers Rob. "A real demon, ohshitohshitohshit . . ."

"I also wanted to meet this guy," says Dagon. He hunches down so that he's eye level with Rob. "Hey, bud, I'm Jael's uncle." He holds out a massive claw.

Rob's face is pale and sweaty, but he shakes Dagon's hand.

"See, there," says Dagon. "Nice, firm handshake. Or it would be if you'd stop shaking. Look out for my niece, right?"

Rob nods spastically.

"And if you hurt her, I'll hang your guts on a fence for the crows to eat."

"Not cool, Uncle D," says Jael.

"Just kidding," he says. Then he smiles so that his teeth splay out in rows. "Sort of." He stands up and looks around at them all with his shiny black eyes. Then he sighs happily. "This is shaping up to be the most interesting thing I've been involved in since that whole Knights of the Round Table thing."

Then he disappears again, leaving only the stench of rotting fish behind.

straight to hell
17

Jael wakes up to a slice of sunlight streaming through her blinds. The first clear sky in days. Probably the last glimpse of the sun for months. She's learned that once the rainy season sets in, she has to cherish moments of light like this, soak them up like a camel storing water. She lies in bed with her eyes half closed and lets the sun warm her face for a little while before she gets out of bed and starts her day.

After she showers and dresses, she goes to the kitchen for some breakfast. When she opens the refrigerator door, she finds a platter full of freshly cut fruit covered in plastic wrap. Apples, oranges, strawberries, cherries, mangoes, apricots, peaches, kiwis, and bananas—a rainbow of juicy sweetness so perfect and ripe that she smells it through the wrap. She stands there with the fridge door open and considers it for a moment, trying to decide what it's for and if her father will notice a few pieces missing. She hears footsteps behind her and turns.

"Good morning," says her father. He doesn't actually smile. That would have been too weird. But he nods to her pleasantly as he pulls out the milk from the fridge and makes himself a bowl of generic cereal.

"Hey," says Jael. She watches him as he sits down and begins to eat his cereal. She can't remember the last time he ate breakfast.

After a moment, he looks up at her and says, "Are you going to eat that breakfast or just look at it? You're wasting electricity with that fridge door open."

Jael looks at the platter. "This is for me?"

"Yes," he says, and goes back to eating his cereal.

"Thanks," she says.

"Sure," he says.

She pulls out the platter and peels back the wrap. She inhales deeply, savoring the bouquet of sweetness and citrus.

They eat breakfast together for a little while in silence, then her father says, "You know, this generic cereal is pretty terrible. It gets soggy so quickly."

"Yes," says Jael. "It does."

As she leaves her house, Jael glimpses someone turning the corner out of view at the end of the block. She gets a strange tingle of recognition. Tall, thin, with wild black hair . . . Jack.

She walks quickly down the sidewalk toward where she saw him turn. She's not going to let this guy get the jump on her like the Mons did. As she walks, she flexes and clenches her hands, feeling them get hotter and hotter. Whoever he is, he was able to put her entire class, including Father Ralph, under his spell. Well, when she catches up to him, she'll show him he's not the only one with a little magic.

"Jael!"

She spins around, and a ball of fire ignites in her fist, cocked and ready to throw.

"Holy shit!" says Rob, shielding his face. "It's just me!"

She smothers the flame with her other hand. "Jesus, Rob. Don't sneak up on me."

"I guess not," says Rob. Then he grins. "That was pretty sweet how you did that, though." He flaps his hand in the air. "Foosh!"

"Yeah, uh-huh," says Jael, glancing back in the direction that Jack went.

"So where were you going?" asks Rob. "School's the other way."

"I thought I saw . . ." Then she shakes her head. "Never mind. So what are you doing here?"

"Walking you to school, of course."

Jael raises an eyebrow at him. "Do boyfriends still do that?"

"This one does," says Rob. "I'm not carrying your books, though."

"Yeah, that would be a little silly," she says.

"Considering your super demon strength," he says with a grin. "Hey, by the way, meeting your uncle was awesome."

"Yeah," says Jael. "He's pretty cool, huh?"

"I had nightmares last night for the first time in, like, forever."

"Oh God, sorry!"

"No," he says, his eyes bright. "It was so incredible. It was like some crazy superintense horror movie. I mean, scary, sure. But the best dreams I've ever had."

"Okay . . . ," says Jael. "If you say so."

They walk together in silence for a little while.

"You're worried," he says finally.

"Ya think? Sure, I don't have to deal with the Mons anymore. But Belial could show up at any time, and there's this other guy from the bookstore sneaking around. Somehow I get the feeling they're going to be a lot harder to deal with."

"Maybe that Asmodeus guy was wrong," says Rob. "Or maybe he was messing with you."

Jael shakes her head. "Not him. We're . . ." She can't quite find a way to articulate the familiarity she felt with that sad former halfbreed. "I just feel like we understand each other."

"Oh," says Rob, and nods kind of stiffly.

"Wait," says Jael. "Are you, like, jealous of a telepathic ram?"

"What? No!" says Rob, and scoffs. Then after a moment, he shrugs. "Maybe just a little tiny bit."

She reaches out and takes his hand. He looks at her, smiling sheepishly. She leans in a little and slips her arm through his. It feels comfortable. She decides having a boyfriend is pretty awesome.

When they get to school, Father Aaron is standing at his usual post just inside the front door.

"Miss Thompson, Mr. McKinley," he says. "Good morning."

"Morning, Father," says Rob.

"Uh, Rob," says Jael. "Do you mind if I meet you in homeroom?"

"Huh? Yeah, sure," says Rob. He awkwardly removes his arm from hers and continues down the hall.

"Hey, Father," says Jael after a moment, "is Monsignor okay?"

"He's better than he deserves to be," says Father Aaron. "The bishop has asked that he retire, effective immediately. We're telling the students it's due to health concerns. He'll live out his remaining days safety cloistered away in a remote monastery. His classes will be split between Father Ralph, your father, and me."

"Who will be my—"

"That hasn't been determined yet. Everyone will get his or her new teacher assignment by tomorrow." He says it like he's dismissing her.

But she stays.

"Was there something else, Miss Thompson?"

"Yeah," says Jael. "Thanks for not . . . making assumptions about me."

"Miss Thompson," he says with the same glowering expression as always. "You are a student in my care. Nothing more. And nothing less. Is that clear?"

"Perfectly, Father," she says.

"Good. Now go to class."

The Mons's sudden retirement is announced by Principal Ou over the PA system and there are a lot of rumors, but none of them have anything to do with the truth. Britt doesn't show up, but Jael isn't too surprised. She knows they're going to have to talk eventually, but Jael isn't quite ready for that yet.

But other than an awkward glance exchanged with Father

Ralph in the hallway, the whole day goes eerily well. Jael can't shake the feeling like she's holding her breath, waiting for the other shoe to drop. So it's almost not even a surprise when she runs into Jack on her walk home from school. He's just standing on the sidewalk, like he's been waiting for her. He looks like when she first met him in the bookstore, a college student with long, wild black hair and sharp blue eyes.

"Nice to see you again, Jael," he says cheerfully. His hands push back the sides of his old sports coat and he tucks them into a slick pair of distressed jeans.

"Hey, Jack," she says. "What do you want?"

"Quite a job you did on that priest yesterday," he says casually, like they're talking about the weather. "It's been a long time since I've seen an exorcism blow up in someone's face like that. Had me in stitches for hours."

Jael isn't about to ask how he knows about the exorcism. "I didn't think it was funny," she says.

He shrugs dramatically, his pale blues eyes sparkling. "Well, you're young yet. You'll grow to appreciate things like that. I'd be the first one to admit, it's an acquired taste."

Jael feels like she's past getting jerked around by people, and she's about to ask this asshole who or what he really is when a sudden gust of wind comes up and blows his long hair back for a moment.

He's missing an ear.

Belial.

"Shit," she says, and tries to run. But he grabs her by the neck and jerks her into the air. She flails around and gasps for breath that barely comes. She tries to poke his eye or pull his hair or kick him in the balls or anything to get him to let go, but he keeps her at arm's length, just out of reach.

"Ah yes," he says, patting the old wound on the side of his head with his free hand. "A parting gift from your mother. Something to remember her by, I suppose." His smile takes on a hard edge. "And believe me, I will never forget. Or forgive."

His smile curls all the way into a snarl, then he slowly presses his thumb into the soft skin under her jaw. She gasps and makes a weird barking sound, like a seal. Her vision narrows and spots start to appear. Consciousness begins to slip away.

Then he loosens his grip enough for her to breathe. She gulps at the air greedily.

"Oh, I'm not going to kill you," he says. "Not right now, anyway. If I had been able to find you when you were a baby, I would have gobbled you up without hesitation. But now . . ." He brings her face up close to his and she can see rows of sharp little teeth. His breath smells like static electricity. "I'll tell you frankly, I was somewhat undecided how to handle you for a little while. But once I saw just how weak and ineffectual you are, how easy to manipulate, I thought, perhaps she can be of some use, in her own pathetic little way."

"Do what you want to me," says Jael in a hoarse voice. "I won't help you with whatever scheme you've got planned."

"Planned?" asks Belial. "No, no, my dear. The 'plan' already happened. It started several hundred years ago. This"—he gestures around them—"is precisely what we wanted. War, poverty, disaster, et cetera. It's all going like clockwork. Which makes it a bit dull, I'm afraid." He pinches her cheek. "And that is why I enjoy your antics so much. When one lives forever, a laugh now and then is very much appreciated. That delightful romp with the priest is only the beginning. I have such marvelous entertainments in store, my little clown freak."

He tightens his grip again, and she gasps.

"Oh, to be sure," he says, "I'll kill you eventually. I must, you see. You are utterly repulsive. It's only the heaps of pain and torment I plan to inflict on you that makes touching you even bearable. Halfbreeds are an abomination that don't belong in Hell or Gaia."

"I am all mortal and all demon. I have a right to both places."

"Oh, that's lovely," he says, giving her a winsome smile. "Who told you that? Your uncle? Or perhaps your mother, right before I tore her to pieces."

She takes a swing at his face, but he catches her wrist and holds her out at arm's length again. His grip suddenly gets so cold it feels as if her wrist and neck are encased in ice. He seems larger now. As big as Dagon. His skin takes on a silvery sheen, and his features sharpen until they look like they were carved with a chisel. Everything about him becomes jagged and sharp, panes of broken glass and ice. His hair curls out to either side, like two thick black horns.

"Ah yes, I can tell already I've made the right choice. This will be quite a lot of fun," he says, his dry, crackling breath on her face. "You know what? I am going to do you a favor. Give you a little clarity. So that when you hear these charming opinions from your family, you'll understand where they're coming from."

He pulls her close to his chest, pinning her arms to her sides. He presses his crystal cheek against hers.

"This may be a little uncomfortable," he says.

Ice spreads rapidly out from his body and encases her in a gleaming, jagged shell. She screams and strains against him one final time, then her scream is cut short as a layer of ice covers her face.

There is nothing but darkness and pain. Sight, sound, and even thought are not possible. There is only the endless, raw scrape of ice on skin. She spends a moment or a year in the ice tomb. It doesn't matter, because there is really only one endless moment of hopeless, crushing agony.

At last the ice crumbles away. She sucks in ragged mouthfuls of dry, hot air, unable to see anything other than splotches of dark, flickering colors. Her body throbs with the echoes of pain from the ice. She hears snarls and cackling laughter and the sound of tearing meat, and she knows that she is somewhere else.

Belial drops her to the ground, which feels like rough stone. She struggles to her hands and knees, straining through her blurry vision to make sense of this place.

As her eyes gradually recover, she sees that they are in a vast hand-carved cavern of a hall. The only furniture is a rectangular table that stretches hundreds of feet long. An airplane-size chandelier hangs overhead. It looks like the skeleton of a giant octopus, if an octopus had bones. Many different creatures crowd around the table. Some are squat and round, others impossibly thin. Most of them seem to be a mixture of animal and human. One tall, thin creature looks like a man with mule legs and a giant peacock tail. Another has three heads: one man, one bull, and one ram. Wasn't that how Asmodeus described himself? But now he's acting like he doesn't recognize her. Not that she blames him. Then she sees two that she knows she's seen before. Baal, the giant oxlike demon who tried to attack her when she was eight, and Amon, the wolf-headed demon with the snake tail that attacked her and her father when she was a baby in Haiti.

All of the creatures drink from seashells, gourds, or skulls. They stuff chunks of dripping, quivering meat into their mouths. None of them seem to notice Jael or Belial.

Amon slithers up from the bench onto the table itself.

"Where's the bread!" he howls.

"Bread! Bread! Bread!" the others yell.

Jael sees movement from a small doorway in one corner of the hall. Her uncle squeezes through, balancing a stack of platters in each hand. His scales are dry and cracked from the heat.

"Coming, coming . . . ," mutters Dagon.

The stuff on the platters doesn't look much like bread. Most of it is greasy and ridged with bits of sharp bone. It seems to move sluggishly across the platters.

Dagon hurries over to the table, but when he gets close, Baal sticks out an iron hoof and trips him. The platters of strange bread go flying. Some pieces make it to the table, others crash to the floor. Dagon falls on his face and Baal steps on his back. All the creatures laugh and cheer, "Crush him, Baal! Crush him!" as Dagon struggles to get free of the massive creature. At last, Baal releases him and turns his attention to the meal. The rest join him, climbing onto the table or scrambling under it as they fight over the slippery chunks of spilled bread. Dagon gets slowly to his feet, clutching his back as he makes his way through the doorway and into the kitchen.

"There, you see?" whispers Belial into Jael's ear, his razor lips glinting in the ruddy light. "Your uncle knows his place in Hell."

Amon lifts his muzzle up from the pile of food in front of him. "Belial?" he barks.

The others look up as well.

"What do you have there?" asks Amon.

"It's none of your concern," says Belial.

As soon as Belial's focus is turned toward Amon, Jael makes a dash for the small service door her uncle used. Her cold limbs scream at her, but she grits her teeth and keeps running.

"What is that?" screeches the peacock man.

"Meat!" howls Amon.

She hears flapping, creaking, slithering, and scratching as the group of demons follows after her.

"Stop!" she hears Belial say. "She's mine!"

"But, Your Grace," whines Amon, "isn't that—"

There's a brittle snapping sound, like dry twigs, and a sad, doglike whimper.

"Anyone else?" asks Belial.

Jael slams clumsily into the door, wrenches it open, and

hauls herself through. She jerks it closed behind her, looking for a lock or something to keep it shut. There's nothing.

She assumed the doorway led straight to Dagon's kitchen, but instead she's in a narrow hallway lit by a foul-smelling phosphorescent fungus that clings to the ceiling in shapes like handprints.

"My dear." She hears Belial's voice behind the door. "Where in Hell do you think you're going?"

She hears a chorus of cackling laughter as she lunges away from the door and careens down the hallway as fast as her wobbly legs will let her. She tries not to notice that the glowing fungus is creeping down the walls toward her.

She reaches a T-shaped intersection where she can go left or right. Both alleys look exactly the same.

The fungus on the walls is on her level, now. Thin tendrils reach tentatively out to her.

Far behind her, the door to the banquet hall slowly creaks open.

"Oh, Jael, dear . . . ," calls Belial.

Jael takes the passageway on the right.

The farther she goes, the less fungus there is, and the darker it gets. Soon she has to keep her hands out in front of her because she's afraid of running into a dead end. After a short while in the darkness, she has no idea if she's missed other passageways or if she's even in a hallway anymore. Her footsteps sound different, no longer a tight echo. She reaches out a hand but doesn't feel walls in any direction. She is completely exposed, utterly lost, and stumbling through impenetrable darkness. Panic starts to take hold, and her breath comes in short, ragged gasps. She feels dizzy and lightheaded, so she hunches over with her head between her knees.

As her breath slows down, she hears a steady, quiet rumble off to the right. It sounds like rushing water. Maybe it's where her uncle lives. She heads toward the sound, still keeping her hands out so she won't run into a wall. After a few minutes of fast walking, she trips and falls forward onto the bottom of a stone staircase, slamming her palm onto the edge of one of the steps. The pain of impact shoots through her body and she curls up on the gritty steps, clutching her hand until it passes. Then she gets back on her feet and climbs.

As she ascends, the sound of rushing water grows louder. A dim, ruddy glow comes from somewhere ahead of her. At the top, the stairs taper off as they lead to a narrow outcropping, where the path simply ends. She peers over the edge and sees a canyon twenty feet deep. A river flows through the center of the canyon, but it isn't water. It's lava.

"Ah, there you are." Belial's voice echoes from the darkness at the bottom of the steps. She whirls to face him, but the only thing she can see are two luminous blue eyes getting slowly closer. "I thought you might run for the kitchen. But perhaps you already knew your uncle wouldn't be able to help you."

Jael looks down at the seething river of lava, then back at the approaching eyes of Belial.

She jumps.

There's a moment of weightless queasiness, then she hits.

The orange liquid is thicker than water, so she doesn't sink down too far. After a few hard kicks, she breaks the surface.

She scans the edge of the canyon, but Belial isn't following. Maybe it's too hot for an ice demon. If that's true, she might have stumbled onto the perfect escape. Now she just needs to figure out how she's going to get out of Hell.

All her clothes have burned off, of course, but she quickly shifts her skin to look like clothes. At a time like this, it seems like a very silly, mortal thing to do, but it makes her feel better. Then she begins to swim with the current, moving to the center of the river and downstream. After a while, the cliffs on either side slowly shrink down until the shores of the river are only slight hills of black volcanic rock. It looks a little jagged, but Jael is getting tired of swimming, so she decides to head for shore.

But the lava is so thick, it feels like she's swimming through oatmeal. After a few minutes, she's only made it halfway to the riverbank. Then the current picks up. The surface gets choppy. Quick slaps of bubbling orange splash her face. A little bit makes it into her mouth and the sudden searing pain leaves her gasping.

Then she sees a large fin, like a shark's, jut out of the lava about twenty feet away. She stops swimming and tries to keep her head above the surface with as little movement as possible. The fin veers off to the right and makes a slow, wide circle around her. It's a glossy pitch-black, like obsidian, with jagged edges. For a moment, its head breaks the surface, and milky quartz eyes glare at her. It cuts through the strong current and thick lava easily as it circles, getting closer with each revolution.

All of her attention is on the fin, so it takes a while for her to look past the tightening circle to see the choppy current downriver. Then her ears pick up the deep roaring sound of a waterfall. Or would that be lavafall?

She needs to solidify this lava. Then the shark thing would be trapped and she can just walk to the riverbank. She can't believe she didn't think of it earlier.

She pleads with the lava, extolling every virtue of coolness and solidity that she can think of. But it mocks her. It heats itself up even more, then sloshes around and hurls itself into her mouth and eyes. She gives a yelp of pain. Clearly the elements of Hell aren't interested in helping her out.

The obsidian shark is close enough that she can see rows of diamond teeth. Her skin may be tough, but she's pretty sure it's not *that* tough. She makes a break for the riverbank, her arms and legs flailing wildly. But the creature speeds up and launches itself into the air, then descends on her in a wall of diamond teeth.

There's a roar and flash of fur, and the shark is knocked away. Jael struggles to turn herself in the rough current. The shark is wrestling with a three-headed demon. It's Asmodeus. The ram and bull heads slam furiously into the side of the obsidian creature while the man head turns toward her and nods solemnly.

Then she goes over the falls.

When she hits, she shoots all the way to the river bottom. For a moment, the lava pounds down on her from above and holds her pinned there. Her lungs scream for air and she thinks to herself, *Is this it? Am I going to die now?*

But then that image of her mother comes into her head again. Those piercing green eyes do not show weakness. They do not give up.

Jael forces herself up against the pressure of the lava and kicks off from the bottom as hard as she can. Her eyes are burning and she has to clench her teeth to keep from taking an involuntary gasp. Finally she breaks the surface and swims wearily to the riverbank. Despite the searing heat of the lava, the bank is covered in ice and snow. She climbs up onto a snowdrift, panting and coughing. The illusion of clothes does absolutely nothing to protect her skin from the snow and freezing winds. But at least she can breathe.

"You know, my dear," says Belial, looming over her with piercing eyes and an easy, glittering smile, "it's really best to stay with the tour guide on your first trip to Hell."

Jael pulls herself up onto her knees, looking for an escape. From the lava riverbank, the snow-covered field stretches out past her line of vision, broken only by scattered outcroppings of jagged ice. The sky is a dull gray, and mottled black storm clouds scuttle quickly from horizon to horizon. She tries to get to her feet, but she stumbles in the deep snow and falls over.

She feels Belial's hard crystal hand close around the back of her head. Then he lifts her into the air.

"The Grand Duchy of the Northern Reaches," he says, slowly rotating her around so she can get a good look. "Isn't it lovely? I do the landscaping myself, you know. In fact, over there you can see one of my favorite spots."

He gestures to a small cluster of neatly pruned hedges huddled in the snow. It's an odd burst of green in the otherwise colorless landscape.

"Does it look familiar?" asks Belial. "No? You were much too young to remember, I suppose."

He takes hold of Jael's upper arm and drags her over to the hedges.

"Allow me to introduce you," he says. "Jael Thompson, meet Astarte, your mother."

Jael looks up at him, blinking stupidly.

Belial says, "Oh, they didn't tell you that part, I suppose. You see, Jael, souls cannot simply cease to exist. Mortals die and their soul goes to wherever it is they go. But not demons. Our souls are . . . stuck, if you will. So when I ate your mother, she didn't cease to exist. Nor did she flutter off to some afterlife. She just changed shape and composition."

"Composition . . . ," Jael says, and looks back at the cluster of hedges.

"Yes, my dear," he says pleasantly. "I digested her and shit her out here. Then I planted some hedges. Demon manure makes excellent plant fertilizer. These hedges have adapted to the climate remarkably. Thanks to your mother. Or what's left of her."

Jael struggles against Belial's cold grip and he lets go. She drops to the ground, then pushes her way through the snow, first at a stumble, then on hands and knees until she reaches the hedges. The leaves are a glossy dark green with sharp ridges.

"Mom?" she says.

"Oh, she can't understand you, I'm sure," says Belial. "In fact, I'm fairly certain that she doesn't really have a consciousness anymore. After all, she's spread out among twelve hedges. A bit hard to concentrate, I would imagine. I suppose she could eventually get herself back together. But she'd have to evolve one step at a time. In a few thousand years, she might reach her original state, assuming she managed to hang on to enough memories to remember who she is." He shrugs and strides over to Jael. "It will be interesting, regardless."

"This isn't her," says Jael. "You're lying."

"Your doubt is understandable," he says. "Go ahead and touch her."

Jael reaches out and puts her fingertips on one of the leaves. A series of confused images floods through her mind, too blurry to make out. Then, for just a split second, she catches one clear image. It's a baby, only a month or two old, in the arms of a man. The baby has curly black hair and bright green eyes. The man is in his thirties, with brown hair and fewer wrinkles, but there's no doubt. It's Jael's father.

"Mother," she whispers. Tears start to well up, but she fights them off. They sting the corners of her eyes as they freeze.

"You may have noticed that I keep her immaculately pruned." Belial reaches out and snaps a branch from one of the hedges. He holds the branch up and picks the leaves off, one at a time. "I'm not sure if this causes her pain, but I like to think so."

The leaves drop to the snow around Jael and she stares at them numbly for a moment.

"I'll kill you," she says quietly.

"Sure you will, my dear," says Belial, and he pats her on the head. "And with that, I'm afraid this concludes your tour of Hell. You're not ready for the truly upsetting places in my humble home. But I hope you've gained a better understanding of how your little family fits into the big picture here. The bottom of the heap. You, my dear, are filth beneath even them. And I am slowly, lovingly scraping you away bit by bit. You see, I am not some gourmand bent on a quick, gluttonous binge of brutality like Beelzebub, my dear brother to the south. No, I am a connoisseur of suffering who appreciates the anticipation nearly as much as the consummation. I will take your friends and family and destroy them from the inside out. I will bend you to my will, force you to do truly terrible things. And then, finally, when you have run out of uses, I will devour you. If you have proved entertaining enough, who knows. Perhaps I will be kind enough to shit you out here with your mother so you can finally be together. Although I fear your halfbreed nature might befoul Hell even then."

He laughs, a sound hard and shrieking, like a buzz saw on sheet metal. Then he lifts up one foot and shoves it down on her back, pressing her face into the snow. She struggles weakly as he continues to push down on her. She sinks deeper and deeper into the drift. It seems bottomless. Then she suddenly breaks through the other side and she's lying on the sidewalk, back in Seattle.

Her father is making dinner when she walks through the front door.

"How'd it go today?" he asks from the kitchen.

This is the part where she's supposed to tell her father that it's all over. That they're completely screwed. But she doesn't.

"Great," she says with as much enthusiasm as she can muster. She goes up to her room and quickly pulls on some real clothes. Then she starts hunting through the piles of half-clean laundry on her floor for her phone. If Belial really plans to get at her friends, Rob is the most obvious target.

But of course she melted the phone in her room two nights ago. So she goes back downstairs and calls Rob from the kitchen phone, keenly aware of her father's presence as he cooks dinner.

"Hello?" says a woman's voice.

"Hi, Mrs. McKinley?" says Jael cheerfully. "This is Jael Thompson, Rob's friend?"

"Ah, yes!" says Mrs. McKinley. "Jael! We've heard so much about you! Rob just won't stop talking about you. So when are we finally going to get to meet you?"

"Oh, uh, whenever Rob asks me over, I guess," says Jael.

"Right, right, well he can't hide you from us forever!" She laughs, then continues to make small talk for several minutes. Jael forces out calm, upbeat responses, fighting the urge to scream. At last, Mrs. McKinley says, "Well, Jael, it's been lovely chatting with you. I suppose you really called to talk to Rob."

"Is he available?" asks Jael.

"Of course! He's been standing here glaring at me for a little while now."

"Great!" says Jael with real enthusiasm. Belial hasn't gotten to him yet.

"Hold on one sec," says Mrs. McKinley.

There is a muffled sound, then, "Soooo, that's my mother," says Rob.

"Hey," says Jael. Her father is setting the table right next to her. "Um, how's it going?"

"Uh . . . fine. Why?"

"No, just wondering," says Jael. "So, what are you doing tonight?"

"I'm in for a real exciting time," he says. "It's family Scrabble night at the McKinleys'."

"Oh, so you'll be in your house all night, huh?" she asks.

"Yeah . . . Hey, are you sure everything is cool?"

"What? Of course. I think that's a great idea. You should definitely spend time at home with your family tonight."

"Okay, you're totally freaking me out now. Is this code or something?"

"By the way, that was really nice of you to walk me to school this morning. How about I return the favor tomorrow? I'll swing by your house tomorrow morning and we can walk together."

"All right, so I'm starting to think you don't want me to leave my house unescorted. . . . Bets, should I be worried about something?"

"You bet!" she says cheerfully. "So, you just have fun at home tonight and I'll see you tomorrow morning."

"Jael," says her father. "Dinner's ready."

"Okay, well, gotta go!" she chirps.

"Wait, Bets, can't you just —"

She hangs up and takes a slow, deep breath, waiting for her

heart to slow down a bit. Then she turns and sits calmly at the table.

Jael and her father eat in silence for a little while, Jael with her leftover squash, her father with a sandwich. Then he puts his sandwich down and looks at Jael.

"I was terrified," he says.

"What?" asks Jael, her pulse shooting back up.

"Yesterday," he says. "I was so sure I'd lost you."

"Oh," says Jael.

"It was like I was back in Haiti, helpless to save you. For all the things I've done to protect you, I realized that you were right. I never considered anything past your physical well-being. I've never really been much of a parent to you. Your mother . . . would not have been pleased." He looks down for a moment, squeezing his hands together in a fist, almost like a prayer. Then he looks back up at her. "I'm sorry it took that fear for me to realize it. But I'm going to do everything I can to make up for it."

Jael bites her lip and smiles. She's wanted to hear something like that for so long, but it tastes sour now. Empty. Because it will all end soon. And she doesn't even have the guts to tell him.

"Everything okay?" he asks.

She nods and somehow manages to pull it together enough for a sincere-looking smile. "Yeah, totally."

"I know," he says. "You're worried that I'll be teaching your religion class?"

"Uh . . . yeah," she says, forcing a laugh. "A little."

"Well, don't. Father Aaron volunteered to take yours."

"That's great," says Jael. "What a relief."

That night, Jael sits on her bed and seriously considers running away from home. Maybe it's not too late to do what her mother did. Draw Belial away from everyone she cares about.

Then she catches the smell of spoiled fish.

"Hey," says her uncle. He plops down on the bed next to her, the box spring groaning in protest. He sits there with his elbows resting on his thighs in a strangely human pose.

"I saw you at the feast hall today," he says quietly. "With Belial."

She nods.

"You okay?"

"For now."

"He take you to your mother's grave?"

"Yeah," she says. "If that's what you want to call it."

"Sorry you had to see all that," he says. "A long time ago, it was all different. . . ." He trails off into silence.

"You said that before," says Jael. She doesn't mean for it to come out bitter, but it does.

"Belial was just a petty sprite named Jack Frost, and your mom and I were . . . well, I guess you might have called us gods."

"So . . . what happened?"

"Things changed," Dagon says. "People changed. The whole damned world changed. It didn't want magic in everyday life anymore. And us? We reflect what the world wants us to be. And right now, that's demons." He's silent for a while, lost in thoughts or memories Jael can't even guess at. Then he smiles slightly and looks at her. "But things changed before. They can change again."

"Sure," says Jael, but she can't really muster up any confidence in her tone.

The sound of Jael's father putting away dishes travels up from the kitchen.

"You didn't tell your dad," says Dagon.

"You think I should?"

"It's up to you," says Dagon. "I've never been good at deception."

"He says he's cool now. That he believes in me. But something like this, I think it would turn him right back and he'd just want to move to Alaska," says Jael. "And it's not like he could do anything about it."

"Probably not," Dagon says.

She leans back against the headboard and shuts her eyes. "Why?" she whispers. "Why does Belial hate me?"

"Revenge. For what your mother did," he says. "And because you're a halfbreed. He's obsessed with purity. Demons aren't what they used to be, and he sees halfbreeds as one more step toward utter degradation."

"Yeah, he said something like that."

"The other thing is, you could screw up what he and the other Grand Dukes are doing. They've had it their way for hundreds of years. It was the halfbreed Merlin who helped them consolidate their power."

"Merlin really was a halfbreed, then? That's what Rob thought."

"Smart guy," says Dagon. "Yeah, it was that asshole Merlin who helped turn everything upside down. So it stands to reason only a halfbreed could make it right again. In other words, kid, you're dangerous to the Grand Dukes' status quo."

"Asmodeus said I have all this power or something. But how, exactly, am I so kick-ass dangerous?"

"You can influence the elements on Gaia."

"But *all* demons can do that."

"Not on Gaia they can't."

"I thought . . . isn't it supposed to be a demon power?"

"Yeah, but the elements only pay attention to someone who belongs here. And us Hell-born demons don't. The weaker ones have to possess mortals just to be here. And even those of us who have been around awhile and are strong enough to be here without a host are really only here in spirit."

"You feel real enough. And so did Belial." She shudders involuntarily at the memory of being encased in ice. "So wait, if demons can't do anything on the mortal plane, how'd Belial take me to Hell?"

"Spirit isn't limited to a single plane. It's on all of them at once. You could say it's what they have in common. So demons can affect spirit regardless of what plane they're on."

"So Belial attacked my spirit?"

"That's all demons can ever do on Gaia. But that can be pretty serious if the demon knows what he or she's doing. And Belial is one of the best. A demon can also project their own spirit outward. Your mother would do that often, as fire."

"Uh, yeah, I've had a little experience with that," says Jael, and clears her throat uncomfortably. "I almost burnt Rob's face off this morning."

"It can be very powerful," says Dagon. "But you have to be careful, because you can expend too much of your own spirit that way."

"What happens if you do that?"

"Well, for full demons, they get weak, then eventually dissipate into an incorporeal state. It can take months to recover from that."

"What about halfbreeds?"

"I don't know," he says. "You probably just die."

"Oh."

"But as long as you're on Gaia, you shouldn't need to use spirit all that much. Try to use the other elements as much as possible."

"Right," says Jael. "Because that's where I have the advantage over Belial. On Gaia, I have all five elements; he only has one."

"Exactly," says Dagon, his black eyes sparkling. "Look, you've got amazing potential, kid. Your mother believed it. I believe it. It sounds like you've got Asmodeus in your corner. I think even your dad is coming around. And I bet there are people you don't even know who believe in you. The only one who doesn't is you. And that's the trouble. If you don't have faith in your own abilities, it's never going to be anything more than potential."

"But how do I do that? I can't just *decide* to believe in myself."

He gives her a gently teasing smile. "Well, that's the trick, isn't it?"

• • •

Britt doesn't know how long she's been walking, or why. She moves slowly through the night, her arms hugging her torso tightly. She shivers now and then, as if an icy wind has just passed through her. She recognizes the world around her, the streets and houses of northwest Seattle. But it all looks strange to her now, filled with ominous shadows. In her ears, she hears the shriek of an old man. A priest. The *Mons*, that's who it is. Weird that she couldn't remember him for a moment there. But why was he screaming?

Jael. Something happened to Jael. She was . . . possessed? Can that really be true? But Jael had been acting strange lately. She talked about it with Jack and he told her to talk to the Mons. And when she talked to the Mons this morning . . . Wait, was that this morning? No, it was . . . a different morning. Yesterday? Or a week ago? How long has she been walking out here? Out in the wilderness, among these dark, inscrutable houses. She remembers that the Mons wasn't strong enough to defeat the demon. The darkness had won. God had abandoned them. . . .

But then she sees a light ahead. It shines white and pure in front of her, and it pushes back the darkness.

"Brittany . . . ," calls a voice from the light.

Maybe she's dying. But she doesn't care. She's so cold, so scared. She runs toward the light. She sees a figure stretching a hand out to her.

She pauses for a moment.

"Jack?" she asks.

"Yes," he says, his voice like a thousand volts of electricity that wipe out all thought, all fear. "It's time you know who I really am. You have been so helpful, so brave. But I must ask one more task of you if we are to save your friend Jael from the darkness that has her in thrall."

"Anything," says Britt as she walks toward the light again. Toward him. And as she gets closer, he changes, growing larger, more beautiful. His skin shimmers like crystal, his eyes blaze with such an intense blue that she feels as though he can see into her very soul. "Jack," she sighs. "You're an angel. . . ."

Belial smiles as he gathers her into his hard, shining arms.

"Something like that," he says. "Now, my dear. To work."

trip trap

18

The phone rings at around eleven o'clock. Jael is lying in bed, trying without success to get to sleep. The sound comes from the kitchen so abruptly, it makes her flinch.

Maybe it's Rob, she thinks. She needs to get that phone before her father does. She scrambles out of bed and heads for the staircase. She hears him opening the door of his bedroom, so she just vaults the handrail. A moment before impact she asks the air to slow her down so that she lands quietly on the hardwood floor.

She slips into the kitchen and snatches the phone off the cradle just as her father enters.

"Hello?" she says quietly.

"It's Aaron," says a harsh voice. It takes Jael a moment to realize that it's Father Aaron on the line.

"Father? What—"

"Jael?" There's a pause. "Put your father on the phone."

Jael turns to her father, who looks half asleep and irritable in his pajamas. But she tells him who it is, and he snaps suddenly awake. He takes the phone from her and says in a calm, quiet voice, "Yeah?"

He listens for a few moments, his face set in that old neutral expression she's known her whole life. His eyes flicker over to Jael and he says, "There's no reason to bring her into this."

He listens to the response, his mouth set.

"But what if—" He is cut off by a shout on the other end so loud Jael can almost make out the words from several feet away. Jael's father listens a few more moments, then says, "Okay, we'll check."

He slams the phone hard on the cradle and stares at it for a moment. Then he turns to Jael.

"Get dressed. We're going over to the Broughers' house."

Sick dread lies heavily in Jael's stomach during the short drive. Of course Belial went after Britt. Why didn't she think of it sooner? Britt was the vulnerable one, especially after that exorcism. She remembers now that the last time she went to the Broughers' house, Ms. Brougher was on the phone with someone named Jack. He was probably setting this all up even back then.

They park out in front of the house. But her father doesn't open the car door. He just sits there, staring out the windshield.

"I like to know what I'm walking into," he says. "Aaron has been watching the Broughers since he noticed Heather displaying some erratic behavior yesterday. The sort of behavior that might suggest demon tampering or possession. Neither of them showed up at school today, and they aren't answering phone or e-mail. He's concerned that something may have happened to them. If you know anything about this, if you even have a suspicion, I need to know about it. Now." Then he just waits.

"Belial found me," she says.

"When?" His face is still neutral.

"I guess he's known where I was for a couple of days now, but I didn't realize that until today."

"You saw him?"

"Yeah."

He nods, almost to himself. "Game's up, then. It's almost a relief."

"Sorry I didn't tell you right away, Dad. I just—"

He holds up his hand. "No point in that now. Let's go."

They climb out of the car and walk up the steps to the front porch. Jael notices that the piles of junk have been neatly organized, which unnerves her. Jael's father knocks on the front door. They wait a few moments, but there's no answer.

"Is there a key?" he asks her.

She nods and points to a crucifix hanging next to the door.

He takes it down and turns it over. The back has been hollowed out and a key stuck inside. He laughs to himself, a short humorless burst through his nose, then takes out the key and unlocks the door.

"Stay behind me," he says. It's stupid, of course. Jael could take a lot more damage than her father. After all, he's just a mortal. But there's a strange confidence about him now. It dawns on Jael that this is not the first time her father has had to face things that could crush him in an instant. That old firm decisiveness she hasn't seen in a few days is back. And while that quality makes for a crappy dad, maybe it makes for a good demon hunter.

He pushes open the door and calls out, "Heather?"

Silence.

"Brittany?" he calls.

Nothing.

He walks slowly, quietly into the house, and Jael follows close behind.

"Dad," she whispers, and points to the walls. All of the crucifixes have been turned upside down.

He nods and continues through the living room.

A very faint humming comes from the kitchen, accompanied by a wet, scraping sound.

"Dad," she says again. He looks back at her questioningly. He doesn't seem to be able to hear the strange noise.

"The kitchen," she whispers.

He nods. "Stay back," he says, and starts making his way over.

Of course, Jael is right behind him as he enters the kitchen.

"Jael," snaps her father, "I said—"

But it's too late. She's already seen it.

The Brougher kitchen is a long, narrow, brightly lit room with lots of cute country kitsch. Ms. Brougher sits on the floor, her feet tucked under her. She's wearing some of Britt's clothes, which are painfully tight on her, and her thick blond hair is pulled up in uneven pigtails. She's rubbing a sheet of sandpaper on her cheek in slow, circular motions and humming to herself. When Jael and her father come in, she looks up at them and smiles. Patches on her face, arms, and hands are reduced to bloody, raw muscle and tendon.

"The wrinkles come right off!" she tells them cheerfully. "I'm young again!"

Jael's father kneels down beside Ms. Brougher and gently pulls the hand with the sandpaper away from her face.

"That's amazing," he murmurs soothingly, like he's talking to a child. Except he never talked to Jael like that when she was a child. "How did you learn about such a wonderful thing?"

"Oh, it's so obvious, I can't believe I didn't think of it myself!" she says, and tries to continue rubbing her face with the sandpaper. He holds her blood-streaked arms at her sides.

"Yes," he agrees. "Who told you about it?"

She frowns for a moment, like she's trying to think of the answer, but then her smile widens even more and her eyes get glassy.

"Oh, it's just a miracle!" She sighs.

"Heather," he says to her a little sharply, like he's losing patience. "Where's Britt?"

"Who?" she asks.

"Your daughter," he says. "Where is your daughter, Brittany?"

"No, no," she says with a sly smile on her ravaged face. "I'm much too young to have a daughter!" Then she looks him up and down suggestively. "You know, I don't normally go for older men, but for you I'll make an exception." Then she leans in, her bloody lips puckered.

"Okay," he says with forced cheerfulness as he holds her at arm's length. He looks over at Jael. "Sorry, honey, I'm going to need you to take a look inside and see what's going on here. Can you do that for me?"

"O-o-okay," she says. She kneels down beside her father and looks at Ms. Brougher, trying to ignore the bits of skin that dangle from her cheekbones and chin.

"Ms. Brougher," Jael says quietly to get her to make eye contact.

"Ms. Brougher?" she says in a horrified tone, her eyes rolling around. "That's my mother's name!" Then she giggles in a high-pitched whinny.

"Heather!" says Jael.

Ms. Brougher's eyes meet Jael's for just a moment, and that's all she needs. She dives quickly down into Ms. Brougher's soul. Or what's left of it. It just looks like a big clump of ice, silent and still. Jael touches it tentatively, expecting a welter of memories and emotions to hit her. But there's nothing.

"What do you see?" She hears her father's voice from far away, like an echo.

"He's completely frozen it," she hears herself say.

"See if you can thaw it out," her father says

She begins to stoke her inner fire. It isn't hard. All she has to do is think about Belial and what he's done to Britt's mom. And if he's done something like this to Britt, then it doesn't matter if he's stronger than Jael. She's going after him, and she's not going to give up until one of them is dead. Screw school and a normal life. She will dedicate herself to getting this bastard who ate her mother and tortured her friend. She will make him pay for everything he's done.

She looks back at the sad clump of ice that is Ms. Brougher's soul. She blows a slow breath like a hot desert wind across it until the ice starts to run, then crumbles. Brilliant life explodes all around her, like a lush garden suddenly appearing from beneath a bed of frost. She wants to snatch it up like she did the fire, to bring it inside and feel it roar within her. She wants to . . .

Then Ms. Brougher screams and Jael is suddenly back in the kitchen with her father. Ms. Brougher screeches like an animal, her hands extended clawlike in front of her.

"My face! My hands! God, what happened to me!" she wails. She's sobbing and flailing about. Jael's father tries to restrain her, but she's pumped full of adrenaline and easily knocks his hands aside.

"Heather!" he shouts. "Please! Calm down! We're here to help!"

"Brittany! Where's Brittany?" she moans.

"We're trying to find her," says her father. "Please, I know you're in a lot of pain, but we really need to find Brittany before —"

"My face! Why the hell does my face hurt so much?! Where's Brittany? BRITTANY!"

Jael's father is trying to wrestle her to the floor.

"Dad, should I . . . "

Her dad shakes his head. "I can handle this," he says. "Just go get some first-aid supplies so we can get her cleaned up."

She knows she could hold Ms. Brougher down much more easily than he can, but it doesn't seem like a good time to argue. She hurries down the hall to the bathroom. She grabs gauze, tape, antibiotic cream, and anything else that looks like it might come in handy. On her way back, she hears a phone ring. The cordless sits on the back of one of the easy chairs. She grabs it, thinking maybe it's Father Aaron checking up on them.

"Yeah?" she says as she carries the supplies back to the kitchen.

"Jael?"

She freezes.

"Britt?"

"Yeah."

"Uh . . . you okay?"

"I'm better." Her voice sounds hollow and indifferent.

"Oh," says Jael carefully. "Well, that's good."

"Can you come meet me?" asks Britt. "I'm calling from a pay phone down at that coffee shop on Thirty-fourth in Fremont."

"Uh, yeah, sure. I'll be there as soon as I can."

"Oh, great," says Britt without enthusiasm. "See you soon."

Jael puts the phone back on the charger. A quiet calm settles over her. She knows that it's a trap. She just hopes Britt isn't so far gone that she can't bring her back. Because Jael will bring her back, or die trying.

Back in the kitchen, Ms. Brougher has settled into a low whimper, clinging to Jael's father with bloody hands. Jael tosses the medical supplies to him.

"I'm going to get Britt," she says, and turns to go.

"What?" says her father. "Jael, wait! What are you—"

"Dad, you can't leave her here alone. But someone has to get Britt." She heads for the front door.

"Wait! Jael! Shit!" he yells at her. "How will you get there?!"

"Run," she says, and she's gone.

Jael sprints down the sidewalk, stretching her body as far as she can. Her breath moves evenly in and out and her muscles buzz with heat as houses flicker past on either side. She can barely hear her footsteps. It's almost as if she's walking on air.

And why can't I? she wonders. So she starts calling out to the air beneath and in front of her. *Let's see how fast we can really go.*

Her next step lands an inch off the ground and she skates along with a smooth, frictionless glide. She soon picks up so much speed that the world is little more than a whirling blur. Despite the serious shit-storm she's headed for, she can't deny the rush of this moment.

Then there's a loud crack and blinding pain, and she sprawls out on the asphalt. She's just run into a brick wall.

It takes her a second to get her breath back, but otherwise she doesn't feel too bad. She climbs to her feet and looks around. She's already made it as far as Ballard, where the street runs diagonally, which is why running in a straight line brought her into a supermarket parking lot.

"Maybe not quite that last," she mutters. But she can't help but smile a little as she dusts off the bits of debris from her jeans. The wall looks like someone went at it with a sledgehammer. She did that.

Then she starts to run again.

Jael finally slides to a stop in Fremont, a funky little

neighborhood on the shore of Lake Union. A block farther down she sees the coffee shop. Britt sits at one of the little sidewalk tables that overlook the houseboats strung along the lakeshore. She's hunched forward, oblivious to the beautiful view, just staring at the curb. She's still wearing the same clothes Jael saw her in the day before. Her hair is a blond haystack.

Jael walks up to her cautiously, but Britt doesn't react. So Jael finally says, "Britt."

Britt looks up at her, and it takes a moment for her eyes to focus. One corner of her mouth twitches spastically, and her lips are dry and cracked.

"Hi, Jael."

"You doing okay?"

"Yeah. Yeah, I am. Doing okay." Then she stands up, slowly, like she's sore. "Come on. I want to show you something."

"Uh, sure," says Jael. It's such an obvious trap. But then, since she can't refuse it anyway, maybe that's the point. She can almost hear Belial's taunting laughter as she follows Britt down along the lakeside until the sidewalk passes beneath Aurora Avenue and the George Washington Memorial Bridge. Then Britt turns up a steeply inclined side street that runs beneath the bridge.

Jael says, "Do you want to, uh . . . talk about—"

"I understand what happened," says Britt.

"You . . . you do?"

"Yes, of course."

Jael waits for more, but Britt just keeps walking up the hill, her eyes again distant and unfocused.

"So . . . ," says Jael. "What do you think happened?"

They reach the top of the hill. Nestled into the spot where the slanted street meets the base of the bridge is a twenty-foot-high statue of a troll. It's hunched forward, long hair partially covering its brooding face. The endless rains of Seattle have stained and eroded its face so that its one exposed eye seems to weep. In one hand it clutches a life-size VW Bug.

"Trip trap, trip trap," mutters Britt.

"What?" says Jael.

"Huh?" says Britt. Her eyes grow wide in the harsh yellow streetlight. She suddenly smiles, the corner of her mouth still twitching, and a thin line of drool rolls down her chin. "Monsignor was unworthy of performing the exorcism. So God allowed you to defeat him. But I have found someone who is worthy." She turns toward the troll, and Jael follows her gaze. Three figures in white monk robes now stand at the base of the statue, their hoods pulled low over their faces.

"Britt . . . ," says Jael.

"This is Brother Jack of the Ancient Order of Vetis," says Britt, her voice dreamy. "And he is here to exorcise the demon from your soul."

Belial steps out from the line and pushes back his hood. He's in his mortal form, but his long black hair sweeps up to the sides, suggesting his horns, and his pale blue eyes glitter like gems.

"Jael, darling," he says. "What a delight to see you again so soon."

"Britt, you've got to snap out of this!" says Jael in a low voice. She grabs Britt's arm and shakes her. "This is the guy who killed my mother!"

Britt's crazy eyes waver slightly, and her fixed smile droops.

But then Belial calls out, "Remember what we talked about, Brittany!"

"Yes, Brother Jack," says Britt, her smile lighting up again, the twitch working overtime. "It's exactly like you said."

"Britt!" barks Jael. "I will drag you out of here by your hair if I have to."

"Do what you want to me, demon!" yells Britt, throwing her arms around Jael. "I will do whatever it takes to save my friend from your evil clutches!"

"Britt! Stop it!" says Jael. She tries to peel her off, but she doesn't want to hurt her in the process.

"Don't worry, Jael," whispers Britt. "I know you're still in there somewhere. I won't give up on you, even if I have to burn with you in Hell."

"Touching, isn't it?" says Belial. He's right beside them now. He lays a pale hand on Britt's matted, dirty hair. "See what her love for you has reduced her to?"

"Okay, asshole," says Jael. "You got me. Now, let her go."

"Jael, my darling, you're missing the point entirely," says Belial. "I already had you. The real fun is using you to destroy this sad little creature and watching you suffer for it."

"Britt! Can't you hear this? What is wrong with you?"

"Some mortals are astonishingly easy to beguile," says Belial. "She only hears what I want her to hear. Her mother was a rush job, but this one I spent some time on. I slowly infected her spirit until I became almost an extension of it. Then I began, very carefully, to change it. If you're too rough about it, they usually just go mad, like her mother, and are useful only as a distraction. But if you do it just right . . ." He taps Britt on the forehead. "That's enough, dear," he says to her. "We can take it from here."

Britt lets go of Jael and collapses to the ground like a doll.

Belial turns back to Jael. "If you do it right, you have a very fun and useful toy! Now, I brought some old friends of yours along. Well, perhaps 'acquaintances' is the more appropriate word." He steps back and gestures to the two cowled monks behind him. "Boys?"

The two monks step toward her. Beneath their hoods, they have human faces, but their eyes flash with a luminous glow that is anything but mortal. One is massive, with hulking shoulders and an almost square head. The other is tall and thin, with a long nose, pronounced overbite, and glittering amber eyes.

"I believe you've met Baal and Amon already," says Belial.

"My, my little girl," says Amon, leering at her. "How you've gro—"

Jael slams him in the chest with a fireball and he flies backward into one of the cement pillars supporting the bridge. She snaps a second fireball at Baal, who staggers, but doesn't fall.

"Put him down," says Jael, and a blast of wind responds by slamming Baal to the ground so hard that the asphalt cracks beneath him.

While the two struggle to rise, Jael slings Britt over her shoulder and makes a break for an intersecting street. There's a mass of people just a few blocks away. Belial has kept a low profile so far, and Jael hopes he won't attack them out in the open.

But then Belial calls out, "Brittany! A little assistance, please!"

Britt suddenly explodes in a fury, scratching and biting at Jael like a wild cat. Jael grits her teeth and holds on to her as she runs. Britt starts bucking and flailing until her leg gets caught between Jael's legs. Jael can't stop in time, and she trips. She hears a sharp crack as Britt's leg breaks, then they both topple over in a heap.

Once they're on the ground, Britt hisses and spits, still clawing at Jael's face with her fingernails. Jael tries to contain her without making her broken leg worse.

"Thank you, Brittany," says Belial.

She goes limp. As Jael struggles to untangle herself, Amon and Baal come at her from either side and slip a loop of thin wire around each of her wrists. They hold the glittering wires with thick leather work gloves, and when they pull in opposite directions, the wire, cut into her skin and draw blood. She sucks in a breath and swallows a scream as they stretch her arms out to either side.

"It's silver, if you're curious," Belial says, nodding at the wire. He grins wide enough for her to see his sharp little teeth. Then he lifts the unconscious Britt up by her neck and holds her at arm's length. Her eyes are rolled back in her head so that only the whites show. Foamy yellow spit dribbles from her lips. She's covered in scratches and bruises, and her lower leg is tilted sideways like a half-broken tree branch. Still holding her aloft, Belial walks back toward the troll statue. Amon and Baal follow him, half dragging Jael across the asphalt by the silver wires.

They stop in front of the troll and Belial gazes up at the massive sculpture. Amon and Baal hold the silver wires so tight that Jael's arms are stretched out to the sides as far as they will go. Every time she strains at the wire, it slices deeper into her skin. Blood runs down her forearms and drips from her elbows to the asphalt.

"Ah, 'Three Billy Goats Gruff,' wasn't it?" says Belial, still looking at the troll sculpture. "Trip trap, trip trap! Who's that tripping over my bridge?" He pats the stone troll's massive fist fondly. "Charming story. And there's a moral, too. Crossing bridges is dangerous stuff. So is wanting more than you deserve."

He regards Britt for a moment, then lets her drop to the ground.

"On your feet, girl," he says.

Her head jerks up and she slowly gets to her feet. Jael can hear quiet crunching sounds as the bones of her broken leg grind together.

"Sister Brittany," says Belial. "I believe your friend can be saved, but it will take a serious sacrifice."

"Anything," Britt whispers, her mouth slack. "I'll do anything."

"But are you worthy?" asks Belial. "You have so many sinful thoughts in that head, you little whore."

"Yes, yes, yes . . . ," whispers Britt. Tears collect in her glassy eyes.

"You must beat out the sin before you can save your friend."

"Yes . . ."

"You know what you must do."

"Yes." Then she hobbles slowly over to the statue, her broken leg bowing out more with every step.

"Britt, stop!" yells Jael. She struggles against the wire until her arms are slippery with blood, but she can't shake the loops. They have cut so far into her flesh that they're embedded in her skin.

"Belial, that's enough!" she yells. "I'll do whatever you want."

"No, my dear," he says. "It's not nearly enough. And you're already doing what I want you to do. Suffer. Which I am enjoying immensely."

Britt reaches the statue. She clasps her hands together in prayer. Then she smacks her forehead into the gritty stone fist. When she lifts her head back up, a dark bruise is already forming.

"More, Brittany!" shouts Belial. "Beat out all the sin! Make yourself clean!"

Britt slams her head into the stone again, then again. A purple lump grows on her forehead.

"Britt! Stop!" yells Jael.

But Britt keeps pounding her head into the troll statue. A spot of blood is starting to form on the stone. She sways from side to side in between each hit, clutching the statue for support. A pointed jut of bone is clearly pressing against the inside of her jeans.

Jael turns to glare at Amon, and he looks back at her with a smug grin. She stares into his eyes, trying to drill down into his soul to grab at anything she can. But there is nothing. No passage. Only his cruel amber eyes.

That doesn't make sense. Everything has a spirit, even demons. She felt her mother's spirit in those hedges. Belial himself said that demons had a soul. So why doesn't she see anything past his eyes? It really seems like there's nothing there.

There is nothing there, says the air. *Something is occupying the space*, it says, *but it's not there.*

There's nothing standing there, says the earth. *Something is pressing down, but there's nothing there.*

Her uncle told her that Hell-born demons are only in Gaia in spirit. The reason she can't see the spirit in Amon's eyes is because he is *all* spirit. But if Amon is only spirit, then he's just another element she can influence.

"Go," she says.

Amon flinches and his human appearance melts away to reveal his true form, the wolf-headed serpent creature. But then he shakes his head and growls at her, giving the wire an extra-hard tug. She can't force him any more than she can force any other element to do something it doesn't want to do.

"Fine," she says. "Let's see if I can *convince* you to leave."

She asks the air in his lungs to leave. It does so, gladly. Amon's eyes go wide as the vacuum begins to turn his lungs inside out, and he drops the wire, clutching at his throat.

She brings her free hand up, ready to hit him with a fireball. But then something slams into her so hard that she flies through the air and smacks into the stone troll's face. Baal has changed into his true form—the ox of iron, wood, and stone. He charges at her again, his eyes blazing within his stone ox's face. Jael holds her bloody hands clasped together, stoking the rage within.

She remembers that image of him stepping on her uncle. She remembers how terrified she was of him as a little girl, and the nightmares that followed for years afterward. When she releases that rage, a jet of fire blasts Baal's face so hard that both he and Jael are knocked off their feet.

Jael struggles to pick herself up off the ground, but her hands aren't working too well and she feels dizzy from blood loss. Baal's wooden parts blaze with fire now, but he is able to get back to his feet. He snorts and smiles a crumbling ash grin. He paws the earth, preparing to charge.

"Sing," she says, and stretches out one pale, red-soaked hand.

As Baal begins his charge, the fire that clings to him grows higher.

"More," says Jael, and she stands her ground.

The flames thicken, burning almost blue with heat. Baal roars in pain, but continues his charge.

"More!" says Jael.

The flames leap up high enough to touch the bridge overhead. There is a thunderous crack and Baal crumbles, skidding in several directions at once.

She looks at the smoldering pieces of Baal that still struggle to rise, then at Amon, writhing on the ground, clawing at his throat. Their spirits are weak now. Easily commanded.

"Leave Gaia or I will destroy you," she says.

They disappear.

Jael turns to Belial. He has also shed his mortal form, and his razorlike body glitters coldly in the streetlight.

"Well," he says. "It appears I may have underestimated you."

"You and me both," says Jael, and she hits him in the face with a fireball.

He hisses with a voice like steam, clawing at his face. Then he hurls a sheet of ice at her, but she waves her hand and it melts, the water splashing the concrete in front of her. She tosses another fireball at him, but he's ready for it this time and easily knocks it aside.

Jael gathers the silver wires that still hang from her wrists and comes at him, skating on a layer of air. He pauses for a moment, confused. It's all she needs. Just as she's about to run into him, the air flips her up and over him. As she passes over his head, she loops the wires around his neck. She lands behind him and pulls as hard as she can, ignoring the searing pain in her wrists. The wires pull tight around Belial's neck. He claws at it for a moment, panic on his face. But then his eyes narrow, and he grabs at the wires between them and hauls Jael toward him.

"Please," she says. "Help me."

The earth rumbles beneath them. Belial's eyes go wide for a moment. Then the ground beneath him splits open and swallows him up to his shoulders.

"You can't kill me, you idiot!" he snarls.

"I don't need to," she says. She winces as she pulls the wires from her wrists. Then she gives them a jerk hard enough to make him gasp.

"What are you . . . going to do," he wheezes. "Wish me away . . . like you did . . . those fools?"

misfit

She takes a deep breath, gathers everything she has, and screams, "*I banish you!*"

He flickers, then disappears.

For a moment, there is silence. Jael takes a slow, deep breath as the adrenaline begins to fade and the pain in her sliced wrists gets louder.

But then Britt turns from the statue, wobbly on her broken leg, her face a mass of blood and dirt. She laughs like crackling static. "Stupid halfbreed!"

"Get out of her!" shouts Jael, and grabs Britt.

"Come in and make me," Britt snarls.

Jael dives into Britt's soul. The mess she finds is even worse than Ms. Brougher's. It's one giant frozen mass of jagged edges. The air is biting, noxious, and Jael almost gags.

A large white worm burrows into the soul as if it were dirt, leaving gaping holes behind. It pauses for a moment, waving its eyeless face in her direction, then quickly turns and begins to tunnel deep into the center of the soul.

Jael scrambles across the soul, slipping, stumbling. She catches the worm's tail just as it's about to disappear. The worm feels like she's grabbed the coils of a deep freezer. It's so cold, the skin on her hands starts to crack and split. The thing wriggles like a cord of stringy muscle as she hauls it up out of the hole. It whips around and catches her cheek, leaving a long, red ice burn. She stumbles backward, still holding the worm, and her foot touches a small section of a memory that hasn't been frozen over.

Abruptly, she is inside Britt's kitchen when Britt was five years old. Britt sits at the table, eating a peanut butter and jelly sandwich while her mom sits on the floor with a bottle of wine in one hand and a phone in the other. The sound of the dial tone is so loud it almost drowns out Ms. Brougher's quiet sobs. This was the moment that Britt understood that parents are just people. That they aren't invincible, and there are many things they can't, or won't, fix. . . .

Jael is back among the icy shards of the soul. She staggers across the uneven surface as she tries to hold on to the wriggling worm and keep her footing at the same time. The worm bunches up, then snaps its midsection at her face. She jerks back, just barely avoiding it. But she slips and falls into another memory.

She is at Britt's eighth birthday party. The sound of girls' laughter can be heard in another room. But in this room, the bathroom, it is just Britt, biting her lip so she doesn't cry, and her thirty-year-old cousin telling her she'll go to Hell if she tells anybody. . . .

Jael comes out of the memory, gasping for air. The worm has its tail wrapped around her neck. Ice spreads out onto her shoulders and up to her chin. It feels like her head is being squeezed from her body.

She tries to gather some heat, but there's nothing in this place to pull from. It's going to have to come from within. But she can barely stand. She needs . . . something. She's hungry. Empty.

She nearly falls into another memory, but she catches herself on a small frozen shard of Britt's soul that juts out from the rest.

That's all she needs. Just a bite. Just something to bring

some warmth back in. If she doesn't do it, they'll both be dead anyway.

The worm squeezes harder, and the skin on her neck cracks like frozen concrete.

Jael breaks off a tiny piece of Britt's soul and swallows it. It hits her stomach like a bomb, sending warmth and raw power out to every inch of her body. She rips the worm off her neck and holds it up above her head.

Belial's voice shrieks, "I will destroy you! You freak! You abomination! You—"

"Go to Hell," she says.

Fire engulfs the worm, and then there's nothing left.

She brushes her hands across Britt's spirit. It leaps back into life, flickering and dancing with a joy so beautiful and hypnotic, Jael wants to reach out and—

No. No more. She's had a taste and she wants it all, but she wrenches herself out of Britt's soul and stumbles back onto the asphalt.

Britt lies in a heap on the ground. Jael drops down next to her and leans against the rubble of the troll's massive fist.

"J-J-Jael . . ."

Britt looks up at her through unfocused, blood-encrusted eyes.

"It's okay, Britt," pants Jael. "I . . . we did it."

"Jael, I'm . . . I'm . . ." She shuts her eyes and tears cut through the drying blood to stream down her bruised cheeks. "Hurt."

"Yeah," says Jael. "You are."

Jael's body still buzzes with power, so she shakes off her own pain, kneels down, and gently picks Britt up. Then she turns and sprints all the way to Swedish Medical Center in Ballard. It's late and no one's out. She skates down the middle of the street on a cushion of air, careful not to jostle Britt's broken leg. The whole time, Britt presses her face against Jael's shoulder and whimpers quietly. Jael doesn't know whether it's out of pain or fear. Probably both.

In a few minutes, they're at the hospital. She walks through the sliding-glass doors of the emergency room and lays Britt on the counter. The nurse stares at her.

"Broken leg," says Jael. "Among other things."

Then she turns and runs out before they can stop her.

As she speeds up Seventeenth Avenue, she thinks, *Broken soul, too. But who's going to fix that?*

She continues north toward home. But the burst of energy is nearly spent. The pain in her throat, hands, and wrists becomes more and more insistent. She feels cold again, dizzy. It gets harder for her to stay upright. She's lost a lot of blood. By the time she reaches her house, the air not only supports her feet, but her hands as well, as she fights to stay upright. She staggers through the door, her vision dim and her own harsh gasps like thunder in her ears.

Her father runs toward her, yelling her name. She tries to reach out to him, but she misjudges and falls flat on her face. She tries to push herself up, but her hands aren't listening to her anymore.

"Father . . . ," she whispers.

Strong, fishy-smelling arms lift her up from the ground.

"I'm cold . . . ," she says.

Her uncle wraps her in blankets while her father rummages through the closet for first-aid supplies. The two of them are yelling at each other. She can't really make sense of it. But she sees the tears in her father's eyes, the anguish in her uncle's expression, and she understands.

"It's okay," she says hoarsely. "I did it."

They stare at her.

"Did . . . what?" her father asks.

"I kicked Belial's ass," she says.

Then she passes out.

healing

19

Jael's father insists that she stay home from school the next day, and she doesn't argue. Her throat is so sore she can barely swallow, and her wrists hurt so much she can't even lift her bag.

She lies in bed, her wrists bandaged in big lumps of gauze, and her neck wrapped from her collarbone to her chin in gauze so thick that it looks like a neck brace. She thinks it's a little excessive, but it gave her father something to do other than freak out while she told him what happened. Or most of what happened.

"I've made as many fruit smoothies as I could," he says as he peeks into her bedroom. "I put them each in individual glasses in the fridge."

"Thanks, Dad."

"I put a pack of straws on the kitchen table," he says. "So you don't have to keep lifting the glasses."

"Cool."

"Try to avoid using your hands. Get as much sleep as you can," he says.

"Will do."

"Dagon will be by in a little while to check on you."

"Great."

"Are you sure you don't want to go to a doctor?"

"Dad, how are we going to explain to them that if they want to stitch me up, they're going to need a silver needle to pierce my skin? I'll be fine. It's healing really fast."

He lingers in the doorway. "Can I get you—"

"Go to work, Dad."

"Okay, okay. See you tonight."

A little while later, Jael makes her way down to the kitchen. She has to eat almost constantly while her body directs all its energy toward healing itself. She tries not to think about the fact that the little piece of Britt's soul she took is helping her recovery as well. She only hopes that Britt can recover too.

She grabs a smoothie from the fridge and sits at the kitchen table, staring out the window at the mottled, slate-gray clouds.

"And there is the greatest niece who ever lived!"

Dagon appears next to her, his grin so wide she can see halfway down his throat.

"Hey, Uncle D," she says.

"Belial is trying to hush it up, but the rumors are flying all over Hell."

"Why didn't you tell me I could do something like that?" asks Jael. "Banish demons."

"Because I had no idea you could do something like that,"

says Dagon. "I don't even think Merlin could banish a Grand Duke."

He sits down at the table. It's too small for him, and he looks like an adult in a kindergarten room.

"Can Belial . . . come back?" asks Jael.

"Nope!" says Dagon. "No one you kick out can come back. Unless you invite them back, of course."

"Yeah, well I'm definitely not going to do that," says Jael. "So . . . that's it, then? It's over?"

Dagon's smile fades. "Oh. Well, no. I mean, the other Grand Dukes aren't going to be pleased. It makes them all look bad. And a lot of their power is based on intimidation."

"Other Grand Dukes? As powerful as Belial?"

"Yeah, there are three others," he says. "And they each have a few generals. And all the lesser imps, of course. Then there are those outside the control of the duchies. Like . . ." He glances at her and she must be looking a little panicked because he stops, and then says, "Well, Hell's a big place. Lots of people are going to want to take a shot at you."

"Yeah . . . ," says Jael, suddenly feeling tired.

"Listen," Dagon says. He leans in very close, his black eyes glinting ".Jael. Life does not give you too many victories, especially ones like this. You better damn well appreciate them when they happen."

She lowers her eyes. "You're right," she says. "I know I should. But . . . there's something else. Something I didn't mention when I was telling you and Dad what happened."

Dagon waits.

"Things were pretty bad and I didn't think we were going to make it, so I . . . I ate a piece of Britt's soul to give me a boost."

Dagon leans back, his chair creaking loudly.

"Ah," he says.

"Yeah."

"Well, that explains a lot."

"Is she going to be okay?"

"Well, you didn't eat the whole thing, did you?"

"No, no, just a little piece."

"She'll probably be fine, then."

"So . . . it'll grow back?"

"No. She's never going to get that piece back. Something will always be missing."

"But what?"

"Who knows? Mortals are funny things. You might not even notice a difference in her. Most likely, it'll be a smaller change than the one you're going through."

"Me?"

"Oh yes. A demon isn't really an adult until they've tasted a mortal soul. It's a rite of passage."

"But I don't want to eat people's souls!"

"And you don't have to do it ever again," says Dagon. "But you did it. You're on the other side of the line now. You understand the real relationship between demons and mortals—predator and prey."

She knew it all along on some instinctual level. From the

first time she saw Rob's soul. Even now, despite her guilt, she feels the hunger deep inside, and it brings a flush to her cheeks.

"You look tired," says Dagon.

She nods.

"I have to get back to work, anyway. Why don't you lie down for a little while."

"Yeah," says Jael. "Good idea."

He helps her over to the couch, and she immediately drops off to sleep.

When she wakes up a few hours later, Dagon is gone, but there's an old yellow envelope sitting on the coffee table next to her. It's sealed, and it has the jagged handwriting that she recognizes as her mother's. The bandages make it hard for her to get the envelope open, but eventually she figures out that if she coaxes a little steam under the flap, the glue dissolves.

> *Dearest Jael,*
>
> *If you are reading this, then you have truly become a demon. Whatever state of existence I am in, know that somehow, some way, I am proud of you. This letter has been in Dagon's safekeeping all these years because there are some things no mortal can handle, not even your father. Understandably so—one of those is the consumption of mortal souls. Most demons look at it in the same way that mortals look at eating the flesh of animals. Some do it, others do not. Even in my darker days, I always viewed*

it as a terrible thing that should only be done in the most dire of situations, and even then done as delicately and as sparingly as possible.

I have no doubt that you would not have done it unless it was absolutely necessary. Even so, you probably feel a tremendous amount of anxiety about it. And that is good. You should never be comfortable with it.

As you explore your new power and identity as a demon, don't forget that you are also mortal. It is vital that you do everything you can to maintain that balance. Of course, since it is so rare for someone who is both demon and mortal to survive as long as you have, I don't really know how you should go about doing that. Hardly anyone does. When you are ready, seek out the demon known as Abigor. He was Merlin's father, and perhaps knows better than anyone what surprises and challenges might be in store for you. He owed me a few favors and has already pledged to assist you, should you call upon him.

Continue to deepen your connection to the elements. That is essential. But it is just as vital that you maintain strong bonds with your mortal friends. Do not use this experience as an excuse to avoid them. Cherish and protect them at all costs. If you give yourself in love, you will never lose yourself.

Love,

Your mother,

Astarte Thompson

A part of Jael wishes she had this letter before. But she knows that she wouldn't have been ready for it. She's barely ready for it now. She sinks back into the old stuffed sofa and closes her eyes, trying not to recall the warm rush of Britt's soul coursing through her.

Then she hears Rob's familiar footsteps come up to the front door, and a hurried knock.

As soon as she opens the door, he starts talking in one hurried rush. "Bets! Are you okay? You were all freaky on the phone yesterday, then you didn't show up this morning like you said you would. Your dad passed me in the hall at school and didn't tell me anything, just said, 'Come over!' Don't people know how much that can freak a guy out? I was all set to skip school, but Father Aaron was watching me like a hawk. Like he knew something was up, too! Why can't anyone just tell me what happened?!"

"If you take a deep breath and sit down," says Jael, "I'll tell you."

"Okay. You're right."

Once he's a little more calm, she tells him almost everything about last night. Maybe someday she'll tell him the one missing part, but not today. When she's done, he just gives her a satisfied smirk.

"Well, well, well. I don't want to say I told you so," he says. "But . . ."

"Yeah, yeah, you were right all along," says Jael. "Thanks. For believing in me even when I didn't. It means a lot."

"You want me to fix those bandages?" he asks. "I mean, no offense to the Mummy King look, but your dad has no idea what he's doing."

"I don't know . . . ," she says. "They're probably still pretty gross."

"Bets, I'm a skater. I can handle a little blood. Trust me."

"All right."

His gentleness surprises her. He carefully unwraps the tangle of gauze that her father swathed her in. The wounds already look a lot better than they did last night. The frostbite on her hands and neck has settled into little more than a minor burn. Only her wrists still look raw and a little bloody.

"It's the silver," she says.

"I thought that was werewolves," he says.

"There's no such thing."

"I'm not dismissing anything at this point."

He puts new bandages on, and Jael has to admit they're much more comfortable and functional.

"Thanks," she says.

"Of course," he says.

"I have a favor to ask," she says. "I want to go visit Britt in the hospital."

"Okay . . ."

"And, um . . . can you come with me? I would just . . . feel better."

"Sure," he says. "But I don't really get what you're worried about."

"I don't know how she's going to react to me."

"You saved her life."

"I don't know if she knows that. And anyway, I'm also the reason she got dragged into all this."

"You can't think like that," says Rob. "You didn't choose any of it."

"But if I had disappeared, like my mom did . . ."

"He probably would have done the same thing or worse to draw you out anyway."

"I guess . . ."

"No 'I guess.' Belial is a total ass-faced goon. It's not your fault. Period."

She looks at him for a moment. At his open, earnest face, and his sparkling if somewhat scattered soul. And she smiles.

"Fine," she says. "But will you still come with me?"

"If you want, I'll follow you all the way to Hell," he says.

"I really hope it doesn't come to that."

As Jael and Rob walk down the bright fluorescent hallways of the hospital, Jael keeps her bandaged hands deep in her pockets. Even though Rob did a good job on the bandages, they're still obviously homemade, and Jael doesn't want some nosy nurse looking too closely.

"Hospitals give me the creeps," Rob says.

"Nobody likes hospitals," says Jael.

"Doctors and nurses probably do."

"You'd be a good doctor."

"Nah. Western medicine is too invasive, you know? Drugs and surgery, that's all they do around here."

"So you'd rather be a . . . what?"

"A healer," he says. "A magician. A shaman."

She stops in the middle of the hallway and stares at him. He chews on his lower lip, and looks everywhere but at her as a slow blush creeps onto his face.

"You're dead serious, aren't you?" she asks.

"Yeah," he says.

"All the alchemy and chemistry stuff. That's all for this, isn't it?"

"There was just one thing I was missing," he says. "One thing that stopped me from going any further. To be a real healer, or shaman, or whatever the hell you want to call it, you have to have faith. You have to believe in something. And I didn't. Until I met you."

"Whoa, whoa," says Jael. "I'm not some kind of god or anything."

"No, no," he says. "I don't want to, like, worship you or anything weird like that. But I feel, deep in my gut, that you are important. That you are doing something important. And it's my job to help you do it." He looks up at her now, and his hazel eyes are strong like she's never seen before. It's almost unnerving. "I believe that. Does that make sense to you?"

"God, you sound like my uncle! Do we have to do this in a hospital hallway?"

"Come on. I've been wanting to say that for a while, and I finally said it. Just give me an answer."

His gaze is too direct, too honest. Now it's Jael's turn to

avoid eye contact. "I get how you could think about it like that. Maybe. But that's not how I feel at all. There's no grand plan. No secret destiny that I'm supposed to fulfill. I'm just trying to survive without hurting people in the process."

He shrugs, and that easy smile of his comes back. "Maybe that's what I'm supposed to do. Help you believe too." Then he just continues walking down the hallway to Britt's room.

"Okay, all this self-empowerment talk is really starting to . . ."

But then they're at Britt's room, and the words evaporate from her lips.

"I didn't realize she was that bad," whispers Rob.

Britt is asleep in bed. Bandages cover the top half of her head, and her face is a mass of stitches and swollen bruises. Her leg is raised in some kind of pulley contraption, with stabilizing pins protruding out of both sides from the middle of her shin to the middle of her thigh.

Britt's mom sits next to her bed. Her own face and arms are covered in bandages. She looks up at Jael, her eyes red and raw and exhausted.

"Hi, guys," she says. "Thanks for coming."

"How's she doing?" asks Jael.

"She's stable," says Ms. Drougher. "The thing they're most concerned about is—"

"Jael?" says Britt, her voice cracking and popping like an old vinyl record. Her eyes are crossed.

"Yeah, Britt. I'm here." She walks over to Britt's bed.

"I need to get some fresh air," says Ms. Brougher. "I'll let you guys have some privacy."

When Ms. Brougher is gone, Britt smiles faintly. "She's been here the whole time. I don't know if she's even gone to the bathroom. . . ."

"So, how are you feeling?" asks Jael.

"The drugs they've got me on are pretty intense, so I don't really feel much pain. But I can't see too well right now. My eyes won't focus."

"Do you remember what happened?"

"I guess I got kidnapped by some cult. When I got here last night, I was pretty messed up and screaming about monsters and demons. . . ." She swallows, and it sounds like it hurts. "The police think they drugged both me and my mom. I don't remember a lot. Some guy with these really intense blue eyes. A lot of time wandering around the city . . . and for some reason I remember the Mons, Father Aaron, and Father Ralph . . . but I know that can't be true. It's like a dream, you know? Most of it doesn't make any sense."

"Do the police know who did it?"

"I don't know," says Britt. "They don't tell me much." She squints toward the doorway. "Someone else here?"

"Hey, yeah, Britt," says Rob, and he steps a little closer. "Sorry, I just didn't want to get in the way."

Britt closes her eyes and smiles slightly.

"Rob McKinley and Jael Thompson," she says. "I totally called that, like, a year ago."

"So is there anything we can do?" asks Jael.

"I wish I could watch TV or read a magazine," says Britt. "I wish I could see something clearly."

Rob nudges Jael's foot. Jael looks back at him and he's cocking his head toward Britt and mouthing silently *"Heal her."*

She mouths back, *"What?"*

He points at the spot between his eyes.

Jael looks at Britt, who seems to be falling asleep, then back at Rob.

He nods encouragingly.

She reaches out hesitantly and touches her fingertip to the same spot on Britt's head. She asks Britt's eyes to focus.

Britt's eyes snap open. She sits up slightly in the bed and looks directly at Jael. "My eyes . . . ," she says. She looks around the room. At Rob, at the machines in her room, and finally at her own broken leg.

"Thank God," she says with a sigh. "That was the worst part. Not being able to see how bad it was. Anything would have probably been better than what I pictured in my head."

"You can see fine now?" asks Jael.

"Yeah. How weird is that? Something must have just slipped back in place."

"That's great," says Jael.

Britt leans back in her bed. "Ouch, she says. "That was maybe a little more movement than I'm ready for." Then she looks back at Jael and a frown rumples up the bandages and stitches.

"It was you, wasn't it?" she says.

"What?" says Jael, unable to hide the panic in her voice.

"You dropped me at the hospital."

"Oh," says Jael. "Yeah."

"I thought so, but I didn't tell anyone." She looks down at Jael's bandaged hands. "They hurt you too, didn't they?"

"Yeah," says Jael.

"I'm sorry you got dragged into it."

"No, it's their fault. Those guys that did this to us."

"They're still out there, aren't they?"

"No," says Jael. "I . . . took care of them."

"You . . . ," says Britt. "How?"

Jael just continues to look down at her hands.

"I don't want to know, do I?" asks Britt.

"No."

Britt looks up at the ceiling and takes a slow, deep breath. "Thanks," she says.

Jael nods.

The little machine attached to Britt's IV whirs as it dispenses medication.

"And thanks for coming to visit," says Britt. "You too, Rob. Nobody else . . ."

"Of course we came," says Jael. "What are best friends for?"

"I remember . . ." Britt's eyes are getting hazy and her voice sounds dreamy. Like whatever was just put into her IV is really knocking her out. "I said some stuff to you, didn't I? Mean stuff. I can't really remember why, but . . ."

"It's okay," says Jael. "It's over."

"Yeah," says Britt, and her eyes close. "It's over. Water under the bridge. Trip trap, trip trap . . ." Then she's asleep.

"I can't believe she forgot everything," says Rob as they're walking through the halls to the exit.

"She hasn't," says Jael. "I think she remembers all of it. She just doesn't understand or believe it." Jael thinks of the memories she saw in Britt's soul. "She's really good at believing what she wants to believe and ignoring the rest."

"I guess we all are, in a way," says Rob.

"Not me," says Jael. "Not anymore."

They walk on in silence for a little while.

"How did you know I could do that?" asks Jael. "Heal her."

"No idea," says Rob with a shrug.

"Skater Zen," says Jael.

They step out of the bright, harsh hospital and into the dark, wet night. The wind and rain greet Jael like eager puppies. She stops a moment and just stands there, breathing in a smell so fresh and alive that it washes away all her tension.

She looks up into the night sky at the endless expanse of stars that spreads in all directions. She feels it pull at her spirit. This time she doesn't fight it, though. She rides it like a wave. She trusts that it won't let her fall. It's cold out there among the stars, and lonely. But that's okay. She's been both of those things and she knows it won't kill her. Since she stays calm, she is able to see that it is terrible, but also beautiful. And when it's time, she slips right back down to the ground and into her body where she belongs. She shivers and sighs.

"Uh . . . ," says Rob. "Everything okay?"

"Yeah," says Jael. "It is."

They take the bus back to Jael's house. When they're

at the door, Rob says, "I got to get home. You sure you're okay?"

"Yeah," says Jael, and she smiles. "Thanks for coming."

They stand there for a moment. Rob seems suddenly a little nervous. "So . . . do you have any plans for Friday?"

"Well, I was planning on kicking it with a few angels, but . . ."

Rob stares at her.

"Kidding, Rob. Kidding."

"Are angels real too?"

"How would I know?"

"I don't know . . . maybe . . ."

"They probably do exist, but I'm pretty sure they wouldn't be interested in hanging out with me."

"Well, anyway," he says. "Are you doing anything?"

"No, why?"

"My mom said I could borrow her car."

"Wait, are you . . ."

"A real date," says Rob. "You know. Dinner, movie, the works. You can even pick the movie."

"Like, a dumb romantic comedy?" she asks.

"The dumbest you can find."

"How about a dumb, foreign romantic comedy?"

"I do not fear subtitles."

"But I don't want you to pay for everything," she says.

"Pay?" he says. "I'm totally hurt. If there's one thing I'm good at, it's exploiting hookups from friends."

"Right," says Jael. "The amazing McKinley hookup."

"Great," says Rob. "See you tomorrow at school?"

"Yeah, I think I'm ready," she says.

He steps in quickly and kisses her, soft and sweet. Their breath mingles and she leans into him, holding him, but not too tight this time. When she's this close, she can feel the hum of his soul through his skin and it's enough. It's just right. They are together.

"Good night," he whispers into her ear. He slips away, looking back at her with that smile, then walks down the street humming to himself.

Jael stands there for a little while, watching him go, his taste and smell still lingering. She's beginning to understand that she has to savor these little moments, hold on to them for as long as she can. They always seem like they will last forever. But they don't. So she has to take them as they come.

When Jael walks into the kitchen, she is greeted by an unexpected sight. Ms. Spielman sits at the kitchen table with her father.

"Ah, Jael," she says as she stands up. "Your father said you'd had an accident and I wanted to see how you were feeling."

Jael gives her father a look, wondering what kind of accident he told her about. He just nods encouragingly to her.

"Yeah, I'm feeling okay," she says.

"Well, I know rock climbing is very popular," says Ms. Spielman, "but could you stick with the more moderate cliffs for a while?"

"Sure," Jael says.

"Oh, good," says Ms. Spielman. She turns to Jael's father. "Paul, see you tomorrow."

"Of course," he says, and smiles.

"Jael, I brought a get-well card signed by your class, but I must have left it in my car. Why don't you come with me to get it?"

"Okay," says Jael. As she follows Ms. Spielman out to the street, she says, "That was nice of everybody."

"Well, of course," says Ms. Spielman as she unlocks her car door and leans in to pick up a card. "Your classmates adore you."

"They do?"

"Certainly. It's almost as if they can't help themselves." She hands Jael the card.

As Jael takes it, Ms. Spielman looks at her bandaged wrists.

"Yikes," she says. "Looks like that hurts."

"It does a little," says Jael.

Ms. Spielman reaches out and takes hold of Jael's wrists. It's so unexpected and it happens so fast, Jael doesn't have time to react. But instead of more pain, she feels a sudden warmth, then all the pain is gone.

"What . . . ," she says as Ms. Spielman releases her wrists. She rotates them experimentally, then opens up the bandages. She is completely healed. She looks back at Ms. Spielman. "How . . ."

"Remember, Jael. There are many mysteries in life. And not all of them are monsters."

Ms. Spielman winks at her, then gets into her car and drives away without another word.

Jael walks slowly back into the house.

"Dad," she says. "You can do magic, right?"

Her father looks up from chopping vegetables at the counter. "To an extent. Why?"

"Are there other mortals out there who can do magic?"

"There are all different kinds of people who do many different kinds of magic. Some priests truly have the power to exorcise demons, and sometimes other abilities as well. And then there are priests or ministers in other religions. For example, my friend Poujean is now a powerful and well-respected *bokur*, or priest, in the Vodoun religion of Haiti. There are also mages — mortals with a demon familiar that they can channel magic through. That's what I am. Or was, really. There are oracles, who can tell the future to a greater or lesser extent. Empaths can read spiritual auras. And of course, a wide variety of witches and healers, all with varying abilities." His eyes narrow. "Now, why do you ask?"

"Well," says Jael, rubbing one of her wrists. "Either it's those awesome smoothies you made, or else Ms. Spielman just totally healed my wrists."

"I see," says her father. "I had a feeling she was more than she appeared to be."

"So . . . should we do something?"

"Did you thank her for healing your wrists?"

"Uh . . . no."

"Then you should do that."

"Right."

After dinner that night, Jael and her father wash and dry the dishes together.

"I still can't believe it," he says as he rinses the last dish and hands it to Jael to dry. "That we don't have to hide from Belial anymore. What an incredible relief." He shuts off the water and turns to her. A broad smile creases his face, and for just an instant Jael sees the man her mother loved.

"Yeah," she says. "About that, Dad . . ."

"What?" he asks, his eyes narrowing.

"Well," she says, "Belial isn't the only Grand Duke of Hell."

"Sure." He nods. "There's Lamia, Grand Duchess of the West; Aguares, Grand Duke of the East; and Beelzebub, Grand Duke of the South. And that's not even mentioning the less-civilized provinces outside the duchies."

She stares at him.

"What?" he says. "You thought I didn't know? That I was under the impression that our troubles were over?"

"Um, kinda," admits Jael. "You're acting like it's all no big deal now."

He holds out his hand to her. Hesitantly, she puts her hand in his, and he brings her in close.

"It's a very big deal," he says quietly, his eyes locked onto hers. "Don't ever doubt that. Every moment we live is a moment stolen from fate. The difference is that before, I didn't think we stood a chance. That we would be cut down by the first marauding demon to cross our path. But now you have shown me that we do have a chance, however slim.

"Your mother went on and on about your potential and I always thought it was just the normal talk of an adoring mother.

But now I believe her. And your uncle. And you. Now I have hope. And for an aging, jaded demon hunter, *that's* a big deal too."

"It's so crazy to think that you used to be some kind of international demon hunter," Jael says.

"Oh, sure," he says. "Your mother and I . . . we were quite the team."

"Wow," says Jael, and shakes her head.

He smiles at her teasingly. "What, you think we fell in love and then immediately had you?"

"How would I know?" says Jael. "You never talked about her."

"Yes," he says, his smile fading. "You're right. Because I didn't want to lie to you about her, but I also didn't want to tell you the truth about her either." He shakes his head. "Probably not one of my better decisions."

Remember that it has been difficult for your father as well, her mother had said in that first letter. *He has carried a burden no mortal should ever be asked to carry.*

"It's okay, Dad," she says, and pats his hand awkwardly.

He looks back at her, a hint of gratefulness in his expression. "Sometimes I think I wasn't really cut out to be a father," he says.

She smirks at him. "Ya think?"

He smiles ruefully. "I'm a pretty good demon hunter, though."

"Good," she says. "I might need one at some point."

"Which reminds me . . . ," he says. Then he turns abruptly and leaves the kitchen. She hears him rummaging around in his room for a moment, then he comes back with something long and thin, wrapped in a wool blanket.

"I should have given this to you already," he says. "Then maybe you wouldn't have gotten hurt so badly last night." He shakes his head and sighs. "But I was still holding on to the illusion that I was the strongest one on our team."

"Team?" asks Jael.

"Before, I gave you the knife that was your mother's. That's used mainly for sacred rituals and magic. But this . . ." He unrolls the wool blanket to reveal a sword-length silver-bladed crucifix, the crosspiece forming the hilt. It gleams brightly in the light. "This was mine, and it is used mainly for kicking rogue demon ass." He holds it out to her.

She stares at him for a moment, not quite able to take it in.

"You're . . . serious?" she asks.

"Jael, my daughter. You are now officially one of the most feared and hated beings in Hell. A status, I might add, that I once proudly held. It's time for you to learn how to defend yourself."

Sometime around midnight, Jael decides to ask for a thunderstorm. She doesn't want to make a habit of messing with the weather. It seems irresponsible. But tonight she feels a little bit like celebrating.

She opens the window over her bed, takes out the screen, and climbs up so that her feet dangle over the windowsill. She takes a moment to breathe in the cool night air, then she asks the evening winds if they know how to make a thunderstorm.

They aren't sure, they say, but they'll ask.

She waits. After a little while she begins to wonder if the air has already forgotten. But then the winds rise up around her, peppering her with mist. The wind brought back spray from the sea. So she asks the spray if it can bring her a thunderstorm.

It says that it may take some time, but it will try.

So Jael waits some more. The wind laughs joyfully as it reports on the progress. The sea is talking. The clouds are coming. The wind cannot recall something like this happening for a very long time. Its laughter grows loud and rough, swirling among the trees and ruffling the grass with an almost manic playfulness. It licks at the bottoms of her dangling bare feet and slides in between her toes.

Dark clouds gather, first in small clusters, then in fronts that roll in like a stampede of galloping horses. A few raindrops strike her shins. The clouds crowd in eagerly, bustling and rubbing against one another until they form an impenetrable wall of dark chatter. A single bolt of lightning slices through the sky, followed a few seconds later by a crack of thunder. Then the sky opens up and rain comes down in torrents.

Jael lies back on her bed with her feet still sticking out of the window. The rain blows into her room and drenches her. She breathes in deeply and sighs.

In every drop of water, gust of air, speck of earth, and crackle of lightning, she hears the same thing: This world is alive. And it loves her.

A little while later, the storm notices that Jael has fallen asleep. The rain tapers off. The clouds sneak away like they're trying not to wake her. The wind caresses her cheek one last time, then disperses in all directions. It carries with it the memory of this funny girl with the sad green eyes. And it carries with it a little bit of hope that things might change. That the world might become what it was supposed to be.

In her dreams, Jael lies on a wintry field in the midst of a small cluster of hedges. The roots of these hedges all mingle and overlap. She puts her ear to the soft snow in the spot where they are most concentrated. She can just barely hear a faint song rise up through the earth.

"Mother," she whispers. "I love you."

acknowledgments

Thanks to everyone who helped me tell Jael's story. To Zach Morris, Mark Levine, Scott Pinzon, Heidi R. Kling, Pam Bachorz, Adam Meyer, Debbie Levy, Deborah Schaumberg, Michelle Zink, Lauren Bjorkman, Kurtis Scaletta, Aprilynne Pike, and Megan Crewe for their thoughtful criticism and encouragement during revisions. To the Debs, a marvelous group of writers that I feel so lucky to be a part of, for their unfailing support. To Emily Sylvan Kim for finding the right home for Jael's story. To Barry Lyga and David Levithan for their sage advice on the often baffling world of publishing. To my editor, Maggie Lehrman, for once again pushing the story to be its very best. To my publisher, Susan Van Metre, for allowing me to tell the stories I'm most passionate about. To my mother, Gini, and my stepfather, Tom, for supporting me during my own teenage quest for identity. To my father, Rick, for getting me hooked on epic fantasy stories in the first place. And to my sons, Logan and Zane, who keep it all in perspective.

Lastly, I want to thank Dr. Paul Jurkowitz, my high school religion teacher, for his knowledge, his humor, and his spirit of adventurous inquiry.

about the author

Jon Skovron has never really fit in and has no plans to start now. After twelve years of Catholic school, he went on to study acting at a conservatory program for four years before returning to his first love, writing. *Misfit* is his second novel. His first novel, *Struts & Frets*, was published by Amulet in 2009. The *Washington Post Book World* said, "Skovron perfectly captures that passion—sometimes fierce, sometimes shy—that drives so many young artists to take the raw stuff of life and transform it into something beautiful." Bestselling author Cory Doctorow said, "*Struts & Frets* will feel instantly authentic to anyone who's ever felt the pride and shame of being an outsider." Jon lives with his two sons outside Washington, D.C. Visit him at www.misfitbook.com.

This book was designed by Chad W. Beckerman. The text is set in Cochin, a typeface designed by Georges Peignot and named for the eighteenth-century French engraver Nicolas Cochin. The font incorporates a mix of style elements and could be considered part of the Neorenaissance movement in typography. It was popular at the beginning of the twentieth century. The display type was designed by Sammy Yuen.